# LOOKING
## for the
# MAHDI

# LOOKING
# for the
# MAHDI

## N. Lee Wood

ACE BOOKS, NEW YORK

ن ۚ وَٱلۡقَلَمِ وَمَا يَسۡطُرُونَ ١ مَآ أَنتَ بِنِعۡمَةِ رَبِّكَ

بِمَجۡنُونٍ ٢ وَإِنَّ لَكَ لَأَجۡرًا غَيۡرَ مَمۡنُونٍ ٣ وَإِنَّكَ

لَعَلَىٰ خُلُقٍ عَظِيمٍ ٤ فَسَتُبۡصِرُ وَيُبۡصِرُونَ ٥ بِأَييِّكُمُ

ٱلۡمَفۡتُونُ ٦

. . . By the pen and that which it writes therewith,
Thou are not, for thy Lord's favour unto thee, a madman.
And lo! thine verily will be a reward unfailing.
And lo! thou are of a tremendous nature
And thou wilt see and they will see
Which of you is the demented. . . .

The Holy Qur'an
Surah LXVIII, Al-Qalam
Verses 1–6

*For Norman,
my friend,
my partner,
and my champion of a divine madness.*

# ACKNOWLEDGMENTS

Many thanks to the following people who aided and abetted in the writing of this book:

Susan Allison, Scott and Suzi Baker, Elaine Block, Chris Bunch, Anne Choller, Allan Cole, Craig Copetas, Roland Gilles, François Landon, Doris Lessing, Pat LoBrutto, Bob McCabe, Mike and Linda Moorcock, Hans-Peter Otto, Stephanie Laidman Tade, Erik Thoraval, Hassane Tlili, Jim Williams, and to l'Institut du Monde Arabe, Mme. Bibi, Mohmed Smaiel, Djaffai Mouliti, Azoua Yakhou and all the rest of the regulars at "Le Onze" in Paris.

## AUTHOR'S NOTE

The country of Khuruchabja is imaginary, and should not be considered representative of any existent country, its peoples, language, culture or religious beliefs. With the exception of historical personages and occurrences, all characters and events portrayed in this book are fictitious; any similarity to actual events or to real people, living or dead, is purely coincidental and unintended.

All quotes from the Koran used in this book are adapted from the 1930 English-language translation, *The Meaning of the Glorious Qur'an*, by Mohammed Marmaduke Picthall.

# ONE

My name is Kahlili bint Munadi Sulaiman, I'm a journalist. Or I was. I still work for GBN, Global Broadcasting Network, where I've been for nearly sixteen years, mostly doing feed-ins for the bubbleheads as a Staff Broadcast Editor. I don't know if you could properly call what I do now "journalism."

I did my fair share of field correspondence during the Khuruchabjan War, securing a brilliant reputation for myself by blipping high-speed feeds for simultaneous reports out of a battered PortaNet while doing all the exciting bullet-dodging and "human interest" stories on dying children I ever wanted. If you do a really bang-up job, you get promoted to a nice safe desk, where nothing more dangerous happens than the Government tries sneaking a tap on your Netlines. Most field reporters I know consider promotions the kiss of death by boredom, but while it's great for swapping a few anecdotes at the Press Club, I had no desire to go back into the field. I was quite happy with my dull, boring career as an anonymous broadcast editor behind a nice big desk and my feed-in Net.

Which was a shame, according to GBN's editor in chief, Arlando. He had been pushing for years to get me to go back into the field and cover the Middle East, saying I had all the "right stuff" for field reporting in that part of the world. Let me try to explain it in the simplistic terms our viewing audience can understand: I'm *ugly*. Among other things. Arlando meant it as a compliment. But while being simply ugly was one of my foremost journalistic qualifications for that particular kind of field work, it's also why I did feed-ins for the prettily coifed and polished bubbleheads.

I'm the brains that writes the words delivered with such perfect accents by the earnest-looking immaculate blonds. I'm the questions that elegant silver-haired anchormen with the penetrating eyes interrogates heads of state with. I'm the puppeteer.

Don't get me wrong, I'm not complaining; I liked my job. I even like bubbleheads, those who're good at it. GBN wasn't the top News Network, networks battering each other for ratings position just to survive ever since Turner had blown us all off the map and made us reconsider our strategies over the last few decades. But we were still prestigious enough to be able to hire talent. It still takes a certain amount of skill, savvy, and grace under pressure to be a decent bubblehead; looks aren't necessarily all you need.

When bubbleheads do their job well, you wouldn't even know I exist, which suits me fine. I like anonymity. I wasn't so ugly as to be noticeable; I mean it wasn't like you'd puke to look at me. I'm short, but I'm not a dwarf, and if I hadn't controlled my weight strenuously on a steady diet of cigarettes and bad coffee, the traditional *haute cuisine journaliste* for the last umpteen million years, I'd have been what you could regard as "squat." By the time other girls in my junior high school started comparing the lace on their training bras, I was being taken to the doctor and given a long, complicated rationale involving my mother's hormone imbalance during pregnancy, which didn't make me feel the least bit better about my tits being wasp-sting size and unlikely to ever get much bigger.

When I started working, I had very long hair and wore plenty of eye makeup and big shiny earrings, because without them, it was difficult for most people to discern my sexual orientation. Even then, I sometimes got some suspicious looks. I was a quite normal heterosexual female trapped in the body of a bull dyke.

But it came in handy during the war in Khuruchabja. It hurt to cut my hair short (I kept the braided remains tied with a pink ribbon in my undie drawer for years before I finally threw it out), but with a scrubbed face above a suit and tie, stop plucking the fine mustache on my upper lip and drop my voice so it rumbled slightly, and I was routinely addressed as "sir," no questions asked.

As a woman, I was as homely as a mud fence, but as a *man*, the same features were judged as "craggy," or "distinguished"; not at all handsome, but the kind of face you'd expect a dusty, weather-beaten field reporter to have, a trustworthy but forgettable face. A face that GBN could use for live reports on the eight o'clock news and you'd never think twice about it. This is Kay Bee Sulaiman in Bumfuck, Khuruchabja, reporting live for GBN Network News. Yeah, right, *now* you remember me. Thank you, it was an interesting experience, but I didn't want to be a man for the rest of my life.

Women may have come a long way, baby, but there are still parts of the solar system left where being male is a definite advantage. There *were* no women field reporters in Khuruchabja, except me. It's hard to do decent reporting if you're covered head to toe with fifteen yards of heavy red wool and banned from all male company except immediate family. Khuruchabja took its misogynist religious laws very seriously, and I continually ran the risk of being sliced and diced into tiny pieces if found out. But it was worth it, in the end. Paranoia keeps your edge sharp, and I always got the kind of stories to feed the bubbleheads a steady diet for high ratings. When I came home I retired my masculine camouflage, accepted my little awards, hung them up on the wall behind my nice safe desk and gratefully disappeared.

Feed-in editing is relatively easy work, if exhausting. GBN's Net is constantly absorbing huge amounts of information twenty-four hours a day, everything from live blips transponded directly by GBN field correspondents from PortaNets via our own secured independent satellites, to old-fashioned AP modem services from over a thousand network bureaus and hopeful freelancers glowing endless green lines of text across the bottom of the Net. Print editors read in three or four lines of copy simultaneously to edit the mass inventory down to digestible lumps. Holo editors splice the hot blipped-in raw footage pouring in from hordes of maniacal correspondents into shape for replay seconds later. Everyone coordinates with the engineers to mesh all this chaos into one seamless whole. Our motto is "You Are There, Global News As It Breaks," since instant news and live coverage makes it that much harder for certain governmental parties to censor out what they don't like.

The idea is not only to have quality news coverage, but to have it *first*. You wouldn't think that a two-minute lead over your competition would mean network life or death, but that's where the news has gotten to. For years, GBN struggled just to keep in the race. Then we struck pay-dirt, leapfrogging into second place by not only having up-to-the-minute worldwide coverage, broadcast internationally, but depending on the signal decoder in your holoset, having the news brought to you in your choice of a dozen languages, not dubbed or subtitled, but with simultaneous anchors. Which means a *lot* of bubbleheads, all of them at least bilingual or trilingual.

Then we feed the bubbleheads, either simply letting them read off the standard monitor, with editors just whispering a few names and places in their ears so they pronounce the foreign words and names with some degree of accuracy, or directly by audio lines into tiny mikes implanted next to bubblehead tympanic membranes.

Some of the older bubbleheads do have real talent, and we let them do what they want, ask a few incisive off-the-cuff questions. A little honest spontaneity isn't bad on occasion. The smart ones like developing their own style, and usually read off the monitor. But we vigorously discourage prima donnas. The hell with what their union contracts say. The days of Dan Rather and Diane Sawyer superstardom with multimillion-dollar salaries are long gone. Those bubbleheads whose main capability is simply hitting the marks without flubbing their lines, which is the majority, prefer audio, a sort of delayed parrot response, sometimes right down to the intonation. That way they don't have to think too hard. All they have to concentrate on is looking and sounding like the interchangeable professionals they are.

I was so ass-deep in bubblehead swamp, murmuring sweet nothings into the delicate shell-like ear of Tricia Kwong, GBN's seven to eleven in the morning English co-anchor, I didn't notice when the alligators started biting.

"Arlando's waiting for you, Munadi," Penley said in a tone that indicated he was repeating himself for at least the third time. "Unplug and get up there."

"What?"

"The boss wants to see you. In his office. Now." Penley was

already screwing his pickup into one ear, squinting at my Net while he jacked in, and took over feeding Baby. On holo, Tricia continued looking straight into the camera, ad-libbing through the few seconds of changeover without batting an eyelash or dropping a beat. True bubblehead pro.

Arlando was everyone's concept of a terrific boss: If you were doing a good job, you never saw him. He made his wants and needs known through the Net, few face-to-face conferences necessary. Only if you screwed up, or if a ton of shit was hovering overhead, would you be called to see him up close and personal. In the privacy of the elevator on the way up, I made a quick sniff at my armpits and tried patting my hair back into shape.

Arlando looked even more nervous than I felt. He stood up as I knocked and entered. Two other men were with him in his office.

"Kay Bee Munadi . . . Sulaiman," Arlando said to the shorter of the two. That in itself was unusual. On those extremely rare occasions when I did any domestic reportage that required a name on it, I always used the name "Kay Munadi." I hadn't used the "Sulaiman" in a decade. I turned, holding out my hand as the boss continued, "Cullen Laidcliff." Laidcliff stood up, smiling tightly, and gripped my hand with more force than necessary. I had him pegged in two seconds. Government. Probably Fed narc or CDI midlevel stooge. I smiled my iciest company's-coming smile and didn't bother taking him up on his handshake challenge.

"John Halton." Arlando said, and I had to turn to shake the other man's hand. I've described myself; you might have some understanding of my instant reaction:

Jesus Christ on a bicycle, he's *gorgeous* . . .

Too gorgeous . . .

Certainly too good-looking to even look at someone like me . . .

Most likely just another plastic bubblehead . . .

Egotistical, narcissistic, talentless, probably gay . . .

I hate him.

All this went through my head in the time it takes to shake a man's hand. His grip was warm, firm without being confrontational, and he held it just a fraction longer than required, smiling affably. He turned me on. I despised him for it.

Introductions over, John Halton sat slightly removed from

the rest of us, an observer sitting by the door. Bubblehead for sure, I was convinced. I sat down, casually glanced at the Government stooge, then at Arlando. "So what's up?" I asked cheerfully. If you exude confidence, maybe the shit will miss.

"How's your Markundi?" Arlando asked.

That surprised me. Markundi is a complex patois of Arabic influenced by Persian and Northern Pashto, an obscure dialect I hadn't used in ten years. "Rusty. I haven't spoken Markundi since I left Khuruchabja. But I don't think it'd take me too long to do some brushing-up. . . ." I was thinking they needed an interpreter.

"That's okay," Laidcliff broke in, waving the problem away with a flick of an impatient wrist. "John's Markundi is perfect."

Perfect. Not good, not fluent . . . *perfect*. It's not like Markundi is your garden-variety college-level language course, either. I couldn't help glancing at Gorgeous George. He was still smiling that bogus little smile and had dropped his gaze down to examine the back of his hands resting on his knees. He didn't seem 'umble, just completely outside the conversation.

"That a fact," I said, for lack of any other intelligent response. Arlando was looking peculiarly uncomfortable.

"We need someone who speaks passable Markundi Arabic and is familiar with Khuruchabja, especially someone who knows their way around the locals' particular cultural idiosyncrasies," Laidcliff was saying, with the nasally tone of someone who obviously considers any culture other than his own "quaint" and inferior. "You've been there, you know the ropes, and you won't attract undue attention, you being an Arab yourself."

"I'm an American," I said coldly.

"I meant of Middle Eastern extraction." He grimaced.

"I'm as American as you are." I wasn't going to give this bigot the satisfaction. "One hundred percent, born in the U.S.A." He snorted, but let it pass.

"In any case, we need someone the natives will trust, at least to some extent."

"'We'?" I asked. He *had* to be the fucking CDI.

Laidcliff smiled his greasy, Government-clown smirk. "Someone unconnected with any official Government organization," he clarified, without clarifying anything.

"What for?"

"To deliver a package."

By now the usual Jeez-what'd-I-do-wrong nervousness had

gone, and I was, I confess, thoroughly pissed off. Even if this patronizing jerk was too young to remember the Khuruchabjan War or the effect his employer's meddling had had there, *I* wasn't, and I remembered it all too well. So did Arlando, so it surprised me he was sitting still for this shit.

"No problem," I said, eyes wide and innocently obtuse. "I'll be happy to look up the number for Federal Express's Overnight Delivery. Give me a couple minutes, I'll go get it for you."

Laidcliff scowled. "I'm not amused," he said.

"You're not Queen Victoria, either," I snapped back, and stood up. "And I'm certainly not a delivery boy, I'm a journalist. Khuruchabja isn't Jupiter; *mail* your goddamned package." I jerked a thumb at the bubblehead. "Or send him. After all, his Markundi is *perfect*—what the hell do you need *me* for?"

"You've got a valid passport," Arlando said.

That made absolutely no sense, until the bubblehead looked up and said quietly, "I'm the package."

To be a decent journalist, you've gotta know a lot about a lot, and put puzzles together fast. I could practically feel the tumblers clicking into place in my brain. John Halton was not a bubblehead. He was, no pun intended, Government property.

He was looking at me now, that same unassuming smile in place. I kept staring at him with my mouth hanging open while the Government weasel lectured.

"The Exalted Pillar of Allah, His Most Excellent Lawrence Abdul bin Hassan al Samir al Rashid has had some trouble keeping his congregation in line after some recent and rather unpleasant ecclesiastical confrontations in Khuruchabja. Larry needs a good bodyguard who can also double as a military advisor, someone whose impartiality and loyalty he can absolutely rely on.

"So"—Laidcliff grinned and nodded his head in Halton's direction—"we're giving him John. But it would be rather . . . indiscreet for our Government to deliver him directly. I think you'll agree we can't just stick a few stamps on his forehead and drop him in the nearest mailbox. You're to take Johnny here as baggage up to the Clarke Orbital Station where we'll have documents ready that can pass Khuruchabjan scrutiny with flying colors. You'll stay at the Hilton for a week before you both fly to Nok Kuzlat. Spend another week or two doing a little sightseeing. Take a vacation, have a good time. Then you leave, John stays." Laidcliff smirked. "You can even do a story or two while you're there, on the local rug factory or something, make it look good."

I'd never seen a fabricant up close and personal before; not that many people ever had. Those few I had seen were usually filmed hovering protectively around the President and other lesser dignitaries, their human Secret Service partners seeming clumsy and feeble by comparison. My naked curiosity kept me busy gaping at Halton to pay too much attention to the creep. But it started sinking in, anyway. "Why me? Not *me*, but why a *journalist*, for crissakes? I could just walk out of here, plug a story like this on the Net and watch GBN's ratings go out the roof!"

Laidcliff had folded his arms, looking at me as smug as a cat. "You wouldn't get three steps," he said arrogantly.

I felt my face go cold, then flushed. "You fascist little fuck—" I said, or started to say before Arlando cut me off.

"Don't threaten my people," he said to Laidcliff, no emphasis in his voice. "Ever." Arlando could be really scary when he wanted.

There was a very long, chilled silence. Then Laidcliff languidly shrugged. Score: zip to zip.

Allow me to pause from our regularly scheduled programming to explain something here: See, it's every government's job, even ours—*especially* ours—to make news and then try to hide it. It's the media's job to catch them at it, then report as much of it as they can. The Fourth Estate has always manipulated the Commons, and the Second has always controlled the top of the political pyramid.

The entire history of media and government has been one of painful coexistence, which rose to an ugly carbuncle during Vietnam. The Government learned, much to their horror, the power that television had to win over the hearts and minds of the American people. The new battleground became the manipulation of public opinion polls. By the time of the Gulf War, they'd trained their own slick PR folks, nice joes all, friendly, witty and totally useless. Lots of neat Hollywood special-effect pictures of things blowing up to keep the drooling pack happy. Someone even got hip and started dubbing in the sound effects.

At first, the only real news was what they *wouldn't* tell you, but the media agreed that during a conflict restrictions were necessary for the safety of Our Boys and Girls in Uniform. It chafed, but was respected . . . until a couple of those nice, friendly Pentagon briefers got caught lying. That sparked the first grumble of rebellion, the media no longer willing to settle for sanitized scraps. The military threw bigger bones, and the reporters showed larger teeth. Compound this with far less sophisticated censorship and misinformation by countries the Americans were supposedly allied with, and newspeople were most unhappy.

Less than fifty of the more than a thousand reporters in the area were ever allowed out of the hotel rooms where they were confined. Reporters started pushing the edges of the official press pool, like a school of hungry piranhas, with wars under the wars under the war. The more the military squeezed the pools, the more reporters struggled to wriggle through their fingers. Some were caught by the enemy, some by their own people. Some even quarreled with other newsdogs over access to what little information they could find, but most ended up without film or stories. The few who did made their careers.

By the time the Americans yelled "cut" and rolled their credits, two entire countries were in ruins, cities destroyed while jackals in assorted uniforms roamed through the carnage and quarreled over the spoils. Scapegoats were tried in kangaroo courts while burning oil wells blackened the skies. One U.S. President was still getting in a few last licks while the moving men were trotting his furniture out the back door of the White House.

But the Gulf War was the media's first major victory since Vietnam, and no time was lost regaining territory. Not only were our "smart" bombs not terribly smart, but our dumb bombs not nearly as effective as the military would have liked us all to believe. Instead of cheering as victorious troops rolled into Baghdad, Mr. and Mrs. Couch Potato in Peoria watched an endless flood of refugees on prime-time news, babies dying of cold and cholera, desperate people struggling for food and medicine beaten by "allied" troops at their borders. The media reminded people Back Home that winning battles doesn't win a war. A lot of information was literally buried in the desert forever, thanks to those patriotic military types perceptive enough to carry out damage control, arms and legs sticking out of the sand where bulldozer tanks had quickly buried enemy soldiers. But it had all begun to grate against the American ideal of The Good Clean War. Public opinion once again slowly began to swing.

The Government pasted together a series of Middle East peace conferences, anxious for what once had been sure-fire foreign policy coups while avoiding futile domestic concerns. Instead of public opinion polls reflecting the news, the media turned the polls into the news itself, making and breaking anyone who got in their way. "Polls Prove President's Popularity Plunges! Throw the bum out . . ."

Meanwhile, the Middle East went back to business as usual. While the West continued in its blind, fumbling arrogance to bring Truth, Justice and the American Way of Doing Business to the Middle East, the Saudis and Kuwaitis went back to their traditional feudal repression, and the Israelis and Palestinians bickered endlessly over land and what color the wallpaper should be for the next peace conference. The Jordanians sneaked in badly needed oil from the unrepentant Iraqis, the Iranians continued their call for the murder of American civilians for the greater glory of Allah, Egyptians started shooting tourists and the Algerians started shooting each other. The Syrians ganged up on the Lebanese, and the two together ganged up on the Libyans, while Qaddafi's wardrobe simply got more bizarre.

It was a long time before an exhaustion hailed as peace settled over the desert. By then, most of the reporters had packed up and left, and the unlucky stragglers had to sift through the picked-over remains. The American appetite was, and is, distinctly selective: The number of 50mm tank-piercing uranium-depleted bullets littering the deserts scaled into billions, but somehow that never made it to film at eleven. The soaring number of miscarriages in Bedouin women, and the incidence of two-headed sheep, were as far off and easily ignored as the low-level radiation pulsing in the shifting sands. Once in a while, maybe, a nice air strike against the fanatical desert ragheads was good for a few extra points in the President's popularity polls, regardless of which President it was, but eventually that too got old.

Americans have always cherished our do-gooder Lone Ranger image while increasingly loath to take on anything bigger than an anthill. It was fun to kick a little Muslim ass, beat our chests a bit, get even for all the hostages murdered, airplanes bombed, avenge all the insults and injuries, real and imagined. Iraq was a spineless pussy. Somalia was just a bunch of fifteen-year-old schvugs. We dood the voodoo in Haiti, but while Bosnia was at least white, they were Muslim and didn't have any oil. Besides, that was Europe's problem. We got dragged into Khuruchabja against our will, Brer Rabbit.

There will always be a new crisis to feed the audience's insatiable appetite; another world leader assassinated, another crash on Wall Street, another earthquake, another nation declaring bloody independence, another Presidential campaign and another President, another economic rival to bash, another juicy movie star murder scandal, another civil war, on and on and on. That's news. *Le plus c'est change.* The fickle Public Eye turned elsewhere.

But the traditional way of covering news was destroyed, never to return. The media had matured, the Fourth Estate becoming a power in itself to be reckoned with, forged in the fire of discontent. The evolving democracy of electronic information fed a world hungry for news, faster and harder. Dusty Bedouin tents sprouted illegal satellite dishes wired to tent poles, avidly sucking up the same airwaves being pumped into Kansas City living rooms. The media stormed the beaches of Mogadishu with Klieg lights and cameras before the Marines even got their boots wet. Photographers in Sarajevo and Bihac could boldly tread where armed UN troops feared to go. Reporters reached rebel Chechen lines before Russian troops even knew where they were. When the war in Khuruchabja began, journalists had already booked up every available hotel room.

Nationalities mean less than journalistic affiliations, our news "borders" jealously guarded. We have our own weapons and ways of protecting our people while we keep various governments relatively in line by the constant threat of exposure of their nefarious activities. They keep us from getting too cocky and overconfident with the usual lies, subversion and oppressive autocracy.

But as I sat listening to Laidcliff, it didn't appear to be our turn at bat.

"You're a bona fide journalist," Laidcliff continued. "John'll be going to Khuruchabja with you as a GBN photographer. It's about as unconnected from our offices as you could get, a perfect cover."

"And what's going to keep me from blowing the lid off it the second I get back?" Of course I knew what. I wanted this cretin to spell it out. "You gonna give me the 'we know where you live,' or 'you'll never work in this universe again' routine?" He could threaten me, but whatever deal he'd worked out with Arlando robbed his intimidations of teeth. The Feds can be very nasty. So can we.

"No," he said. "I don't think that's necessary." Then he looked at Arlando. "Is it?"

The boss looked like he'd eaten a very large turd. Hmm.

"I'm *not* going back to Khuruchabja," I heard myself saying calmly. *Where I almost didn't come back from the first time*, I didn't add. That didn't faze Laidcliff. "It's not my job to plant spies in foreign governments, that's your forte. *My* job is catching you spook assholes at it, which you're making painfully easy."

"John's not a spy, he's merely an advisor," Laidcliff said, as innocent as a two-year-old with chocolate on his mouth.

I laughed harshly. "Please. And what were all those infrafusion bombs with your fingerprints all over them, then? Oh, right, I remember: 'industrial farm equipment.' "

"You can't pin that one on us," Laidcliff said, his eyes narrowing. "That was before the State Department merged . . ."

"Calm down, both of you," Arlando said quietly. Like outraged schoolchildren, we stopped bickering while glaring daggers at one another. Halton still sat erect in the corner, eyes brightly alert like a well-trained police dog interested in the peculiar antics of his masters without understanding any of it.

"I couldn't even get a decent story out of it, so there's absolutely no incentive for me," I said to Arlando, and then to Laidcliff: "And I've never responded well to threats, so go fuck yourself." I smiled sweetly.

"I never said there wouldn't be any incentive." Laidcliff pretended to be amused. "You only asked what would *prevent* you from disclosing this story."

I thought about that for a moment, then eyed Arlando again, speculatively. He merely raised an eyebrow, which said volumes. I wondered if he'd been bribed or blackmailed, but either way I knew I was going to be dragged back to Khuruchabja whether I wanted to or not. I decided I'd better make the best of a rotten deal.

"You want something leaked, it comes to me first. *Exclusive*. And it'd damn well better be good and plenty." It wasn't much, but it would at least be something. Leaks are about the only real means of semi-honest communications between the media and government. Competition in the news biz is cutthroat fierce, and GBN was struggling to hold on to second place. We're number two, we gotta try harder just to stay afloat.

Laidcliff grinned, sharklike. "Just call me Son of Deep Throat." Triumphant, he could afford to be facetious. We ran over the scheduling details; then everybody except me stood up. "See you tomorrow," Laidcliff said to me, and then to Arlando, "Pleasure." He slapped Halton lightly on the shoulder. "Let's go, Johnny."

Halton turned to the boss. "Goodbye, sir," he said, polite beyond belief.

For a moment Arlando hesitated, then held out his hand. "Good luck," he said. I admired Arlando for that. *Real* class. Halton shook his hand as Laidcliff snickered. Halton glanced at me and didn't even make the attempt. I had no desire to touch him. Again.

"See ya 'round," I said with a mock salute. Halton nodded and followed the clown out.

Arlando allowed me to sit in his office without saying anything for a few minutes, letting me think while I adjusted to the ton of shit that had fallen straight down on my wee widow head. Arlando was one of the very few who knew what I'd gone through in Khuruchabja and why I didn't want to return. Finally, he said, "You could still back out, Munadi. I can't force you to do it."

I snorted. It was pro forma, we both knew it. "Gee, thanks, boss."

"Look, just run the errand and get back here, okay? It's not an assignment, there's no story. *Don't* get involved."

Whatever shit they had on Arlando, it had to be nasty. "Fine with me," I said sourly. "But you're gonna owe me a big one."

He grinned and nodded. "So how do you want to play this?"

I sighed. Damn. I fingered a lock of shoulder-length hair. I'd just had it done real nice, too.

"Same as last time."

Arlando called Documents while I went for a haircut.

# TWO

"**G**ood afternoon, and thank you for flying American Orbital," the woman behind the privacy desk said, all professional smile. "May I help you, sir?"

I set my one suitcase down next to a shiny new PortaNet and handed her my tickets. It's a bad habit for journalists, but as I watched her thumb through the papers quickly, her perfectly manicured long nails (mine had looked just as good the day before) rasping against the infosensitive surface, I had her categorized. Not pretty enough to be a bubblehead, but smart enough to roll with the punches. "Passport, please?" She looked up.

Laidcliff had supplied First-Class tickets on the Orbital, not as a courtesy, but because the check-in at the Admiralty Lounge provided more privacy. He and Halton stood behind me as I handed the woman my passport card.

I have two, both valid and legal . . . more or less. My private passport gives my name as Kahlili and my sex as female. Then I have my special passport with my journalist visas for certain kinds of field work, one I hadn't used in years, which was identical to the other. Except that my first name was initialized to "K.B.," and my sex masculine. When I had arrived in a white shirt, its crisp silk tie tucked neatly into a suit, and my hair cropped into a crew cut, Laidcliff looked like he'd have a hernia stifling his laughter. Halton didn't even blink. I hadn't expected him to.

Opaque shadows flickered across the privacy screens on either side of the receptionist's desk, other passengers checking in. The only audible conversation was our own.

"Will you be traveling alone today?" She glanced at my entourage.

"We're together." I jerked my thumb in Halton's direction without looking at him.

"Window or aisle seat?"

"Aisle."

The woman asked the usual questions, adjusting the orbital tickets. My lone suitcase chugged away down the belt, while she security-scanned the PortaNet I'd take as carry-on with me. Then she slid my passport into the reader, and pushed the handpad a fraction of an inch toward me. I placed my right palm down on its white surface and her holoscreen popped up the appropriate image, albeit a little thinner and younger. It beeped and spit out my card. She handed it back to me, her professional smile intact.

"Thank you, sir." She turned her attention to Halton. Her smile for Tall, Dark and Handsome was definitely brighter than it had been for me. "Passport, please?"

"He hasn't got one," Laidcliff said, obviously enjoying himself. She looked surprised, then even more surprised as he flipped open his Government ID. My assessment of her, however, was right. Laidcliff unfolded Halton's paperwork, and she read through it quickly and competently. This time when she looked up at the fabricant, her eyes were impassive.

"I'll have to have this authorized by my supervisor," she said. "Would you please wait here for one moment?"

"Nailed in place just for you, sweetheart," Laidcliff said, leering.

Her professional smile twitched a millimeter, her only hint of distaste. She returned shortly, accompanied by an older version of herself, cool and efficient. Silently, the supervisor checked through the documents, then handed them to me.

"You're willing to affirm you're the owner of record, Mr. Sulaiman?" she asked me politely.

"Pro tem," I muttered as I folded the documents and shoved them into a side pocket of my PortaNet.

"Excuse me?"

"Yes," I said clearly, straightening up. "I'm declaring Mr. Halton is indeed my personal bodyguard."

Since that's what the paperwork said. It's rare, but not unheard of, for the obscenely rich to own fabricant bodyguards like Halton, or for the Government to assign them as perks to high-level bureaucrats, who're generally members of the obscenely rich in the first place. The obscenely rich, of course, don't usually fly commercial, so the orbital personnel's experience would have been limited.

Journalists, who mainly fly Economy, naturally don't have salaries large enough to afford luxuries such as their very own fabricant, but the Government goon busy sniggering into his shirt tie behind me brushed aside any peculiarities about the situation.

"Everything seems in order," the supervisor said, handing Halton his ticket. "If you and"—she hesitated—"Mr. Halton would like to wait in our refreshments lounge, we'll call you before boarding."

I slung my PortaNet over my shoulder and headed for the lounge without bothering to see if the Dynamic Duo were following. I hated the whole thing, just wanting it to be over.

A skinny kid in a formal waiter's suit took our orders, and if the gossip had spread, he didn't give any indication. Halton wasn't drinking, and Laidcliff, predictably, had a Gordon's gin and Nouvelle Perrier. I ordered a straight Scotch. No ice.

"A *real* man's drink," Laidcliff quipped.

"Fuck you," I said quietly, and sipped it as he chuckled. I waited for him to make some kind of stupid comment about my sexual preferences as well, but he spared me that. I think I would have decked him right there if he had, proven my "manhood," as it were. For someone who wanted me to ferry goods into hostile territory as a favor for an organization I wasn't fond of anyway, Laidcliff wasn't being very appreciative. But I'd dealt with his kind before and knew that rudeness was a congenital defect. An enlightened and charitable person shouldn't hold it against him. Too bad I'm not an enlightened, charitable person.

After an interminable wait of ten minutes or so, a blue-uniformed Orbital hostess appeared. "First Class is now boarding at Gate Seven," she said and the lounge rustled with closing briefcases, pocket PC's snapping shut and tickets doublechecked.

Laidcliff traipsed after us as we queued up in the short First-Class line. "Well, kids, have fun," he said as we handed tickets to the attendant at the gate. "Drop me a postcard, Halton."

"Yes, sir." Halton's little smile never wavered.

"Talk to you later, Kay Bee," he said to me, then laughed and leered suggestively. "He's all yours."

At that moment I decided I'd get Laidcliff, one way or the other. He was only your typical Government jerk, and any retribution would certainly be petty, but for the next few hours I enjoyed myself as I ran various creative revenge scenarios through my mind.

I leaned over toward him, touching him lightly on the arm, smiling as sweetly as possible. "Don't worry, honey," I said in a low, sexy voice. "I'm saving myself for you." I puckered my lips and blew him a silent kiss.

His reflex was lovely to watch. His eyes told him I was a man before his brain kicked in and reminded him I was really female. Then he glanced around hastily, afraid someone would see and think he was with a faggot. It was my turn to snigger and leer. He walked away fast, his neck red above his collar.

An orbital flight is pretty much like one on any other plane, although most of my flying experience has been in Cattle Class, hard seats packed together like sardines, plastic meals, surly overworked attendants and never enough magazines or pillows. But it's better than Coffin Class, otherwise touted as the "Extra Economy Sleeper Fare." Underneath us, packed tight in the shuttle's belly were stacked rows of comatose clients who'd "sleep" the entire trip, no need for flight attendants or meals or coffee. If we blew up, they'd never know, which some considered an advantage. If I go down in flames, I want to *be there* when it happens.

I've always hated the idea of a separate First Class on planes. We're all supposed to be living in an egalitarian society, at least in theory, right? There was something distasteful about sitting with the snobbish aristocrats being catered to hand and foot while the unsavory sight of ordinary people commuting from one place to another, jammed into seats packed so tightly together it was hard to keep their knees out of their nostrils, was kept at an aesthetically isolated distance.

On the other hand, I do like the idea of all the free booze you can swill to make the time go faster.

"Would you care for champagne?" the male flight attendant asked politely as we waited to take off.

Laidcliff had soured my fondness for Scotch. "Screwdriver, if you've got it. Double vodka."

"Of course." He gazed soulfully at Halton, his smile sultry. "Anything for you, sir?" he practically purred.

It hurt, illogical as that was. I was incapable of attracting a man no matter *which* sex I was.

Halton looked at me and waited. "Don't ask me, I don't give a shit," I said sharply. The attendant drew back prudently, mistaking my anger for jealousy.

"Would you have a single malt?" Halton asked.

"Glenfiddich okay?"

"That'd be fine, thank you." When the attendant went on to the next sybarite porked out on the marshmallow-soft loungers, Halton said quietly, "I don't get drunk. But I do like the taste." He seemed completely relaxed and composed.

"You don't need to explain anything to me," I said acidly. I was neither relaxed nor composed. I wanted the alcohol to settle the jitters in my stomach. Halton watched me for a few moments, his aloof eyes assessing me calmly, then left me alone after that.

The shuttle took off and I drank screwdrivers as fast as the attendant could bring them while Halton slipped his whisky and leafed through the glossy Orbital magazine. Outside the window, the sky grew a deeper blue. I couldn't see the ground from my angle, but I knew the curve would be visible.

It wasn't a long flight, but when you fly First Class, they have to let you know you're really flying *first-class*. It was two o'clock in the afternoon Eastern when we took off, close enough for them to consider it dinnertime. The pilot had barely pulled the wheels up on the shuttle before the attendants were bustling down the aisle passing out the silverware. Real silver. Linen napkins. The caviar was Caspian Sea beluga, the poached salmon with fettuccini was served on Limoges porcelain, and the coffee was fresh-ground Blue Mountain. I ate because there wasn't anything else to do, and besides, someone else was paying for it. But I followed the coffee with another cocktail.

The next screwdriver was served in a sipcup with a Velcro bottom to fix it to the lounger's tray, a sure sign we'd be cutting the gravitational umbilicus presently. I'd consumed enough vodka to ease the tension that had crept up to lodge between my shoulder blades the day before. My full stomach made me lethargic and my head felt lightly numbed. When I looked out the window again, the sky had turned black.

Halton glanced at me, his eyes slightly wide. He unsnapped his safety belt and let his body float a few inches off the lounger, grinning at me in astonished delight, a wide honest kid's grin. I laughed, forgetting for a moment.

"First time on an orbiter?"

He pulled himself back down and refastened the safety belt, slightly abashed, or so it seemed to me. It was likable, that moment of embarrassed diffidence. "Yes," he admitted. "I'm not exactly a world traveler." He paused, then, "The fact is, this is the first time I've ever been outside of Virginia."

"Really?" I chuckled. "Well, you've sure got that suave and urbane air of sophistication down pat."

"Built-in." I returned his smile before I remembered what he was and who he worked for. I'd been conned by better.

"No doubt," I said coldly.

I immediately felt like a clod; he blinked and for a brief moment his eyes were hurt and sad before his polite little mask slid back into place. The reserved expression was flawless. I was surprised; it hadn't occurred to me that fabricants could feel pain. I considered apologizing, then reasoned that was exactly what he wanted me to do. Halton was just another CDI operative trying to manipulate my sympathies for his company's covert schemes. I had no intention of giving them any more cooperation than I had to, and tried to convince myself that apologizing to a biomachine would make about as much sense as begging pardon from a microwave oven. I didn't do a very good job of it.

Halton went back to perusing his magazine, and staring out the window when the orbiter rolled over so that the Earth was now above us instead of below. I dozed off at some point during the flight, waking up in time to notice one unwinking star growing brighter than the others. On the tube set in the back of the seat in front of me, Chad McQueen was swooning in Allison Eastwood's arms, both of them scantily clothed and artfully sweating in an African jungle indigenous only to the back lots of the Vancouver Screen Studios. Halton was listening with the Italian-language plug in one ear while scanning through a plastic-covered issue of *Cosmopolitan*.

Another hour went by, most of which the shuttle spent braking speed, nudging itself into alignment as the Clarke Orbital Space Station grew bigger and bigger. In the airless vacuum of space, everything looks closer than it really is. By the time we docked, the beginning of an intense hangover had bunched up my frontal lobes in its malicious fist. We had to wait on board as the shuttle was lowered down the spike elevator, feeling the illusion of gravity beginning to pull at us. It was less than Earth's, but not light enough that we'd bounce around like kangaroos.

The Hilton was only one of several international companies on the Clarke Orbital Station. The Station itself was a huge, double half-wheel, something like the fairground ride called the Hammerhead that I knew as a kid. Docking bays were dead center, one side open for incoming and outgoing shuttles, the other side attached to a solar-collector span perpendicular to the station. The collectors stayed still, while the station rotated on the axis like a huge, slow top in geosynchronous orbit. Two mammoth spokes going to either end of the station terminated in smaller spokes connected to a curved series of arches, the two ends rotating around each other—"South Pole" side for business and leisure, and the "North Pole" side for you-don't-wanna-ask-too-many-questions. Each Orbital Station—there were only three then, the fourth hadn't been finished yet—was built with the Poles far enough apart so that the Coriolis effect in the two rotating halves was minimized.

Minimized or not, just like my childhood Hammerhead ride it still had a tendency to make some people feel like puking, especially new arrivals who've consumed a gallon or two of vodka screwdrivers beforehand. The bellhops waiting at the South Pole Hilton shanklock quickly and efficiently took my PortaNet out of my queasy grip, deposited us and our luggage aboard their little shuttlecart and whizzed us off to check-in before I threw up my beluga and salmon.

I spent the next few hours splayed out across my hotel room bed, groaning piteously and getting up only to vomit. Once, Halton knocked cautiously on the door that separated our suites.

"Are you all right? Is there anything I can do . . . ?" he called through the locked slab of real Earth-grown walnut, exactly the right amount of anxious concern in his voice. I wondered if he'd had to rehearse to get the tone so perfect.

I lifted my head off the pillow just long enough to gasp out, "Piss off!" before I clamped a hand over my mouth, rolled off the bed and staggered toward the toilet again, head spinning.

Finally, there wasn't anything left in my stomach to get rid of; time and my overworked liver cleaned the remaining booze out of my bloodstream. I slept fitfully, then woke up in twilight, the hotel room "windows" set to provide the appropriate light from whatever time zone you came from or planned on going to. It didn't help; the Coriolis made me feel disoriented anyway. I'd get used to it, so they said. I checked my watch. Dinnertime. Or maybe it was breakfast.

The water pressure in the shower wasn't quite what I would have liked, but it was hot and the steam helped clear my pounding head. My short hair felt odd under my hands, but at least it dried quickly. It was cropped short enough that I didn't really need to even run a comb through it. After eating a couple of aspirin, I sat wrapped in a towel on the edge of the bed and smoked a cigarette while staring at my masculine reflection in the mirror. I blew an ironic kiss at myself.

Dressed in fresh clothes, I stopped to consider for a moment before knocking on Halton's door. "It's unlocked," I heard him say. When I opened it, he was dressed and on the bed, reading a book. Propped up against the headboard with his legs stretched out and crossed at the ankle, he looked at me expectantly over the book.

"I'm going to dinner," I said, guessing at whichever was correct, and added reluctantly, "if you'd like to join me."

"Thank you, that's very kind, but I've already eaten from room service."

"Ah—" I spotted the covered remains on a trolley waiting for the cleaning crew to take away. "Right." I felt vaguely bad, wanting to at least make peace and not knowing how. I hadn't had much practice. I fumbled for a moment before I shrugged. "Well, then. See you tomorrow."

He looked as if he wanted to say something further, then just smiled that annoying phony smile. "Good night."

I ate alone, leaving most of the food on the plate, my guts still rebelling, before heading back to my room. Halton's room was silent, no light showing underneath the connecting door. Flicking on the TV, I dialed through the channels, blowing friendly raspberries at our competition, until I found GBN News. Keying in the English version, I watched Lewis Marlow's truncated head float at the foot of my bed, earnestly delivering the late evening stories.

Lew was okay for a bubblehead, a little vain, but a nice

enough guy even when he wasn't on camera. I found him rather amusing on the air. He was so audio-sensitive, I could tell who the puppeteer was just from the inflection in Lew's voice.

"Hi, Rylla." I waved bleakly at Lew's image. "Give 'em hell, sweetheart."

I fell asleep alone in a strange bed, far from home, while bubbleheads sang me sweet lullabies.

# THREE

alton was up and ready by the time I knocked on his door for breakfast. He let me in, then slipped a sheet of hotel notepaper in his book to mark his place and set it down on the bureau. It was an old-fashioned print novel, not even a bookreader. I looked at the dogeared cover in surprise.

It was a scandalous Hindustani-language romance novel. The cover illustration showed a Brahmin princess, dripping gold jewelry, valiantly resisting the charms of a dark, handsome Mogul while perched atop an elephant, no less, her sari in precarious disarray, barely covering her formidably-sized bosom, her head thrown back on an impossible swan neck as her kohl-ringed eyes rolled imploringly toward the gods.

"What the hell are you reading?" I asked, my curiosity getting the better of me as I looked at the graceful Sanskrit letters embossed with worn gold foil.

"*Lord Ramachandra's Captive Princess,*" he said.

I nearly laughed. "A trashy bodice-ripper romance novel? I wouldn't have thought that kind of thing would interest you."

Halton wasn't embarrassed in the least. "I'll read anything, and this was all they could find at the desk besides magazines," he said. "They're good for passing time. 'No brain, no strain,' I believe is the expression."

I snorted, and we left for breakfast. Between my orange

juice and Eggs Benedict, however, we were interrupted by a jovial fat man pressed into a very expensive suit and carrying an AI briefcase.

"Kay Bee!" he called out in delight. "Haven't seen you in ages! What a pleasure running into you here. Why didn't you tell me you were coming? We could have taken the same shuttle, caught up on old times. . . ."

I didn't know him to spit on. He shook my hand vigorously, then turned to Halton. "And you must be John Halton, Kay Bee's holo photographer. Elias Somerton, nice to meet you." He pumped Halton's hand with equal enthusiasm.

Cloak and dagger time. I grinned. "Jeez, Eli, old man," I said with gusto, "I didn't know you were coming. How's the wife and kids?"

"Oh, fine, just fine. Mind if I join you for a few minutes?"

"Not at all, sit yourself on down." I waved a hand at an empty chair. "So, she didn't press the divorce after all, huh? You dumped your mistress, then?"

Somerton's eyes flashed warningly, and his pitch dropped about twelve octaves. "Don't press it," he growled as he slid his bulk into the vacant seat. He smiled and blathered as the waiter eyed us, deliberating whether or not this newcomer would need his own place setting. "I won't barge into the middle of your meal," Somerton said, back up to full volume. "Got a meeting in"—he shucked his wrist out of his suit sleeve and inspected his watch—"half an hour, but let me write down a number. Let's get together for dinner or drinks or something. You on Clarke Station long?"

That satisfied the waiter, and he ambled off. Somerton set his briefcase on the table, and opened it. The thing was apparently smart enough to keep its mechanical mouth shut while Somerton rummaged through its compartments.

"The key is for a storage locker on Level Two. You'll find optic equipment for Halton and all the documents you'll need to get into Khuruchabja," he said in a barely audible voice. "Once you get to Nok Kuzlat, someone will contact you." His voice jumped decibels. "Here we go, I found it." He pulled out a pad and pen and scribbled something totally illegible before he ripped off the sheet of paper and shoved it across the table in my direction. No doubt the key was underneath.

I rested my chin on one hand, elbow propped on the table, in an effort to keep from bursting out laughing. "Don't you think you're overdoing the spook melodrama just a little?" I said in a normal voice. "It's sort of like a bad holo, only you're not good-looking enough to play the leading man."

He shot me a look that could have melted glass. "Just do your job, and we'll do ours." He stood to go, the broad grin at odds with the cold eyes. "Hell, wish I had a bit more time, Kay Bee. Stay in touch, won't you?"

"Oh, you bet, Eli old son," I agreed cheerfully, a little louder than really necessary, "Cheerio, best to the family." Somerton's jaw muscles clenched as he grinned his toothy grin, furious, and departed.

"Christ, what a pompous ass," I said to Halton. "Friend of yours?"

Halton shook his head. I picked up the paper like a kid opening up a Cracker Jack Surprise. Sure enough, a magkey to a storage locker was underneath, number stamped along its edge. "Gee, looky, looky what I done found," I said to Halton.

"Are you *trying* to call attention to yourself?" Halton asked seriously. There was nothing admonishing about his tone, just curiosity. It took all the fun out of it, and I slipped the key into my pocket without responding.

"Goddamn cheap secret agent bullshit, royal pain in my butt." I grumbled the litany to myself.

We finished the rest of our breakfast without speaking.

I had to ask directions to Level Two, and stopped to ask again for the way to the storage area from a janitor dressed in horrible yellow overalls. He seemed dumbfounded that any-body would actually stoop to bothering to talk to him, and the resulting directions were so garbled, we spent a half hour bum-bling around in the bowels of the Operations Section before someone noticed and steered us in the right direction. If anyone came asking if we'd been noticed, I think we'd be remembered. Hey, who said I ever *asked* to be a spy?

The locker was smallish and narrow, the kind used to hold a sweat jacket and a pair of track shoes rather than a suitcase. The HoloPak equipment had been broken down into sections in order to get it stacked inside, but there wasn't enough to be overly cumbersome. Not that it made that much difference to me, since I wasn't the one who would have to lug it around. At the bottom of the locker was a fat industrial-strength envelope. I picked it up while Halton was slinging the last of his discon-nected HoloPaks over his shoulder, and handed it to him.

He looked at it, turned it over, then held it back out to me. "It's unmarked," he said, as if that explained anything.

"So what? It's obviously for you, open it."

*Something* flickered through his eyes, expressionless and glacial. Totally inhuman. "You are in charge," he said. "Until the proper documents have been signed and provided to His Excellency, you are still the legal owner of record."

"Like hell," I muttered, but took the envelope back anyway. I slid my no-longer-tapered-and-Chrysanthemum-Amethyst–polished fingernail under the flap and tore it open. Inside were several official-type visas and credentials for Khuruchabja, one set for K. B. Sulaiman, GBN Journalist, and another for John Halton, GBN Photographer, as well as a passport card in the name of one John Halton, American citizen. Another was a set of blank Bill of Sale–Transfer of Ownership documents in both English and Arabic, with the particulars to be filled in at a later convenience. No mention of what the specific merchandise might be, of course.

And an unmarked microflake.

"Oh, goody," I said sourly, holding it up to the light and watching the rainbow colors sparkle through its translucent surface, "now we get to play international smugglers as well as spies." I slipped the flake back into its holder, and put it in my wallet next to my cherished Visa Express card. "This wasn't mentioned in the job description. Maybe I'll just flush the damned thing. I didn't agree to risk my ass smuggling for Uncle Spam."

I handed Halton his passport card. "That might create some unpleasant repercussions for you later," he said absently. He wasn't being funny. He was holding his forged passport almost warily, examining it with minute care. I paused, watching while he touched the back of the card gingerly, as if he could feel the data stored within it with his fingertips.

"*Now* you have a valid passport," I said quietly.

He looked up. "It's not valid," he said. "Simply an adequate enough imitation to pass any inspection."

"What's the difference?" I snorted.

He looked back down at the card before putting it away in his own wallet. "Everything," he said in a lifeless voice.

It was an awkward moment, at least for me, as we stood silently, looking at each other. I wavered for a moment, unable to let my guard down even when I wanted to. Finally I gestured with my chin toward the HoloPak equipment. "You know how to use that stuff?" I said gruffly, changing the subject. "All of it?"

We would be traveling as the usual stripped-down field crew; Halton would double as his own sound man, and I would be my own director. Not that we were doing anything more than playacting.

"Yes, pretty much."

"Fine." I closed the storage locker, key in the lock, and we walked away, heading back out to the hotel to drop off Halton's extraneous equipment. "Then I don't have to waste my time teaching you. Let's dump this crap."

We went to his room first. I noticed how abnormally clean it was as he set the equipment down carefully on the hotel's ersatz Louis XIV desk. Even after the maids get through with a room, there's usually some indication that there's someone actually occupying it. The usual accumulation of spare change on the night stand, odds and ends scattered on the bureau, a bathrobe draped on a door hook, an extra pair of shoes sticking out from under the bed, anything.

While Halton busied himself unzipping and reorganizing the HoloPak sections into their proper units, I strolled over to the bathroom door, pulling it ajar with one finger to peek in. In mine, I had toothbrush, toothpaste, mint-flavored waxed floss, hairbrush and comb (superfluous), a brand of men's cologne I could tolerate as "after-shave," armpit grease, shampoo and conditioner, nail kit, shaver (also superfluous, but good camouflage), a bottle of "prescription antihistamines," which would actually harmlessly suppress my menstrual cycle for a few extra weeks, another of real aspirins and a shaker of pink-tinted medicated talcum powder, all spread out over the marble counter with haphazard negligence.

Halton had a single navy blue ditty bag, brand-new, zipped shut and set neatly on the shelf below the spotless mirror.

I took a step back into the room, regarding the pristine bathroom and feeling vaguely affronted. Halton stood watching me. Wordlessly, I crossed to his closet, sliding the doors open. His single suitcase was set neatly on the top shelf, the combination lock reset at 0000. Three dress shirts with ties, a suit jacket, two pairs of pants. All hung with painful precision. Pulling open the drawers, I examined various pairs of socks, rolled immaculately, and several pairs of underwear, as neatly folded as the day they came out of their shrink-wrap package. One impeccably folded sweater. One equally impeccably folded sport shirt. An extra pair of shoes were squarely aligned next to the drawers. I stared at them with a clouded sense of outrage.

I closed the closet doors, scowling, then brushed past Halton to yank open the drawer of his bedside stand. Nothing but the hotel's usual *Interdenominational Spiritual Guide in Seventeen Languages*. No pen, no scraps of paper with doodles or numbers scribbled on them, nothing. Halton hadn't been carrying anything more than his suitcase—no valise, no pocket PC, not even a bookreader. The only personal object in the room was the romance novel, and a borrowed one at that. There was nothing in his room that indicated a human being lived here.

"Is there something I can help you find?" Halton asked.

"Nope," I said, slamming the drawer shut. "Just snooping."

He had his head tilted as he studied me. "Is it because I'm a fabricant, or are you rude to everyone?" he asked. There was no insult or anger in his voice, only curiosity. But he'd caught me off guard. Whatever vacillation I'd felt vanished.

"You're a CDI agent," I snapped. "That's reason enough." It was as close to the truth as I cared to go.

"I see."

I stepped up close to him, having to crane my neck to look up as I stared at him in growing anger. "Do you?" I asked sarcastically. "Do you really? I doubt it."

His eyes were mild, looking back at me without fear, without reproach, without much of *anything*, actually. I looked at those innocuous brown eyes and saw nothing in their depths. Just like the room, nobody home. At least he wasn't smiling that goddamned pretentious smile.

My hands had balled into fists, and I was shaking with a nameless, irrational rage. Thinking I'd fly apart if I didn't get the hell out of there, I stalked over to the connecting door and slammed it behind me as I entered my own messy, very humanly disheveled room.

"Jesus Christ, Jesus fucking Christ," I breathed to myself, "pull it together, girl . . ." I was sweating, prickly heat and adrenaline trembles making my head throb. I sucked in several deep breaths before I could trust my fingers to handle a fragile cigarette. "Pull it together . . ."

If I lost my temper this early in the game, what would happen by the time we landed in Khuruchabja?

# FOUR

I don't know what Halton did for the rest of the afternoon, but I ended up prowling the length of the Station arch, already feeling cabin-feverish. There was only a moment of embarrassment; I stopped to look at a display of ladies summer fashions in a shop window with a bit more interest than most men might exhibit. The clothes had a nice cut. The tailoring, I thought, might make me look a bit more tall and svelte, if you can imagine a tall, svelte toad. A passing salesclerk glanced out at me with a strange expression that jerked me back into my adopted persona. Besides, I'm an autumn person, and they didn't have a *thing* in my colors.

By evening, I'd walked out my jitters, gotten my head back on relatively straight, started thinking about what the hell I was going to do for the next five days before we headed for fun and sun in Khuruchabja.

I went back to the hotel room to change into some decent clothes for dinner. It had been a long time since I had masqueraded as a man, and my reflexes were still very much in female mode. To most women, men's clothes look comfortably simple, almost bland when compared to strapless pouf dresses and high-heeled shoes. But there's a style and specific manner to men's wear that is nearly as complicated as women's, if more subtle. Halton knocked on my front door as I was struggling with the snaplinks on my dress shirt.

"Open," I called out, knowing if it wasn't him, it certainly wasn't someone I was going to be able to keep out anyway.

"Have you had dinner?" he asked. He gave no indication that the earlier unpleasantness had ever occurred.

"No," I said, and the snaplink popped off. "Goddamn it, help me with this thing." I shoved my sleeve out at him as he retrieved the fallen link off the carpet. As he slipped it into place through the fabric, I asked, "You?"

"Not yet." The snap clicked securely.

"Thanks." I looked at him as I shrugged into a dinner jacket. He simply waited. I shoved my hands into my pants pockets and sighed. "So let's go eat something. I saw a place up the main arch seemed like it had a decent menu."

Actually, it hadn't looked all that wonderful, but I hate eating in hotel restaurants all the time. If I was going to be stuck here another five days, I might as well check out the competition. The wine list was pretentious, entirely French and atrociously overpriced, but so long as Halton's playmates were picking up the tab, who cared? I don't even remember what I ate; it was neither bad enough nor good enough to be memorable.

For the most part, our initial conversation stayed in the safe zone with Halton asking benign questions and me telling the usual amusing Press Club anecdotes I'd garnered for just such mindless activity. But somewhere between the main course and the cheese, Halton put his wineglass back on the table with the same precision with which he folded his socks.

"It has puzzled me," he said, both voice and eyes level, "why you haven't asked me more questions. About myself. You certainly seem to have some strong feelings about fabricants, but I would have thought a journalist would have had more curiosity."

I was pleased that I had walked out the major part of my tension and hostility that afternoon, and easily kept my temper under control. Truth was, I was angry at being forced to return to Khuruchabja, angry with CDI and Arlando both, but most of all I was scared pissless. Not that I'd admit it to anyone, especially not Halton.

Of course, I *was* curious; not many civilians had ever seen a fabricant, never mind having dinner with one. Some people still believed they were an elaborate hoax, like the moon landing had been a sham filmed somewhere in the Arizona desert. But I'd read the investigative reports and the Congressional hearings transcripts. I damn well knew there was a listing for fabricants in the U.S. Military's secret mail-order catalog, under *Weapons, Biological*.

I finished chewing whatever delicacy we were sampling before I spoke. "Being lied to annoys me," I said in a reasonable tone. "So why bother? What are you going to tell me that I can't look up in *Jane's*, or get out of the Government information service? I'm doing my best to take notes, and I'm sure there's far more to you than the approved official literature covers. But would you really tell me something they won't? Any juicy classified confidential secrets I could ferret out?"

"Is it really the same thing reading a manual about a new military fighter as it is to see it up close, interview the pilots, try to talk your way into a personal flight?" he countered.

I held up my butter knife, conceding the point. "Touché." I thought for a moment, then grinned wickedly. "Okay . . . so tell me something about your love life."

He blinked, probably the closest he got to an offended expression. "What would you like to know about it?" Cool, real cool. Imperturbable.

"You a virgin?"

"No." He paused. "Are you?"

I laughed. "No. Believe it or not, there *are* men out there who get off on fucking really ugly women. Make porno magazines, even, find them right between the animal sex and transvestite bondage issues." He didn't seem to find that funny. He didn't seem to find much of anything funny. "So—" I lobbed the conversation back into his court. "You got a regular girlfriend, or do fabricants just indulge in mindless orgies with each other?"

He leaned back in his chair, scrutinizing me as if trying to come up with the correct answer to give his college biology professor.

"I don't know about other fabricants," he said slowly. "My sexual experience has been limited to human beings. There are also, it seems, women who get off on fucking fabricants. I wouldn't know if there are any porno magazines made about it." His voice was calm. I was the one blinking with astonishment. He smiled, that ghastly little smile. "I've been told I'm a fairly decent 'lay,' however. One woman called me a miracle of modern science, technology's most advanced dildo."

"Jesus," I said, shocked.

His expression didn't change as he said, "It doesn't bother me. I'm used to cruelty." He looked down to pick up his wineglass, sipped, and resumed eating his dinner as if this conversation had never happened.

My face burned with sudden shame, chagrined by my own malice glaringly mirrored in the casual heartlessness of that unknown woman. His hand rested on the table and I reached out to cover it with my own. "I'm sorry, that was mean."

Apologizing to your microwave oven, Kay Bee? Maybe . . .

He froze, studying my hand for a moment. I had to make an effort to keep it there. Then he turned it over, placing his palm against mine. He inhaled, and looked up, appearing more human than I'd seen him before.

"No apology is necessary. I offered to answer questions, and that one certainly wouldn't be in the official Government guidebook." He smiled, this time a warm, seemingly genuine smile. "It didn't hurt my feelings. And yes, I do have feelings, and they can be hurt."

I felt a strange rush of emotions—guilt, anger, resentment, fear—all swirled up in a nebulous cloud of forlorn desire. At that moment, another couple walked by our table, the woman's odd glance reminding me that two men don't generally hold hands in public. I carefully extracted mine.

"I would have thought the Government wonderboys would have designed a *homo fraudulentus* without emotions, all that sentimental stuff mucking up analytical thought." I tried to keep from sounding sarcastic, to show I was actually capable of discussing the subject without being confrontational.

"I don't think the designers would want to, even if they could, which I doubt," he said. We slipped into the dialogue with no more awkwardness than we would have discussing account ledgers. "Fabricants aren't mechanical androids or AI computers; they're a biological construct. The DNA may be off-the-shelf recombinant configurations, but the matrix into which the structure is programmed is based on the fundamental human mold. Fabricant bodies, including the brain, are structurally equivalent to humans. They have a normal cerebrum, cerebellum, limbic system, hypothalamus, pons, medulla, everything that goes into constructing an integrated working brain."

I noticed that he repeatedly referred to fabricants as "they" rather than "we," an interesting observation I kept to myself.

"Nature has had millions of years in which to perfect the human machine, and fabricant brains are simply a variant on the model," he went on. "A fabricant medulla functions to keep my heart beating and my lungs working in exactly the same way as your natural human medulla does for you."

"*Exactly.*" My doubt was obvious.

"For the most part, yes. There aren't too many alterations or additions that can be made on the basic model without ultimately impairing the essential functions. In order for fabricant brains to work properly, each part must be able to perform its assorted tasks in synch with every other part. For me to respond to a danger stimulus, my body temperature must rise, my heartbeat speed up, adrenalin dumped into my bloodstream. In other words, I must be able to feel fear."

"Your basic 'fight or flight,'" I agreed. "But what about things like morality, aesthetic appreciation, spirituality?"

He nodded, smiling now as if he really was enjoying the conversation. "Then you're getting into the abstract emotions, which really depend on a more complex integration of working parts, don't they? Fabricants are not humans. Their brains are comparable but not identical to human brains."

It was a strange conversation, very civil in an elegant atmosphere. Other conversations buzzed around us at nearby tables, high-powered businessmen, with frowns and heads bent over pocket PC's; rich kids in their stylish clothes holding hands and staring into each other's eyes through the candlelight. We looked like any other normal dining duet chatting, although I doubt anyone else was discussing a subject matter both as esoteric and personal as this.

"My specialization is as a linguist, just to use my particular design again as an example," Halton continued, using the correct fork and knife on his entree. "My brain has been specifically tailored to facilitate an increased capability for languages. Most human language and speech centers are predominantly left-hemisphere; both my hemispheres have multiple, integrated speech and language centers. In human brains, the neurochemical secretion which stimulates these speech centers and aids young children in imitating sounds, learning a language *fluently* without an accent, begins to disappear by about the age of five or six. In mine, it never will."

"How many languages *do* you speak?"

He looked at me thoughtfully, not as if he had to stop and count, but as if reluctant to boast about himself at the cost of *my* feelings. "Not counting differences in regional dialects or accents, twenty-seven."

"Shit." I couldn't help it, I was both jealous and astounded. "All *perfect*, no doubt?"

He didn't answer that. "The point I was leading up to," he said, addressing his plate, "is that if you fiddle with the design in one area, there may be other changes along the chains of integration. Do fabricants feel the same emotions in the same way that humans do? I don't know. Their brains are different; it's possible that the way they interpret emotions is different as well. One side effect of my language capability is that I don't have a dominant hemisphere. I'm truly ambidextrous. That in itself has no particular significance, but I believe the designers themselves don't know to the last detail what effects other alterations might ultimately have."

That chilled me. "Frankenstein and his monster, hmm?"

He stopped eating. "I don't think it's quite that drastic," he said quietly and looked me straight in the eye. "Do I seem like a monster to you?"

It was my turn not to answer the question. We sat without speaking until the waiter whisked away plates and brought coffee and dessert menus. I avoid sweets, but I ordered a cognac. A double.

"I'll have the same," Halton said, handing his menu to the waiter.

After he left, I said, "I thought you don't get drunk. Just drink for the taste. Another side effect from all those minor adjustments in your synthetic brain?"

"Not . . . exactly." The vague little smile was back. "Nanos."

I laughed, a nervous explosion of muffled sound. "You're *punked*? Jesus Christ, they built you with everything except the goddamned kitchen sink! *Tell* me you're not Super Spy."

"I'm not Super Spy," he said, dead serious.

I stopped laughing. "Then exactly what the hell *are* you?" I was getting pissed off again.

"I'm just a fabricant." The voice was carefully controlled, indifferent. "That's all."

"That's like saying you're just an infrafusion bomb, that's all.

Just your ordinary run-of-the-mill little old harmless explosive device sitting around going tick tick tick."

Again, I saw that cold *something* flicker across his eyes, arctic emptiness blowing through a lifeless abyss. Chilly goose bumps rose on the back of my neck.

The waiter came with the cognacs. "You got any cigars?" I asked him on impulse.

"Certainly, sir," he said.

He brought a wooden tray, hand-rolled brown Havanas in varying sizes nesting in their aromatic cradles. I picked out a Romeo y Julieta, seemed ironic enough of a statement for me.

"Want one?" I asked Halton.

"I don't smoke."

"You wouldn't," I retorted, but kept any other pointed remarks to myself. Other ears were listening. The waiter offered me the guillotine to snip the end, then lit the cigar for me. I'd made far too many mistakes today, time to really get down deep into the role I had to play. I puffed white smoke into a halo around my head.

"Thank you," I said to the waiter and he went away.

We sipped, I smoked in silence. Finally, I couldn't help it. It just came out. "Shit. Nanopunked," I said. And shook my head in disbelief. "I sure didn't read *that* in the Owner's Manual."

"It's not that unusual," Halton said. "Humans were modifying themselves with nanos before there were fabricants. Even before nanotechnology, they altered themselves with electronic devices. Nanos are not classified material. You could have nanos tailored for you if you wanted them."

His voice was as impersonal as always, but it seemed to carry a hint of defensiveness, or maybe an appeal. Or maybe I was just reading things into it which weren't there.

"No, thanks," I said accusingly. "I don't stick things in my body I can't get out again if I change my mind later."

"Do you have a car?" Halton asked.

The abrupt change of direction baffled me. "What?"

"Do you own a motorized vehicle of some sort?"

I narrowed my eyes, suspicious. "Yeah."

"What kind?"

"A GM Mitsubishi,"

"Is it AI'ed?"

I had no idea where this line of questioning was going. "No, it's an economy car, a Temperance. Map computer, autopilot, that's about it."

"Have you named it?" He had the same flat look, eyes steady.

"What do you mean?"

"Many people give their cars pet names. Have you given your car a name?"

I thought about my first car, a gas-guzzling land whale, one of the last American solo-produced monstrosities, which I bought in lousy secondhand condition for very little money. It was a dented dark blue sedan, practically drove itself even before computerization. I'd called it Miss Violet before the thing upchucked and died for good on me in the middle of rush-hour traffic during final exams. Then I called it "You piece of shit" and had it hauled off to Auto Purgatory.

"No, I don't name my cars," I said. "Why?"

"Many people do. They give inanimate objects names and expend a great deal of affection and attention on them while knowing intellectually that the object itself is incapable of returning, or even recognizing, the devotion lavished on it."

I picked up the gist. "And you're not an inanimate object, that it?"

He ignored the question. "Do you have a pet like a dog or a cat?"

I leaned back, one arm draped over the back of the chair as I puffed on my cigar. "Yes, I had a dog when I was a kid. She was a German shepherd mix I got from the pound. Yes, I gave her a name. Her name was Kooty. Yes, I lavished affection and attention on her, which she recognized and responded to, without any problem."

"She had teeth? Was carnivorous? Occasionally aggressive?" The deadpan delivery was grating on my nerves.

"So what are you getting at?"

"She had the capability of doing physical damage to you, yet you were never afraid of her? You trusted her?"

I signaled the waiter for another cognac. The last one wasn't doing much for me. "Kooty was a dog. You're not a dog. You're a very dangerous humanoid biomachine designed and built by the people who brought us orbital laser weapons, great big infrafusion bombs capable of blowing up the moon with a single shot, tiny little smart bullets programmed to kill only the selected target, and God only knows what else. You may be a little young to remember the war in Khuruchabja—" I was startled by his fleeting smile, but failed to see the humor in that bloody conflict. "But I was there. I've seen what your bosses' toys are capable of doing to human beings. You're their creature, Halton. Your only loyalty is to the Men on the Hill, so *don't* try jerking me around, okay?"

He didn't even stop to think about it. "There are four hundred seventy-five operational fabricants currently in active use in five different governmental departments," Halton said quietly. I stared popeyed at him. He waited, scanning my face, his eyes moving back and forth as he studied me.

*That* certainly wasn't part of the "approved for public consumption" literature in the Government information handouts. I sat straighter, stubbed out my half-smoked cigar and paid attention.

"Each design specialization is broken down into five subsectors, controlled under two main sectors depending on eventual application. Each sub-sector is divided into categories with units of ten identical fabricants, each with fifty more nonactive recombinant embryos in deep-cold storage. My fabricant designation is subcategory Halton, series John. Central Defense and Intelligence has two sub-sectors for its exclusive use, as well as ancillary fabricants on loan to other departments. My sub-sector is part of CDI's exclusive quota." The facts were delivered in a precise, cold recitation.

"This is classified information you're giving me, Halton. I'm a journalist . . ."

"Seven hundred sixteen experimental fabricants were terminated over the original development period of ten years," he went on, unshakable, "due to defects from natural causes, design flaws and unforeseen or unacceptable progressions in the construction process."

Even Congress hadn't been able to squeeze exact dates and figures out of the mealy-mouthed CDI spooks they'd dragged into the hearings. No one knew how long CDI had been developing their fabricant technology, nor how many there were. It had it all been buried under the National Information Security Act. "You're not supposed to be telling me this," I said, nearly whispering.

He didn't falter. "Over the past seven years, sixty-two successfully completed and functional fabricants have been lost in covert operations while in place and engaged in CDI or other Government-supported actions . . ."

"Are you . . . ?"

". . . thirty-nine fabricants have been terminated by CDI or other Government departments after failing to complete their assigned missions, and seventeen fabricants have successfully completed their assigned missions, then been terminated for reasons of irreparable physiological damage or psychological contamination."

"Shut *up*, Halton." I was suddenly very afraid, for him, for myself, paranoid that someone was listening. I suppressed the desire to peek under the table. "If they find out you're shooting your mouth off, what happens then?"

"I would be immediately terminated," he said, without hesitating. *"Will you trust me now?"*

He was leaning toward me; his dark eyes bored into mine. I swallowed, and sat back. My heart was racing, and I had to pull myself in tight to think.

"Providing this isn't more disinformation," I said slowly. His expression didn't change. "You could be lying, telling me just what I'm supposed to think, so you—or they, through you—can manipulate me the way they want. That *is* how they operate, and there's no way I can corroborate this information, now is there?"

Halton closed his eyes, holding them shut for the space of several heartbeats, then exhaled and sat back, defeated. "I haven't lied to you," he said, almost wearily, "but I concede that there isn't much I can do to prove it without ending up dead as a result."

"Even if it's true, why tell me? Why hand me a loaded gun?"

"Because I need you to trust me. I need your help," he said simply. "I don't want to end up like other expended fabricants."

I watched him as he sipped the last of his cognac, his hands steady, eyes impersonal. The rest of my brandy sat untouched.

"You proposing some kind of bargain, is that it?" I asked finally. "Are you offering to trade information in exchange for GBN's help, maybe get you out of CDI?" I thought of old Cold War films, shadowy-eyed men in trench coats and slouch hats hanging around in rain-soaked alleyways. "Do you want to defect?"

He took so long to answer, I thought he wasn't going to. He stared into his empty snifter. "Not . . . exactly."

I wasn't sure I really trusted him, or believed his story. Our coffee cups were empty, cognac gone, the cigar ashes cold. Our waiter began to look impatient; we were cutting into his rate of turnover and another tip. He hovered persistently nearby, and the chances of being overheard increased tenfold. I motioned for the check, which arrived almost instantaneously, and paid it on my GBN corporate card without bothering to look over the charges. I just wanted to get out of there.

We stepped out into the busy main drag. On a Station, the official time is synchronous with whatever time zone it happens to be in orbit above, but since most everyone arriving is zoned to a different time anyway, Clarke Station was the space city that never slept. Restaurants opened and closed by their own clocks; most ran twenty-four hours a day, willing to serve whatever meal your stomach told you it was time for. Shops were almost all continuously open, it seemed; so were cinemas and "night" clubs. The street outside was as jammed at "midnight" as it was at "noon."

"Okay, let's go back to the hotel," I said, as he fell into step beside me. "Maybe we *should* talk."

He shook his head. "Our rooms are bugged."

"Now you tell me." We strolled up the street, heading for a community park at the center. "Hell, for all I know, *you're* bugged, Halton. Maybe they've put teeny-tiny nanocameras inside your eyeballs and not even you know about it."

I was joking. He took me seriously. I got a chance to verify that his hypothalamus did indeed work at least analogously to mine; he blanched, and looked shaken.

"If they have," he said, his voice calmer than he appeared, "I'll know about it soon enough."

*Then* I believed him.

# FIVE

I'd gotten an idea from the janitor we'd asked directions from on Level Two. As long as we were stuck here for days before the next flight down to Sun City, I figured we should keep busy. After all, we had all this great new GBN equipment we hadn't even checked out yet. I decided to shoot a feature piece on the Station's unseen community; my specialty, a "human interest" story. Also, I thought it might be a good idea to resurrect "Kay Bee Sulaiman" with a smaller story first while "Kay Munadi" was on vacation.

Halton didn't say much for the first few days as we walked around scouting possibilities. I suspect he was waiting to see if someone would show up on his doorstep and blow his expensively cultured brains out the back of his skull. When they didn't after a few days, he spent an afternoon searching out and crippling listening devices in both our rooms. But we didn't talk about much, not even then. Our relationship was uneasy, if cordial enough.

We found the janitor in the ugly yellow coveralls. I stuck my hand out and grinned. "Hi, Kay Bee Sulaiman, GBN Network News?" Always approach it as a question, never seem too aggressive.

"Yeah, I 'member you," the janitor responded. "I mean I

watch GBN, all th'time, really, but you were the guys got lost th'other day? That was you, right?"

This time, I had the field pak part of my PortaNet slung across my shoulders, and Halton was toting the holocamera, with extra slipclips on his belt in case we needed more footage.

"Yeah, that was us." I chuckled depreciatingly. "It's a big Station, easy to get lost in if you don't know your way around."

Yeah, yeah, he was nodding and grinning in complete agreement. He looked back and forth from me to Halton, expectantly. "This's John Halton, my holo optics man."

Halton slipped his shoulder out from under the holocamera rest to shake the janitor's grimy hand. "Hi, just call me John, how you doin'?" Halton said smoothly, with a casual Californian intonation. *Perfect*, I thought, with just a twinge of envy.

I'd run Halton through the usual GBN protocol as if he were just another rookie, which was exactly what he was. None of this "How do you do, ma'am, very fine, thank you, sir" bullshit. Come on too formal and you look like just another uppity rich puke these people are sweeping the floors for.

Guy's name was Randy Something; I could look it up. Used to be Stations hired just the cream of the crop, at first only those ultimate astroheads straight out of college, then topline executives and company careerists once it started going more commercial, at least at the South Pole. The North Pole was still reserved for hush-hush shit. Who knows if there were even any live people there to clean up after? Maybe Secret Santa had his double-agent elves do it.

Once the rich boys and girls came up to play, however, the college sophisticates weren't the type to be mopping gilded toilets or changing coitus-perfumed silk sheets. There's always been an underprivileged underbelly keeping things neat and tidy for the rest of us, and eventually, Stations had them, too.

Randy and the rest of the Service Engineering Department were neither stupid nor uneducated. Service is as necessary as any other work, and the Service people were proud of the job they did. Getting hired on a Station was a relatively prestigious position at any rate, and the pay certainly wasn't bad. But Randy wasn't the type to rise in a rags-to-riches story from what was still technically the gutter to the penthouse. He didn't mix with the affluent business types, just did his job, hung out with his Service peers and stayed invisible.

We shot a shitload of footage, lots of man-on-the-street-type interviews, lots of background shots of dancers undulating in glittering nightclubs, to cut later with silent footage of Randy riding his little cleanercart down a deserted corridor. The noisy clatter and tinkle of porcelain and silver in exclusive, crowded restaurants, overweight executives spouting corptalk and mergerbabble, contrasting with the quiet lunchroom conversation as Randy and his crew discussed various diets to keep their weight below the required economically viable liftoff/kilo rate. The chaos of high-powered entrepreneurs bustling down the Main Arch, to cut in later with another janitor emptying garbage bins in the hushed solitude of the vast Waste Recycling Center.

"You wanna film me doin' this?" one of Randy's fellow Service employees said, her face screwed up in disbelief. "By *myself*?" She was in charge of the night-shift cleaning crew in the public toilets on Level Four. Halton had the top of his forehead jammed into the hololens cover, the little digital flyeyes projecting from either side of his head like some comic insect.

The rest of the crew stood behind Halton, grinning and trying to stifle the giggles. We could edit the sound later, but I wanted to keep it down to a minimum.

"You're right," I said quickly. "That wouldn't look authentic, would it? Need another person in here, give it a genuine feel, you're absolutely right." Actually, that wasn't what she meant at all. She was the boss. She didn't clean toilets; she told other people to clean toilets. But it was my show and I didn't want her getting too involved in the directorial end of things. She was still the boss, however, so she got first crack at "Hi, Mom," but I wanted a shot of somebody pushing a brush around a toilet bowl.

Dubiously, she picked her backup choice out of the group all going "Me! Me! Aww, c'mon, pick *me*!" and we got the pictures of two middle-aged, dignified women in immaculate uniforms silently scrubbing out the ladies' loo.

The flyeyes followed them as they went from stall to stall. "That's right, don't look at the camera," I said softly. "Just pretend we're not here . . . John, swing it around this way, get her reflection in the mirror . . ."

As great journalism goes, this wasn't exactly Pulitzer Prize material. Since it wasn't hot news, I had to script and cut it myself, before blipping it to Central. A calculated social commentary piece GBN would use as filler on a slow night, I still like to think it was well done, that I hadn't lost my touch after years of sitting behind a feed-in desk.

It was also interesting to see how Halton handled the optical machinery. He could simply pick up any piece of equipment and figure it out in about ten seconds flat. But journalism is more than pointing a camera in the right direction and a recitation of cold, dry facts.

The camera never lies, but a good cameraman can certainly edit what it sees. Close in on a shot and you can turn a few dozen beered-out kids into a whole city beseiged in a riot. Pull back on a shot of a politician's fiery speech to show a legislature full of empty seats, and you can thoroughly puncture his hot-air balloon. I explained the concept briefly to Halton, he nodded, and that was it. You never had to tell him anything twice.

It was as if he'd done field work for years. I watched without any sense of pride, since I hadn't done much teaching. What I felt was a vague indignation and anxiousness, the kind you get when someone says, "You can be replaced, you know." Sort of what I imagined the tall Cro-Magnon man might have sneered down his Aryan nose at some dark and hairy, beetle-browed Neanderthal: *This planet ain't big enough for the both of us. . . .*

Because that's what someone like Halton meant to me. Anything I could do, he could do better than me. The six-gadzillion-dollar man—stronger, faster, smarter, cleaner, better-looking, more talented—you name it, John Halton had it. And if he didn't, there were nine more exactly like him where he came from. He made me nervous.

The night we filmed the potty patrol, we went back to the hotel to take a nap before the next scheduled shot. My watch bleeped me awake and I banged on the connecting door.

"Let's go, it's a long walk," I called out, running a comb through the stubble of what was left of my hair and tucking in my rumpled shirt. He opened the door within two seconds. I couldn't help staring.

Everything was in place. The shirt was still unwrinkled, his hair unmussed.

"Didn't you take a nap?" I asked suspiciously.

"Yes, of course," he said, serious.

See what I mean?

We trammed it to the shanklift, heading out to the peripheral edge of the South Pole, a place normally off-limits to the general public, but we'd pressed enough palms and filmed

enough "Hi, Moms" to get an invite. There, we set up a tele-
photo shot, and filmed, I'm not kidding, a space cowboy riding
his electric manure spreader away from the camera, down a
long, long row of experimental crops glassed in under the wide
black heavens above, pinpoint cold stars gleaming. We had
timed and angled the shot to pick up the Earth low in the distance, and waited until the sun peeked out over the edge, shooting a nimbus of glorious color through the Station's periphery
and silhouetting our tiny Lone Ranger riding off into the sunrise. Barely got it into the slipclip, too, before the Station rolled
far enough to ruin our perspective.

God, it was hokey. Gloriously wonderfully tearjerker hokey,
it'd be a hit, I was sure of it. But we had nine slipclips worth of
footage to cut and edit into a two-minute and a five-minute
short, plus a full-length twelve-minute version, before boarding
time for Khuruchabja the next morning.

We hustled ass back to the hotel, with the intention of
shoving my TV holoset through the connecting door into Halton's room to use in tandem with his set as editing monitors. It
was bolted to the floor.

"Phone!" I bellowed somewhere mid-curse.

"Yes?" Why do all phones have that same insipid, androgy-
nous voice? Give them a goddamned gender and be done with
it.

"Front Desk. Now."

Once they'd figured out what we needed, it took about an
hour to find somebody from Maintenance who knew how to disconnect the TV from the floor while I pulled out what was left
of my hair. After we got the TV moved, I called Room Service,
and had them send up a half-case of Budweiser, the real Czech
stuff, not that watered-down American crap, a tub of ice to keep
it cool and a couple trays of anonymous finger food.

We plugged in the PortaNet to one monitor, and the
HoloPak to the other, sitting cross-legged on the bed or the floor
while we blipped and snipped, going over the edited clips and
cleaning up sounds, re-digitalizing the images to sharpen the
depth, magnifying some cuts, reducing others, intersplicing this
with that to see what the effect would be. I paced around pro-
jections, making sure all the angles fit, then ran them back, over
and over, until my eyes started burning. For a while, the joy of
work even made me forget Halton was a CDI fabricant, and I
snarled at him for his opinion of this shot or that angle as if he

were any other all-too-human cameraman. Six and a half hours later, I had my three pieces, each ending with our little farmer far from Mother Earth in complete silence for several seconds, no commentary necessary, other than the sound of the manure spreader humming along, to spoil the overall impact.

Then the voice-over: "Kay Bee Sulaiman"—long pause—"Clarke Orbital Station"—another long pause—"for GBN Network News."

The end.

I leaned back, cracking stiff backbone joints and groaning. We'd been sitting on the floor for hours, and my butt had fallen asleep. Halton still looked like he'd just been unwrapped from the box. I looked around the room and chuckled.

Empty beer bottles littered the room, some of the dead soldiers leaking fluid, foam-rimmed dark spots on the carpet. Slip-clip cartridges were scattered on the floor and the rumpled bed, detritus of food crumbs and greasy chicken bones sprinkled liberally about for good measure.

"Ah, jeez, Halton," I teased. "We've mussed up your pretty room. What a shame."

He glanced around, and said without a trace of irony, "The cleaning crew will take care of it."

My jaw dropped and I burst out laughing, clutching my sides and rolling over onto the rug as he looked at me with an innocent, puzzled expression. That just kept me going. I laughed so hard, my eyes teared up and I thought I'd pee my pants. I was tired and punchy, and it just felt good to laugh.

I wheezed back into some sense of self-control, and said, "Maybe we should have filmed this room and *you* as the last act. Jesus, Halton, you're so fucking *perfect*." I wiped my eyes, and handed him one of the last two beers left in the tub. "Here, why don't we finish these off before we crash."

He took it and drank it. We leaned back together against the side of the bed, watching the fuzz of dead air hover as the monitor projected nothingness.

"You did okay," I said finally, a little reluctant. "I gotta admit. Good job, Halton." I bounced the end of my half-finished beer lightly on the end of his knee, a gesture of semi-drunkish camaraderie. Y'know, the fellow journalist buddies kind of shit.

I was smiling, feeling mellow, feeling like we'd just done a good job, and my body was tired with the pleasant ache that comes after a well-done story. He looked at me, strange poker face hiding whatever was going on in that deluxe manufactured brain.

The next second, I was standing, backed up against the wall, quivering with outrage and panic while he just sat on the floor gazing up with ingenuous surprise. The son of a bitch had just tried to kiss me.

"You did a good job, but not *that* good," I spat out. "Just what the fuck was that all about?"

"I'm sorry," he said quickly. "I misread your intention."

"No shit!"

"May I explain?"

I held my hands up, warding it off. "Hey-ey, I don't think I want to hear it—"

"*Please*, Kay Bee . . ."

I was panting like I'd just run the three-minute mile, heart boinging around in my chest like mad. I didn't say anything, too busy trying to catch my breath, get myself back under control, and he took that as a "yes."

"When I told you my sexual experience was limited, I didn't define how limited it really is. I understand *sex* well enough; the kind of women I've had intercourse with simply made their propositions direct and unambiguous."

Christ, he didn't even have the euphemisms down.

"I haven't had much exposure to people outside CDI; I've never been on an outside assignment before. It's important for me . . . *essential* that I learn how to analyze different people's emotional states—that's what I was telling you about fabricant and human brains not seeing or feeling things in exactly the same way."

I haven't had all that many men put the make on me in my lifetime, either, and I was well aware they usually had pragmatic ulterior motives for the sudden, undying passion. I didn't like it any better than the next woman, and loathed myself whenever I gave in. But most of them had at least had the courtesy of maintaining the illusion of lusting after my body, and my self-esteem wasn't exactly in a position to challenge anyone on it. Halton's blunt admission that I was just a guinea pig for his impersonal curiosity about human emotions blew away any warm feelings I might have been developing toward him.

"So learning the art of seduction is just another part of your assignment, is it?" I had the jitters under control, and scorching anger was taking its place. The words came out venom. "Your bosses teach you all the right tricks to get me to fall in lust, blow in my twat and I'll follow you anywhere? Or is this just another part of your deal? Am I supposed to be so grateful that a hunk like you would jump these homely old bones, I'll risk my ass for you?"

He hadn't moved from the floor, his hands palms down by his side on the rug, legs still stretched out casually, crossed at the ankles. His eyes watched me with detached calm. "It's not like that," he said quietly.

"I'll just bet," I sneered.

"You were sexually attracted to me when we met, before you knew I was a fabricant," he said. I felt my face flush. "The other night at dinner, when you asked about my love life, you had strong sexual desires then, which I presumed I had been the stimulus for."

"God," I said, mortified. "I didn't realize I was being so obvious."

Halton looked suddenly embarrassed. "You weren't," he said, and held up one hand, palm facing me. "Nanos. Chemical sensors. I could read it when I touched you."

My skin crawled, and I think I wanted to kill him at that moment. Nothing could have better driven home just how inhuman he was. "You don't touch me again, *ever*. You got that?" I hissed.

He nodded. "Yes." The steady expression was the same, but his face had paled.

"I've been told I have to spend two more weeks with you, turn you over to Sheikh Larry, nothing more, and hopefully I'll never lay eyes on you again. Unless you've got something more than a bunch of unverifiable numbers or your fabulous mechanical prick on offer, you got *nothing* that I or GBN are willing to stick our necks out for. Meantime, you just play your role, and don't you forget mine, not for a second, not even in private. I'm a *man*, and I don't fuck other men."

I could feel the rage beginning to unglue my seams again. At any moment I'd start smashing things, which I really didn't want to do and chance destroying six and a half hours worth of edited work. I had to get out of there. My legs felt like frozen rubber bands as I crossed to the connecting door and jerked it open.

"And I *especially* don't fuck robot spies," I said in a low voice, to keep it from quavering.

"I understand," he said softly, still sitting on the floor.

"I hope to God you do." I slammed the door shut behind me and spent the next few hours lying on my back, chain-smoking and staring at memories crowding the ceiling, hating myself.

# SIX

I blipped the story down to GBN and wiped the slipclips before we packed up and checked out. I was nervously packing the microflake in my PortaNet, trying to stuff it casually into a side pocket ("Microflake? In *my* PortaNet? Jeez, Officer, how the hell'd *that* get in there?"), when Halton asked me for it. I'd hesitated for just a moment, then given it to him. What the hell, he was paid to do the spy-schtick, not *me*. He went to the head for a few minutes, returned, and we left the room without a word. Maybe he'd flushed it—I didn't really care, just so long as I didn't get caught trying to enter Khuruchabja with illegal substances. I wasn't going to rot in a Khuruchabjani prison for fifty years so CDI agents could send love letters to each other.

Going through Orbital Passport Control, I was more nervous than Halton, but I already knew that wasn't unusual. He handed the Orbital officer his bogus passport card without blinking an eye, laid his steady hand down on the pad. The reader beeped a contented Okay, and spit it out, no problems.

The Orbital down to Cairo was pretty much a rerun of the one up, this time with filet mignon and port-sautéed pears. Halton and I didn't talk much on the flight, and I didn't drink much this time. Khuruchabja is, technically, alcohol-free. They frown heavily on people smuggling liquor into the country, even if you're bringing it inside your own bloodstream. We set down at

Helwan InterOrbital, and had to race to catch the only connecting commuter flight from Cairo to Rawalpindi in the Republic of Independent Punjab, with a dozen stops along the way, including fabulous downtown Nok Kuzlat.

The decrepit puddle-jumper was only fourteen hours behind schedule, remarkably on time for that part of the Middle East. At least five hundred passengers were waiting for a place in the seventy-seater plane, all of whom carried four times their weight in ratty luggage, boxes tied with string, extra-large duty-free bags filled to ripping capacity with plastic-covered clothes, bottles of French mineral water, stuffed toys, disposable diapers and Belgian chocolates. A few even held crates of various animal species, all adding their barks, mews, cackles and bahs to the overwhelming noise. We fought our way through the screaming, furious mob to the gate and were waved through by the grace of a fresh 100-*écu* note.

While there were plenty of people in Cairo anxious to get on the plane, most of them were not getting off at Nok Kuzlat. You have to remember that Khuruchabja hasn't really been of world-wide importance for much other than some of the most spectacularly bloody, vicious fighting the world had seen. It has a few tiny oil deposits, not even sufficient for its own population's energy needs, and no other natural resources that any other part of the world covets. Its indigenous population is a loose collection of rabid ultra-fundamentalist zealots, whose only interesting occupation seems to be continuous internecine squabbling. It has some minor strategic value, a sort of buffer zone between two countries who *really* hate each other's guts. But Khuruchabja itself is too far from anything else anybody would want, and too small to be much more than a nuisance to its neighbors.

The last time I'd been here, Khuruchabja was being run by a group of extremists calling themselves the National Behjar Democratic Brotherhood, who knew as much about democracy as I know about quantum astrophysics. Their monomaniacal leader, al-Husam, had the charisma of the Ayatollah Khomeini, the lunatic mania of Qaddafi and the chutzpah of Saddam Hussein. But except for the occasional car bomb and hostage-taking, they'd been no more than the usual nuisance. Then the Brotherhood managed to catapult Khuruchabja to the front line of world attention after the forerunner of the CDI helped them get their grubby hands on a couple of small infrafusion devices.

Unfortunately, al-Husam promptly welshed on whatever covert agreement he'd made with the CDI, and was threatening to use the bombs in the name of Allah on his most detested Enemies of the Week, which would have severely altered the landscape and real-estate values of the countries immediately bordering his chosen target.

The despised American devils and their traitorous puppet allies, of course, couldn't allow such an occurrence, and the people responsible for creating the mess in the first place were keeping rather quiet about it. Technically, since it was an internal affair, direct action against the Behjars, the then current semi-legitimate government of Khuruchabja, was not recommended. The UN went through its usual futile attempts at negotiations, one broken cease-fire after another, before giving the inevitable okay for intervention. The Western powers managed to persuade the various countries allied in the Damascus Coalition "Peacekeeping" Force to stop quarreling with each other long enough to play with the newest high-tech toys in the name of Muslim Unity. The U.S. and Common Europe jockeyed with each other over who got to be Executive Producer and which general got the credits as Director.

Every news organization sent in its own battalions of reporters, PortaNets strapped to their backs. This war, our military didn't bother with the press pool farce. But also, this war, the military gave the media some stiff competition of their own, a PR battle for the viewing public's limited attention span, with their exclusive fighter gun and missile cameras bringing back spectacular high-definition digitalized holo footage of explosions in full living color with wraparound Dolby sound. With their consciences salved that our bombs were "guaranteed-100%-*this*-time-not-to-harm-civilians, video war addicts went into prolonged orgasms.

Mankind's weapons get "smarter" and more sophisticated, but our political acumen doesn't appear to evolve at the same pace. In spite of a few minor adjustments, the story unfolding was pretty much the same as the last one, and the one before that, the end result being lots of people dead and homeless, property destroyed simply to get back to square one and start the process all over again. The Have-Nots will always resent the Haves, and stir up trouble. The Haves will always squash them in the end, to keep them from getting any of *theirs*, and the news will be there to preserve those precious moments as they occur. Nobody has ever been able or willing to solve the underlying problems—especially in *this* part of the world—that have caused all this misery in the first place.

While all of Khuruchabja's military bases were outfitted with modern airfields, Nok Kuzlat's civilian airport didn't have quite the same degree of amenities. It had a single runway, the dirt and potholes covered by a thin layer of cracked tarmac and oil. A charred litter of less fortunate planes decorated the sides of the strip. The airport had no tower, no radar, the only item of hightech being a tattered red wind sock which usually hung lifeless from a pole. Of course, when there was wind, it would have been impossible to see the sock through the blowing sand, anyway.

The decrepit puddle-jumper wobbled its way to a spine-crunching landing at Nok Kuzlat in the middle of the afternoon. It was unbelievably hot, the white glare of the sun boring down with an almost perceptible weight. My clothes began clinging with sweat to my skin. I had also somehow managed to forget about the smell since I was last here. Now the exotic perfume of the Middle East came back in a pungent assault: a mix of dust, urine and gasoline.

We debarked in the middle of the runway, filed past a surprised-looking pilot and down a rickety ladder pushed up against the side of the aircraft. The two dour-looking men holding the ladder in place didn't seem too concerned we might slip and break our necks. Halton, I, and seven other businessmen of various nationalities clambered down cautiously and trekked across the airfield into Khuruchabja's quaint version of Customs. The terminal wasn't much more than a mud-and-concrete imitation of a Quonset hut, shaped much like the ovens the locals cook their flat bread in and with about the same internal temperature.

"Welcome back to the ass-end of the universe," I muttered to myself. The last time I'd left Khuruchabja I hadn't any intention of *ever* returning.

We avoided baggage claim, as the Nok Kuzlat International Airport didn't have one. Since Halton and I were carrying only two small suitcases and the PortaNet, we quickly passed our fellow passengers struggling along with their four and five suitcases, various duty-free bags and chicken crates, since the Nok Kuzlat International Airport didn't have baggage carts, either.

First stop in the cigarette-hazed terminal was Passport

Control. The hostile child with a submachine gun slung over his shoulder glared at us from behind his glassless window.

*"Fha'rmâan wah veesah,"* he demanded curtly.

We handed him our passport cards, along with the thick sheaf of our Khuruchabjani visas. The visas were absolutely essential, as the passport reader had apparently been out of service for the past decade. He took his sweet time thumbing through the visas, checking our names against those in a book the size of the Manhattan Yellow Pages. After appropriating several sheets with holoflats stapled to them, along with a 25-*écu* note sandwiched between them, he liberally garnished the remaining documents with a big rubber stamp, obliterating any vital information with beautifully ornate Arabic calligraphy. Finally he waved us through to Customs.

One thing Khuruchabja Customs is, if slow and primitive, is thorough. Their passport reader might be defunct, but their metal detector and X-ray machines were functional to the point of lethal radiation. If they believed I looked too suspect, they could decide to check to see whether I was using my asshole as an extra luggage compartment. Of course, once I'd dropped *my* drawers, I could use the opportunity to kiss my sweet feminine ass goodbye. A few of our fellow travelers were jerked out of line and expertly frisked, then marched off under armed guard to God knows where, just to make the rest of us paranoid. But for the most part, Khuruchabja officials make a great show out of inspecting foreign journalists' equipment with minute care while leaving our bodies alone.

"Please give me your wallets, open all luggage and lay it out on the counter," the surly kid with a razor-thin mustache said in Markundi, then, eyeing our Western clothes suspiciously, repeated in English, "Money. Bag put here, open now. *J'ahkzhil!* Quick!"

By now I was sweating with nerves and heat, and tried blathering a few friendly words of Markundi to impress the kid with my gallantry in learning his language. I'd forgotten a lot of the finer points of Markundi and it showed. His lip curled in derisive humor as he rifled through our wallets, toting up my *écus*. The Khuruchabjans counted hard currency to make sure visitors exchanged their money at the government's official rip-off rate rather than on the street at the black market's more realistic value. Every purchase we made thereafter had better come with a receipt, and any discrepancy found in the total on the way out would be severely penalized. He jotted down a figure before handing our wallets back, minus his inspection fee. No receipt for that, of course.

He turned his attention to my small suitcase, rifling through it and confiscating my after-shave (I might want to drink it), my two ballpoint pens (I might stab someone with them), pried the pinhead-sized ion battery out of my watch (I might use it to make a bomb), and my cigarettes (he liked the brand). Then he pointed at the PortaNet. "Put that up here, too. Open it."

Halton squinted at the kid quizzically for a moment, and smiled skeptically. *"Puridehz?"* he said, in strangely accented Markundi. The kid blinked rapidly in surprise, and grinned back, indecisive. "You *are* from Puridehz, aren't you? I *thought* so. . . ."

They babbled about cafes and streets in some northern town I had no idea existed, and the kid scribbled an address for his uncle's place we ever got to Puridehz look up the family and say hello from him stuck in the goddamned army for another two years miss his mom's cooking looking forward *insha'allah* God willing to going home. . . .

The kid piled everything back into my suitcase without much more than a cursory look, barely glanced at Halton's before turning to scowl at the man shuffling behind us, and we were through. We walked through the glass gates toward the gaggle of taxi drivers waiting to descend on us.

"That was slick," I said to Halton under my breath. "Thought you'd never been outside Langley."

"Get it out of books," he said, and we were swamped in the deluge of unwashed humanity clamoring for our business.

The airport was conveniently located some ten miles outside the city limits, and Nok Kuzlat, shimmering whitely off on the flat horizon, is much too far to walk to find a hotel. There is no train or bus service. The unsuspecting Western traveler arriving in Khuruchabja's capital city suddenly finds himself at the tender mercies of grinning dark-skinned men with unshaven faces under a mound of checkered yardage wrapped around their heads.

"Taxi? You maybe want taxi?" they whisper as conspiratorially as if they had dirty postcards or stolen watches under their qaftans. "My taxi very good, very cheap, get you there quick." Then there's the calculated confusion as one claimant declares the other a fraud and a cheat, trust only him, with the insulted party objecting strenuously with words or fists, whichever he's in the mood for. Finally, one or another wrestles the helpless luggage away, tries to make a twenty-yard-line dash with it for his taxi and stuff it into his trunk without being tackled, which apparently scores the touchdown. It doesn't matter which one in the end; they're all identical run-down junkers barely able to clatter along over spine-snapping potholes, and the fares equally extravagant.

Our driver, a wizened old man of around thirty-five named Samat, declared himself the victor as he pitched my captive suitcase and Halton's HoloPak into his trunk, slammed down the lid and jumped up to sit on it, grinning ear to ear. I'd managed to keep hold of the PortaNet, getting my shoulder wrenched for the effort, and we got into Samat's fifteen-year-old Ford Suzuki, on our way to the Nok Kuzlat Grand Imperial Hotel on Hajara Boulevard.

The seats had been covered with a frayed Persian carpet which hid but didn't do much else for the vast amount of torn and missing foam padding underneath. The antique air conditioner wheezed and moaned vigorously, barely making a dent in the temperature. It wasn't that far from the city suburbs, and we plunged into the midst of narrow, crooked streets, bisected at impossible angles by other narrow, crooked streets. Samat negotiated them with enthusiastic breakneck speed, barely missing innocent pedestrians attempting to use the same thoroughfares, since sidewalks seemed entirely lacking.

I hadn't been in Nok Kuzlat in more than a decade, and at that time bombs and fires had done a lot to alter the city's ambience. Also, to a certain extent, the outskirts of Nok Kuzlat looked pretty much like any other slum area that accretes itself along the perimeters of more prosperous city centers in this area of the world. It was a strange mixture of modern opulence and primordial misery: new holosets flickering in the windows of decrepit tin-roofed shacks; an electric toilet abandoned in an alleyway next to rabbit-warren apartment blocks with an open sewer trickling past the front doors; children running in the dusty streets half naked, playing with the broken pieces of technological wonders cast off by their rich city cousins; an old, bent woman completely covered in embroidered red wool, flicking a switch at a half-dozen skipping goats as she herded them past a man dressed in a Western business suit and kaffiyeh talking into his remote PC modem.

I wasn't paying much attention to our route, since I've long accepted the theory that taxi drivers will always take you far out of your way, the longest possible circuit in order to confuse you into paying four times more than you should. The bleak slums and devastated apartment buildings all looked pretty much the same; it wasn't like I knew Nok Kuzlat like the back of my hand.

But I did notice when Halton began glancing out the window and into Samat's rearview mirror, his eyes alert and wary as he studied our friendly taxi driver chattering away in some incomprehensible Markundi accent.

"What is it?" I demanded in English. He didn't have time to answer before Samat slammed on the brakes and turned around to lean across the seat, black teeth grinning over an antique but quite deadly fletchette pistol pointed at us. Dust-blurred forms of men moved in to block the light outside the windows. "Ah, shit," I said, disgusted. "This is really getting ridiculous. . . ."

The doors were yanked open, and we were invited to accompany our new friends into the cool, dark sanctuary of a bombed-out building conveniently located right on that very street. Samat sped off in a squeal of balding tires and rooster-tail of dust, probably a real taxi driver on his way back to the airport to see if he could find another group of kidnappers willing to pay big money for stupid infidels.

Inside the building, my eyes adjusted to the gloom. It looked like it might have once been a cafe, but had the distinct reek of having been uninhabited for some time. Pigeons cooed unseen in the shadows overhead. The largest of the five men had his arm crooked around Halton's neck and an Israeli-made Eclipse pistol pressed firmly against his head. Halton wasn't resisting. Two others had me pinned between them by either arm, and the remaining two were busy dumping our clothes and equipment in a jumble onto a floor splattered with pigeon crap.

A puff of smoke wafted across the shaft of light filtering down from a hole in the wall far above us, and I made out the vague silhouette of someone seated behind a small table, smoking a cigarette. All of a sudden, I really wanted one, too.

"You know, you people should think about hiring a new scriptwriter for this shit," I said to the shadow. "I've seen old TV reruns with more originality—"

"Shut up," the shadow said in a husky woman's voice. She was definitely not a native Anglophone, but her accent was very pretty. My escorts decided to lift me off my feet for emphasis, making my shoulder sockets ache.

Finally the two men rooting through the remains of our luggage sat back on their heels. "It's not here," one said in Markundi.

"Perhaps one of them has concealed it upon his body," the woman said in her lilting English.

The man who'd spoken turned to stare at me; a stiletto materialized in his hand, snipping the air. He smiled thinly. "Perhaps we should look," he said. Right. Sure. Always pick on the littlest guy first.

Clichéd or not, this had *not* been part of the original plan. I had a sinking feeling I knew what they were looking for. The man with the knife stepped closer to me. He seemed like an ordinary kind of guy, not what you'd think of as a villainous Snydley Whiplash twirling his mustache. No bulging biceps, no rotting teeth, no livid scar etched across his evil face. Just your everyday working type.

Do you know that if you kick a woman in the crotch as if she had balls, the resulting physiological incapacitation is very similar? Well, okay, maybe not *exactly* the same, but when he kicked me with a steel-reinforced boot, I heard the bones in my pubis go crunch. I don't know if it hurt as bad as it might have had I been a man, but it was bad enough, believe me.

My escorts allowed me to drop to my knees on the dirty floor, where I clutched my injured parts, moaning. Then the guy who'd kicked me did a little dance step and kicked me again, neat and square with his toe in the solar plexus, sending me sprawling. Someone had studied his anatomy diligently in school. He got in a couple of extraneous blows to the head and neck, more for general pain than for disabling any potential defense, before I was jerked up and spun around to fall in the arms of one of his friends. I hung there like a drunk, completely paralyzed as agony shuddered through me.

They tore my shirt as they dragged my pants down around my wobbling knees, laughing. I got spun around to face the guy with the knife again. He appeared indistinct through my tears.

"It's a *woman*," someone gasped, and I was ignominiously dropped on the floor on my bare ass. Once let go of, I promptly curled up into a fetal position, trying to do nothing more strenuous than whimper piteously.

Things happened pretty fast after that, none of which had to do with me. A snap, a strangled scream, another crack, and the guy holding Halton fell down with his neck broken. The Eclipse pistol spit twice and two more went flying like disjointed rag dolls tossed aside. From the floor, I watched the shadow at the table start to stand. A second Eclipse spat-spat as Halton *flowed*—I can't think of any other way to put it—from one side of the room to the other. The fourth man with the gun died, little pieces of his chest puffing out of his shirt. The man with the knife threw it at Halton and died before it was halfway through its flight. When it reached its target, the target had long gone. The knife thunked solidly into a wall, quivering. Startled birds fluttered high above us.

It had taken only a few seconds. Five men lay motionless on the floor. The woman was standing up now and took a single step into the column of dusty light, illuminating her like a theatrical stage light. She had an Eclipse as well, this one pointed at me.

Halton froze, his gun trained on her.

She was beautiful in the way only Arab women can be, breath-stealingly beautiful, golden-skinned, almond eyes, black hair down to her waist. A tiny glint of a gold stud in both perfectly curved ears. Expensively tailored Western dress that hugged a flawless figure. She stared at Halton, and spoke in Markundi, her tone one of awe and helpless frustration.

"*Yah'malahjinn.*"

The hand on the gun pointed at me wavered, her finger tightening fractionally against the trigger.

He shot her.

She fell down, and that was it, really.

Halton stood looking at the woman's body for just a second more, still holding the Eclipse at the ready with one hand bracing his wrist, dust motes filtering down over them both in the glimmer of sunshine. Maybe he was admiring her, even dead. Maybe he just wanted to make sure she *was* dead.

It was suddenly very quiet, kinda pretty, even, except that I hurt a whole lot. Then Halton was kneeling next to me, his Eclipse clattering to the floor. The faint, acrid tang of its burnt explosive bit the air.

"Kay Bee . . ." He reached out to grasp my shoulders to

help me sit up, then hesitated with his hands inches from me, his face genuinely anguished.

I grabbed hold of the front of his shirt, struggled to pull myself up. He gripped me by my elbows, and I could feel him trembling. I looked him straight in the eye, then vomited all over his immaculately shined shoes.

I sure was spending a lot of time puking up airplane food on this goddamned trip.

# SEVEN

Somehow, Halton got our stuff back into the suitcases, and, somehow, he got us a ride to the Grand Imperial, and, somehow, he got me past the front desk and up into the room. I could barely walk, every step making the inside of my thighs scream all by themselves.

He laid me out on the closest bed and peeled my clothes off gingerly, careful to avoid touching my bare skin. I honestly couldn't have cared less at that point. I had several large bruises beginning to swell and darken, the worst of which was between my legs. He found an ice machine somewhere, and when he laid crushed ice wrapped in a wet washcloth against my injured crotch, I had to fight not to shriek in agony. He dragged a chair up next to the bed and sat motionless, his hands resting lightly in his lap, getting up once in a while to change the ice pack, or dab gently at the oozing cuts congealing on my forehead and chin.

I think I slept. Sort of. I'd open my eyes, not like I was waking up, but I wouldn't know where the hell I was. I'd move, the pain would shoot up my torso, and I'd see Halton's impassive eyes watching me in the gloom.

I heard the faint noise of traffic, aware there was more of it than there had been before. I realized dumbly that the night had passed, and blinked open gummy eyelids. Halton still sat in the chair by the bed, his head bent slightly, eyes shut. He was breathing regularly, sound asleep. Hmm. So that's how he kept his shirts from wrinkling.

I only moved my head a fraction on the pillow, and he opened his eyes instantly, alert and gauging me critically.

"Water?" I croaked out, my lips cracked from mouth-breathing all night in hot, dry air. My tongue was parched and fuzzy, and I couldn't work up enough spit to wet my lips.

Wordless, he got up and ran tap water into a plastic tumbler, imitation cut crystal with the hotel's ornate crest embossed in scratched and faded gilt. When he bent to lift it to my mouth, I said peevishly, "I can hold it, just help me sit up, will you?"

He did, conscientiously not touching my nude body any more than necessary while trying not to be obvious about it. My hands still shook badly, and I spilled some water down my chin, wiping it away with the back of my hand. It felt wonderfully cool.

Halton didn't seem so fresh-pressed; he looked a little haggard around the edges. I kept seeing him move unearthly fast across a dusty cafe room, the dull snap of bones breaking, the flash of the Eclipse spitting, how beautiful the dead woman looked crumpled on the floor after he shot her. I've seen people die before, some of them up close and personal, but the sheer speed and efficiency with which Halton had killed scared me.

I was staring at him. It probably didn't take a mind reader to see what was written on my face. His eyes wavered, pained; then he looked away. "I've never killed anyone before," he finally said in a low voice.

*Could have fooled me.* I shuddered. But that was definitely a subject I didn't particularly care to bring up anyway. "Where's the microflake?" I demanded, unemotional.

For an answer, he stuck a forefinger in the side of his mouth, between his upper lip and his teeth as if digging at something caught between his molars. It stuck there a second, then pushed in further up. And up. And up. I could see the bulge it made against his cheekbone, and the lower lid of his eye pushed half shut. When he extracted his finger, the microflake rested on its tip.

"I have certain extra cavities in various parts of my body where people are not likely to look," he explained.

"That," I said, "is gross."

He gave it to me, and I handled it carefully, holding it up

to the early morning light. It was surprisingly dry, winking dully. It seemed harmless enough. "She called you something," I said pensively. ". . . *Yah'malahjinn?* Your Markundi is better than mine."

"It's a kind of mythological mechanical demon," he said. "Somewhat analogous to a Jewish golem." He didn't sound offended.

"Hmm." My mind was starting to work again, slowly. She had certainly seemed rather surprised. She had known about the microflake, known it was coming in on us, but *didn't* know Halton was a fabricant until it was too late. Very odd.

I continued to hold it up, eyeing it thoughtfully. "She seemed to want this rather badly," I said finally. "And she wasn't too polite about asking for it."

He took a deep breath, looking a little less frazzled. "Yes," he said. "So it seems."

"I wonder if we can crack it." I sat up and slowly put my legs over the side of the bed. And cried. I'm entitled, I'm a woman, it's in my contract. Besides, it *really* hurt. Halton didn't try to assist me or stop me, but mutely handed me my shirt. I had to have help getting into the pants, though.

We got the PortaNet and the HoloPak hooked up to the single Chinese model TV holoset the hotel room boasted, which of course didn't fit any standard jacks. I wished we'd brought an AI pocket PC with us as well, but the rather more orthodox Khuruchabjani muftis get the willies around machines that hold intelligent conversations with people. Something about trapped souls. Apparently Allah doesn't like them, and what Allah doesn't like isn't legal in Khuruchabja. At least openly, anyway. We finally got the jacks linked into the holoset.

Microflakes are made for containing extremely compressed layers of data, enough condensed information to hold half the Library of Congress squashed down into an opaque square two millimeters thick and no bigger than the nail on my little finger. They're multiple layered microDRAM-chips grown on a molecular level, *very* expensive, and you're not likely to find them on sale at your corner Mom and Pop Computer Shop. It takes a fairly sophisticated AI reader to unlock and unfold these layers, something that was a bit much to ask of a jury-rigged PortaNet and Chinese holoset. We could unfold about two simple layers before the thing balked; like seeing the cover art on a bookchip and only getting to read the title page.

All it said was, "Confidential. Restricted Access. Authorized Personnel Only." No shit.

I was sweating and cursing as we took turns bending over the PortaNet. Halton wasn't having any more success than I was, but concentrating on breaking into the flake made me forget some of my aches and pains. The phone rang, and I jumped about three feet in the air, landing hard on the chair. My pubis reminded me I shouldn't be doing any calisthenics for a while.

It also reminded me that I was royally pissed off.

"What!" I yelled.

"Kay Bee Sulaiman?" a man's voice on the other end asked, his tone slightly puzzled. I hadn't bothered to get up and turn the screen on. And didn't intend to. Not with my face the way it looked at the moment.

"Who wants to know?"

"Elias Somerton," he said promptly.

That wasn't Somerton's voice. "Well, hi there, Eli old buddy! How's your therapy coming along? Your kid out of detox yet?" Halton looked at me quizzically. I was feeling my old self coming back on-line.

"We don't have time for childish games, Sulaiman," the voice said, with a slight, but annoyed, English accent. "You and your holo optics photographer are expected tonight at His Excellency's Presidential Palace. There will be a formal dinner, nine o'clock. His Excellency is receiving the British Assistant to His Majesty's Foreign Secretary."

"Wow, and we're invited? Is it like black tie, or what?"

"You're just another reporter, Sulaiman—cover the dinner like any other GBN assignment. Do your job, got it?"

"Got it, bwana." I saluted even though the man on the other end couldn't see me.

"His Excellency has agreed to speak to you after the dinner. Wait for him to approach you."

I opened my mouth to say something about the microflake, then clamped it shut, temporarily distracted from thinking up wisecracks. I suddenly remembered, maybe a little too late, that the phones in Khuruchabja were routinely monitored. Especially those of foreigners. "Sure, no problem," I said.

"There had better not be," the voice said and hung up.

"CDI doesn't hire too many finishing school grads, do they?" I said to Halton.

"No, I don't believe so," he answered seriously.

I shook my head ruefully. "Jeez, Halton . . ." Then I had him stick the microflake back up his extra nasal fistula. It was probably safer there than anywhere else.

Khuruchabja's capital is neither as rundown nor ultramodern as you might assume. It's true that when God was busy parceling out national resources, Khuruchabja got the short end of the stick, one of the major reasons for their last war. They have few assets available to turn into ready cash in the same way as their rich Saudi Arabian and other Persian Gulf cousins do. The semi-friendly competition for the cutting edge on high-tech military toys had been exclusively reserved by the Israelis and the Americans between themselves for decades, with only occasional input from the French and British. Like every other Middle Eastern nation, Khuruchabja's offensive military power has been kept frustratingly third-rate. With the brief exception of the infrafusion threat.

Also, once the IMF got through "refinancing" Khuruchabja's national postwar debt, a good many Khuruchabjani citizens would be calculating their profit margins on investment stock only by the amount of wool it had growing on its back for generations to come.

Despite the customary Islamic duty of consecrating their worldly possessions by handing out a generous *sadaqa-t* to the needy, citizens of rich countries preferred to give alms to their native peasants, and let other countries worry about their own poor. There had been any number of complicated proposals for divvying up Middle Eastern oil wealth more evenly throughout the Arab world, none of which was ever found acceptable to those in control of the oil. For one thing, the "Arab" world isn't all Arab. Why should rich Arabs just give away the money Allah so obviously had intended for them by putting all that oil under *their* sand in the first place to a bunch of Persians? Or Kurds? Or Turks?

That question aside, there's the problem of "good" Arabs, meaning all those rich and comfortable Haves that do a lucrative business with the rest of the modern world, versus "bad" Arabs, the Have Nots that keep on creating trouble. Why throw good Arab money away on rabble-rousers like the Yemenese or the Palestinians? Or the Khuruchabjans? Even if national differences could ever be ironed out, there's always the next hurdle of which Muslim sects are the True and Pious Followers of the Prophet Muhammad, and which are nothing but a bunch of blasphemous reprobates spreading dissension and heresy. Royal families and presidents-for-life in various Middle East countries have been balancing on the delicate tightrope between secular progress and Islamic shar'ia law for decades, with only limited success.

Of course, if these arguments get shaky, the self-respecting Arab could always wrap himself in his emotional heritage, deeply offended, to play on the inexplicable guilt of the West and the radical fears of Muslims everywhere, Shi'ite or Sunni, rich or poor. How dare these imperialist Zionist-loving Western lapdogs usurp the rights of our faithful brothers of Islam and dictate how Muslim money should be spent, these traitorous bloodsucking infidels who have brought nothing but war and butchery to our holy sands? It is an Arab problem, which should be solved only by Arabs.

Right. Any century now.

Charity has always begun at home, and altruism always stops at the border, no matter whose border it is. No one cares what's going on in some other country, so long as it's not a plot to take *their* money away from *them*. The end result being, of course, that some Islamic countries are shamelessly rolling in dough while two miles away, across the border, homeless Muslim children starve in the most abject poverty imaginable. But before you go getting all self-righteously indignant, bear in mind we *Americhurjas* have had the same thing in the States ever since Polk ripped off large chunks of Mexican real estate and turned what was left into part of our own personal Third World right next door.

Khuruchabja is still an old, old part of the world, and there have been many borders drawn with a sandaled foot in its shifting sands over the centuries. Before Muhammad, the Persians and Sumerians carved great monuments here to their winged-lion gods, and the last remnants of the migratory Bedouin tribes still find shelter for their flocks in the shade of ruins. The Romans forged roads across the hostile deserts on their way to more hospitable vacation spots, and left behind a good number of sunken baths and arched aquaducts in the wastelands, a wealth of other statues and temples to other forgotten gods. The caliphs spread out into an increasingly complex fusion of Umayyad rule, uniting a new Muslim empire that embraced all of Khuruchabja in its enlightened collective grasp. Nok Kuzlat blossomed like a desert flower in the rain, and muezzins warbled from hundreds of minarets calling the thriving faithful to rich, opulent mosques.

Until the whole thing collapsed under the Abbasids and Shi'ites with the same petty secessionism that still tears apart empires and nations all over the globe. The wealth of the Muslim empire slipped away to places like Baghdad and Mecca and Damascus and Medina, while Nok Kuzlat's mosques, having no dearth of faithful, suffered from the lack of funds in their pockets. A brief rally under the Ottomans revived hopes of a united empire, the Turks occasionally stopping by to pay a Big Brotherly visit and a handy contribution to the city fathers.

The Ottomans were not exactly loved and adored by all their subjects, but they at least were Islamic. At the turn of the twentieth century, the British crushed the last great Muslim empire under the heel of colonial imperialism; then the Americans started sucking away the dreams of a united Islamic state along with the oil and their business monopolies. Nok Kuzlat went back to being a third-rate city eking out an existence at the edge of the desert—bitter, resentful and forgotten.

A partially dismantled ancient city wall demarcated the actual Old City center from the slums that had grown up around the perimeters. The city center itself had been relatively unscathed during the past war. Einsteinian missiles had carefully dissected communications centers and government buildings from architectural treasures while the outskirts took the brunt of the devastation, stupid bombs being sufficient to eradicate the messy chaos infesting the 'burbs. A compact collection of archaeological wonders and modern high-rise office buildings, the old city was punctuated by the green and white minarets and gold domes of all those mosques built during Nok Kuzlat's glittering heyday.

Khuruchabja was one of the last Muslim countries still collecting the religious donations that all Muslims were required to pay, since there were too few rich and generous businessmen to keep the cream floating on the top. The *zakat* created a steady drain on the already meager finances of average Khuruchabjans, but Islam was the law, and the law was to be obeyed. Or else. The faithful anted up their taxes to the holy IRS, and Nok Kuzlat continued to kid itself into believing it was actually a world-class city.

His Excellency, the Most Glorious and Sanctimonious Lawrence Abdul bin Hassan al Samir al Rashid, Beloved Servant of the Almighty and Merciful, Omnipresent and Invisible, Eternal and Everlasting Allah, Rightful Descendant of the Prophet Muhammad, Adored and Revered Titular Royal President-for-Life of All Khuruchabja, was the son of the second cousin of the uncle of the brother-in-law of the last potentate of Khuruchabja, inheriting his enviable position in the time-honored manner of his father and forefathers: by assassination. His illustrious predecessor had managed to keep the rabid wolves at bay for a few years longer than most, many of them members of his own family. He'd actually started working out some minor reforms within Khuruchabja in an attempt to win Western approval in the form of foreign aid for economic development, which might have helped to raise the standard of living for most of his subjects to a more modern level comparable to the vastly richer, secularized Islamic countries outside Khuruchabja's borders.

Of course, this kind of moral contamination by the satanic West didn't sit well with His Excellency's overabundance of xenophobic fundamentalist sects. Economic development would bring the taint of the West with it, leading to unspeakable horrors, like whiskey and rock music and—Allah forfend!—barefaced women tourists in shorts. It was, after all, these same godless infidels who had dropped most of the bombs on Khuruchabja, they reminded the monarch, disregarding the argument that the Behjars had been the enemy and the West had helped the Damascus Coalition to "liberate" Khuruchabja. Tiring of all this erudite debate, one of his most trusted bodyguards pulled a marketing sample of Israel's very first, brand-new Eclipse specials from under his robes and blew the ex-President to Paradise.

That's how it's traditionally done. I could understand why Sheikh Larry wanted to tap an outside employment agency for his bodyguard service.

Usually, one strong man is knocked off by another in a bloody game of King of the Mountain, brother pitted against brother, religious factions vying against secular. But when the dust cleared, a lot of job candidates on the short list were dead, while nobody had much idea exactly who was in charge anymore. The muftis and ulemas had to scramble through the old family photo album to dredge up Larry, the last male scion of a semi-royal family severely anemic from repeated bloodletting within their own ranks.

On paper, Larry looked okay. He was educated, graduated with honors from Yale, did a few years as well at Oxford. He dabbled in yachting and horse racing, hobnobbed on occasion with the various other international remnants of obsolete royalty still leeching off public monies, but otherwise didn't appear to have much else to his credit, good or bad. He'd been prepared to embark on a lifelong career as one of dozens of Khuruchabja's typical royal family brats, a spoiled playboy leading a scandalous lifestyle in the decadent West. He'd probably been just as dismayed and petrified to find himself unexpectedly elevated to the pinnacle of power as a good many of his subjects were to have him there. He'd only been Top Banana for a few years, and spent most of them holed up in his Royal Presidential Palace with the bed sheets pulled up over his head, allowing various court toadies to battle each other for power and authority as they pleased, all in his glorious name.

But apparently he was beginning to peek out once in a while, like a groundhog checking to see he still had a shadow, and taking his first tentative steps at actually ruling the place before he too followed in the footsteps of his blessed and exalted ancestors, off the customary exit stage left.

I spent the day resting, and managed to score a bit of hashish from the Room Service kid. Alcohol might be illegal but black Turkish hash and Yemenese qat were imported openly by the ton. It took the edge off, but the pain was too sharp to allow much of a buzz. The sun set, and the air conditioner perked up as I changed into my other "good" suit, which was pretty much the same as the first one, except cleaner, and kept an ice pack on both upper and lower bruises until curtain time. The cuts and scrapes didn't look nearly so bad as I'd feared, once they'd scabbed over. One eye sported a half-moon shiner, in lovely holocolor.

We had the hotel call a taxi (we checked before we got in; it wasn't our friend Samat), and arrived at the palace gates a lit-

tle before nine. I wasn't expecting a mad crush of reporters jock-
eying for position, hysterically waving press passes as if the king
of England were arriving from Buckingham Palace. Neverthe-
less, it took the better part of an hour simply to have our credentials checked at the gate before we were politely escorted
inside to Security. Once inside, we were subjected to a security
check similar to the one we'd experienced at the airport, after
which a car whisked us the quarter-mile distance to the immense Presidential Palace, where our credentials and choice of
evening wear were again inspected. Inside, I met my fellow
journalists, the usual gang of idiots lounging about listlessly
while waiting for the show to start.

I hadn't been a field correspondent in over a decade and
nobody'd ever seen Halton before, so I didn't expect to bump
into anyone I knew. I wasn't disappointed. Most of them were
desperate freelancers and amateur second-stringers from a half-
dozen Third World countries; the rest being younger machos
out serving rotations through Correspondent Purgatory, breaking in on the worst possible assignments. I'd never met any of
them before.

In fact, it was a bit gratifying when one of the kids from
TVN cable news squinted and said, "Sulaiman? Kay Bee Sulaiman? Weren't you the guy here during the war? Got the first
clips of the air strike against the Bayjars?" He pronounced it
just like he would have spelled it, and I tried to keep from winc-
ing.

"*Behjars*, and yeah, that was me."

"Hey, wow, man, that was like rilly great stuff." The kid was
grinning and stuck out his hand enthusiastically as he introduced himself, "Jefferson Carleby, just call me Carl," he said,
eyeing me with deference. No doubt in a moment he'd confess
he'd cut his milk teeth on my live reports. "What happened to
you after that? I mean I haven't seen you do much else
since—"

"I got promoted to Broadcast Editor. Went to a feed-in
desk. This's a one-time special assignment only.

"Aww, man, that's awful," he said. There were more sympathetic heads nodding in unison at my tale of contrived woe.
"That's typical, waste of talent. Shit, I grew *up* on your stories . . ."

I entertained Carl & Co. with a few amusing Press Club anecdotes I could have rattled off in my sleep, and Carl repaid the favor by bringing me up-to-date with some of the newest electronic toys for journalists. Kids are always up on the latest gizmos, and Carl enjoyed impressing one of the aging legends. I was happy to let him press a couple of the gadgets on me as tokens of his esteem. I would have been more interested to know how he got them through Khuruchabjan Customs. But they might come in handy, especially here.

Halton followed me around at a suitable, casual distance, his holocamera suspended on his chest, where it was ready to snap up to his eyes whenever I gave the signal to start shooting. He'd recovered his self-composure, and traded some laid-back shoptalk with a couple of the kids. Once I strolled within earshot to eavesdrop. Bullshit about places and people he'd never been or met, liberally spiced with cinematographic jargon. But very smooth, believable bullshit. *Get it out of books.*

Typically, the notables all kept the press waiting well after the appointed hour, but finally we were all allowed to troop in and get our footage of Western dignitaries in ridiculously tight suits and dress ties, or equally tight military uniforms garnished with decorations for obscure achievements, as they shook hands with their Eastern counterparts dressed up in their best beads and bed sheets and grinning just as hypocritically.

I saw very few of the men who had been powerful influences on the new government that took over just after the last war. The political tide swept strangers in and out of power with an almost seasonal regularity. The only one I recognized who recognized me didn't seem overly thrilled to see me waggling fingers at him in a friendly-like greeting. He'd been on the opposing side a few changes back, bitterly feuding with the very men he was now obsequiously glad-handing and flashing teeth with. Given the chance, I knew, he'd as soon stick a knife in his buddy's belly without a twinge of conscience. Khuruchabjan politics is not for the faint-hearted or scrupulous.

Once we'd wasted enough slipclips on this crap, we got to film silent servants dressed in actually tasteful clothes seat this collection of creeps at a long table heavily supplied with ornate saltshakers every two inches in honor of the Assistant to the British Foreign Secretary, a chinless, fidgety man who looked like this was the first time he'd ever sat above the salt in his entire life. There were, naturally, no wives present.

Sheikh Larry had taken over his kingdom at a young age. He was now about twenty-three or four, still trying to grow a mustache, dark and thinly handsome with a practiced sneer of disdain on his face as he gravely shook hands with men he knew despised him. He'd learned to treat the press corps like the best of them; when he was on camera, they didn't exist. Sort of like the guys in black in Kabuki theater who move the props around; you're not *supposed* to notice them. He was still camera-sensitive enough to pose very carefully, shoulders back, chin high, get my good side, guys.

But he had a healthy respect for us news rats, and while we were leaning up against the back wall, HoloPaks humming at low speed just in case anything more exciting happened than someone dropping gravy in his lap, another contingent of servants passed around trays of canapés and drinks for the press.

There wasn't going to be much happening until after dessert, so I leaned back and washed down another couple of heavy-duty aspirin with a glass of Khuruchabja's pride, Chateau du Vieux Mouton. Or maybe it was Faux Moufette, but it was still awful. Nothing is quite as bad as unfermented ersatz wine. Yuck. I'd asked one of the waiters for *hrarak*, a sort of peppery drink made from dates and aniseed, a specialty of the mountain people of Khuruchabja. He looked at me as if I'd asked for a glass of horse piss.

We were waiting for the after-dinner part of the festivities, when we were all scheduled to retire to a truly huge and hideous hall in the palace so that various reporters could chat with the dignitaries of their choice. This, I assumed, was where and when I was going to meet Sheikh Larry. But I snapped to my senses when I noticed some aide-de-camp type stroll casually up to the dining table and discreetly whisper something in the Boy King's ear. The kid paled, then nodded his head a fraction. A quick glance around the press pool told me I was the only one to cop to the change, the rest of the children too cranky and bored. It was past their bedtime.

The aide stood aside, and Larry picked at his food apathetically for a moment before he stood up. "My cherished and esteemed friends," he said, "please excuse me for one moment, if

you will. A minor matter requires my attention." Which is usually diplomatic code for "Back in a sec, I gotta take a leak," and
he walked slowly and calmly out of the room.

Nobody else seemed to think this was anything to be concerned about, but I nonchalantly signaled Halton. We mean-
dered closer to the entrance of the dining hall. I caught a quick
peek out at Sheikh Larry engrossed in heated conversation with
his aide and another man, this one dressed in the plainer, more
serious uniform of a professional military officer, before one of
the servants closed the door with an aggrieved look directed at
me.

"I do believe," I murmured to Halton, "there has been a
slight change in our program."

Sure enough, Larry didn't come back. The aide returned
with flowery apologies, and the dignitaries fluttered around a
bit, not quite certain of what the protocol was at that point. Reporters, suddenly aware that the night was going to be a complete bust if they didn't get *something* in the can, hastily
badgered their selected targets before Sheikh Larry's butlers arrived with hats and coats for the kiddies and genteelly kicked
the press pool out.

"Would you care for a lift back to your hotel?"

The limo pulled up next to the sidewalk outside the firmly
locked palace gates where Halton and I had been standing, me
frantically trying to hail a cab for the better part of an hour.
What few taxis I'd seen had sped up as they passed, the Presidential neighborhood more dangerous with trigger-happy paranoid guards than the darkest ghetto alley. Most of the other
kiddies had already given up and grumbled off on foot. I wasn't
up to walking all the way back to the hotel, although I was giving serious consideration to putting a few streets between us
and the Palace gates.

A polished black window hummed down to reveal a smiling, affable sort of chap with an exquisitely posh English accent.
I'd seen him seated amid the British camp during dinner, not really able to tell by the saltshaker his level in the government hi-
erarchy. He wasn't wearing one of the wedding-cake uniforms,
just a simple gray silk business suit, rather plain, really, by comparison.

I stole a look at the driver, a reflex our friend Samat had instilled in me. The chauffeur could have been a robot, an impassive, dark Semitic type with wraparound sensor glasses that matched the limo's smoked bulletproof glass.

"To whom would I owe the favor?" I asked. He could have been Jack the Ripper, and I wouldn't have cared. The PortaNet was too heavy and my body too tired and aching to be so picky at midnight.

He smiled more broadly. "To no one, I assure you. It would be my pleasure, and I confess, it is I who would be indebted, if you are indeed the same Kay Bee Sulaiman who covered the previous Khuruchabjan conflict."

"Indeed I am," I said. God, if he didn't open that damned car door in a few more seconds, I was gonna start singing "God Save the King" and asking for crumpets with my tea. Desperation time.

He signaled the driver, who got out and smartly opened the door for us. The limo was a brand-new model with an old-fashioned design, arranged so that we could sit facing each other. I climbed in and sat down gratefully, trying not to make my problem too obvious. The car pulled away and we cruised down a mostly deserted Qaiyara Avenue, as insulated from the sound and smell of the outside world as if we'd been in a private plane thirty thousand feet above it.

"May I introduce myself?" The Brit in the two-thousand écu sterling suit extended his hand. "My name is Thomas Andrew Hollingston Clermont," he said. I was waiting for "the Third," but apparently he was an original model. "I'm in the British Consulate's Public Relations office as an advisor to Mr. Hoyle." Mr. Hoyle was the Assistant in the British Foreign Office, who had sat with a stiff upper lip plastered on top of his overbite after his host had so unceremoniously run off. "I recognized you in the palace, and couldn't help taking advantage of the chance to meet you, our mutual professional interest being what it is."

We shook hands. Halton gave Clermont his name, adding "GBN photographer," and we finished the round of pleezed-ta-meetchas. As I was the senior correspondent, Halton would sit back and play respectful rookie, watching with his eyes open and his mouth shut.

"Thanks for the lift," I said.

"Not at all," Clermont said. I caught him looking speculatively at my shiner, but he was, at least on the surface, too polite to ask any pointed questions.

I wasn't. "So maybe you could tell me what His Excellency was so upset about?"

Clermont raised an eyebrow. "I didn't notice His Excellency appeared to be upset," he said. It was hard to tell with that supercilious public school accent if Clermont was being arch or not.

"Well," I said, "it sure looked to me like he had a king-sized bug up his ass when he was conversing in the hallway with the major."

Clermont's eyebrow looked like it would crawl all the way up his forehead and fall off the back. Gee, Mom, did I say something wrong?

"You're certainly observant, Mr. Sulaiman, which I should have expected, considering your reputation," he said. At least he wasn't doing the usual government two-step shuffle. "Actually, I suppose it will be common knowledge by tomorrow morning, in any case. I see no harm in telling you now. His Excellency has had a death in the family."

For a bereaved man, Sheikh Larry had looked more scared and pissed off than sad.

"That's too bad," I said. "Anybody close?"

"His youngest wife, Khatijah." Clermont sighed theatrically. "Such a pity, really. Beautiful girl, good family, educated, bright. His Excellency was very fond of her, although they'd only been married a few months." He paused, then said in Markundi, with a perfect accent, *"Yah hawalla il-lâahch,"* adding, "A great loss," just in case I didn't understand.

Suddenly, I had this creepy feeling. Like, I knew *exactly* what Mrs. Sheikh looked like. Probably last seen wearing a very nice tailored suit with a tacky hole in it. And I had an even creepier feeling that this fortuitous ride wasn't coincidence, either. Clermont was watching me with studious calm.

"Yeah, a real shame. Was she sick long?"

"Khatijah?" Clermont laughed, a refined chuckle. "Never in her life. She was a born athlete. I believe she met His Excellency at Oxford, where she was a member of the equestrian club." He did his melancholy-sigh number again. "No, it appears to have been an unfortunate automotive accident. Her car was hit by a truck and forced off the road. The truck driver's tire blew out, and he lost control of the vehicle. Both Khatijah and her driver were fatally injured when their car turned over. The national police are investigating the site now, and I'm sure there will be a complete announcement by the Palace tomorrow." He brightened slightly, as if he'd just had a thought. "I don't suppose any other journalists know yet, which puts you a step ahead of them, doesn't it?"

I was still digesting the news. Larry was going to some length to cover up the nature of his wife's death. "Yeah," I agreed. "Sure looks like an exclusive to me. Thanks a lot, Tom."

He blinked rapidly a few times over his plastic cordial smile, and let the familiarity pass. "My pleasure." The limo pulled up to our hotel.

"Please—" Clermont pressed a business card into my hand as we were shucking the PortaNet and HoloPak out on the sidewalk. "I'd be honored if you should choose to ring up the British Consulate during your stay here. If there's anything we can help you arrange, do call on us." He smiled with a calculated, shy look. "I'll be forthright in telling you we could use all the PR we can get—we're not a large contingent here. This is, after all, Khuruchabja. I certainly have the utmost respect and admiration for the work you did here during the war, and can't tell you how pleased I am you've returned. I'm sure we'll be seeing each other again. Perhaps we can be of mutual benefit. I hope you don't think I'm being too forward."

"Not at all, Tommy. We'll keep in touch. Cheers, luv."

Ta-ta and all that. Off he went, and I looked at his business card like it had a particularly vicious strain of infectious virus smeared all over it. Jeez, creeps come in all sizes and packages.

"He was lying," Halton said quietly as we trudged across the spacious lobby to the elevators.

"No shit, Sherlock," I said. "Not even I have to have nano-enhanced senses to guess that. The question is, about what? He certainly made it a point to tell me all the juicy details, didn't he? Question is, *why*?"

I fumbled with the lock to the room and took two steps inside before Halton grabbed me by the arm. I looked at him questioningly. "It's still early," he said, not looking at me. His eyes were studying the room. "I have a couple of questions on the HoloPak. Would you mind having a coffee with me before we turn in?"

I glanced around the room. Nothing seemed out of place. "Sure, no problem."

"We can leave the equipment here." Halton's voice was casual, but his entire body had gone as alert as an Irish setter quivering with one paw up and nose pointed at invisible poultry hiding in the bushes.

We dumped our stuff and went down to a coffee shop around the corner, a smoky, dingy place half-filled with unshaven men staring lethargically at us with droopy eyes. The coffee came in two chipped demitasse cups, thick black mud heavily spiced with cardamom and raw sugar. A radio on a shelf over the bar played a selection from the Markundi hit parade, a thin, wailing ululation accompanied by a *ghabah't* flute. It would never make the Top Forty, but it covered our conversation.

"The room has been searched," Halton said, once the brooding kid who brought the coffee had shambled away.

"You made that fairly obvious," I told him. "What I want to know is, how could you tell, and why did you make such a point of leaving the equipment?"

He sipped his coffee, eyes scanning the room. I got the feeling that if I'd asked him later to sketch each face he'd seen that night, he could have done it with as much precision as a holoshot. "I know the room was searched because things are not exactly in the place I put them."

"What about the maid? They *do* clean rooms here, y'know."

"The maid would not have taken such care to attempt replacing my bookreader, or your jacket, in precisely the same place and way." That made sense, in a kind of paranoid way. "I wanted to leave the equipment, because they will want to search that, too. While we are here, they are in the room, looking."

" 'They'? 'They' who?" He shrugged. All this secret agent stuff was making my already raw nerves even worse. "Then what the fuck are we doing sitting here instead of someplace where we could see who 'they' are?"

"Because if we can see them, they can see us, and then they would *not* examine the equipment."

I sipped my own coffee. It was cooling rapidly, the thick,

cloying taste making my mouth feel fuzzy. "Maybe I don't *want* them examining my equipment." I was just feeling cranky and argumentative, that's all.

He looked at me speculatively. "Is there anything illegal hidden in it?"

"No."

"Then they won't find anything. I'll have to do a more thorough search, but if they've returned, we can assume the room has been bugged."

"*I* assumed the room came that way already," I pointed out. "They usually do, this part of the world. Phone I'm sure is wired."

"Phone's only a wiretap, not an open monitor," he said calmly. "I crippled everything but the phone last night. It's all ordinary equipment, old Chinese manufacture. Cheap junk malfunctions all the time—it's not unusual. But if they heard us leave the equipment, we'll know the room's been professionally miked."

I looked at him, unintentionally staring at the part of his face concealing the microflake. He smiled, that phony, thin smile. Not even a dimple showed.

"I want to crack that goddamned flake, Halton. I find it just awfully *weird* that we've been here over twenty-four hours and nobody's managed to ask me nice for it."

"Without an AI reader, I doubt it will be possible."

Great. But, I was thinking, all I was supposed to do was deliver Halton, and split. Arlando had made it clear I wasn't supposed to play secret agent, and all the extra fun and games so far had only gained me a lot of pain and aggravation. So why did I want to delve any deeper and risk *really* getting hurt?

Because, jerk, even though I'd retired my Kay Bee Sulaiman secret identity and jockeyed a desk for twelve years, I still had illusions that I was first and foremost a *journalist*. It was my *job* to sniff out the news, and there was a lot the newsmakers were trying to hide while using me at the same time. My pride had been injured, never mind other parts of my tender body.

Also, because I was just plain pissed off. Even then, I didn't believe I was in any real danger of getting killed over this crap, just seriously inconvenienced, a grim but acceptable risk for professional journalists.

I sat there brooding, trying to think of a way to get my hands on an AI reader, until Halton judged we'd given the snoops enough time to root through our equipment.

Upstairs, I opened the door and waited, looking at Halton. He scrutinized the room, and said, "Thanks, Kay Bee. I don't think I'll have any more problems on the HoloPak."

Well, hell. It didn't look like intelligent conversation was going to be included on our list of hobbies for a while.

# EIGHT

We got a call about seven the next morning from the Deputy Minister of Information and Culture advising us that His Excellency would see us at ten. The screen had the telltale hairline ripple of a tapped system. I checked my eye in the bathroom mirror, and found it was worse today than it had been yesterday, but not as bad as I'd worried it would be. My crotch was recovering somewhat, and I managed to dress by myself, to my vast relief.

Halton and I left, equipment ready, shortly before nine, and arrived at the palace with only five minutes to spare. It wasn't that the palace was far from the hotel, but that morning rush-hour traffic crawled at a rabid snail's pace. We could have walked in less time.

The palace's security screen was just a pinch tighter than it had been the previous night, searching our equipment and walking us through the sensor, followed by a quick and alarming pat-down which made me glad I'd taken a few precautions, padding my undershorts with a wad of the same material I once used to stuff in my bra. They didn't get too familiar, and after they were satisfied that we weren't concealing any guns, knives, bombs, booze or girlie magazines, we were escorted through long, long halls decorated with mirrors and French masters in heavy gilt frames, red velvet chairs with carved lions' feet, Grecian and Roman statues on jade-marble pillars.

The interior decor was a mad fusion of vaulted rococo ceilings covered with frescoes, walls veneered with the most gorgeous ornate tiling imaginable, marble floors in elaborate designs, rich Persian carpets hiding most of it, carved wooden screens overlooking the wide courtyard atrium, huge fountain splashing peacefully. We passed endless arched doorways, tasseled brocade curtains screening off a series of *ma'gâlees*, reception rooms. One door was open, and I caught a glimpse of a young boy in a Western suit sitting on the floor with his pet monkey sharing a plate of figs.

Complete with a matching set of surly guys in brown khaki and mirror-shades strolling the grounds and toting machine guns, the palace could have been straight out of the *Arabian Nights* as interpreted by the Marquis de Sade.

It was rumored that the palace sat on top of the Boy King's personal underground bunker far below us, the best twentieth-century German technology money could buy. German engineers had built a number of these palace fortresses in several Islamic countries at the end of the last century, along with a scattering of poison-gas plants. They'd had a long historical expertise with both bunkers and toxic gases, and later had reason to regret sharing these rather esoteric specialties with various Muslim leaders. That part wasn't included on the tour, however.

Sheikh Larry was in his playroom, a two-thousand-square-foot chamber with its own sunken fountain, deep white velvet couches tastefully arranged on pale Art Deco camel-hair rugs, chandeliers with real cut-crystal tinkling overhead in the slightly aromatic breeze from a hidden air conditioner. A twelve-foot-high brass aviary held a dozen pure white macaws screeching at each other. A half-dozen or so of the Boy King's highest advisors, all elderly men with snowy beards and bleached qaftans, lounged at a respectful distance, looking bored and irritated. All that white hurt my eyes.

The Pillar of Allah, Beloved and Exalted Potentate of Khuruchabja, His Excellency was dressed in a pair of faded Levi's worn at the knees, a pair of scuffed Adidas track shoes, and a T-shirt emblazoned with an iron-on photo of the deranged-looking lead singer from the French rock group Brain Damage. He lay supine on one of the immaculate white sofas, his legs draped over its back, and wiggled the controls of a holovideo game, projected above him and, from my point of view, wrongside up. Tiny green tanks fired at spaceships roaring upside-down beneath them. A miniature UFO hit one of the dwarf tanks, and it exploded in realistic fire and smoke before it completely vanished. No unsightly dead bodies left lying around to clutter up the playing field.

Another alien craft followed the fate of the tank, and the game froze, a trumpet sadly blaring out the mourner's march. Inverted Arabic script floated across the screen, indicating playing scores.

"Hah!" Larry said. "Beat *that!*"

A dignified elderly man stood up from the group watching the Sheikh's game, strolled over to a nearby chair, and with a resigned air, picked up his own set of controls. The projector flipped the perspective to an upright vantage, and as antique Mirages and Mig 34's screamed overhead, ersatz tanks fired a barrage of weaponry at alien flying saucers. Goose-stepping soldiers began tossing phantom artillery at hordes of creepy-crawlies springing up out of thin air. They looked like tomatoes with legs, and when hit, exploded with a blossom of red and a muffled *splat*. It was the weirdest holovid game I'd ever seen. The minister reluctantly working the controls was doing so with his distaste barely concealed.

Larry rolled off the couch like a gymnast doing a back flip, landing on his feet. "Hi," he said, in a perfect American accent. "You're Kay Bee Sulaiman from GBN?" He was eyeing Halton with undisguised interest.

"That's correct, Your Excellency," I said. "John Halton, my holo optics photographer.

"Yeah, right," he said, grinning. Nudge, nudge, wink, wink. If the kid made it any more obvious, they'd have to import more neon. "You guys were supposed to do some kinda 'in-depth' piece on me—you know, 'meet the king' sort of shit."

"That's about it, Your Excellency—" I hesitated, eyeing his clothing. "It'll take only a minute to set up our equipment . . ."

"Sorry, but I guess you've heard. The palace is in official mourning, so no pictures now. Maybe later on. Right now, I thought we'd just talk, get to know each other, discuss how you're gonna film it, that kinda thing. A king's gotta be dressed for the camera." He laughed. "But a king's still got an obligation to his audience. The show must go on, right?"

He didn't look like a bereaved husband. Regardless of *how*

his wife had died, I would have thought he might have shown a little more sorrow. Somehow, I liked him better when he'd been stuffed into his tight wedding-cake uniform, hair slicked back, and scowling. This boy seemed no different from any other pampered rich snot I could have found soaking in a jacuzzi in some Beverly Hills ultra-private club.

The original game plan had been set up this way: We were to do an extended interview of the kid, take about a week or two, after which he would "offer" Halton a job as his personal PR consultant. Halton would accept, and I'd sign over the paperwork in private, then go home. No one outside a handful of people would ever know Halton was a fabricant. It seems Allah doesn't approve of fabricants in Khuruchabja any more than He does AI's.

But now it seemed I wasn't even going to get a story to justify my own trip, even one I wasn't interested in. I was still a journalist, and the thought of wasting my time, never mind slipclips, on this cocky, narcissistic brat was annoying. *Just do it, Kay Bee. You're paid for the time, and the slipclips can be better spent on something else.* I swallowed my ego, and got down to work.

Halton dumped the now *verboten* HoloPak in the corner and sat off to the side, out of the way but where the kid could still eyeball him. I started doing a half-assed exploratory interview, at least allowed to record on audiochip instead of scribbling notes. I had been told to keep it all trivial and light, the kind of toothless chat show bah-bah wah-wah questions like, "If you were a teabag, Your Excellency, what flavor teabag would you be?"

The kid was more than happy to give me his complete background from the time he was three years old and tried to stuff the maid's cat down the electronic garbage disposal. I practically fell asleep listening to him prattle on vacuously. Where was the serious, aloof young man I'd seen at dinner? That should have been my first clue, and I wasn't paying attention. Halton was doing his part, his current one, which consisted of doing less than I was.

We were being watched by the king's advisors from a circumspect distance. The kid's opponent lost his last tank to invading hordes of Monster Zucchinis from Outer Space, breathed a weary sigh of relief and retired to the back benches with the rest of his buddies.

Larry broke off long enough to glance at the old man's score and laugh. "Is that the best you can do, you old fart?" he called out to the stoic minister. "I'm gonna have to rewrite the damn programming to make it easier for you." The old man looked back steadily without saying a word. Perhaps he didn't speak English.

"Al-Hasmani's okay, but he's just no challenge. You play?" the king abruptly asked Halton.

Halton shrugged his eyebrows. "I could learn."

"You wrote the programming?" I asked, eyeing the phantom Marching Mutant Munchies as they devoured tanks and fighter jets in midair.

"Sure," the kid bragged. "It's pretty easy, really. All you have to do is take something like the IBM 8 MicroModel 470 for the basic holo paradigm with a track-link conditioner to upgrade the HB display, and interface it with an A-Zed-190 timing sequencer and grafting on some standard ComPleet-catacode logistics for the tanks and the planes. Then, for the Alien Veggies . . ." There was a lot more of enthusiastic computer babble about hologames, which interested me not in the least.

"Very impressive," I finally managed to interject, and steered the conversation back toward his personal history. He seemed happy to prattle on about anything at all, so long as the theme was himself. I changed chips in the recorder after another half-hour, stifling my yawns and trying to keep my mind from wandering to more interesting subjects, like lunch. The alien vegetables must have been having a subliminal effect on my appetite.

"So after Yale, I applied to Oxford to do some post-grad studies on the influence of nineteenth-century British imperialism in the Middle East on the current popular culture and mythology in Islam." He grinned. "It seemed appropriate." I must have fogged out of paying attention. I blinked at him stupidly for a moment. "You know," he prompted, "Lawrence of Arabia?" He laughed. "My grandmum was half English, loved all that kind of mystical shit, even badgered my father into naming me after the greatest English hero in the Middle East. Christ, I'm just glad she didn't name me after Glubb Pasha! Can you imagine? 'His Royal Highness, Sheikh Glubb'?" He nearly fell off the sofa, laughing. "Anyway, Grams had this crazy idea I was going to be another Lawrence. You could use that as an angle, couldn't you? She was the one who insisted I go to Oxford, more because it was T.E.'s alma mater, rather than because it was a really good school."

"Which is where I understand you met your wife, Khatijah?"

I couldn't have done better had I farted in the middle of High Mass at Notre Dame. For a brief, tense moment, the kid lost his brainless computer nerd cum born-again yuppie act, observing me narrowly, eyes shrewd. Two of his ministers, I noted from the corner of my eye, also reacted, including old al-Hasmani. Yup, definitely English-speakers.

"Khatijah is . . . was . . . *one* of my wives, not my senior wife. Muslims are still allowed four wives in Khuruchabja, as you're well aware. Khatijah and I hadn't been married all that long. In any case, that is part of my private life, which is not open for discussion or examination." He seemed to remember hastily that he was in mourning. "It's just too painful for me to talk about right now."

Sure. In any case, anything more personal than the rambling nothings of Sheikh Larry's public life was going to be unlikely. I wrapped up the wah-wah's and made an appointment with one of his secretaries (a portly minister who scratched in a large vellum-paged book with a quill pen, I kid you not) to return when the king would dress up for the camera.

Oh, goody, I could hardly wait.

We trudged out of the palace with little more than we'd come in with. Halton didn't look in the least discouraged, but then he was only playing at being an Intrepid Reporter.

It was only half past noon, the day was young. "We might as well get some lunch," I said, "then walk around, see what we can find for background shots."

I had something else on my mind, so I guess I was only playing, too. But then, *everybody* was only playing at their roles. So what else was new in Nok Kuzlat?

# NINE

The weather was already searingly hot, and we found refuge under the shade of a solitary acacia tree left standing in an abandoned construction site turned impromptu public park in the Old City. Birds rustled in the thorny branches, snapping up the insects attracted to the scattering of yellow flowers. The scarred bark of the tree still bore traces of a fire, a gnarled survivor.

We sat in what had once been the home of some government building, a faded and graffitied sign proclaiming this to be a reconstruction site. The bombed rubble had been bulldozed to the sides, and dry brown weeds grew in the furrows, as far as the "reconstruction" ever got. The backsides of windowless office buildings bordered the lot, graffiti-decorated aging service doors chained and locked. The anorexic spires of minarets and the gold gleam of a dome wavered in the distant heat.

The acacia tree was the central feature of a makeshift outdoor restaurant, if the establishment we were currently gracing with our patronage could actually be called that. White-collar workers certainly scorned the place, and the few loyal customers seemed to be the local office buildings' garbage collectors and janitors.

The three sides of the kitchen "walls" were made from old cardboard, sheet tin and canvas tenting. Facing the open kitchen, two rough tables had been cobbled together from scrap boards. I sat on an empty packing crate; Halton perched atop a large rock.

We had one table; the other was shared by a half-dozen grizzled men in dingy workclothes who were sipping coffee and eyeballing us over a lethargic game of dominoes. Occasionally, one of them would get up and shuffle behind the kitchen to piss on the mountain of trash behind the cook tent wall. We wore Western clothing and spoke English, but unlike many other Middle Easterners, the average Khuruchabjan was cautiously aloof. The secret police were known to drop by and ask a few pointed questions with rubber hoses and electric wires if you were too friendly with foreigners, particularly Americans.

I had Halton film the man sweating over the three barbecue grills made from oil drums sawed in half, as I interviewed him. Yes, yes, death to America and the Zionist pigs, he chanted dutifully for the camera, Allah bless the king forever, hang all accursed Western unbelievers headdown over the fires of Hell, would we like to try some of his homemade pepper sauce in our *sha'warmâa's*?

The old man grinned hugely as he broiled speared chunks of mystery-meat *kibbâa'hs*, using the edge of his dirty kaffiyeh to avoid burning his fingers. Behind him, a tiny generator burbled, keeping an ancient refrigerator running.

Actually, it wasn't bad. The proprietor brought us his special "apple juice," tickled we had filmed his humble establishment for our reviled, godless Western but most important news station. It was cold, at least, a bit watered but still tart and delicious. A pretentious little vintage, but a very good week.

Served with wilted mint, yogurt, and pickled vegetables stuffed into a roll of flat bread the chef had fried on the side of his makeshift oven, the sharp, peppery spices in the meat surely killed any lingering bacteria foolish enough to stick around. I wasn't sure what species of animal the meat had originally claimed, but didn't want to know that badly. Our chef handed us our *sha'warmâa's* wrapped in torn pieces of newspaper, along with several more pieces of the tortilla-like bread. I dusted the charred bits off the bread and used it to dip into tiny jars of vegetables, oily mashed chickpeas, an aubergine faux-caviar, and an odd sort of curried tomato and cucumber yogurt mixture, which I guessed was made from sheep's milk. Attracted by the smell, flies buzzed around us.

A skeletally thin cat slid its bony body around my legs begging for a bite. I leaned over to feed it a scrap of meat, then grimaced when I straightened, a sudden shot of latent pain in my crotch. I hissed my breath in between clenched teeth. Startled, the stray cat took off, taking its prize with it.

"Are you all right?" Halton stopped his constant observation of our surroundings to eye me discerningly.

"You're not my mother, so stop worrying about me, okay?" I retorted hotly. "I'm fine. Just fine. So back off."

He looked at me, his expression neutral. "I apologize if I've said something to offend you," he said. I thought I detected a hint of reproach behind his cool voice. "Maybe if you could explain what it is I'm doing to annoy you, I might be able to improve our working relationship."

I *had* been a complete bitch. I sighed, brushing the constant swarm of annoying flies away. "I'm sorry, I'm sorry, I'm sorry. Fucking hell. I don't mean to take it out on you," I said lamely. "It's the heat, it's this place, it's this whole fucking setup pissing me off."

He kept looking at me like he didn't believe me. "I don't know if I could explain it to you, Halton," I took another sip from the "apple juice," feeling the sting of alcohol in my cut lip. "I don't think I really understand it myself. *You*, personally, don't offend me. Even you're being CDI doesn't bother me, or not as much, anyway. But just the fact that you exist at all makes me nervous."

I swatted at the most persistent of the flies hovering around my face. For some reason, the flies ignored Halton. He said nothing, just nodding as if he understood, and finished the rest of his lunch.

"When I was a kid"—I felt compelled to explain something to him—"there was a big fuss about a genetically altered petunia this research group of university botanists wanted to release in the wild. It had an artificial gene spliced into it, not something that was going to give it any edge in competing with wild petunias. They wanted to use this spliced-in gene as a kind of bookmark they could track to see what would happen over multiple generations under various natural conditions." I remembered the term from my college biology. "Genetic drift."

"Petunias." The corners of Halton's lips quirked up, amused.

"Yeah. Petunias. This whole huge organization of people—

environmentalists, Greens, nutcases, whatever—marched on the university, demanding they destroy all the altered petunia plants. At some point things got heated, a brick got thrown through the greenhouse glass, a botanist shoved somebody— who knows what all really caused it? But people got seriously hurt and the greenhouses were burnt down, fields torched." I shrugged. "There were a lot of people suing each other, laws got passed, some of them pretty laughable, some of them just plain stupid and mean. A company allowed to make poison gas for weapons couldn't get permission to grow vats of tailored bacteria to produce cheap insulin."

"All over petunias?"

It sounded pretty silly to me, too. "It wasn't just about flowers; genetic engineering wasn't as sophisticated then," I said defensively. "Facts and rumors got mixed up. Some people claimed that Legionnaires' disease and the AIDS virus were secret biological weapons the Government released, probably accidentally."

"Do you believe that?"

"No." Or not much, at least. "But it scared people, and they ended up arguing so loudly about petunias that nobody noticed when Government agencies like CDI started buying up patents on genes and clonal techniques, including every known strand of human DNA."

The National Institutes of Health in Bethesda had gobbled up every patent on any gene linked to the human brain even before the turn of the century. Defying the EEC cries of foul play, the Recombinant Advisory Committee, a Government review board conveniently controlled by the NIH, had allowed a few select biotechnological companies eager to win FDA patent approvals ahead of their competitors to corner the market on fabricant technology before fabricants were even a gleam in some mad scientist's eye. The Europeans found themselves shut out from even basic access to biological data. American pharmaceutical and gene-therapy companies suddenly found their CEO's weren't researchers or physicians anymore, but Government-controlled sycophants with some interesting ideas of their own.

"But by then it was too late. Nobody had any idea the kind of things they could create."

I flushed, realizing I'd inadvertently insulted Halton. Again. He was listening stoically.

"Things like viral pesticides," I said, covering up quickly. "Some of the precautions were necessary. You don't go releasing modified viruses into the atmosphere as pesticides to kill one species of bug if you don't know for certain they won't hurt other species or mutate into something that might be toxic to people."

Halton stared at me. "I'm not a virus, Kay Bee," he said quietly. "And I'm not a petunia."

"No," I agreed. "You're much scarier than that. When it was still illegal for American doctors to use aborted fetal tissue to cure diseases, only the CDI could have developed fabricants. They had the money and legal immunity that allowed them to play around with human genes."

His chin came up a fraction, I thought. "CDI didn't break any laws. I'm not a virus, but I'm not human, either. My chromosomes were not stolen from human beings; every strand of my DNA is legally patented and designed. Not one gene has been taken from any natural source." His voice held a note of pride I found oddly touching.

I knew the argument. The details of CDI's fabricant technology were a closely held secret, but this much was common knowledge: Fabricants didn't have parents. They were individually crafted organisms, and therefore legally biomachines. The only organism the law considered human was that "conceived of man, born of woman." It didn't matter if it was a test-tube baby or a fetus altered with genetic surgery. What counted was that its origin was one human egg fertilized by one human sperm. If it walks like a duck and quacks like a duck, it'd better have a set of genetic blueprints to prove its parents were ducks. Otherwise, it wasn't legally a duck.

"That's true, Halton," I said softly. "You're not a virus, and you're not a human. What you are is a lethal military weapon. That's what you were designed to be." The impassive expression returned, Halton's eyes unflinching. "We humans are good at developing new weapons. We have the power to completely alter our environment, change ourselves, without necessarily having complete control over what we're capable of doing." I smiled lopsidedly at him. "Your average man in the street is afraid fabricants are really a sort of Hitlerian *übermenchen*, the start of a brave new world which will sooner or later begin culling out the imperfect human riffraff." I thought briefly of the occasional insults and animosity I had endured in school, the blind, jingoistic hatred toward Arabs, fanned by periodic acts of terrorism and war. "Including me."

"Then why do people build things that frighten them?"

"Because we can," I said. "That's part of what it means to be human. It makes no sense, I'll admit. We've built weapons with the power to completely vaporize the planet, slaughter every living thing, turn the Earth into a lifeless stone. Just because we can. Pretty fucking useless, when you think about it."

He had finished his lunch, and leaned back on his rock. Filtered sunlight through the acacia leaves caught highlights in his dark hair, and speckled his tanned, smooth skin. I found myself dejectedly admiring the way his shoulders pressed against his shirt. Pushing away the flutter in my stomach, I tried to think of something else. He took a deep breath, a sad, patient sound.

"So you're still afraid I really am Frankenstein's monster, after all?" he asked. I thought I heard a slight edge of sarcasm in his tone. A damned good-looking Frankenstein's monster. I didn't say it. "Do you honestly believe fabricants are going to suddenly wake up one day, realize their superiority over all you flawed human tinkerers, and rise up in revolt to destroy their own creators?"

"You don't seem to have any psychological impediment to killing people," I pointed out.

"For which I would have assumed you'd have reason to be grateful." I wasn't sure how to take that. Sometimes Halton seemed absurdly naive, then could turn around with biting keenness. "But if you're worried I might have some ideas about mutiny, my designers have already taken care of that. I *am* psychologically inhibited from killing for my own purposes."

He smiled, that strange plastic smile. "You're right. I'm a weapon, but *only* a weapon. I am not a killer." He seemed to be reassured by that, his confidence in the ability of his makers, if not in their intentions, unshakable.

I shuddered. How utterly convenient. *Guns don't kill people*, I remember my card-carrying NRA stepdad saying, refusing to register his hunting rifles racked like art on the living-room wall and calling it civil disobedience. He had slept with a loaded .45 under his pillow, and bought my mom a shiny new .38 of her very own for her birthday, just the right size to fit into her purse. Every other weekend he took us to the rifle range for target practice; no gang of teenaged drug thugs was going to take his family down like weak-kneed liberal wimps. *People kill people.*

People have always seemed to enjoy dreaming up new ways to kill a lot of other people.

"Well," I said, "that's one way to keep your conscience clean."

I got up and bought some more "apple juice" from our genial host. He refilled our chipped glasses with his homemade hootch from a fruit jar kept in the antiquated refrigerator, condensation running down its sides. I brought them back, set one down in front of Halton and turned my back to him. We drank in silence. I watched the kids playing with a scabrous mutt in the smelly mountain of trash piled behind the improvised kitchen, and let my thoughts wander off on their own.

Bad idea.

God knows what Halton was thinking. But I was reminiscing of a time before anyone knew about fabricants, not so long ago, when we didn't need help in killing each other. My senses did a sudden detour, a sickening lurch into a past reality I'd thought I'd managed to suppress. I hadn't had those waking nightmares in years. The breeze shifted, and for a heart-stopping moment I didn't smell the sickly sweet odor of rotting garbage, but the thick stench of blood and burnt flesh and scorched explosives. A kid turned, laughing, his mouth open. I saw the silent scream in a baby's withered corpse.

My skin turned clammy, and I was sweating.

"Kay Bee?" Halton had moved as noiselessly as a ghost, standing with his hand on my shoulder. I started, realized I was panting, my heart racing.

"I'm all right, it's okay, just leave me alone . . ." I blurted rapidly, trying to brush him and my fears away. The welcome surge of anger focused my awareness, blotted out the waking dreams. It was true, I was stuck in Nok Kuzlat. But it was *now*, not then. Kids played with their dog in a rubbish heap. No booby-trapped mines exploded under their feet. The scrawny cat, a flash of orange fur, streaked across a field of broken bricks and weeds. No spotting missile would spear down from the sky to blow it to pieces, no invisible sniper's bullets rip it to shreds.

No child's huge eyes staring at me over the barrel of a gun, small, dirty hands holding it up before . . . *Just staring . . . Before . . .*

I pushed the memory down. Hard.

I hated Nok Kuzlat then, I hated it now. I hated this entire part of the world and everyone in it with the kind of guilty self-loathing only the displaced can feel. I despised the mindless violence and relentless misery, while still bristling at the West's chauvinistic attitude of superiority.

Most of all I hated my parents for being Arabs.

My father was born in the Gaza Strip, and my mother in Kuwait City, neither of them citizens of the countries of their birth. They met and married while working as wage-slaves for some despotic Saudi company and emigrated to America the first chance they got. They lived in what they initially considered luxury, but what was then regarded in the States as poverty-level subsistence. I had been born in Denver, Colorado, and that made me 100% American under United States law. I could even run for President when I grew up.

I don't remember my real father; he died when I was four. My mother promptly threw away her veil and married a half-Irish, half-Italian, all-American cowboy who thought the sun rose and set just for her. Religion was never a problem in our family; Mom never gave up being a Muslim, not entirely. There was no mosque in our small town. I went to a Presbyterian church with my stepdad on major Christian holidays while Mom did her praying in private. God was an abstract that had no particular meaning for me.

My life was not much different from that of any other average American kid. My mother dressed like the other ladies at the local PTA, wore makeup and had her hair done at the neighborhood beauty salon, and worked at our local Sears in the purchasing department. My stepfather was a state contractor who built Government offices. He drove an ordinary car to work with its "Buy American" bumper sticker, drank beer with his buddies on Saturdays down in the game room he'd built in the basement, football or basketball or the World Series blaring from the latest model television set. We weren't rich, but at least my stepdad had steady work and we never really lacked for anything important. I ran around the malls with the few friends I had, grew up on a steady diet of Burger King and Pizza Hut, rode rental horses at the stable, mooned over cute boys and magazine photos of pubescent movie stars, snuck cigarettes with my buddies in the girls' toilet in school. An all-American childhood.

When I was about nine years old, I remember a U.S. Congressman from Georgia or Louisiana, some Southern state, testifying at one of these Congressional panels televised every so often to justify taxpayers' money being wasted on finding out where taxpayers' money was being wasted. The latest "peace initiative" had gone exactly nowhere. While everyone was busy arguing over the old question of Israel's occupied territories, the perpetual sticky wicket in negotiating any peace agreement, Israel kept building up its military arms capability and expanding Jewish settlements on the West Bank and Gaza and the Golan Heights as fast as they could drag prefab trailer homes into them. Then some Islamic terrorist group had set off a bomb in New York's World Trade Center, killing people who probably didn't have too much interest in the cause they had died for, and not furthering favorable American public opinion at all.

The Congressman, an ex–White Citizens Councilman who reveled in controversy guaranteed to get him good news coverage, stood outside the Capitol surrounded by a pack of journalists, thumbs tucked in his belt as he likened the Middle East to a large pack of vicious dogs penned up together, all fighting over a single bone while Israel, an ill-tempered alley cat, sat on the fence and watched them. Every once in a while one dog would jump at the cat, snarling and snapping, and the cat would leisurely swipe at the dog's nose with sharp claws, sending it ass-over-teakettle yipping in pain.

The U.S. Government had allowed this to continue as long as our "national interests"—which translated meant "cheap oil"—were not threatened. But periodically one dog would get too big and mean, and start savaging a smaller mutt, and that interfered with America's interests. Then Uncle Sam would be forced to wade into the pack with a big stick to beat the crap out of the meanest dog, and stand there yelling, "*Down*, boys! *Down!*" The rest of the pack would slink around his legs, glaring at each other, and the smaller mutts would take surreptitious bites out of their fallen companion. The cat would hiss in the corner, a couple of mutts would cough up one or two pale hostages, Uncle Sam would announce A Lasting Peace in the Middle East, shake a scolding finger at the cat, and wade out again. Then the pack would fall on each other, and the fighting resumed, with the occasional snarl at the cat sitting on the fence, licking its paws and sniggering at them all.

It was a hopeless situation, the Congressman was saying in his affable country-boy drawl. Sure them Israelis don't play fair, but whaddya expect from Christ-killing Jewboys? Still, they were a democratic government and most of 'em were at least white. But them Moo-slim ragheads are stuck in the fourteenth century, violent, treacherous, and ungrateful, impossible to do respectable business with and fundamentally incapable of ever evolving into civilized human beings. Now that they're bringing their heinous terrorist activities to our hallowed American soil, we gottah keep our military capacity up, our money to ourselves, and our borders firmly locked against them Third World hordes clammering to overwhelm us and dilute our democratic American Way of Life. Our only hope, our Good (Christian) God willing, is that the fence never breaks.

At the age of nine, news was something shown between cartoons and sitcoms, and it meant nothing to me then. But my mother had burst into tears, scaring me. My dad—my stepdad—didn't know what to do. He put his arms around her and said lamely, "He didn't mean *everybody*, Fadela." She promptly slugged him, screaming hysterical curses at him in Arabic he couldn't understand, and stomped out the door to disappear for three days.

That's the first time I ever felt like anything other than a normal American kid. The Congressman had meant *me*. *I* was an Arab, wasn't I? *I* was the kind of rabid dim-witted cur the Congressman felt so contemptuous of, a dirty, lazy heir of that untamable primitive Bedouin race which over the past century had murdered, terrorized, looted, raped and plundered, bombed airliners, blew up office buildings, destroyed oil wells, damaged their own environment, massacred thousands of innocent people. We were utterly despised and utterly despicable.

My family lived in a small town near Denver. I was short and dark, but obviously not Latino, and some of the kids in my school thought I was American Indian, a notion I started doing nothing to disabuse. Indians were fashionable then, a noble, innocent and historically persecuted people whom whites treated with an inherited guilty conscience. I dropped the name Kahlili, and started calling myself Kay Bee, insisting that my parents do the same. I refused to speak Arabic with my mother any longer. I wouldn't answer her if she spoke to me in anything other than English. I regret that for two reasons: one, because my Arabic is now shitty; and two, because it hurt my mother needlessly. If she had been humiliated by some porky Southern-fried bigot, it only deepened her shame to see her own daughter frantic to deny her heritage.

Later on, when my mother died, I had a brief surge of remorse, actively announcing my Arabishness to anyone who'd listen, parroting various causes with little understanding of any of them. It didn't last long. I bored the piss out of the few friends who could stand to listen to me for any length of time, and quickly discovered after a brief escapade with a *real* Arab renegade that I had little in common with his philosophy, his fanaticism, or his passionate hatred of everything Occidental.

My stepdad had adored my mother but merely tolerated me, which I genuinely didn't mind. I'd catch him staring at me once in a while, totally baffled how someone as lovely as my mother could have given birth to such an unattractive child. But he did his best to love me, in his own way. He was fair, kind, good-natured, and we got along okay. After Mom died, he sent me to a boarding school to finish out the last years of high school. I loved it, thought it was heaven; all the horses I could have ever wished for. He calls once in a while, and we still dutifully exchange Christmas cards every year, although I haven't seen him in almost twenty years.

What I lacked in looks, I made up for in academic achievement, and I was offered a scholarship from one of those vague, oil-rich Arab-American Cultural Leagues, which covered the bulk of my tuition. Not to be outdone, the Kiwanis Club in my hometown cobbled together a half-assed agricultural textbook scholarship. To make up the rest, I sold my soul for the newest version of the Government's nondefaultable student loan; Pay-It-Back-Or-Rot-In-Prison. My stepdad sent a check once in a while when things got lean, but I knew that, all things considered, I was one of the lucky ones; the entrenched damage to the educational system had already been done. Affordable education in America had been flushed down the toilet years before; only the kids of the very rich or those who could qualify for obscure scholarships ever managed to get a college degree. I was certainly one of the few with above-average skin pigmentation, like, y'know, fer sher.

Since I *was* a scholarship student rather than a scion of the leisure class, I somehow felt I had to compete, to show them rich snots that I was better'n them. But after graduating Phi Beta Kappa and *summa cum laude*, with the usual pins and tassels and pseudo-cabalistic college rites, I found that all my shiny new journalist's degree got me was a slightly above minimum-wage job as a glorified coffee girl at a secondary city newspaper. Everybody wanted to be a star reporter, and the competition was just plain cutthroat fierce. I couldn't even get anyone to sexually harass me in exchange for a promotion. My take-home pay didn't even start to cover the monthly payment on my college loan. I was well into my thirties before the IRS had deducted enough out of my income taxes to pay it off.

I quit print and went into television, then just starting to go holo. GBN was a fledgling company, and while they gave me a job title fancy enough to satisfy my ego, in reality I *still* wasn't much more than a glorified coffee girl with a salary to match. Struggling along with one shit job after another, trying to get someone to pay attention to what I could write, once in a while being thrown a bone and doing a "human-interest" report, and it started being hammered home I was going about as far as I ever would.

Then al-Husam and his Behjars stole their infrafusion bombs, and the tiny country of Khuruchabja was suddenly the navel of the news universe. Lo and behold, GBN had a bonafide bilingual Ay-rab journalist in its ranks. I was given a promotion, a cameraman and a PortaNet, and a round-trip ticket to Nok Kuzlat.

Somewhere inside me, I had nurtured this secret belief that I could blend seamlessly into the Arab culture. I had Arab parents, an Arab name. I really *was* Arab . . . wasn't I? I'd be accepted, the prodigal daughter returning to the fold, all that nonsense. I felt smug, my co-workers jealous, when GBN grabbed me from the oblivion of the metaphysical mailroom and sent me off to find fame and fortune in fabulous Nok Kuzlat.

It didn't last long. Maybe if I hadn't been an Arab-American, I wouldn't have taken the disillusionment so hard. What I knew about Arab life and culture was about as much as any American teenager reading Kahlil Gibran and thinking that made us sophisticated intellectuals. *A Thousand and One Arabian Nights* and Indrah Shah's *Caravan of Dreams*; old Valentino silent movies and *I Dream of Genie* reruns; all the endless, stupid fantasy novels with exotic spice caravans, romantic sheikhs and juvenile *Sinbad the Sailor* rehashed ripoffs did nothing to unveil the gritty realities behind the myths.

Well, *obviously* they would have the same kind of moral values and have the same logic as we did. Arabs would think as we do, act as we do, be people exactly like us. Except they dressed funny.

It wasn't that the various Middle Eastern countries and people weren't different—indeed the distinctions between them were myriad and copious; all of them, however, were infinite variations on the theme of frustration and repression. Nations hated peoples, hated tribes, hated families, and everywhere the endless, bloody feuds. In the East, lives were short and memories long; in the West, lives were long and memories short. How could we hope to understand each other?

Cairo, great city of the Pyramids and Pharaohs, was a dusty, crowded slum, the reek of oily exhaust, sewage and rotting produce clotting in your nose and throat, the Nile sludge fermenting with microscopic parasites and bacteria. The relentless noise was everywhere, a solid assault on the senses, the constant throbbing clamor of bargaining, begging and baksheesh.

Riyadh was a broiling nightmare of Thou Shalt Not and greedy arrogance; half the population, obsessed with their Islamic duty, devoted to repressing the slightest hint of pleasure, blanching every trace of color and flavor out of life, and the other half desperate to escape.

The gratitude Kuwait might have once had for Americans was as fleeting as the desert spring. The flying carpets and bottled genies of Baghdad had never recovered from the Iran-Iraq and Gulf Wars. The smiling faces of picturesque Bedouins on the covers of travel brochures never quite matched those of the mutilated old Khuruchabjani men, children with bloated bellies, shrouded women weeping with their claws extended, clutching at your legs and arms as you walked the narrow streets, aggressively begging.

The culture shock was secondary to the unreal horror of death and devastation, an orgy of killing freely indulged in by all sides. Death here was as commonplace and accepted as the ubiquitous flies. Not only weren't Arabs what I'd expected, *we* weren't exactly what I'd believed us to be all these years, either.

Things were not cut and dried, black or white, the good guys not that distinct from the bad guys. All the justified rationales for "softening up" the enemy still meant bombing the piss out of men shivering in crowded bunkers, arguments that twist principles and morals to excuse what still ends up no more than wholesale slaughter; the sanitized vocabulary with words like "attrition" and "collateral damage" to make the blood and death more palatable to soldiers and spectators alike.

What's worse, it was often genuinely necessary. But it was still killing. Finally, I simply went numb. Then I went mad.

Much later, I went home.

Here I was again, a decade later, back in Nok Kuzlat. Kay Bee Sulaiman had returned from the dead, accompanied by a machine imitating a man. I thought it might be time to look up old friends.

And wondered if I was still mad.

# TEN

I watched some of the local news that evening to practice my rusty Markundi, mumbling words to myself. The ecclesiastical-controlled state censors were still very powerful in Khuruchabja, and the local news was mostly Pablum. Needless to say, the unfortunate demise of Mrs. Sheikh had been glossed over quickly, more oratory than information. No photo was shown of the dead woman, but I knew she hadn't died in any car accident.

Khuruchabjan television consisted mainly of the interminable state-run, cleric-approved prayers interspersed with old tapes of sporting events, the Khuruchabjan team always winning, of course, which cut down drastically on the number of televised games. Variety shows were devoted to carefully choreographed exhibitions of love and loyalty to Sheikh Larry, children dancing and waving flags.

Occasionally, wrathful reports of various disgusting atrocities being committed in America's godless inner cities livened up the fare, each played to the hilt. I particularly enjoyed one hydrophobic account about the barbarous ritual practice of publicly devouring charred pork carcasses by alcohol-guzzling men who freely mingled with bareheaded loose women in tight, sleeveless T-shirts.

GBN had made the hotel arrangements, although I'm sure

CDI was picking up the tab. This time Halton and I were sharing the room, since with two beds, separate rooms for two male colleagues would have been an unnecessary expense, especially for journalists on a company expense card. Not that CDI cared; they just wanted everything to look right. It was also, I assumed, so that Halton could keep an eye on me. But the Grand Imperial, in spite of its name, was not the most luxurious hotel in town. It catered mainly to a Western clientele, far reduced from the enormous ostentation visiting sheikhs and flamboyant emirs preferred to something more human-sized in scale.

Our hotel room was not that much different than one in, oh, say, Topeka, Kansas. Slightly larger than the Orbital Hilton, it was big enough for two queen-sized beds, a decent-sized holoset, be it the off-brand Chinese model, various mismatched pieces of veneered pressboard furniture with a modern Oriental-ish design. The carpet was old, with faint coffee stains and cigarette burns. The bathtub had a handheld shower-hose and the faucet dripped, leaving a rust streak. The hot water was merely tepid, despite the broiling temperatures outside, and the toilet burbled constantly, an oddly comforting sound somewhat like a country brook. The air conditioning was marginal at best, the windows having been cleverly designed never to open, turning the room into a sauna by mid-morning. It was, however, clean, the cockroaches respectfully discreet and the bed sheets changed regularly.

Halton had found and rearranged the professional bugs, not so much disabling them as adjusting them to send out normal transmissions of nothing much at all. It seemed unlikely they had been placed by one of his erstwhile confreres, since they would have certainly expected their fabricant to be able to seek and destroy the devices. More likely it was a higher grade of Khuruchabjan secret police, intrigued by our personal visit to His Majesty. Halton wired in one of Carl's electronic toys to broadcast randomly generated sounds, a cough, a sneeze, a toilet flush, a few muttered fragments of pardon me's and thank you's with our voiceprints on them, to filter our real conversation. Still, it did take some of the enthusiasm out of any intellectual discourse.

He was crashed out on the opposite bed, nose buried in a bookreader. He scanned the pages rapidly, methodically, with an expression I'd have expected had he been reading *American Scientist*.

I had to stretch to pick the chipcover off the stand separating the beds. Against the background of a luridly painted Wild West landscape, a demure woman with an impossible décolletage had her head thrown back while feebly repelling the embrace of a dark and handsome half-naked cowboy nuzzling her impossibly long swan neck. Another trashy romance novel. God only knew where he found this shit. At least this one was in English.

"*Love Aflame at Paradise Crossing?*" I nearly laughed. "You really like this stuff?" I asked, holding up the chipcover.

He looked up, blinking. "Yes." He paused before asking, "You don't?"

"Bodice-rippers?" I sneered. "They're badly written carbon copies churned out by illiterate factory hacks following a bunch of demographic guidelines generated by computers. I'd rather read the phone book."

He held up the bookreader. "It's sold more than three and a half million copies," he said. "Literary standards don't appear to be their main appeal."

I turned the chipcover over to read the blurb. "'He loomed above her, a smoldering arrogance in his cold, crystal-blue eyes,'" I read aloud sarcastically. "'But his skintight jeans and embroidered shirt couldn't hide the desire raging in his lean body. Her head reeled, a headiness that sprang from out of nowhere as his strong hands took her, his mouth hard against hers. She gasped when his tongue slipped between her soft lips, his unspoken passion beating like a captive bird in his chest pressed against her heaving bosom. It was a dangerous game they played, each seeking revenge against the other, but the heiress and the cowboy would find their hearts had a stubborn will of their own, their fate indelibly etched in the arroyos and echoed in the tremorous howls of coyotes on the night wind.' *Jeez*, what crap!"

I grimaced and tossed the chipcover back onto the night stand. "It's pornography, Halton. Emotional pornography for women." I felt offended by this cheap novel, deeply angered by its lies. Only stunningly beautiful women were ever the heroines, winning love and unbelievable devotion from equally gorgeous men. Ugly girls need not apply.

He looked at me blankly. "Yes?"

"So if you're reading it to get some kind of insight into what women like, don't bother. It's a cheat, it's not real. Nobody has lives or feelings like that. Women read this junk because they feel something's lacking in their own lives. They get vicarious thrills by reading this phony crap and whacking off their emotions."

As I said it, I realized. ". . . Oh." I had a sudden sour taste in my mouth. "Giving your limbics a good stroking there, Halton?" I asked softly.

He looked back at me, unabashed. "Yes." Then he went back to the book. I went back to keeping my mouth shut and concentrating on the turbaned anchorman lecturing on the corruptive influence of pop music, my face suddenly hot. Halton was still reading when I dozed off to the melodious sound of Markundi invective.

I woke early, having spent most of the night waking up every time I turned over onto some other part of my body that hurt like hell. Taking a shower, I inspected the various bruises, and was happy to notice they were improving somewhat. The half-ring around my eye was more green than purple, but neither color did much to improve my looks. Then I went up to the roof for breakfast.

Halton stayed in the room, uncoupling and replacing the bugs in their original places in case the maintenance crew decided to double check the equipment. I preferred not to tip off whoever was listening that we knew we'd been bugged. Except for the PortaNet. If I found bugs there, no one would be surprised if I deloused it. I had Halton clean the PortaNet before I took it up to the hotel's rooftop terrace cafe. There I could do some private work by myself.

It wasn't that I didn't trust Halton . . . No, actually, I really *didn't* trust Halton; I only trusted him slightly more than I trusted his creators. But I had some resources of my own to play with, and while I was confident that he could snoop out other snoopers, I wasn't all that certain that Halton's buddies hadn't maybe stuck some kind of nano-sized microphones in their fabricant's ears.

The day was beginning to heat up, and most of the hotel guests had already eaten breakfast and gone. The few who remained were lounging in the shade of umbrellas and the terrace canopy, well out of the sun. All the protection I had was a pair of dark sunglasses and a thin coating of Number 8 sunblock.

I picked out an abandoned table at the edge of the veranda, sitting down with my back to the panoramic city view, and opened the PortaNet. The hotel waiter ambled out, blinking in the harsh light. Dressed in an imitation twelfth-century Mameluke outfit with the hotel crest on his turban, he looked more Pakistani than Egyptian. But he'd obviously seen enough insane journalists beavering away over PortaNets in the open air for him to be miffed at being forced to come out in the white-hot sun to take my order.

I ordered coffee, a large carafe of bottled water, figs and dates, goat cheese, coarsely mashed fava beans in vinegar, and the local flat bread drizzled with olive oil. Coffee and water first, breakfast when I'm finished working. He nodded, scribbling. The Grand Imperial Hotel was one of the few in Nok Kuzlat that catered to a Western crowd: the usual collection of ragtag journalists and a few brave tourists, usually healthy blond Nordic hiking types looking for exotic and cheap adventure, as well as roaming bands of Arab businessmen from neighboring countries who had developed chic Westernized tastes. I wasn't eating the local food because I was entertaining some romantic idea about going native. Cultures with limited access to experiencing real Western cuisine tend to have some curious notions about its correct preparation.

I sat with my back to the vista, because unless Spider-Man was crawling up the side of the building to peek over my shoulder, I could keep my transactions on the PortaNet to myself. Blipping wasn't anything that should trigger anybody's alarm systems, or so I hoped.

The PortaNet is the descendant of the original field equipment, bulky independent power generators chugging away hooked up to suitcase-sized transmitters with umbrella-like parabolic disks the size of a two-man camping tent. The PortaNet can be strapped to your back and hooked to the HoloPak for instant real-time relay, or for those less pressing moments, it can fit nice and neat on a cafe table with enough room left for a civilized cup of coffee and the morning newspaper. I could have used the audio equipment, since it's also scrambled into relay codes, but I didn't want to take the chance that one of my innocent-looking breakfast companions didn't have a spikemike jammed in his shorts, aimed in my direction. With the sun-hood over the keyboard, it was going to be damned difficult for anyone to eavesdrop on my transmission.

The waiter brought out my coffee, filled a glass with water

from the imported bottle, and walked off without a glance or a word.

I unfolded the keyboard and slipped in the call card, then hit the automatic send signal, simply an up-link call number for the GBN Cairo Relay station. The PortaNet whirred for a few seconds, searching for an available GBN satellite, found it and caught its attention.

CAIRO RELAY. YO HOODAT?

I chuckled. Somebody *real* on the other end, my fellow American smartass, and suddenly I had a strong wave of homesickness. There's no place like home, Toto.

K B SULAIMAN—I'd almost typed "Munadi"—NOK KUZLAT."

HI SAILOR NEW IN TOWN?

SORT OF. SECOND TOUR SOSDD. It meant "Same Old Shit Different Day," or in my case, "Decade."

TELL ME BOUT IT. HOURLY RATES OFFERED. BACK RUBS HALF OFF THIS WEEK ONLY.

I grinned. THANKS ANYWAY. SENDING RAW CLIPS GBN CENTER. TAG ARLANDO BK PG FILLER. The stuff I had wasn't really even worth sending at all. Arlando would look it over, wonder what the hell I was up to and probably send it down to the basement just in case anyone wanted to look up names to match the faces of the party animals. Otherwise, GBN wouldn't bother with airing any of it, edited or not.

READY.

I blipped, a high-speed transfer which went up scrambled, bounced off the security-shielded GBN satellite and back down into Cairo, where the station would zip it through a second coded channel on its way home, all within seconds.

There was always a chance somebody unfriendly-like might be trying to snoop, and the long separation of News and State had forced each side to devise different networks of information, data transmission and methods of ensuring the other side wasn't listening, while always trying to break in on your opponent.

As the tapes were being blipped, I thought about why I was really calling, hesitant to drag up the bloody past. I was only supposed to be running an errand, not doing investigative reporting.

KICK IT UP A PEG, OK? I finally typed after the footage had been blipped. If there was anyone tapping, that would perk their interest, but I had to take the risk. I was asking Cairo to go to the next tighter security scramble, make it that much harder for little ears.

WHATCHA NEED SAILOR? Cairo came back in a few seconds. The extra scramble would make transmissions fractionally slower, but people aren't machines, and the time lag isn't that noticeable.

LOOKING FOR A FRIEND. CHK BK ARK—I gave him the month and year for the archives—HAMID IBN RAZAILI. APX 45? LAST NOK KUZLAT.

CUT N CALL 10 MN. BYE-BYE.

I shut off the PortaNet, signaling the waiter for another coffee, and waited. My friend in Cairo was sharp and efficient, for which I was thankful. No questions about why I was typing instead of getting on the handheld. No long chats and no "hold one moment while I check, please" which only gives the opposition more time to hone in on a transmission. I had no illusions that given time, *if* the Government was tapping, they'd crack it. There are thousands of journalists all filing reports in dozens of languages every minute of the day. It would take thousands more Government agents whose only job it is to cover each and every transmission they could, to unravel it all. Agents like John Halton. I was taking the chance that they hadn't caught up, and that the scramble would hold.

Ten minutes expired, and I punched in the PortaNet again. The satellite hadn't moved too far, and apparently nobody else had used it to go on-line elsewhere. It was up and running within a second.

CAIRO RELAY. DAT U SAILOR?

YO HO HO.

LST KWN MEHEMET ST 56 BIS. X EL KAASEM. LUCK.

THNX. BYE

I had the PortaNet shut down the next moment. Cairo had known I was in a hurry, and the last transaction had taken less than fifteen seconds. If someone was snooping, they'd have to be damn good. But I wasn't going to let that make me too confident.

I didn't write down the address, just kept it in my head. I had figured that this time through Nok Kuzlat all I'd have to worry about was getting caught squatting to piss in the men's toilet with my shirttails dragging down into the open hole of Turkish jakes. The country wasn't at war, no bombs and bullets to worry about.

But the little chat in the abandoned cafe had set me operating on a much higher level of paranoia. The kind of furious, jittery paranoia I hadn't felt since I was a kid and my father told me God was so powerful, He could watch everything I did and hear every thought in my head. God apparently didn't believe in the right to privacy, and neither did the CDI.

I was folding the PortaNet back together as the waiter brought out my breakfast on a heavily engraved silver tray. "Have you finished, sir?" he said in perfect snotty English, even a trace of Oxbridge.

I was, and he popped an umbrella open over my head with the kind of superior flourish reserved for exclusive use by English royalty and waiters. I sat in the shade and ate slowly, thinking as I watched the baked air shimmer across the rooftops of Nok Kuzlat.

# ELEVEN

Under the baleful eye of the maitre d', I swiped an orange from the buffet table to take down to the room for Halton. He thanked me politely, put it in his pocket and we casually strolled down through the lobby and out onto Qaiyara Avenue, a busy thoroughfare cutting through the heart of Nok Kuzlat. I had the PortaNet draped over one shoulder like a carryall bag, and Halton had the HoloPak braced against his chest, partly covered by a loose *zhuhba-t* vest to make us less conspicuous.

The desk clerk had stared at me as if I were insane when I asked if he had a more current city map. The one he'd given me had been published in 1942, in Russian Cyrillic. New maps were not exactly prohibited, but they were regulated by the government and not handed out freely. Since the natives all knew where they lived, only enemies would want such information. You want to go somewhere, take a taxi, the clerk advised. Taxi drivers know all of Nok Kuzlat. Right. I knew that.

"How good is your mental map, Halton?" I asked. The noise of traffic forced me to half-yell to be heard. Ancient buses wheezed along crowded with people, some hanging on to the sides without a care. Old pickup trucks with bleating sheep in the back vied with new Mercedes and classic BMW's ruining their hydroglide brakes slamming to a stop, honking madly, then stomping on the gas for another three yards. Teenaged boys hauled handcarts stacked high with wares, straining undernourished muscles to their limits. Adding to all the entertainment were hundreds of shoppers and shoppees, dashing in and out of traffic with goods for sale, goods they'd bought, goods they wanted *you* to buy and were being thoughtful enough to bring right to your car door, whether you wanted them to or not.

"I can find my way around," Halton said. I'd bet he could.

"How's your radar?" He glanced at me, puzzled. "Do we have any unwanted company following us?"

He didn't look around, or hesitate. "Yes."

"Shit." I cursed quietly. "CDI?"

"No. Too obvious, too clumsy," he answered. He didn't seem concerned about it, and probably he wasn't.

"Can we lose them?"

"If you like."

I liked, and we had the first fun I'd had since we arrived in this shithole, walking briskly and turning quick corners, slipping through the endless coffee houses to come out in connecting back alleys. We jumped a fence into the back end of a covered suuq, buying things from the tiny stalls along the narrow bazaar streets at a near run. I draped a cheap rug woven with hideously bright colors over my PortaNet, and Halton's HoloPak ended up stuffed in a rattan-type suitcase. Both of us now had checkered kaffiyehs covering head and shoulders, held precariously in place with cheap beaded cords jammed around our crowns. I had bought the shabbiest-looking native wrapcoat from an elderly man's pile of secondhand clothes laid out on a piece of cardboard on the ground, doing a token bargaining at breakneck speed, then handing him far more money than it was worth and tugging it on regardless of possible lice, as we scurried off. The old man's eyes were both delighted and contemptuous of this sudden windfall from yet another stupid Western tourist.

This kind of amateur night wouldn't have shaken arthritic fleas off a bald dog, but somehow we lost our tail, and emerged at the edge of the slum growing along the border of the city center.

I told Halton where I wanted to go, and not to make it a direct route, either. We wandered, stopping occasionally to sniff whether or not our tail had caught up, then headed down El Kaasem Avenue deeper into Nok Kuzlat's ghetto where the

sleaze hadn't been varnished into sanitized, touristified "quaint-
ness." The poverty here was very real, and very grubby.

El Kaasem Avenue twisted and turned chaotically around
tenements and old buildings, as if the buildings had been
plunked down whole and the road forced around them. Other
streets, not even wide enough to be called alleyways, perforated
El Kaasem at odd intervals, the stench and squalor intensifying,
and the helpful English subtitles on street signs completely van-
ishing as we finally located Mehemet Street. We were lucky
Mehemet Street even had a sign, still having illusions it was a
part of the city proper.

Number 45 bis Mehemet Street was a sort of convenience
grocery and hardware store, a tiny, dim shop, vegetable racks
made from stacked wooden crates on the outside, a few carcasses in various stages of dissection hanging in the window as
enticement. There was no name written on the door or window,
only prices listed in Arabic script on scraps of paper shoved into
the cracks between the window frame and dusty glass. No English. This wasn't a place the usual gawking tourists would find
easily or would be welcome in.

A group of elderly men loitering by the door eyed us with
hostile suspicion, gnarled hands languidly brushing away the
omnipresent flies. A pair of small boys pulled a mangy goat tied
on a rope past us, their own skin as patchy as the animal's, their
eyes runny with the yellowed grime of untreated infection, as
they squinted up at the strangers invading their territory.

"Hamid's come up in the world," I remarked, smiling to
hide my anxiety. I was suddenly afraid, wanting to turn around
and go back.

The door hung precariously on rusty hinges and whined
loudly as I pushed it open, no need for a bell to signal the arrival
of customers. Inside, a teenaged boy dressed in a stained smock
peered out at us, warily curious. On either wall were shelves
crammed with a little bit of everything, boxes and bags labeled
in Arabic rising close to the ceiling, the top shelf holding various
brass pots and cooking utensils, carpentry tools, dangling daggers in dull pewter-colored scabbards. I knew Hamid would also
be the local money-changer as well as having a few odd pistols,
rifles, grenades and spare ammunition available for his regular
patrons. The narrow room terminated at the opposite end,
screened with a beaded curtain, the faint outline of a staircase
behind it.

I asked for Hamid, and the kid called toward the back, keeping his contentious eye on us. Down the stairway came a short, round, powerfully built figure, a white butcher's apron tied around his middle, not bothering to hurry. I was grinning uneasily, my nerves tense as he swept the beads to one side and squinted at us for a moment before he recognized me.

"*Yah salaam hkhala khee'dha!*" Hamid blurted out, and fell upon me as if I were a long-lost brother back from the dead. "Peace to you, and the blessing and mercy of Allah, Kay Bee. I never expected to see you again!" He was kissing both my cheeks.

"Hamid . . . Hamid . . ." I was wheezing, trying to catch my breath. I don't know if I was more relieved or surprised.

"Ahmat—" He turned to the kid. "Do you remember my son, Kay Bee?" I should have guessed.

Ahmat didn't recognize me. Only seven when I'd seen him last, the stoic little boy clutching the hand of his father and staring at the ruins of his life had grown up into a dark-eyed young man with whip-thin strong muscles in his arms. He stared at me gravely, as if trying to superimpose this strange face on a blurred memory and whatever stories his father might have told him.

"Jamilah!" Hamid bellowed, still holding on to me as if to prevent me from running away. "Come here! *J'ahkzhil!*"

"Hamid . . ."

"*H'asaleet ilb-araka!*" Hamid was running on. "My house is blessed with your return, I've always wondered what happened with you after the war, where the hell have you been keeping yourself, anyway, you never wrote, you never called . . ."

He was beginning to sound like my mother. More than that, we both knew it was a charade, acted out for the benefit of the curious hanging around the doorway. While I'm sure his emotions were genuine, when he pulled away from me I could see the sharp, gauging eyes boring into me, wondering what I was doing here. He glanced around the street, alert to any suspicious types who might be watching and reporting, before smiling reassuringly to his friends and firmly closing the door behind us.

A woman shrouded head to toe in a henna-dyed cotton aba'ayah, all but her eyes covered with an embroidered yashmak, came down the stairs to stare out through the beads at us in curiosity. Hamid introduced us to his wife, Jamilah, before he sent her back upstairs into the family's apartment above the store to make coffee for their guests.

Hamid ibn Razaili had been a lot younger, a lot thinner and a lot more sour, the last time I'd seen him. He was a few years older than I, a displaced *fhalell'ha*, born in the ruins of a remote village of Khuruchabja. While I had been pestering my parents to buy me a pony, he had been riding a secondhand bicycle, no tires on its metal rims, carrying contraband across half-swept mine fields, making a fragile living doing business with rival armies.

By the time he was fourteen, his father and older brothers had been killed off one by one in factional violence. His widowed mother had died from a combination of exhaustion, too many childbirths and untreated syphilis. His sisters had all expired from the extensive list of diseases widespread in the country; one from typhoid, another from cholera, one bled to death after a miscarriage, another bled to death after she'd been stabbed by a jealous husband. Orphaned and alone, he fled into the slums of Nok Kuzlat. Nowhere else to go, getting too old to prostitute his body for food, he had been pressed into the army and chosen to remain there, rising as far as his non-blue blood would allow him.

In Hamid's second year in the army, Khuruchabja had briefly joined in a small conflict between Shi'as and Sunnis duking it out for possession of a border town already ground into bits, useless to whichever side was ultimately victorious. The officers had abandoned the front lines, exhorting the ragged farm boys they left behind to fight on to glorious martyrdom. After shrewdly appraising the situation from his pitiful foxhole in the sand, Hamid had stuck his hands in the air, handed his antique rifle over to the nearest Damascus Coalition soldier he could find, and rode in the back of a flatbed truck to spend six months in a "relocation camp."

There, he met the first Westerners he'd ever seen, learning his English from an American Air Force sergeant stationed in Kuwait, a homesick rancher with a sixteen-year-old son back in Wyoming worrying about his pimples, virginity and the high-school prom. Hamid was no naive teenager—his childhood had been brutal, nasty and short—but he was a survivor, knew how to trade cigarettes and hashish when he had them, and smiles and innocence when he had nothing else. English was just another tool he could use in a never-ending chain of bribes given, baksheesh taken, staying alive.

He was still in the Khuruchabjan army years later when I'd

hired him as my driver to take me out to the front lines. Then, he supported the Behjars, with the nominal allegiance necessary for whichever faction held power. Money and survival, not politics, was his main concern. Like most other drivers in the motor pool for the local army contingent, he made a little extra tax-free cash off journalists desperate for transportation out to where the actual fighting was going on. Unlike most other drivers, however, Hamid actually knew how to drive.

The Behjars had secreted their infrafusion bombs, holding on to the capital of Nok Kuzlat and most of Khuruchabja while attempting to exterminate pockets of resistance fighters begging for help from the West and the allied Damascus Coalition. When public opinion polls finally allowed the West to send cavalry riding over the hill in the form of black unmarked jets and bombers screaming overhead, the Behjars lost ground quickly.

Hamid didn't seem to care that he was on the losing side; he'd been on the losing side before. He didn't have strong political beliefs of any kind, didn't much care if the journalists he hauled back and forth from the front lines were from countries siding against his employers. Journalists, even the most ignorant wandering *al-wabâhr* understood, had no country. They were strange creatures dressed in their own version of uniforms, bright, gaudy Hawaiian shirts to clearly demarcate them from soldiers. They asked foolish questions in their clumsy accents and seemed delighted when their own Western leaders were called blood-drinking bastard sons of diseased pigs.

Hamid's uniform was secondhand, and he wore sandals on his feet, a frayed, checkered kaffiyeh on his head. The belt around his waist was old, the leather repaired, but the gun inside his holster was polished and clean, as functional as the man himself regardless of how he dressed.

The driver always came with the jeep, since each driver was responsible for his machine, not daring for any price to hand over the keys to a stranger. Hamid drove me and the idiot optics kid GBN had stuck me with around for several weeks, anywhere we requested him to go. He asked no questions and said even less, silently watching and listening for planes overhead, ready to turn the sandjeep off the road if it seemed that bombs were imminent. He could look at the burnt corpses of villagers slaughtered outside their bombed houses with a dour, impassive face, holding the edge of his kaffiyeh over his mouth and nose to filter the stink, languidly brushing the ever-present flies from his eyes while we filmed.

The nation-state is still a relatively novel idea in the Middle East, one of those strange Western ideas that ignores the longer history of land divided between tribes, political ideology not enough to replace traditional blood ties. The dead weren't his family, the killers not his tribe, it was not his fight. He didn't pretend to understand the politics killing his countrymen, the senseless civil war sucking Khuruchabja's neighbors into the conflict. He was but a simple soldier; his sole ambition was to stay alive and make a little money. At least that's what he claimed.

Contrary to what the West wanted to believe, al-Husam and his Behjars had come to power by popular demand, and the charismatic leader had enjoyed wide support among Khuruchabjans for quite some time. With the sudden power of infrafusion bombs in his hands, it seemed to many in the country that the time had finally arrived for evening up the score after years of humiliation from the imperialist Zionist scum and their sycophants—traitorous, greedy, oil-rich Arabs. The average Khuruchabjan was a faithful Behjar enthusiast—

Until desperate Behjars started killing Khuruchabjans wholesale in the capital, their paranoia agitated by rumors of rebel terrorists hiding in the twisted alleyways of the slums. Hundreds disappeared in the night, the mutilated bodies of some dumped in their family's doorways as a warning, others never seen again. Soldiers herded women out of their cloistered quarters at gunpoint and into the streets as instant rent-a-crowds, eyes wild with either fervor or fear, chanting their praise for the Behjars and their hatred for the rebels in front of cameras. Once the camera crew had finished, the chants were abruptly switched off and the trembling women vanished silently, escaping like so many henna-shrouded ghosts back inside their anonymous stuccoed houses until the next staged rally.

Hamid introduced me to one of the Behjars in charge of organizing these mock rallies, a nasty little army colonel who was singularly unapologetic about the rent-a-crowd's patent phoniness. A great admirer of American history, he told me it was not the Arabs who were becoming Westernized, but the West which was becoming more Arabic.

"Especially you Americans," he said with a smirk. "You

think of all Arabs as deceitful liars and traitors. We can't help it; that's the Oriental mind-set, yes?" He spoke English with an unsettling Midwestern twang offsetting his melodic Arab accent. "But Americans, ah, these are the masters of lies! The fabled Gulf of Tonkin attack with six mythical Russian Swatow gunboats launching their invisible torpedoes, that lie gave you how many years of Vietnam, yes? A great lie, ingenious! And your late President Reagan, very clever, such a magnificent liar! He make himself President dealing in hostages just like a Syrian; he lies to Iran and your Contras; he just say no to drugs with his left hand and with his right he buys and sells to Peru and Colombia and Panama."

He chuckled, an evil little snicker. "But I like best his little lies, so pleasing, yes? He filmed Nazi death camps in the Second World War, so he say. Such admirable talent that he could do this thing without even leaving his country. He tells this story to his Israeli friends, who know he is lying. Such a grand comedy!"

The colonel was laughing, a raging, furious laughter. It was both fascinating and appalling to watch. Hamid sat silently listening, with only the glow of a cigarette butt he sucked to life occasionally showing the glint of narrowed eyes.

"Then you Americans lied to Saddam Hussein to trick him into a war. And you lied to the Palestinians and the Israelis; you lied to the Soviets when there were Soviets, and the Russians when there weren't. You lied to the South Americans, to Europe and Japan. You lie to the Mexicans and the Chinese, everybody. Now you lie to the Khuruchabjans, but most of all, you lie to yourselves.

"We have learned much of your sophistication, yes? But we Arabs pale into insignificance beside your glorious deceptions. And you, you Western journalists, you report these lies, to what difference? Do the great American peoples rise up and cry out, no more lies! No more! No, lies are for children who are afraid of the night. They comfort you, so you cherish them, keep them safe. You journalists, so proud of your truths, do you know what truth is anymore?"

He hawked and spat, a gummy wad of tobacco-yellowed phlegm missing my foot by inches. Hamid smiled, a humorless crease across his unshaven face.

"And what is the truth, then?" I shot back, not so much angry as curious. "Tell me, Arabs never lie anymore?"

"Of *course* we do. It is an art and our heritage." The colonel glared at me with pure hatred. "You have become more Arab than we will ever be Western. But listen carefully, for this time I speak the truth: The difference between Arabs and Americans is that we know when we are lying, because we believe our own lies as we tell them. Then we forget them and make new lies. You Americans tell lies without knowing they are lies, because you don't believe them at all, yes?"

Yes. It made no sense, and it made all the sense in the world.

Early one beautiful blue morning, the air still chill, Hamid had driven me and my optics kid out toward a small town along the provincial border rumored to be under siege by cut-and-run enemy forces. We were competing with a wolfpack of other journalists, ever hungry for copy, the more blood and guts the better. There had been a brief skirmish between two inept factions during the night, a lot of wild gunfire and noise but with little damaging effect. The main casualty seemed to be a goat run over by a heavy-armored gunjeep on its way out of town. We filmed a wizened old woman lamenting the goat's rather gory death.

"*Bodies!*" one of my esteemed colleagues was shouting furiously at no one in particular. We tried to ignore him as he stamped through the dusty village streets, crazed with frustration. "Where are the goddamned *bodies*! We need *bodies*!"

But while we were elbowing each other to interview the excited villagers, Hamid's army radio had whispered to him of worse horrors. He literally grabbed me and the optics kid, and drove as fast as the army jeep could take us over the potholed road back to town.

Crude gasoline bombs, large barrels mixed with fuel, explosives and scrap metal, had been placed at selected houses in the wee hours of the morning. They'd looked exactly like the harmless propane tanks many of the families in the poor suburbs depended on for heating and cooking, painted with the familiar green and white logo of Nok Kuzlat's local fuel company. No one had noticed an extra tank here and there against a house. The bombs had gone off as housewives turned on their gas stoves to prepare family meals, blowing everything in a ten-meter radius into a shattered crater.

The surrounding houses were all badly damaged, the innocent injured standing outside the windowless ruins, pressing cloth against bloody gashes from the scrap-metal shrapnel as they waited for ambulances slowly pushing their way through milling crowds. But the center of the blast left nothing standing, nothing alive, nothing recognizable as once being a place where people had ever lived.

The Behjars made two mistakes that morning. The first was placing one of their bombs at the wrong house. Their intended target had lived one street over. The other was blowing up Hamid's family. We drove up to a screaming crowd still teeming around in panic and confused grief, then pressed our way through to the crater. A neighbor woman recognized Hamid, tearing at her clothes as she wept hysterically. She clutched a small boy to her voluminous robes, half suffocating him.

Hamid took the boy from her, holding him tightly by one hand. Together they looked down into the crater that had once been their cramped little home. His oldest son, seven-year-old Ahmat, had gone early to the school at the mosque where he learned reading and writing from the Holy Qur'an. Hamid's crippled uncle, his elderly mother-in-law, his wife, their three teenaged daughters and infant son, were all killed in the blast, their charred, dismembered corpses being dug out of the rubble and laid side by side on the cracked pavement. Bits and pieces of Hamid's house surfaced from under shattered bricks— a corner from a picture frame, a tea glass miraculously intact, the leg off a chair, a cast-iron frying pan with its handle missing, the scorched remains of the meal his wife had been making still sticking to its round bottom. It resembled some bizarre art show carefully laid out by a demented modern artist: *I call my latest creation Surreal Horror.*

A soft whir behind me snapped me out of my shock. The optics kid was filming Hamid and his son, standing silently at the edge of the crater while his neighbors jostled behind him, wailing. Hamid looked up slowly at the camera, a glaze of disbelief on his tanned face, too stunned to even weep. He turned to look at me, something deeply ominous behind his eyes. My skin rose in cold goose bumps.

"Stop," I said to the kid quietly while I kept staring at Hamid. I didn't know why. The whir of film continued. I whirled, knocking one of the flyeyes out of kilter with a sudden angry slap. It snapped, hanging from a wire thread. "Stop filming."

The kid dropped the holo down onto his chest, startled and

indignant. "What are you talking about? We've got it, man—it's *exclusive*, this is great stuff!"

I knew it was. "You're fired. Get the fuck away from me."

The kid eyed me with incredulity, then stomped off in a huff, fiddling with his broken flyeye and muttering. Turning to stare down into the crater, I found to my own surprise I was crying. "I'm sorry," I said to Hamid, a man I barely knew. "I'm so sorry."

"*Allah ahk'bahr,*" he whispered hoarsely. God is great.

God is great. God is good. Thank You for our daily catastrophe, without which I'd soon be out of a job.

He took his young son by the hand and walked away. That evening, I hunted down one of the few illicit bars in Nok Kuzlat and drank a couple of Coca-Cola bottles of whiskey before the owner got nervous I'd be seen leaving drunk, and cut me off. That was the day I knew I was starting to lose it, knew I'd seen all the dead bodies, all the children's corpses, all the misery and stupidity I was ever going to be able to stomach in the name of Truth, Justice and the Public's Right to Know. I was staring down into the dark mud of my third lukewarm coffee when someone sat down across from me.

It was Hamid.

"Peace to you," he said quietly.

"*Insha'allah.* If God wills," I said, unable to wish him the blessings and mercy of Allah, who so obviously had turned His face from Hamid. I hesitated, then said, "*Yah hawalla il-lâahch.*" Markundi, like most Arabic tongues, has an abundance of customary formulae for every event in life. It makes so much more sense than the Western philosophy of blindly ignoring anything bad until it's rubbed in your face, then leaves you waffling around trying to come up with something to say. In English, I'd have been left stupid and inarticulate in the face of Hamid's calamity; in Markundi, there was ritual comfort for us both.

He nodded, his eyes dry and bloodshot. "God is merciful," he said, his voice husky. The sweet smell of hashish clung to his clothes. "He has spared the life of my firstborn son, and I thank Him for His compassion and benevolence." The words were sincere, but completely devoid of emotion.

That in itself was unusual. Arabs are among the most intensely emotional people in the world, flying to the extreme reaches of joy and grief, love and hatred, gratitude and treachery. This quiet, composed man should have been tearing his clothes and weeping, firing his rifle into the air, searching out the company of his brother Muslims to help him express his anguish, not sitting here quietly with a Western journalist.

I watched him carefully. "He has opened my eyes," Hamid said, watching me with equal wariness, "and filled my heart." Simple words. Simple emotions. Hamid was not a simple man.

"You have great courage, my friend," I said.

He smiled. "Do dead men have courage?" I had no answer for that. "I have decided," he said, "that I am tired of this fighting. I am sick of innocent people dying to satisfy the appetites of greedy men who care nothing about those they claim to love, in whose name they kill us. We are only cattle to be used and slaughtered at their whim."

So it has been in these lands for thousands of years.

"Also, I am tired of foreigners who say they know what is best for us. The Damascus Coalition doesn't care what happens in Khuruchabja, and the West will only fight for money."

"What can you do, Hamid?" I asked fatalistically. "You are only one man."

"These words these men spout in their high speeches, this call for 'democratic progress,' the 'people's will,' 'freedom of expression,' 'constitutional representation,' what use are these to us? What do we *fhalell'hin* know of these? Are cattle capable of understanding?" He was not being contemptuous; he was comfortably resigned to his place in this society. But it is a poor farmer who doesn't take proper care of his cattle.

"These words aren't meant for us, they're for you, you Westerners who prize useless words like these above all others. Our leaders have learned from you how to say those words which can buy them money and influence from the West, but they mean nothing. Your words are poison. You are all fools, you rich people in your rich countries. This is what you should be telling these rich people who see you on the television. You should tell them they are like stupid donkeys to be deceived by men who kill innocents and call this justice and righteousness. You must tell them this."

There was no scorn or anger in his voice, and I sat with my eyes dry, my ears burning. "It's just not that simple, Hamid—"

"These men must go," he said, cutting me off. I imagined I saw the pure demented light of an ancient *hashshâshin* shining in his eyes.

"Then they will be replaced by men just like them. Nothing will change."

He nodded. "Probably. A wound cleaned may fester again. Or it may heal. That is up to Allah. But it must be cleaned, nonetheless." He laid a man's ring on the table in front of me, a broad gold band with the insignia of a high-ranking Behjar officer engraved on its face. The man's finger was still in it.

"I will avenge the death of my family. The guilty must die." Hamid looked at me, unblinking. When I nodded, his hand closed around the ringed finger and it vanished. We walked out of the illegal bar together, an unspoken agreement between us.

He took me into a world of madness then. He built his own private network of resistance rebels. Orphans and outcasts bereft of their traditional interrelated family ties became their own tribe, forged their own loyalties. They were not the loose group of disorderly maniacs the Behjars had mistaken his family for. These were quiet, serious men, some mere boys. They were shadows flitting through doorways, speaking with glances, silent killers.

Still in the Behjars' army, Hamid drove me around for another month, taking me deep into war zones with the berserk nonchalance of a man who doesn't care if he's killed. An untapped source, it was a journalist's dream, a living nightmare. I ignored my bureau chief's dire warnings, going where no sane reporter dared to.

I smoked Hamid's hashish with him as we crouched in rain-soaked trenches while bombs rippled through the ground. To keep warm we shared bottles of whiskey I bought from soldiers. My feelings deadened, I covered the bloodshed with unseeing open eyes, telling the West that they were fools and stupid donkeys in a terminology they could understand, with a calm voice and professionalism that sealed my reputation as a Fearless War Correspondent.

Hamid was able to take me, along with the equally insane optics kid GBN ordered me to hire back, deep into the Behjars' domain. Doors opened with the right spoken words, and I was so close to the blast that took out one of the last of the Behjars' military strongholds, my eyebrows and lashes were singed off. I coughed acrid smoke out of my lungs for weeks.

I was still young and numb enough to believe our Hawaiian shirts were somehow bulletproof. We learned better; I was shot in the foot climbing over a wall, the optics kid was killed by a mine four days later. After that, Hamid insisted on giving me a pistol, a small timeworn heirloom, his eyes almost shy as he affirmed my manhood with that ultimate of Arab confirmations. I shrugged, stuck it in my pocket and learned to limp. I found a decent freelance optics stringer desperate to crack the networks to replace the kid. We became machines, watching death and destruction, dedicated to preserving it for the masses to savor.

I knew Hamid collaborated with other insurgent factions, then sold them out if he had to, and I didn't care. He discarded his uniform and slipped through the dark, sowing a careful garden of death and mistrust in his wake. Most of the Behjars' top leaders were eventually either killed or escaped into exile. Those who remained were frantic to hold on to whatever power they had left. But by the time the Damascus Peacekeeping Coalition finally got around to invading Nok Kuzlat, they were pretty much finished.

Hamid murdered quietly and efficiently those people he thought responsible for the death of innocents. I knew better. We were all guilty, but it was getting me the best footage of the Behjars' downfall possible. The conflict was so terrifying, so huge, there was no possible way to understand, to make sense out of the violence and chaos and killing and hatred.

Then there was the child. In a darkened doorway. The tiny hands around a gun, black cylinder pointed at Hamid's back. He doesn't see. I shout, Hamid twists away. The child lifts the gun, turning toward me. The antique pistol is somehow in my hand. His face is as delicate as an angel's. Sometimes I wake up in the night, seeing the dark eyes staring at me. Just before. I kill him.

I had thought my feelings were already numbed, but I'd been wrong. Something in me died, then, something nameless and vital.

Hamid later returned the favor, pulled my ass out of the fire a few times, too, and I lost count of what the score was. Whatever it was that bound us, it was not friendship or loyalty, but something more primitive and inexplicable.

When the Behjars' fortified headquarters in the center of Nok Kuzlat was stormed, we had all the excitement we could film. I had the exclusive, yelling into the camera to be heard over explosions ripping through the background, hoarse shouting that al-Husam had been assassinated, the demoralized Behjars surrendering en masse, the Damascus Coalition peppered with the odd American soldier out of Saudi Arabia capturing the infrafusion bombs intact. Victorious rebels linked arm in arm danced through the ruins with ecstatic bliss, waving rifles and howling. I could almost feel the bubblehead at GBN Center creaming with joy to be the one lucky enough to have the com when it happened. I felt no joy.

The troops were mopping up through the rubble when I walked in on Hamid just in time to watch him cut the throat of a Behjar officer with no more emotion than had he been slaughtering a chicken. It was our friend, the colonel who admired American history so much. He'd been on his knees, hands tied behind his back, eyes white with terror as he begged for his life. When Hamid turned, bloody knife in his hand, the optics man had him on the holocamera with his face clear and unmasked. The dying colonel at his feet kicked feebly as his life gurgled out. Reaching over, I punched the slipclip out of the camera.

"Hey!" the guy protested, then shut up when he saw my face.

"You know you don't film him," I said quietly. "Those are the rules." Then I dropped the clip to the floor, smashing it under my heel. Hamid smiled grimly, nodded, and that was it. The optics man ranted on that I'd gone stark crackers, but he didn't quit. We were all more than a little mad by then, including him.

I knew if the tables had been turned, the colonel would have murdered all of us with no more compassion than Hamid had shown. Or I had. We were not in Kansas; this was no chivalrous battle between knights in shining armor. The line between what the West considered good and evil was lost here, no mercy given because none could be afforded. I think by that time I really was clinically insane. I slept as peacefully as a baby at night, and covered the carnage with the hunger of the starving.

Somewhere during the fire-bombing of the Behjars' last retreat and the coverage of occupying troops pouring into Nok Kuzlat, Hamid gravely shook my hand and disappeared. So did a lot of the old Behjar regime, bodies popping up here and there with their throats cut.

Victory inevitably turned to revenge. After the new government set up by the occupying powers began settling old scores with their defeated enemies, they became edgy when several of their own associates mysteriously joined the mutilated bodies dumped in alleyways and garbage bins. The government started publicly hanging members of their former allies and their own loyal rebel execution squads. The UN moved in with refugee aid as the Coalition withdrew. By the time the new regime was overthrown in a military coup and replaced by a newer, even more vicious regime, I'd left Nok Kuzlat. For good, I'd thought. I'd prayed.

I accepted my little awards at a civilized ceremony, and went to work on the feed-in desk. The waking nightmares started shortly after I got back, and I finally started seeing a shrink, covertly. No one other than Arlando ever knew. My glib medley of predigested Press Club anecdotes covered up a lot of torment and depression.

Once in a while I'd see hints of Hamid's work, keeping tabs on the rise and fall of Khuruchabja's seasonal governments until Sheikh Larry's predecessor ascended the Presidential throne. The violence gradually died, the people exhausted after a decade of blood.

While it was one thing for the Behjars to have stolen infrafusion bombs, or so it was publicly claimed, the infighting that went on long after they had fallen was no heartbreak for the U.S. Government. The goal was to keep Khuruchabja unstable, but weak. If Khuruchabja was too busy arguing over internal politics, they weren't likely to ally themselves with one neighbor or the other outside their borders, keeping the broader region fractured and factional, malleable to what the West considered proper influences on world security.

Now I smelled a rat. And if there was any rat-shit to sniff out, Hamid would probably know about it.

I took off my shoes as we entered the family's *ma'gâlees*, a small living room above the shop, and Hamid seated us at a place of honor for his guests, on a genteelly worn sofa and chair around a carved and inlaid wood table set low on the floor. As Hamid settled into a chair, I politely admired the family photos decorating the walls between ornate Qur'an calligraphy in worn gilt frames. A collection of small nicotine-stained *narghileh* pipes was arranged in an English knotty pine teacup cabinet; the family's good tea set shared space on a table in the corner with an eclectic set of French demitasse cups and saucers.

Ahmat sat next to his father, while small children played outside the doorway, peeping in and giggling once in a while. Jamilah brought the long-handled brass *ibik*, and poured us cup after tiny cup of potent coffee while feeding us the little sweetmeats she was hurriedly making in her immaculate kitchen.

Hamid had changed dramatically over the years. The thin, dour man who had stared at me over a severed finger had been transformed into a chatty, laughing man. But his eyes were still sharp, the *hashshâshin* warrior still watching me, eyeing Halton, evaluating.

"You've done okay for yourself, Hamid—a grocery store, of all things," I said.

"Allah has been kind to an old man," he said.

"Old, my ass. You have one or two more years on me, my friend, and I'm not old."

"Is it always the years that make us old, Kay Bee?" Hamid smiled, and I saw the bitterness in the wrinkled lines radiating from his eyes. "I became too slow, too fat, to remain a young troublemaker sprinting over rooftops. I had Ahmat to think of, as well."

Ahmat grimaced, the universal disdain boys have at the crux between being a child and leaving home as a man. "And so . . . ?" Hamid shrugged. "I found myself a good woman with wide hips who could make healthy sons, and became a respectable man in the community. I have important responsibilities now. I bought a miserable little grocery so that at least my family will never starve, and created Old Hamid the Grocer." He indicated his plump torso with an actor's flourish.

He had allowed Jamilah to remove her yashmak and loosen the h'jab around her face, a sign we were accepted as close friends of Hamid's. Her face was round and plain, but she had beautiful, intelligent eyes. Hamid obviously adored her, although his masculine pride made him attempt to hide it. She entered with another tray of sweetmeats, setting it down on the low table. Hamid brushed her hands away as she attempted to serve us, and she *tsked* with affectionate impatience.

"Eat," Hamid urged us, adding the old peasant's idiom, "Or I will be forced to divorce my wife."

I ate a flaky pastry filled with crushed dates and glazed with honey. "Where would you find another wife who could make anything as delicious as this?" I asked.

"The same place I found this one, in a French cooking school. But perhaps I should look for another," he said, "one who can't cook as well, but with a sweeter disposition. My wife has been to University where she has learned too many foreign ideas. Women should not learn to read, it is very bad for their minds. They lose their proper virtue and honor when they think too much. I need another wife, a stupid wife who doesn't read and who will respect me."

Jamilah didn't seem too worried about his opinions, her rueful half-smile proof she'd put up with Hamid's banter too long to be upset by it.

"The love between a man and a woman is a fine thing, is it not?" Hamid said, one eye on his wife, "but the love between men, this is a strong, pure love. Only the love of Allah is greater, don't you agree?"

Seeing as neither Halton nor I were *men*, I demurred politely.

"That is why a true man needs more than one wife. It is part of the natural way of life. Lucky are we Muslims to be able to have more than one wife"—Hamid was teasing—"unlike you wimpy Western men with your half-naked harpies marching through the streets like common prostitutes shouting for votes and driving-licenses instead of making their homes clean and giving their husbands sons."

"Muhammad had many wives," Jamilah reminded him archly as she refilled our tiny coffee cups, "for all the good it did him. They fought among themselves and deceived the Prophet, and for all their trouble still gave him no living son for an heir."

"In that respect, the Prophet was unlucky," Hamid declared. "But I have always had good luck with my women." He was looking at Ahmat and added more quietly, "And my sons."

A little girl of about four had clambered into his lap to steal a square of pastry. "What about your daughters, Papa?" she said, her mouth decorated with sticky crumbs, brown eyes wide.

He laughed, grabbed her and kissed the crumbs from her face as she squealed in delight. "May Allah see you grow up to be beautiful and lucky enough to have a husband as good as me!"

I was smiling, but a tremor of cold shot through me as an image of Hamid, standing with his young son silently on the edge of a shallow crater, superimposed itself on this happy family. Clouds, they bring rain and joy, they blow away again on the breath of the wind—who can hold the clouds in his hands? Pride and fear shone in Hamid's eyes.

"You still keep in touch with old friends, Hamid?" I asked casually, watching him over the lip of my coffee cup as I sipped.

He said nothing for a moment, then looked at Halton. Halton was back into his automaton mode, being inscrutable. I answered Hamid's unspoken question. "No, I can't trust him," I said. "But he's saved my life." Hamid would understand that very well.

He considered, then tickled the little girl before he brushed her from his lap. He turned to yell at the gaggle of children loitering around the doorway. "You kids go out and play! Out, out, *out!*" They giggled and jostled each other, ignoring Hamid's order until Jamilah shooed them away with a wooden spoon waved threateningly in the air. She closed the door, and returned to the kitchen, quietly shutting that door as well. Ahmat remained seated, as sullen and brooding as his father had once been.

"It is hard not to see old acquaintances in so small a city at least once in a while," Hamid said carefully.

"Would you know anyone who might have access to AI equipment?"

Ahmat glanced at me, startled, then tried to mask his expression. Hamid smiled woefully, shaking his head. "My son scorns the ways of old men like his father, thinking we are all daft and ignorant. He is like Jamilah—he's studied an entire year in University, you see, so he thinks he knows all the secrets in Allah's universe. But he's still as transparent as water."

Ahmat colored, a deep flush of red creeping up his neck and cheeks. His father laughed, putting an affectionate arm around the boy's stiff shoulders. "Yes, my son knows a great deal about computers and other accursed Western toys," he said proudly.

"Ahmat," I said, addressing him as a man, not as a child. "Maybe you could do us a great favor? I need to find an AI reader quickly."

Father and son exchanged looks, a silent understanding passing between them. Ahmat stood. "Come on, then. I'll take you."

"Old Hamid the Grocer must open the shop," Hamid said, getting laboriously to his feet. I didn't believe for a second he was as feeble as he pretended to be, had no doubt those old legs were as sturdy and fast as they'd been a decade ago. "There are surely people waiting while we selfishly keep you from your business. There is gossip to catch up on which only old men are good at swapping. And since I know nothing of these matters young people learn in their great universities, being only an old and ignorant peasant, I trust you in the hands of my son. *Allah yhishal'limakh*, go with God."

We kissed cheeks; I felt Hamid's strong fingers on my shoulders, the rasp of his beard against my skin. I held him at arm's length, looking into his eyes. They crinkled as he smiled, dark and warm. Only eyes.

"*Mah salaama*, my old friend," I said quietly. "God give you peace."

# TWELVE

Ahmat took us out the back. If the front of Hamid's store seemed grim, the dirt alleyways twisting mazelike behind it were appalling. Blank, mud-colored walls abutted each other in mad confusion, leaving spaces between them barely wide enough for a man. Our shoes made sucking noises as we picked our way through the slime and rubbish, the smell of sewage and rot strong. Cockroaches scuttled in panic. Broken wood lattices in small windows above our heads hid eyes that I knew followed us.

The maze widened into a dirt-paved street, and children seemed to coalesce around us, a growing feral pack with hate and hope in their eyes as grubby hands picked at our clothes, begging for money. They chattered in a clipped Markundi slang. I had a hard time looking into their ravaged faces, eyes and noses runny with dirt-crusted mucus. Ahmat walked in front with his back stiffened, brusquely pushing the children aside and slapping away the more aggressive.

I glanced at Halton, wondering how he interpreted this small sample of human poverty and misery. The feeling of desperation intensified, and I was keeping my hands firmly on anything I didn't want to see vanish. A bony, grime-stained hand nimbly attempted to separate Halton from an unprotected part of his HoloPak. The child's eyes went wide as Halton effortlessly plucked the Pak back. Then the mob scattered as Ahmat grabbed the kid's hand and broke a finger. The beggar child stumbled away, howling in pain and fury. As cruel as Ahmat seemed, under Islamic law the child might as easily have lost his whole hand. A rock spattered into the wall as another retreating ragged child cursed us, his aim wild.

Ahmat glared at me, dark eyes bitter. The children were only another reminder for him of the endless, grinding deprivation in Nok Kuzlat, a glaring statement of Khuruchabja's demeaning inequities, and the West's indifference.

When Ahmat had led us through the labyrinth of back streets until he was satisfied we were completely disoriented, we ducked into a squalid cluster of rooms behind a walled-in empty courtyard. Inside, our eyes adjusted to the gloom. Ahmat rapped his knuckles in a coded rhythm against a locked door. After a moment, solid locks thunked open and the door creaked ajar, a pair of bespectacled eyes blinking at us.

Inside, the room was clean, brightly lit. Three young men straightened from old-fashioned flat-screen monitors to stare at us distrustfully, their faces reflecting the oscillating light. Cables connected an odd assortment of computers, AI frames, old holosets, faxerox machines, dozens of obsolete South Korean-made underboard interfaces siamesed together. A venerable laser printer hissed to itself in a corner, churning out a growing pile of pages.

"*'Ahchlan*, Ahmat," the oldest of the bunch greeted our guide, straightening to examine us suspiciously. He was in his late thirties, the rest barely out of their teens. "What's going on?" He was self-assured, dark eyes intense. A charismatic personality, obviously the leader and patron of this small group.

"Friends of my father's," Ahmat said, and sat down, pointedly away from us as if to separate us from any question of his loyalties.

The man regarded us for a moment, then nodded with formal politeness, his hands spreading to greet us. "Be welcome," he said, and swept a long rug-covered bench made of crates clear of manuals, program chips, and various pieces of electronic paraphernalia, to make room for us to sit.

"*Ih'salaam*," I said, and we sat.

Ahmat did a quick round of introductions; the older man's name was Ibrahim al-Ruwala, the voice of authority. The others were all either his younger brothers or cousins. Then we sat staring at one another, the boys glancing uneasily at each other as the silence drew out uncomfortably. Shit, might as well cut right to it, I thought.

"I understand you may be able to help us with some AI equipment," I said in awkward Markundi.

"Maybe," Ibrahim responded in English. "What have you got?"

I had Halton turn his face to the wall before he produced the flake. Let them think he got it out of a false tooth, but people who stuck fingers up into their sinuses might look a bit too weird. He handed the flake to Ibrahim.

After inspecting it, Ibrahim looked at us, his eyes shifting between Halton and me as he deliberated. "You'd need some top-line AI stuff for this," he said. He waved a depreciative hand toward the jury-rigged system. "I'm afraid we might not be of much help."

"Halton?" I asked quietly.

He'd already scanned the hodgepodge. "It'll work," he answered simply. "The equipment is better than it looks."

Ibrahim stared at him, eyes calculating. I smiled amiably. "Halton's a decent enough computer hacker," I lied, not knowing at that moment how right I was, "but of course, it's your equipment."

Ibrahim grunted. "Okay, so if we do crack the flake, what's in it for us?"

It always comes down to the suuqs, even when dealing in bits and bytes. "What are you asking?"

He grinned. "How about the flake?" he said shrewdly.

I shook my head. "That's no deal for you, believe me. This damn thing's already been more trouble than it could possibly be worth." I indicated the bruises on my face. Ibrahim looked thoughtful, considering. He nodded, giving up the idea of the flake. His lips pursed as he pretended to think.

"Ibrahim, a PC miniCray," the cousin with the wire-rim glasses blurted out impatiently. "What about a miniCray? Allah, what I could do with one of those babies . . ."

"*Baj'lâash khalâam*, Abdullah," Ibrahim snapped. "Shut your mouth." Then he frowned, his tense eyes glancing at me. "Well," he said reluctantly, "what *about* a miniCray?"

"You'd have to trust me on an IOU, but I could get you one."

Abdullah beamed like a kid at Christmas. While it was obvious who their leader was, the scrawny nerd wearing glasses and peach fuzz on his upper lip was undeniably their principal whiz kid. We argued briskly over exactly which model, more for form's sake. Ibrahim didn't really believe I'd honor any bargain two minutes after we left, but his curiosity about the microflake was too aroused. When the deal was made, Halton and Abdullah started in on the flake.

Abdullah stumbled along for a few moments in English before Halton slipped into flawless Markundi. The kid looked surprised, then began rattling away with Halton in a rapid-fire exchange too fast for me to follow more than a few sentences heavily spiced with Anglicized computer terminology. The rest of us hovered around in the background, kibitzing. New cables were strung from the AI frame to the various computers. I plugged the HoloPak into one of the two wheezy-looking holosets, its murky gray haze shimmering in the air, waiting.

It looked like it was going to take some time. Ibrahim pulled Ahmat to one side for a brief conference while I got nosy and picked up one of the sheets still being spit out by the laser printer. It was the usual polemic denunciation of some obscure local outrage, but even though my Arabic was rusty, I could read a little between the lines. Following the traditional vehement and sensationalist prose vilifying the sordid practices of the culprit in question was the suggestion for a reasoned, objective investigation along with a proposal to remedy the situation rather than the emotional cry to string the bastard up by his nuts in revenge. I smiled.

"So you're from GBN," Ibrahim finally said to me, his chat with Ahmat over. He pointed his chin at the paper in my hand, his arms crossed belligerently across his chest. "A big-shot Western journalist like you must think that's pretty naive stuff, huh?"

"No, not at all. Of course not . . ." I assured him quickly.

"No?" He raised an eyebrow, his lips twisted in an amused scowl. "But it's *supposed* to be naive." He laughed at my puzzled expression. "A nation fed for twenty years on nothing but bland rice can't be expected to be able to digest hot spiced meat in a day. But neither can you expect them to stay satisfied forever on a tasteless diet. Change is necessary, but by incremental steps."

I held up the sheet. "And you're in the process of gradually spicing up your politics?"

He shrugged. "I hope so. Surround the unfamiliar with the familiar until it too becomes accepted. Not too much, not too little. Like the rain, too much and you end up with a devastating flood. Too little, you die from drought. Just enough, and ideas grow like plants. Anchor your roots first in the soil before trying to grow flowers."

"You're quite a philosopher."

He smiled broadly this time. "I'm an Arab," he said.

Ibrahim had graduated, with honors, he emphasized, from a small British-run academy in Istanbul, the closest technical institute he could afford. But his degree in telecommunications and economics was less than worthless in Nok Kuzlat; he worked at night in an industrial laundry, overseeing the antique robotic programs on the huge washers. Frustrated, but unwilling to abandon the country of his birth, he organized the Young Islamics for Contemporary Democratic Reform, a lengthy, high-sounding title for a fraternity consisting mostly of himself, a few of his brothers and cousins of varying degree, and a few nonrelated members like Ahmat and another friend who was apparently working at the moment in a garage.

"We're small, so what?" he said, unconcerned. "We work quietly and stay outside the notice of the government. The problem in Khuruchabja is the delusion that we are an island, isolated from the rest of the world by an ocean of sand. The government prefers to support that myth with the lie that they are keeping pollutants out, when in fact they are only keeping us prisoners within. But sooner or later we will have to admit the truth that we are part of the whole, accept the necessity of working *with* the rest of the world, not against it. And we must do so peacefully."

Ibrahim had a politician's voice, but his eyes were a rarity, those of an honest evangelist's. He *believed* in his arguments, and that kept me fascinated.

"War is just another Western strategy to keep us subjugated and alienated. America is too strong militarily, Europe dominates us economically, our own rich Muslim neighbors won't risk lifting a finger to help us. So what can we do?"

I had a feeling he had the answer to that one, too. And it surprised even me.

"We must give up our guns, if not our anger. We must learn to fight with modern weapons like diplomacy and the media and manipulating world opinion. But to do that, we must become *part* of the world." He held up his hand, fingers down. "First the roots," he said, and turned his hand palm up. "Then the flower." Slowly he closed his fingers into a clenched fist. "*Then* we will triumph."

Beyond proselytism, Ibrahim's other talent was hustling, a consummate PR man wheeling and dealing to beg, borrow and smuggle enough equipment into their secret hide-out to produce a surprisingly extensive underground electronic-bulletin network, while generating a steady flow of posters and leaflets. His cousin Abdullah had never stepped foot into a university but had taken to the computer equipment Ibrahim had acquired like a piranha to steak on the hoof.

While Ibrahim's interest was politics, the younger relatives under his patronage had their own specialties revolving around computers and communications. All of them had ambitions, a fire in their blood, dreams of changing the world. Two cousins had access to the government's central computer library, where they worked evenings as low-level data entry clerks. Ahmat had spent his single academic year studying telecommunications and holoscience, longing to earn his degree in journalism at a good university, maybe in Kuwait City, where the Americans still taught, or even in the dark heart of the reviled, degenerate West itself.

But Hamid didn't make that kind of money, and it didn't seem likely that Nok Kuzlat was going to be developing any cutting edge in the forefront of technological wonders any time soon. In the meantime, the Young Islamics churned out their leaflets, wrote coded E-dispatches to each other through their computer bulletin network, and sent their shaky, amateur holofootage surreptitiously to Amnesty International and the Worldwide Human Rights Association.

"We're through!" Abdullah said in delight. "We got through!" The "Confidential, Restricted Access, Authorized Personnel Only" had given way to a fast progression of diagrams, a split screen of specs beside it. Abdullah's eyes widened even more behind his thick lenses, threatening to pop out of his head. "It's a weapons system—" he said, awed, "diagrams AI'ed for modification . . . It's a whole set of ways to make infrafusion bombs!"

My legs suddenly twitched like they wanted to get up and run to the nearest border, all on their very own. My ears buzzed, nightmare images sniggering around the edges of my vision; I couldn't hear the babble of excited voices in the room or see the excited faces clustered around the computer. Halton was silent, watching the screen in front of him, scrolling slowly through the diagrams pulsing evilly.

"This is not correct," he finally announced.

"What?" Ibrahim said.

Halton had turned to address me. "These diagrams are erroneous. It would be impossible to build a working device from any of these plans. The AI programming is too rudimentary; the entire system is using less than a tenth of the storage capacity of the microflake."

"So what are you saying, Halton?"

He gestured at the screen. "This is a cloaking program. It's hiding something at a deeper level."

Abdullah stared at Halton with astonishment and a growing expression of worship. A true hacker's hero. I must have looked a little astonished myself.

"Can you get into it?" I asked.

Halton glanced at the boy seated beside him. "I think we can," he said. Abdullah beamed.

Ibrahim didn't look pleased; Abdullah was his cousin, and Halton had just cut into his jurisdiction. I stayed quiet, hoping the tension would stay controlled as Abdullah and Halton hunched over the screen, pecking away at the ancient keyboard and conversing in an incomprehensible language, half Markundi, half computer babble. The "weapons system" froze, then vanished, replaced by scrolling lines of algorithmic code, silent black letters marching up the pale screen. I took one look at the stuff crystallizing on the 2-D display and knew I was way far out of my league.

Halton straightened, and turned to look at me with that imperturbable expression. "It knows we're here," he said quietly.

*Brrr.* Cooties crawled up my spine. I suddenly had some sympathy with the muftis who hated AI's.

Abdullah was following the screen with absolute concentration. "Look at this stuff," he said, his younger cohorts crowded around him. "I've never seen any programming paradigms like this. Look!" His finger jabbed at the screen. "And that—incredible, fantastic, it's *poetry* . . ."

Then it balked. Frozen script pulsed on the screen while

Abdullah cursed softly, keys clicking frantically under his sprinting fingers.

"We can't do it," he said finally, and leaned back away from the screen.

"Why not?" Frustration at getting so close jittered my teeth.

"We don't have the equipment." He looked utterly disappointed, not for having failed, but for being denied access to the precious programming.

"It's a holoed AI, like you thought, Kay Bee," Halton said. "But it's asked for specifications not available here."

"Like what?" Ibrahim cut in sharply.

"It's a three hundred sixty-degree hologram," Halton told him. "We'd need four synchroed full-sized holosets for projection, and it refuses to communicate without simultaneous display." He pointed to the two standard holosets in the corner. "They're no good—too old, can't be synched."

Ahmat smirked dourly, *Told you so*.

Jesus H. Christ. A full dimensional AI'ed hologram at that level of self-governing would have been *monstrously* expensive to produce. The damned flake must have cost more to make than Halton. That thought made me uneasy.

But Ibrahim was not a man who liked to be thwarted. He turned to me. "How much money have you got?" he demanded brusquely.

"Not enough to run out and buy four new holosets, if that's what you're thinking."

He held his hand out imperatively. I handed over the contents of my wallet, which amounted to a hundred and eighty-seven Khuru rials and change, or about sixty bucks. He smiled tightly. He was back in charge now, and he wanted us to know it. "In my hands, it'll be enough," he boasted and left.

Half an hour later, he drove up in the most battered three-wheeled delivery car I'd ever seen, oily black smoke from the two-stroke Albanian-cloned Trabant engine belching out the exhaust pipe. The boys scurried out to unstrap the two huge woven baskets tied to the flatbed and hustle them into the dark interior, away from any curious eyes. Inside were four top-of-the-line 90-degree holosets in mint condition, sales specs still pasted on the sides, along with the umbilicus attachments to synch them. I knew they must have cost close to three thousand dollars apiece. They were gorgeous.

I didn't get back any change, either.

"We have three hours, then we have to return them," Ibrahim said, triumphant, enjoying the surprise on my face. "They're being destroyed tomorrow."

"*What?*"

"The *mutawin* confiscated these from people showing illegal holotapes. They plan a public demonstration in the square tomorrow. They're going to burn all the illegal tapes and holosets, whiskey, AI cassettes, music chips, pornographic magazines, books, all the things they've taken."

Along with some of the hapless targets of Nok Kuzlat's self-appointed Muslim Morality Police, I wouldn't be surprised. These *mutawin* roamed the streets preying on citizens who didn't come up to their notion of Islamic standards, lecturing suspected miscreants, seizing possessions with impunity, slapping women around whose excuse for being on the street was not adequate. They were allowed to burst into private homes without warning or warrants, looting whatever they chose, beating the inhabitants or hauling them off to certain mosques as prisoners. They were tolerated, even encouraged by the government, since their brutality kept the population properly subdued while making the *mutawin* a target of hatred rather than the regular police.

Westerners living in private compounds set aside for them weren't exempt from these Gestapo tactics either; the previous year, three Dutch nurses working in a Nok Kuzlat maternity hospital had been abducted, held hostage for more than five months while the EC and Dutch consulate filed a barrage of complaints. After being publicly flogged by the *mutawin*, the nurses were turned over to the government, who promptly threw them out of the country as lawbreakers and agitators. Their crime? They'd been caught drinking champagne during a birthday party when the *mutawin* broke down the door of their shared apartment. When in Rome, best not to fuck around with Caesar and his lions.

"You stole these?" I asked Ibrahim incredulously.

"Of course not," he scoffed. "I rented them. I've got a friend in the *mutawin*." Apparently, even the Muslim League of

Decency still believes in the good old-fashioned values. What's a little traditional baksheesh between close friends?

Ibrahim and Ahmat set the holosets up, cables running in a circle from set to set like an electronic witch's pentacle, I thought.

Abdullah hunched over the computer screen, his bottom lip pushed out as he scowled, his total attention on the world inside the electronics. He conversed with Halton in low tones about the sheer finesse of the tight virtual code, the elegance of the parallax fractal subfoci. They discussed the fine points of concept AI vocabulary and Mitre's tertiary directrix symbolism. Things entirely outside my planet, monkey boy.

A shimmer of hazy gold light coalesced into effervescent bubbles of electronic fire, bouncing off the self-generated holoscreen spun by the four synched holosets. It filled out into a solid tube two meters wide, extending to the ceiling. Spikes of gleaming light shot to either end of the holosets' projection radius. I shook off the uneasy impression of an electronic genie, smoky fingers lazily exploring the insides of the bottle.

"It says it's not happy with the accommodations," Halton said.

Then Abdullah whistled, eyes wide. "Merciful Allah, I don't think I believe what I'm seeing!"

The AI was rewriting its own programming. All by itself.

"Now it's happy," Halton said tersely.

The room exploded with brilliant white light. I squeezed my eyes shut, retinas smarting from the abrupt flash, then cracked them open to squint cautiously into the radiance. The light was so intense, the room looked flattened, annihilating any hint of shadows.

All of us had our hands up shielding our eyes, staring at the figure taking shape in the midst of the column of light. The holosets hummed, forced to the limits of their capacity. The light pulsated, contracting into an oscillating human form suspended in the air, unearthly glorious. Pure white robes like fine silk blew around its body without revealing the indistinct shape beneath it. White fire spun through its hair, illuminating the most terrifyingly beautiful face I've ever seen.

We stood immobilized, staring open-mouthed as it shimmered silently. I was thinking, *Jeez, the boys in CDI's Research and Development labs sure get to smoke some wild ganja to dream up something like this baby*, when it opened wings, slowly unfolding from around its form. Stretching open. Out. Up. The effect was overwhelming. One of the cousins moaned and fell on his knees. The rest of them didn't look too far behind him.

"*I am the Archangel Gabriel*," the thing said. Its voice reverberated through the room like thunder, genderless, musical, hard as granite.

Another cousin sagged to the floor, murmuring strangled prayers to himself in a choked whisper. I frowned. "No, you're not," I said with as much scorn and authority as I could whip up. "You're just a programmed AI microflake being fed into a holo-projection." It was for the benefit of the boys, but the hair on the back of my neck stood up when the hologram inclined its head, its white eyes as blank as a marble statue's boring straight into me.

You're supposed to look at holograms. They're *not* supposed to look at you.

"*Who*," the thing demanded imperiously, "*are you?*" The voice was like fingernails down a velvet blackboard.

Stunned, I stared at it without speaking for a moment; then my brain kicked back into gear. Reaching out, I passed my hand through the field, distorting the projection. It didn't seem to notice. I took three noiseless steps to the right, and grinned in satisfaction as its blind eyes remained glaring at where I had been.

It was sophisticated, I had to give it that. But the illusion was still an illusion. The AI could adjust the projection's attitude by triangulating on the direction of my voice, all remote-controlled from the flake.

I thought about my answer. The AI would remember this conversation, recording it in the flake's memory tracts down to my voiceprints. Anyone who opened this microflake again was going to know someone had popped its cherry. Since CDI had sent it down with me, I didn't figure it would take them all that long to guess who. So what the hell.

"Kay Bee Sulaiman, GBN Network News," I said in my best news correspondent's voice. "I'd like to ask you a few questions, if you don't mind. . . ."

"*You are not the Chosen One*," it interrupted, its eerie voice angry, harsh cracklings ripping through the intonation. It scowled, refocusing on my voice. Its eyes blazed white heat as it turned its head to sightlessly glower at me. I think it was royally pissed off that its ruse had been discovered. *"You are not the Chosen One,"* it repeated.

And shattered into splinters of erupting light.

In the sudden darkness, I heard muttering, hands groping. The lights hadn't gone out, it was just that the hologram had been so bright, the room only seemed dark until my eyes had adjusted. Halton was already at the monitor, tapping into the board as Abdullah stumbled to pull himself up beside him, staring at the screen with dazed awe.

Ibrahim was incensed. He stalked to glare down at the AI reader. "Blasphemy," he said angrily, his voice strained. He was shaking; sweat beaded the hair of his mustache. "Of the worst kind." His eyes rolled toward me, bloodshot. "What kind of insulting bullshit *is* this, Sulaiman?"

Halton turned from where he sat in front of the screen. "It's refusing to come out again," he said.

"I wish you'd stop talking about it like it's alive!" I shouted at him. "It's only a goddamned computer flake! Not a human being!"

Ibrahim darted to pop the flake from the reader, and gasped in surprise as Halton *blurred*, one moment seated in front of the monitor, the next standing by the reader with his hand firmly fastened around the man's wrist. Their eyes locked as he gently took the flake out of Ibrahim's hand.

"That microflake's got to be destroyed," Ibrahim insisted. "It's an affront to Islam and Muslims everywhere."

Abdullah looked appalled at the idea.

"More than that," Ibrahim continued, "someone is making fools of us. This shit is obviously intended to be used in some kind of manipulation, another hoax by the West designed to exploit and cheat us. You can't let this . . . *thing* . . . get out. There would be chaos!"

That probably was closer to the pragmatic truth. Ibrahim didn't quite seem the devout type.

"You're probably right, Ibrahim. Some people are playing a rather nasty game," I said quietly. Halton released his wrist, and Ibrahim rubbed it while watching us both balefully. "But if you destroy it, you gain nothing. Whoever made it can make more. I want to find out who wants this thing and why . . . Don't you?"

Halton and I had some heavy-duty scheming ahead of us tonight.

Ibrahim massaged his wrist, the muscle in his jaw working. " 'Woe unto those who write the Scripture with their hands and then say, This is from Allah,' " he said quietly. " 'Who is an enemy to Allah and to Gabriel.' "

I nodded grimly. "You got that right, kid."

# THIRTEEN

This time I was getting reproachful looks from the waiter as I sat way out on the rooftop, away from the canopied veranda adjoining the interior. I didn't have my PortaNet, and I had the umbrella up to block the worst of the sun's direct rays, so I had no excuse for still forcing him to walk out over white-hot cement in his thin-soled pointy shoes to take our breakfast order, other than I wanted privacy.

And this time, Halton was with me. He sat across the table, eating a plate of various *s'ambusihks*, meat pastries with pine nuts, with his oversweetened coffee. I was sticking to my goat cheese and mashed-bean breakfast, this time with a bit of yogurt.

We were about halfway through our meal when a shadow fell across the table. I squinted up into the vague silhouette standing over us, a thin man in a white linen jacket, carrying a briefcase, the shade of a broad-brimmed hat hiding his eyes.

"Kay Bee Sulaiman?"

"And you are . . . ?"

"Elias Somerton." Then I recognized the English voice from my telephone call. I'd been expecting him.

I snorted. "Lost some weight, there, Eli old boy?"

"Mind if I join you?" Without waiting for permission, he pulled a metal cafe chair up to the table, sitting between Halton and me. He squinted at my black eye while I continued to eat as if he didn't exist.

The waiter ambled out, irritated at the growing number of idiot infidels defying sunstroke. "*Sh'aakhudh qahwâa, suukkahr qa-leel,*" Somerton said haughtily, his accent even more atrocious than mine. I noticed he didn't bother with saying "please," overplaying the last of the British Em-Pah bit, I thought. He didn't see the kid's sardonic salute, or at any rate, he ignored it. The waiter took his time bringing Somerton his coffee, "light on the sugar."

"I believe you have something that belongs to us, Mr. Sulaiman. We'd like it returned now." He rested his briefcase on his knees, balancing it on the table edge.

Showtime. I shoved some cheese and bread into my mouth and chewed, speaking around it. Somerton winced slightly. "What, you want me to give Halton back already? I thought you folks wanted me to hand him over to Sheikh Larry."

I didn't look directly at Halton, but I could see him from the corner of my eye. He wasn't reacting in the least.

"That is not what I was referring to," Somerton said coldly. He looked at my bruised face suspiciously. "What happened to your eye?"

"I ran into a doorknob," I said, this time grinning around a mouthful of mashed beans and yogurt.

"Must have been a rather tall doorknob," he snapped.

"I like walking around on my knees. You meet a better class of people that way."

Halton sipped his coffee, unconcerned, uninvolved.

"Let's skip the games, Sulaiman, shall we?" Somerton said, and shifted the briefcase on his knees slightly.

"Yes," I agreed. "Let's." I swallowed and signaled the waiter, who sauntered out lazily. "Would you please take Mr. Somerton's jacket and briefcase to the check desk?" I asked him in Markundi, handing him twenty-five Khuru rials. The kid beamed. Somerton look alarmed. "It's far too hot to be wearing a jacket, and you look most uncomfortable balancing that case, Eli old buddy."

Halton was looking up at me now, his face impassive. Funny thing, I was beginning to think I understood what was going on behind that bland expression.

"Really, it's quite all right, never mind . . ." Somerton was trying to brush the waiter away. The kid grinned hugely, enjoying not understanding either Somerton's English or his flustered Markundi, while trying to snatch the briefcase away from him.

"Give it to him, or we have nothing to discuss," I said in Spanish, the only foreign language other than Arabic that I can speak with any degree of fluency. Somerton glared at me. I wasn't sure if he understood Spanish or not, but he gave up, and allowed the waiter to strip him of his coat and case.

When the kid had gone, I reached into the pocket of my own rumpled jacket hanging on the back of my chair, and placed a small cube in the center of the table, next to my package of Gitanes. Switched on, it steadily blinked a tiny yellow light.

"What's that?" Somerton scowled at it.

"It's what we in the newsbiz call Raid. It kills bugs. Dead." It was one of the toys I'd gotten from Carl during the Boy King's aborted party. If anyone had a spikemike pointed in our direction, the Raid would spray an enveloping buzzing field in a two-meter radius, totally masking our conversation from outside ears. As an extra added feature, any electronic cooties Somerton was carrying would suffer instant and permanent death. Pretty ordinary stuff, really, one of the other new kids on the block had assured me offhandedly. The fancier ones fed bland, randomly generated conversation into the masking field. A lot of journalists carry them these days for private interviews.

"All right, Sulaiman. If you're quite finished, shall we talk?" Somerton's feathers were all ruffled and he was red in the face. He looked aggravated, not scared.

I smiled, looked at Halton and nodded. Casually, he dropped his hand onto Somerton's knee under the table. Somerton jumped slightly, startled, then froze as Halton squeezed just enough for Somerton to feel the sheer power in the fabricant's hand clamped solidly to his leg. Somerton's face paled. *Now* he was scared.

"Yes," I said. "Let's talk. I have something you want. You have something I want."

"What would that be?" Somerton had regained his composure, but his hand shook as he sipped his lightly sweetened coffee. He put down the cup, his other hand dipping casually toward his waist.

"Keep both hands on the table where I can see them, please," I warned him. He set his hands, palms down, on the cafe table with exaggerated finesse. "C'mon, Eli. What else would I want? Information. Someone else was interested in the little extra package you folks sent along." I pointed to my black eye. "They were very impolite. Rude people piss me off."

I waited, and his eyes widened, shifting from me to Halton and back. Ah. So he did know about the dead bodies in the abandoned cafe. And I'd just told him who killed them. "I have no idea who you're talking about, Mr. Sulaiman," Somerton said slowly. "They certainly weren't anyone from our offices."

I looked at Halton. His fingers gripped Somerton's knee a little harder. Somerton inhaled sharply. "Halton will crush your kneecap, Eli old chum, if I'm not happy with what I hear."

"*You're* CDI," Somerton accused Halton. "You're not supposed to be operating outside company regulations."

Halton looked at him innocently. "I'm not. Check the rules."

I chuckled and leaned forward toward the disgruntled Englishman. "Look, Eli, I'm getting tired of being ordered around and roughed up, while you people expect me to just put up with it. I was 'asked' by your offices to chaperon Halton to Nok Kuzlat in exchange for some very minor journalistic considerations. I was *not* asked to smuggle illegal trinkets. Some rather unpleasant people beat the living shit out of me, something else no one mentioned was going to be part of the agreement. Unfortunately, they weren't in any condition to explain anything when we left. One of them, I believe, was a close personal friend of our boy Larry."

Somerton simmered, his face florid, but remained silent.

I picked up my cigarettes and leaned back in the chair as I shook one out of the pack and lit it. "Now, *I* would like some answers to a few questions myself. Why don't we start with who you are, and what you want."

"You know who I am," Somerton growled, cautiously. He flinched reflexively as Halton picked up his coffee with his other hand and sipped. "And you know what I want."

"Cut the hokey spy shit," I warned him.

"CDI. The microflake." He spat the words out.

"Your name really isn't Elias Somerton, is it?"

He took a breath, and glanced at Halton. "I wouldn't tell you that if you had him break both kneecaps."

I shrugged. "Not important. But maybe you can tell me why, when I was asked to accompany Halton, didn't anybody happen to mention the microflake." A muscle spasmed in his stubbornly clenched jaw. "If you don't tell me, Eli, I won't bother with your kneecaps. I'll just destroy the flake."

That got his attention. "That would have very serious consequences for you, Sulaiman."

"Not as bad as it would be for you, I think." I blew a stream of smoke into his face, à la Bette Davis. Or in this case, maybe, Errol Flynn. He grimaced and blinked rapidly. "Tell you what, I'll just speculate, and you let me know if I'm getting warm. I think you probably really are CDI, but you're part of some kind of schism within the company . . . Or you're working on your own, completely outside official authorization." I waited a few heartbeats. "Or maybe you're a double agent."

Somerton sat stone-faced. I looked over at Halton and raised one eyebrow questioningly.

"Double agent," he said, not looking at Somerton. He picked up his last square of meat pastry with his free hand and took a bite.

Somerton's face drained completely of color, realizing suddenly that while Halton could indeed pulverize his knees, the real reason Halton's hand was on him was to read his body through the sensors in the fabricant's skin. He started to stand, and gasped as Halton kept him effortlessly pinned in the chair. Somerton sat quietly for a moment, struggling to recover his self-possession. With his spine straight, he sipped the last of his coffee and set it down on the saucer with considerable care.

"Who besides CDI are you working for, Eli old friend?" I asked serenely. He kept his eyes down, staring at the empty cup. I sighed theatrically. "Do I really have to run down a list of possibilities until one of them pops up three cherries on the Halton-O-Meter?"

Actually, when I'd arranged this possible scenario with Halton, he'd warned me that once Somerton realized what was happening, the level of adrenaline being pumped into his system would cloud any readable signs, making it difficult to ferret out answers. Doubly so, since it wasn't direct skin-to-skin contact. I'd have perhaps one shot at jolting Somerton off his rails, and hoped he bought Halton's invincibility act.

"Besides, that's time consuming, and the more resistant you are, the more likely I'll be unwilling to give you back your toy. Do I make myself clear?" I inhaled on my cigarette again, hoping I looked cool and nonchalant.

Finally, Somerton looked up, his eyes rimmed red, mad as

hell. "Yes," he said. "Quite clear. Shall we make a gentleman's agreement? I'll tell you what you want to know. Within reason, you understand. Then you give me the flake."

"There are no gentlemen in the espionage game, Somerton," I said, grinning. It was a line from a classic TV holo, but I don't think Somerton had ever seen it. He didn't get the joke. Maybe he really didn't know. "But if you answer my questions, I'll give it serious consideration. Who are you working for besides CDI?"

He hesitated. "Mossad."

"He's lying," Halton said, indifferently.

"It's the truth," he insisted, jaw set in anger.

Oh, shit. If Halton was mistaken, then this little game would be over. "Halton sez you're lying, Eli old sport. Now why would he say a thing like that?"

Somerton swallowed. "It *is* true . . ." he said, signs of panic starting to show around the edges. "In a way."

Bingo.

"What way?"

"The Israelis have had cells penetrating every government and opposition organization in the Middle East for decades, and plenty in Europe as well," he said, almost babbling. "We proposed a mutually beneficial arrangement and they agreed with us that the powers pulling the strings behind the Sheikh to control Khuruchabja had to be stopped. You're right about a schism inside CDI. We used it to infiltrate CDI via Mossad channels in London. The United States doesn't have diplomatic relations with Khuruchabja, but the EC does. Once we were inside CDI, it was arranged for some of us to be assigned to work with the British Consulate in Nok Kuzlat."

"Who is 'we,' Eli? Interpol? MI6?"

"*I can't tell you*," he hissed through his teeth, his calm façade completely gone. He leaned toward me, his face twitching as Halton painfully reminded him of his knee's vulnerability. "But if you give that flake to the wrong people, I can tell you it'll start something that will make the last war here look like a skeet shoot."

"And you're not the 'wrong people'?" He sat back, refusing to answer. "Okay, so maybe you can tell me if Khatijah was working for you."

"No," he said slowly, weighing how much this information was worth. "She wasn't."

"CDI?"

"No."

"Her husband?"

He snorted. "No."

"Shit, Eli," I said disgusted. "How many sides *are* there?"

He smiled grimly, the color starting to come back into his cheeks, his self-control revived. "This is the Middle East, Sulaiman," he reminded me. "How many sides do you want?"

"How about the one on the side of the angels?"

His smile vanished. "You have no idea what you're meddling in," he said, shaken. He didn't seem to care about his knee right at that moment.

I stabbed the butt of my cigarette out, and leaned toward him. "I didn't *ask* to meddle in the first place," I said, a bit more vehemently than I had intended. "You spook assholes got me in the middle of this. Now, why don't you tell me why it was necessary to bring such a specialized AI flake like that into Khuruchabja?"

"Where's the microflake?" he demanded, suddenly obstinate.

I nodded to Halton. I thought he was going to do the disgusting finger-up-the-sinus trick again, but even I was surprised when he slowly smiled, exposing the flake held delicately between clenched front teeth. I wanted to laugh with delight, it was such a great theatrical touch. The kid was learning.

Somerton stared at it, and sank back defeated. He took a deep breath. "All right. CDI didn't send the flake, because they don't know about it," he said. His voice was toneless. "We knew they were sending a fabricant, and thought if we sent the flake along with him, we could get it back from you before he was turned over to the Sheikh. You'd go along with it without too much objection so long as it seemed like part of the original plan. But, somehow"—he rubbed his eyes tiredly with thumb and forefinger—"somehow, it got out that the flake was on its way, and Khatijah's faction thought you were both CDI agents. She'd no idea CDI was sending a fabricant."

He looked at Halton speculatively, as if silently asking if Halton had *really* killed all those people single-handedly. He didn't inquire. We didn't enlighten him.

"So once again, CDI has screwed up," I said bitterly. "You'd think you guys might have learned a lesson ten years ago."

"We did. But the politics have changed somewhat since you

were here last," Somerton retorted, ignoring Halton's hand on his knee.

"I keep up with the news," I said dryly.

"Only if you know what the real news *is*," Somerton returned. I was beginning to like him. Grudgingly. "What you and I both know," he continued, "is that the West gave up years ago on their Holy Grail for a permanent peace in the Middle East. Now the industrialized world 'keeps peace' here by doling out rewards for their client countries who toe the party line, and severely penalizes any that make them uncomfortable. It keeps our oil interests from being impaired. Little Khuruchabja, a hotbed of fundamentalist Muslim hostility, has been kept dicking around for the last ten years, the so-called 'moderates' arguing with the so-called 'conservatives' about how many angels can dance on the head of Muhammad's prick."

Wrong religious analogy, but I got the idea.

"As long as their arguments remained internal, and they only murdered each other, the security and well-being of external states was assured. Any time there has been a sign that one side or the other is getting the upper hand, a few judicious prods here and there keeps the balance even."

"The rich stay rich, the poor stay poor, and CDI keeps Khuruchabja as a nice solid stake poised over the heart of Islam."

Somerton nodded, an almost wry humor in his eyes. "And the dream . . . or the nightmare, depending on your point of view, of a united Islamic front remains just that; a dream."

"And your side . . . wants what?"

I was asking him to try and convert me. He knew it.

"The West's interest, and CDI's interest in an American hegemony, has always been maintaining the status quo. Keep the Khuruchabjan Islamics busy snarling at each other's throats so they don't become any real threat to First World interests, but just rabid enough to make their oil-rich neighbors nervous. A fourteenth-century country is easier to control than a twenty-first. The Mufti of Nok Kuzlat has been foaming at the mouth the past few years trying to whip Khuruchabja into becoming the crux and cradle of yet another Islam military jihad, unite all of Islam and crush the imperialists along with their Zionist cronies into oblivion." He smiled dryly. "Rivers will turn red with our blood, snakes will crawl through our skulls, the usual medieval zealot's wet dream. Whilst he can get various downtrodden Muslims to all agree they hate the Zionists' and imperialists' guts, he can't get them to stop fighting amongst themselves long enough to do any serious damage."

This was an old, sad story I was all too painfully aware of. He seemed to read it on my face.

"What *has* changed, if not the shepherds, are the sheep. It's no more possible for the Islamic world to return to the Golden Age of Muhammad than it would be for Europe to turn back the clock and resurrect the Renaissance, or America to give it all back to the Indians. Younger Khuruchabjans still live within the traditional tribal-family culture, but their awareness of the outside world is a thousand times more sophisticated than their fathers' ever was."

" 'How you gonna keep them down on the farm once they've seen gay Paree?' " I said.

"Something like that, yes. The clerics can rant and rave all they bloody well want, but their children have gone to Western schools, they travel, they have faxeroxes and computers and holo satellite dishes. Their exposure to the West is unpreventable. But yet they're still Arabs, still Muslims. They're torn trying to find a way to reconcile their faith with their desire to join the First World on an equal footing."

Somerton had relaxed once he was on familiar ground. A born lecturer, a bureaucratic spy.

"His Excellency has spent most of his life outside Khuruchabja, and although he may be a little out of touch with his own country and the subtleties of twenty-first century global politics, he fully comprehends the supremacy of the United States as the military overlord of the planet. He knows any military jihad whipped up to fight the West will end up like the last few attempts. While he knows the United States can be pushed pretty far, annoy the sleeping giant too much and even if he escaped being killed or publicly humiliated, he would be beaten militarily, his country ruined."

Somerton was warming to his little speech. "But despite his fondness for electronic toys and his yuppie accent, His Excellency is still a Muslim. His ambitions are still similar to the Mufti's. He would also like to shake off the boot on his neck and unite Islam, but not in fighting any jihad, which he knows is impossible and ultimately self-destructive." Somerton smiled. "He wants to create the modern, twenty-first century version of the jihad, an *economic* jihad to unite Islam and join the First World as an equal among equals. First-rate education, decent medical care, a fair legal system. A peaceful First World nation. But *Islamic*. And with himself as the undisputed leader of the Islamic revolution at its head."

"He wants to be the Muslim Martin Luther?" I asked.

"More of a born-again Ataturk, I'd think," Somerton replied.

"It's been tried before. Iran's 'Economic Revolution'?"

"That was Iran. Too many people, too little money. And far too much bad blood under the bridge by then."

"You don't believe he can do it." I made it a statement.

Somerton shrugged. "With help, maybe. Despite some rather nasty flaws, His Excellency genuinely means well. His problem at the moment is wanting someone else's cake and eating it, too. He's young, he's flexible, in time he'll understand that the benefits of a truly democratic society outweigh the fun of being a dictator."

I wouldn't have put any money down on it. Too many other well-meaning dictators have invented their own forms of "democracy," some of them even honestly progressive and beneficial, only to screw it all up when it came down to the last inning. Somerton knew the history here as well as I did. The Janus nature of saviors and tyrants, the alternating recognition and disapproval from the rich Western powers who often helped them in and out of power with the frequency of a woman trying on shoes.

Ibn Saud had ridden the Wahabi wind of fanaticism and the promise of purified Islam to power, then crushed all of his rebellious Wahabis into obedience, breaking the thorns they'd become in his side. The austere Saud legacy declined into an orgy of looting and bribery and exploitative tyranny lasting generations.

One bellicose Egyptian after another proclaimed himself the latest incarnation of the divine Mahdi and fought the British, the French, the Turks, each other. All they attained was a wealth of popular uprisings, rebellions, massacres, dead martyrs, burnt farmland and a glut of purple Victorian epic poetry. Nasser secularized his country, then alienated the West and lost the Sinai. He played the Americans and the Russians off each other like divorced parents while squandering vast sums of money on the disastrous Aswan High Dam as his own pharaonic pyramid, drowning an immense wealth of archaeological wonders and ruining acres of arable land with salt and pollutants.

Habib Bourguiba's moderate campaign for Tunisian self-rule landed him under house arrest, but once he'd been proclaimed his country's "Supreme Guide," he didn't hesitate to waste Tunisian tax money on building himself dozens of state palaces where he too could hold court in grand style like any other indolent desert prince.

The British secretly helped to overthrow the despot Mozaffar al-Din, replacing him with the popular Pahlavis. When they in turn became too tyrannical, the West changed its mind and helped bring yet another leader to power they believed they could control. The Ayatollah swept away the shell of the Pahlavi Shah's modern reformations in the storm of his Iranian revolution, to the horrified disbelief of the West, and ultimately the exhaustion of his people.

Frightened by a democratically elected party of Islamic fundamentalists, Algeria reacted with a military coup, plunging their country into decades of murder and terrorism, assassinating doctors, intellectuals, journalists, unveiled women, and anyone driving the wrong color car along with any Westerners stupid enough to remain, the bloodshed spilling out from time to time onto European soil.

The royal family in Kuwait repaid the West's liberation of their country by renewed martial law, nepotism, assassination and repression, locked in a bitter struggle with their own citizens who are themselves still having trouble figuring out how to run a country properly after they'd kicked out or murdered their wage-slave work force of Yemenese and Palestinians. It had only taken one egomaniac to annihilate the Ba'ath party's considerable achievements along with the whole of Iraq. Only one madman was needed to destroy the Behjars, replaced in turn by a series of repressive Islamic fundamentalists.

Under the veneer, far too many dictators had revealed themselves to be irretrievably ruthless, bloody and violent. True progressive leaders were very thin on the ground in the Middle East and young Larry didn't seem to be any glowing promise of change to me.

"As far as the United States is concerned," I said, "they would obviously have to openly favor democratic change in

Khuruchabja, but we both know they would secretly do every-thing possible to crush it here. Khuruchabja isn't much of a threat to First World control, but they're useful in keeping every country around them dependent on America's military goodwill. Not to mention that Khuruchabjans help fill a large, cheap labor pool for their rich neighbors who don't care to dirty their hands," I added dryly. "The kind who aren't likely to welcome their janitors and maids as members joining their private coun-try clubs."

Somerton conceded the point with a smirk. "That, how-ever, is in Khuruchabja's favor. They aren't the lazy, conceited citizens of oil sheikhdoms who have to import their labor just to keep their lights on and the water running. The average Khu-ruchabjan knows how to get things done, he knows how to *work*. His Excellency hopes to create his very own Khuruchabjani *wirtshaftswünder*, and entice his neighbors into joining *his* country club."

I wondered how much of it was really His Excellency's idea, and how much had been outside influences pushing in from the sides. Somehow, I had doubts Sheikh Larry had come up with these sophisticated opinions all on his very own.

"That good ol' Protestant work ethic isn't going to do Khu-ruchabja much good without an economic base to start from," I said. "It won't be easy, even if he can unite his own people be-hind the idea. Also, like I said, there's always the Americans."

"In 1945, Japan and Germany were both beaten, their land occupied and their military might completely crushed into sub-mission," Somerton shot back promptly. This was obviously a debate he'd engaged in before. "But in less than half a century, they became economic giants, both of them First World coun-tries. How? Because they had to give up offensive military arms completely. They received huge amounts of money to rebuild their countries once they were disarmed and powerless, and spent very little money on their military thereafter."

He grinned, enjoying himself in spite of his situation. "They rolled over with their bellies exposed, and no civilized na-tion in the world would dream of hurting them. It was easy for the Americans to befriend people they could feel superior to. Americans want to be liked and appreciated, and their former enemies were happy to tell them how wonderful they were."

He put his finger next to his nose. "Everything was co-pacetic," he said ironically. "Then all of a sudden, *surprise*. Somehow their docile little friends had reached up from where they lay on their backs and grabbed the very conqueror who'd put them there by the economic *cojones*."

So he did speak Spanish, after all. I eyed him critically. "Come off it, Somerton. We created our own problems."

"Didn't dissuade anyone from taking advantage of them, did it?"

We were definitely on opposite sides of the political fence, but I found his arguments intriguing. "So that's your game plan for Khuruchabja? Winning friends through surrender and submission? Somehow, I don't think that'll go down too well here."

"That's only one part of the equation," Somerton replied. He was looking smugly pleased with himself. Halton still had his hand clamped around the man's knee, but Somerton seemed to have forgotten him. "Japan and Germany had no choice in their disarmament and occupation, but it isn't necessary to become completely helpless.

"His Excellency has a great respect for the power of democracy, the American ideal of equality for all under the law. He has more faith in the Bill of Rights and the Constitution than the average American." Somerton raised a regretful eyebrow. "As long as it stays in America. He recognizes that it's this same society which rose to become the world's leading military power, and would like to adopt some of the same advantages for his own country but without the disadvantages for himself personally.

"Unfortunately, he suffers from a serious birth defect; he was born without the average American's sense of virtuous cynicism. He believes he can easily manipulate the U.S. Government into paving his road to a disarmed democracy with gold whilst giving up none of his own power."

I shook my head slowly. "Americans are no strangers to the arts of deception. He should remember the financial disaster Eastern Europe had after they 'declared' democracy. The West jumped up and down, cheering and waving flags. Half the Berlin Wall is now on American mantelpieces. We were all ecstatic—until they presented us with the bill. They had the idea that if they declared themselves a capitalist society, that meant we'd give them capital. Except by then we didn't have a lot left ourselves."

I picked up the pack of Gitanes and shook out another cigarette. After a moment's thought, I silently offered one to Somerton. He declined with a bemused shake of his head.

"It took the Germans *years* to recover after they swallowed East Germany," I said, cupping my hand around the tip of the cigarette as I lit it. "And Japan finally bottomed out of its own gluttonous economy; you can't export all those Sony Walkmans and Toyotas and holosets to the States if there's no one left with jobs to buy them because all the work has gone overseas. If your boy is looking for a role model, that one sure ain't it."

Somerton shrugged. "There's another country in the Middle East that once had problems similar to Khuruchabja's," he said. "A tiny country with no national resources, no oil, a harsh environment, surrounded by hostile countries eager to absorb it into their own borders, the outside world alternatively generous with aid or reluctant to help, depending on the caprice of political winds. They created a First World country nonetheless, whilst still remaining strong militarily."

"Israel." It was obvious.

"Exactly."

"Israel's come a long way since Rabin shook hands with Arafat, Somerton, but I still don't think holding up the Jewish state as a model is going to please too many Muslims. Besides which, Israel had some assets Khuruchabja is lacking; a seaport, for one. Nuclear fusion weapons for another. You recall what happened the last time Khuruchabja got hold of infrafusion weapons?"

*I did.*

"Besides that," I continued, "Israel also has long-standing traditional support from the States. She has a large European and American immigrant population, along with about half the brains the Soviets ever produced, highly educated people, all of whom were dedicated to building a Jewish homeland. Khuruchabja doesn't. More than half of the population here are illiterate farmers and shepherds. Far too many of the other half, the educated, the intellectuals, the professionals, packed their bags and got the hell out a long time ago.

"So just how are you going to convince these people that laying down their beloved guns will bring prosperity and rewards from the West, which they despise to begin with, not to mention all the factions within their own government fighting for control with all the usual fascist police tactics?"

I was thinking about Ibrahim's little lecture, roots in the sand, flowers in the desert.

"No one said it would be easy," Somerton agreed. "We have to unite an illiterate common people under one banner they can understand, at the same time giving those expatriate doctors and lawyers and Indian chiefs a reason to come back to the land of their birth. A properly managed economy can be a formidable weapon. Teach those in power a new way to control the purse strings and it might actually allow them enough breathing room to refrain from assassinating one another."

"And with the Archangel Gabriel by his right hand, and the light of your secret society to guide him, our boy Larry has a good shot at that, is that the idea?"

Somerton steepled his fingers on the table. "Our four-teenth-century citizens would rally behind a miracle, whereas our twenty-first–century citizens would be impressed by the display of high-tech AI science. The entire population is tired of fighting, tired of poverty, tired of being bullied by the West on one hand and sneered at by their rich Muslim cousins on the other."

"And the religious ban against AI's? Trapped souls, all that?"

He shrugged one shoulder and raised a sardonic eyebrow. "If the Archangel Gabriel himself gives *Islamic* AI technology the kiss of legitimacy, who's going to complain?"

I sat back, thinking about that. It was an admirable goal, but was it genuine? "What's your assessment, Halton?" I asked. Somerton turned his head to watch Halton, like a kid nervously waiting for a report card.

"My assessment?" Halton looked up at me, his eyes lifeless. "Mr. Somerton speaks fluent English, and judging by his accent, was probably raised in a mid- to upper-middle-class neighbor-hood in the Birmingham area—I would estimate in West Bromwich. He had about two or three years of public school and has spent a large part of his working life in London. He's lived in Canada for the past five to seven years, and by the flat tones of certain vowels, I believe in southern Manitoba, proba-bly in or near Winnipeg. Mr. Somerton's Markundi Arabic is fairly basic, at the level one would find in someone who had recently taken a crash course given to government or embassy personnel assigned to a foreign country. I would guess he understands some Spanish, at least the slang, or has enough of a background in Latin-based Romance languages to infer from."

He mercifully shut up. Somerton stared pop-eyed at him, then guffawed, a sharp, strangled bark of laughter. I glared at Halton, knowing full well what he was saying. *I'm a linguist, not Super Spy.* Very funny.

"I'm impressed," Somerton said. He looked back at me, seeming more relaxed, despite the vise-grip on his knee. "Well, Sulaiman? May I have the flake?"

"Tell me one last thing, Somerton," I said, dodging the question. "Something's bothered the hell out of me, and maybe you can clear it up. Why me?"

He looked uncomfortable, glancing down toward his trapped knee, then at Halton. "What do you mean?"

"It's pretty obvious that CDI didn't happen to pick my name out of a hat. I'm here for a reason. So why a journalist, and why *me*?"

Somerton laced his fingers together and studied them, avoiding my eyes. The silence dragged out for a long moment before he spoke. "The official reason is that you're an Arab-American with experience in this part of the world, Sulaiman," he said slowly. "You're a respected, seasoned journalist. You were here during the last war, and came up with incredible coverage which certainly deserved the awards you were given. People on both sides believe you, they have confidence in your reportage. That, and your fluency in Markundi, gives both you and Halton a reasonably trustworthy cover."

He looked up, his expression determined. "The *real* reason is that you don't do field work anymore. You burned out. You haven't done any first-hand correspondence in over ten years. You haven't been in Khuruchabja since. You're rusty, out of touch and out of shape. You don't know the deep politics here anymore. You don't have a good grasp on who's what. You have a hot temper and an overly high opinion of yourself. Your cockiness is enough of an edge for CDI to influence what you might see, and how you choose to report it."

I could feel my face burning, and it had nothing to do with the morning's heat.

Somerton sighed. "Sorry, Sulaiman. If you didn't have me

hooked up to your organic lie detector"—he jerked a thumb at Halton—"I might have been able to be a little more . . . diplomatic. But you *did* ask." His voice sounded honestly regretful. "So. Did I pass?" he asked quietly.

"With flying colors," I said, keeping my voice low to keep it from shaking. "Give him the microflake, Halton."

Halton released Somerton's knee, extracted the microflake and handed it over. The relief on the man's face was marked, and he placed the flake carefully in a holder in his wallet before he stood up. Rubbing his knee gingerly, he hesitated.

"I realize you're still a journalist, Sulaiman. I don't expect you to keep this conversation secret. But if you report what I've told you too soon, it would not only cause us a great deal of trouble, but innocent people could be hurt needlessly. I'm only asking you to keep this meeting private until you go back. Give us a little time to protect them, that's all . . . Please."

"I'll think about it." Just what I needed: more guilt from the blood of innocents on my hands.

"You could expose me to CDI," he said tersely to both of us. "Blow my cover." Halton looked at him, his expression unreadable.

"If you're so worried about it, why don't you have us shot?"

"We don't work that way," he said, then added dryly, "If we can help it."

"I'm not going to burn you, Somerton," I said, sighing wearily. "I've got problems of my own with CDI to worry about right now."

He glanced at Halton questioningly. Halton nodded.

Somerton nodded, chewing on his lower lip. "We repay our debts." He paused. "We do have a common enemy, Sulaiman."

I glared at him, my eyes dry and burning, wanting him to just go away. "I know. That's why I gave you the goddamned flake. But the enemy of my enemy is not necessarily my friend."

He nodded. "And in the desert, nothing is ever what it seems to be, is it?" he said.

I thought for a moment he was considering sticking out his hand for me to shake, but he smiled grimly, nodded at Halton and walked off to retrieve his jacket and briefcase.

The waiter set the bill down on the table. In the distance, I could hear the electronically amplified warbling of muezzins calling the matinee crowd to services. The cafe was deserted.

Halton sat patiently as I stared blindly out over the rooftops of Nok Kuzlat.

I'd forgotten what as a journalist I should have taken for granted: Nothing packs a punch quite as hard as the truth.

# FOURTEEN

The month before I'd gone to Khuruchabja I had turned the big Four Oh, which at the time didn't bother me in the least. I didn't tell anyone, nobody threw a party for me, no big deal. It's not as if it meant anything, just another day, another year, so what? I'd been secretly proud of myself—how cool, how nonchalantly, I'd passed this middle-age midlife crisis milestone without even a whimper.

I'd been happy behind my feed-in desk. I'd discovered I was not the kind of reporter who plunges fearlessly into the depths of hell, risking life and sanity for the chance to interview Satan himself. Those kind of journalists were rare, eccentric birds, adrenaline junkies in it for the sport. I'd done it, and spent the next few years having intimate tête-à-têtes with shrinks. I'd liked the fame and prestige, but learned the hard way that's not why it's done. The fire in the belly was what keeps them driven.

Mine had turned to ash. I thought I'd accepted that.

Somerton's words had hurt me more than I realized they could. I *had* burned out. I hadn't done field correspondence not just because I didn't want to anymore, but because I was no longer able to. I hadn't cared what the politics in Khuruchabja were for a decade, trying to put that part of my life as far behind me as I could. Any illusions I had about my Arab heritage or the exotic mysteries of the Orient had been thoroughly crushed. I wanted to go home, where it was safe, where life made sense, where I could just be any other ordinary American.

Yet I hated the thought that I was old, so easily manipulated. I'd been played for a fool. I hadn't avoided my midlife crisis; Somerton simply triggered a delayed reaction.

Here I was at forty, running around the desert, disguised again as a man, scared and angry, doing the same job I'd done before I'd turned thirty, when I'd thought it was the way up the career ladder. Nothing had changed except me. I was older, creakier, turning gray and still unmarried, no love life on the horizon. My only passion was my work, which had long ago lost the kind of glamour and excitement I'd fantasized about as a young college graduate.

Being around John Halton wasn't helping any, either. Fabricant or not, Halton was one of the most desirable male creatures I'd ever seen, which was depressing since it only served to remind me that such men never even glance in my direction when passing me on the street. So you can understand why Halton's every indication of intense interest confused the hell out of me. He aroused a libido I thought I'd long suppressed, and I resented it.

I'm too old to do the libido, I thought sourly.

We drove out into the Greater Khuruchabjani Desert, following a dirt road blending almost imperceptibly with the bleak, flat land, the occasional sandblasted wrecks along the side of the road serving as road markers. I wanted to get some footage of the desolate provinces surrounding Nok Kuzlat to intercut with the royal interviews. A kind of ironic commentary both on the land and its people, as well as the Boy King who ruled them.

I also needed some privacy. I needed to get away, lick my wounds and think. I was going crazy in Nok Kuzlat, watching every word I said, glancing around at faces who might be watching us. Out here, they'd have to be really goddamned omnipotent to eavesdrop. I doubted they'd spend the effort watching us on a spy satellite, and if they were, I was determined to bore whoever was snooping to tears.

The last time I'd driven this way, planes had been screaming overhead, the road generally impassable as Behjar bombs blew up convoys of trucks and tankers attempting to escape across the desert to their own countries. Antiaircraft guns and missiles had lit up the night sky. People fled their homes out into the desert in a mad panic, villages bombed into rubble. Both sides had peppered the surrounding desert with vibration-sensitive scatter mortars, supposedly to deter the army engineer crews repairing the roads, or the Behjars raiding and looting the junked convoys. They were also equally effective against a ten-year-old driving a small herd of the family's sheep. That most of the killing was being done by their own countrymen was of little comfort; the farmers and nomadic shepherds had little grasp of the finer nuances of global politics, but they understood terror and death very well indeed.

Now, the desert was silent, empty, the hot gusts whipping up only dust dervishes spinning elegantly across the red sandstone wastelands. In the distance to the southwest lay the mountain range the Khuruchabjans called *al-Ummah'at*, The Mothers, where ancient gods still sang through strange rock formations carved by the windblown sand. On the other side of the mountains lay the border between Khuruchabja and one of its more anti-American neighbors, not that that made the Khuruchabjans like *them* any better, either.

We stopped and shot a bit of footage of a nomadic sheep-herder eyeing us suspiciously as he drove his flock across the road, framed by the shell of an abandoned tank crumpled by a long-ago missile, shards of dull metal creaking in the hot breeze. After the war had devastated the people and the economy and the IMF drove what was left into eternal destitution, none of the businesses from surrounding nations had been willing to risk returning to Khuruchabja, their overall losses negligible, but irritating nonetheless. The two sole highways leading to Nok Kuzlat were left half-repaired, and traffic was minimal at best. Our shepherd only looked back once, his expression obscured by the checkered kaffiyeh twisted around his leathered face. He whipped his flock up the other side of a wadi and disappeared over the next sand dune.

Toward the end of the afternoon it was still blistering hot, the dry air shimmering along the horizon with the illusion of water, nature as apt at contradictions here as the people. I spotted a *madja'* in the distance, and turned the sandjeep toward it.

It was a single room, built of corrugated tin and mud-brick, the door and shuttered window still intact, although it was evident no one had been here in a long time. It had been one of those ambitious and well-meaning Western ideas that never worked, a series of rest-stations for weary truck drivers, shelters from dust storms, that sort of thing.

The water barrel outside had been long drained and the sink and faucets stolen, leaving naked pipes sticking through the wall as if astonished there was nothing to fit to. Cupboards which were supposed to hold emergency supplies of khaki-wrapped UN medical supplies and MRE food rations now held only grit blown in through the cracks under the door. The faded poster on the wall admonishing visitors in five different languages to respect their fellow travelers, take only the supplies they needed and leave the way station neat for the next guest, had been defaced with derisive Arabic graffiti.

Three wooden chairs were all that remained; the fourth chair and most of the picnic-like table had been broken up by a previous guest and used as firewood, a circle of ash and charred wood in the sand-carpeted center of the *madja's*. We dragged two of the surviving chairs out of the *madja's* broiling interior, and sat in the building's shadow.

We ate the picnic lunch I'd had the hotel pack, and drank most of the water, even though it was hot enough I could have practically made tea with it. The sandjeep's engine cackled to itself, expanding metal cooling in the slight shade of the *madja'*.

The sun turned the sky behind the mountains a blood-red, The Mothers stained a deep turquoise. I heard a high, faint call and shielded my eyes to spot a desert hawk wheeling far above us, hunting the small animals just beginning to come out now that the worst of the heat had begun to fade. Wings spread against the updrafts, the hawk glided in the air, a patch of white along its splayed feather tips. It was throat-stoppingly beautiful.

Yes, Virginia, there *is* beauty in the desert. I grew up roaming the Southwestern backlands, hunting Indian arrowheads and trilobite fossils, and had always loved the quiet of desolate, open land, knew how to see more than just heat and lifelessness.

"They're lovely," I said to Halton, still watching the hawk. "So deadly and yet graceful. One of nature's most elegant creatures."

He glanced at me, then peered up at the hawk curiously. I knew from his expression he wasn't seeing the bird the same way I was. I felt sorry for him at that moment.

"Last time I was here," I told him, "I spent so much of my time recording ugliness and suffering, I didn't have much left over for appreciating anything."

I was also getting into feeling sorry for myself too, truth is.

"Running around, trying to keep my ass from being arrested or shot off, trying to keep both armies from confiscating my film. I was too young to really be scared. It was exciting, at first. But I started thinking that too much of news is just people hurting and dying and I didn't want to spend my life reporting that."

Halton was watching me quietly, listening. I've had few friends in my life, and even fewer boyfriends, none of whom really spent much time listening to me. While my girlfriends were going on dates and making out in the backseat, I sat home alone and watched old movies. I'd learned to protect my fragile ego with fast quips and slick stories, but as far as real conversation was concerned, I'd had more honest heart-to-heart chats with the neighbor's cat.

"Now, I'm afraid I've wasted the best part of my life either chasing blood-and-bomb stories, or hiding behind a feed-in desk." Boy, had I caught up with the midlife blues in a hurry, the sight of a desert hawk opening up whole floodgates of self-pity.

"You're not that old," Halton said. He wasn't trying to jolly me out of my depression; he simply stated a fact.

"How old do I look?" I said, smiling wanly. I should have known better than to fish for compliments from Halton.

He shrugged. "A little over forty," he said. Damn, somebody should have taught this guy a bit more tact. I must have looked dismayed. He looked at me curiously. "Is that old?" he asked, ingenuous. "I thought the average person's life span was about ninety years. In the West, at least."

"It's old for starting over and finding a new career, Halton," I snapped. "It's old when you've stayed in one place for too long, and nothing's happened."

It's old when you wake up alone one morning and realize you're going to spend the next forty years waking up alone, but I didn't say that. I looked at his young face, still smooth and handsome, and was envious even if he was a fabricant. "Wait a few years, kid, it'll catch up to you, too."

He looked surprised, then smiled. "How old do you think *I* am?" he asked wryly.

I didn't want to play this game anymore. "I don't know," I said shortly. "Thirty-two, thirty-three." I wasn't thinking.

"I'm twelve," he said. "I'll be thirteen in January." I gaped at him, and he grinned. "But I've been told I look young for my age."

Laughing outright, I shook my head. "So you *do* have a sense of humor, after all."

"Working on it," he said.

"It's sometimes hard for me to remember you're not real."

He stopped smiling, blinked and looked back out at the mountains. "I *am* real," he said quietly.

Maybe, while they were at it, someone could have taught *me* some tact as well. I kicked myself mentally, looking at him as he stared somberly across the empty desert. He had tried hard to do right by me. Hell, he'd saved my life, and I'd just been treating him like everyone else who's ever gotten too close to me, warding him off with verbal jabs and hostility. I owed him better.

I felt a wave of affection for Halton suddenly go through me. More than that. I wanted him. I wanted to make love with him under that wide crimson sky, dress up in harem silks and lie back on a thick Persian rug, feel the weight of him on me as I watched a hawk circle above me, graceful, beautiful killer. I must have been suddenly oozing buckets full of horniness pheromones.

"Oh, the hell with it," I murmured. He glanced at me, puzzled, and I reached out with both hands to grasp his firmly. He inhaled sharply, and stiffened, tense.

"Kay Bee . . ." he said, uneasily.

I pulled on his arms to make him bend over far enough so that I could kiss him, a long embrace that left us both quivering. When he pulled away, his eyes were wide, almost frightened. "You wouldn't still be interested in making love with me, would you?" I asked, this time with me feeling like the shy one. I was terrified he'd changed his mind.

He nodded slowly. "Yes, please," he whispered.

Christ, what kind of education had his former lovers given

him, anyway? I had the sudden image of an Oliver Twist standing with his stiff little penis in one hand, saying politely, "Please, suh, I'd like some more . . ."

We didn't have a Persian rug, but we did have the tarp from the sandjeep, which smelled faintly musty and was far from being soft against the skin. It was marvelous. I still had a phobia about a spy satellite snapping Polaroids of the birthmark on my butt, so we opened the door and window of the *madja'* and aired it out to a tolerable temperature.

John Halton was the best lover I'd ever had, which actually isn't much of an endorsement considering the number and quality of my previous bed partners. But I've no doubts at all that he would have been in the top percent of anyone's class.

We lay on that musty tarp in the gloom of an abandoned *madja'* while he undressed me with as much admiration and wonder as if I'd been a Miss Universe runner-up, exploring my body with virginal innocence. I undressed him, feeling guilty shyness. I'd seen him naked before, but not quite this up close and personal. His muscles trembled under smooth skin, curly hair dusting his chest and legs, not an ounce of extra fat anywhere, and I looked, too. He was way far out of my usual league, and I kept thinking, I don't deserve this, it's too good, any minute now he'll take a hard look at me and *see* . . .

He kissed the side of my neck, and pulled back to smile at me. "Look," he said, marveling, "you've got goose bumps only on one side," and stroked the raised flesh. He kissed the other side to raise goose bumps on that half, playing as joyfully as a child until I was gasping for breath, more hot and bothered than I'd ever been in my whole life.

I lay back against a pillow of sand molded under the tarp, breathing unsteadily as he moved against me, his hands caressing me, gently here, rougher there, as if he knew exactly what I wanted. Suddenly I realized, he *did* know; the chemical sensors buried in the flesh of his hands could read my skin as accurately as any laboratory instrument. He was reacting to my own desires like a feedback mechanism. I was telling him what I wanted as precisely as if I'd been doing it myself, which in effect, I was.

*The world's most technologically advanced dildo,* I thought, unable to help myself, and stiffened.

He abruptly pulled back, eyes worried in the shadows. Shit, maybe he could hear my thoughts as well. "Am I doing something wrong?" he asked anxiously.

You idiot, Kay Bee. He can't read your mind, but he *can* read your fear.

"No, nothing," I assured him, pushing the thought away as I held him tightly. After a moment, he nuzzled me again, his soft lips and rough tongue running against my skin until I was moaning. He slid inside me easily and I locked my legs around his back, the sound of his ragged breathing in my ear driving me up the wall, over the side, and crashing down into the best orgasm I'd ever known. He gasped, shuddering, and I could actually *feel* him coming inside me, waves pulsating all the way through him.

His chest was slick with sweat. He slid off me, and I nestled into the crook of his arm. Both of us panted like dogs in heat. A slight breeze blew through the open door, cooling the sweat on our entwined bodies. It felt deliciously good.

After a while, I smiled up at him and kissed his forehead. "God, that was wonderful," I said.

He grinned like a kid, pleased with himself, and hitched himself up on one elbow to lean his head against one hand. His other brushed across my naked body in gentle patterns, tracing lazy circles with his high-tech fingertips around the tiny nubs of my breasts. It made me suddenly self-conscious, and he stopped, looking at me questioningly.

"I have trouble understanding how someone who looks like me can turn you on," I said lamely. I could feel the heat of a blush crawling uncomfortably up my cheeks.

"Why?" he said, matter-of-factly. "My body needs sexual release occasionally, and my head thinks you're an interesting person. Why is combining the two difficult to understand?"

"Jeez, thanks a whole hell of a lot, Halton," I said cynically, and swatted at him. "You sure know how to make a girl feel sexy."

He smiled, a little uncertain, but leaned over to kiss me, his tongue gently exploring my mouth. Amazingly, I could feel his cock pressed against my thigh growing thick again. His mouth traveled down the edge of my chin, into the curve between my neck and collarbone, as his hands, his wonderfully sensitive hands, caressed my stomach and chest.

"I like the goose bumps," he whispered, his voice muffled against my throat.

Gently, I pushed him back, rolling over to press him down against the tarp. "What else do you like?" I asked softly. "Do you like this?" I kissed him the way he had me, then along his chest.

He reached for my shoulders, and I caught him by the wrists, holding his arms down by his head. "What are you doing?" he asked, bewildered.

"I want to make love to you, Halton, the way you made love to me. Do you like this?" I slid further down, my mouth slowly exploring his perfect body. "Or this . . . ?"

I kept his nano-amplified hands pinned by his side, nuzzling him with my lips and tongue until he was as randy as I was. "Now?" he said, voice hoarse, pleading. "Now, yes?"

"Yesss . . ."

I straddled him, my legs between his, and within moments I came, my body turning as rigid as a surfboard riding the orgasmic wave. Halton was looking up into my face. My coming turned him on, and he followed, his face going round and smooth. Eyes half shut in the rush of euphoria, he murmured, "Oh. Oh. Oh." No contrived macho grunting and straining, and the look of utter bliss on his face quickened a second tingle curling up around the base of my spine ready to course through me. . . .

Yeah, a scientific example of feedback mechanism, only this was pure human, totally natural, the real thing.

We lay exhausted and shaking, a trickle of sweat running down my nose to drip onto his neck. I kissed it, tasting salt. His dark hair curled plastered to his forehead, no longer perfect. I think I preferred it mussed up.

"No one's ever done that to me before," he said softly once he'd caught his breath. "No one has ever made love to *me*."

I hadn't thought so. I suspected the women Halton had known before, who had approached *him* for sex, were both pretty enough to be carelessly self-confident, and selfish enough to use a fabricant as a substitute for what they couldn't get from a real man. At least that was my pet theory, which also fit in nicely with my other pet theory, which was ugly women were better fucks, because we have to try harder to be any competition at all.

I didn't bother expounding on my theories right at that moment.

Cuddling together in the warmth of the *madja'*, we murmured unintelligibly for a while. He dozed off after a few minutes, curled up around me as if I were his favorite teddy bear.

I couldn't sleep, my mind going in circles, vague worries chasing their own tails in the growing dusk.

# FIFTEEN

I was surprised by how deeply Halton slept, as if the sex had shorted out his hyperawareness circuits. I watched him as he dreamed, his eyes moving behind the lids, his fingers curled around my forearm twitching now and then. It was close to evening when he sighed contentedly, and woke up. The temperature would cool off rapidly once the sun began dropping behind the edge of the mountains, but the waning heat was still comfortable.

He smiled at me sleepily, a satiated, very human-looking smile. I stroked him gently, combing his tangled hair with my fingers until he yawned and stretched, then hitched himself on one elbow to look down at me. He kissed my bruised eye.

"Well," I teased him, "I guess you lied to me, then. You were a virgin after all."

His forehead wrinkled as he thought about that seriously. "I don't think so, at least not by the common definition of virginity," he said finally. "I think a better word would be 'inexperienced.' "

I laughed. "Jeez, Halton, sometimes I think you're putting me on."

"I'm not," he insisted. "I'm just new at this."

"Are you *really* only twelve years old?" I asked. "I could go to jail. There are laws against that, you know."

He leaned back, his eyes widened. "Are there really?" He still had trouble recognizing a joke.

"No, I'm kidding," I assured him. I had to stop teasing him.

Wrapped in a comfortable post-coital glow, we talked. That, I also didn't bother telling him, was a first for *me*. My average sex partner usually couldn't wait to get his clothes and his rocks off, and afterwards couldn't wait to get his clothes *on* and split.

After a while, he said, "It is true, about my age. Fabricants are designed to have very short, intensive childhoods, and a much longer adult life span." His face had that barren look again. "Although there aren't many fabricants much older than I am." I assumed there weren't ever likely to be too many either, because none would be allowed to live long enough to grow old. I shivered as he gently held me in his arms.

He needed to talk. His naked body entwined with mine, he was as physically close as we could possibly be, but his eyes were off somewhere else, a million miles away.

Fabricants, he told me in the bland kind of voice a college professor lectures with, are neither robots nor clones. Each fabricant zygote is individually grown around a predetermined DNA "template," human-phenotypic, but not genetically the same. Even his mitochondria were considerably different from anything human. He couldn't get me pregnant; we're not the same species. I wasn't sure how I felt about *that* one.

The nanomachine systems are added sequentially to the growing embryo at various stages of its development before the fetuses are implanted into surrogate "mother fabricants." Originally, they had used chimpanzees before developing a more dependable pinheaded female fabricant with only the most basic of brain stems to keep it functioning. Its specially adapted limbless body is not much more than a large womb cradled by wide, deformed hip bones, allowing the fabricants a full fourteen months development before birth. With every stage of fetal development rigorously monitored and controlled, every hormone and biochemical measured and balanced, the ten resulting fabricant babies were more invariable than human identical twins.

This was certainly strange pillow talk. Almost as weird as our dinner conversation, but I listened carefully, curled up in the crook of his arm.

After their forced delivery, baby fabricants grow at an enormous pace, their education strenuous and rigidly narrow. At about five, they hit puberty, and the massive growth spurt begins to slow. By eight, fabricants are considered to be at their completed adult stage, and from the next few years on, their aging slows to a similar rate as their human counterparts.

Halton had grown up in a small enclave inhabited only by his nine twin "brothers" and his teachers, CDI trainers. His knowledge of the outside world was limited to what the CDI trainers wanted him to know, directing his developing body and mind down the corridors of reinforced preset patterns they determined most useful. A fabricant's first loyalty is to his CDI trainers. In spite of their communal upbringing, the ten little John Halton fabricants had no particular devotion toward each other, no "brotherly" bonds. They didn't even have separate names.

"Don't you care at all about the others?" I asked. "What happens to them, at least?"

He didn't answer for a very long moment, and I twisted to look up at his face. That inhuman, bleak *nothingness* drifted through his eyes, before he blinked, as if coming back from the edge of a barren abyss, and smiled wanly at me. "Yes," he said. "I care."

I didn't press it, just let him talk about what he wanted. "I didn't see my first stranger until I was four years old," he said. Computed in doggie-years, that would have made it the equivalent of about eleven. "And I still think that it was an accident." He smiled, and kissed my forehead, running his fingers through the stubble of my hair distractedly. "She was nice."

He was looking out the open doorway, watching the shadow of The Mothers as it crept across the desert flatlands toward us. "I mean that she was nice because she wanted to be, not because it was a calculated part of the conditioning methodology. She brought in books from the outside, the first different books I'd ever seen. She would read stories to us for fun instead of having us study them for tests." He was quiet for a moment. "I believe she got into trouble for it. They transferred her after that, and I never saw her again." His voice was sad.

"What kind of books?" I asked quietly. I was beginning to get a hint of what made John Halton tick, understand him a little better. It scared me, and it made me want to cry.

"Children's adventure books, fairy tales, mostly. Nothing really subversive." He shrugged. "Classics like *Ivanhoe* and *Treasure Island. Peter Pan*, that sort of thing. I'd never seen any fiction before, so it confused me at first, thinking these were real stories." He was still staring out, looking back in his memory at the first true mother figure the John Haltons had ever known even briefly.

Of course they hadn't wanted her to treat the fabricants as real children, turn their affections away from Big Brother CDI to an actual human being. I could imagine him sitting on this faceless woman's lap, wide-eyed at vast enchanting worlds opening up on the surface of a bookreader, combined with the potency of his first experience with kindness simply for kindness's sake. It affected him deeply, an indelible impression left in his young, growing psyche.

"After she left, my entire subgroup had to have tests done to see if the series should be terminated early for psychological contamination," he said, the flat serenity in his voice not matching the horror of his words. "We were isolated individually, reassigned to new trainers, and subjected to extra tutoring in understanding the difference between fiction and fact. Then we were retested. Fabricants *are* expensive." I almost heard irony in his voice. "The decision came down that we were still within the acceptable parameters."

I heard it, unspoken. "But?"

He shrugged again, helpless. "But," he said. And stopped. He took a deep, ragged breath, and I put my hand against his chest, feeling his heart beating more rapidly. "But . . . sometimes, I think . . . they might have been wrong." He had to drag the words up, twisting out like little vicious snakes annoyed at being disturbed. He averted his eyes. "I'm scared," he added softly.

"Just because someone was nice to you when you were a kid, read you a couple of books?" I was incredulous. "That's ridiculous! You don't really *believe* that?"

"I know," he said quietly, "if I fail on this assignment, I'll be terminated. I think, even if I don't fail, after I return to Langley I won't pass the post-examinations. I'm the third John Halton; the first two somehow failed. They had to be destroyed. I don't know why or how, and I'm afraid if I don't figure it out, I'm going to fail the same way."

He finally looked up at me. "But I suspect CDI has already made that decision. That's why they've placed me with a non-company person. It's not important to the assignment if I'm contaminated by you. I'm expected to perform a certain function, and after I've served my purpose, I'm expendable. I won't be needed or useful again for anything else."

I sat straight up and stared back at him, horrified. "Jesus Christ, Halton, then don't go back! *Screw* the CDI, run away or something. Why don't you go to the ACLU, file a lawsuit and sue the goddamned Government for human rights abuse? GBN would get you a major-league lawyer, we could help you organize fabricants into fighting for their civil rights. . . ."

He was staring at me like *I* was the crazy one. "Kay Bee, I'm a *fabricant*. Fabricants aren't human, they're not people. Their whole purpose for existence is predetermined, they can't function independently. That's outside the designs the CDI molded them for."

"*Us*, Halton, *us!*" I was yelling at him, furious. I jumped up to pull my shirt up over my shoulders, the desert cooling rapidly in the twilight. "Why can't you say it? *Them, they*—you're always talking about other fabricants like they're fucking Martians from outer space!" I was pacing in the confines of the tiny *madja'*, like a caged neurotic tiger. "Didn't the goddamned CDI plug any sense of family kinship into you at *all*?"

Halton had sat up, bare legs curled under him, his hands in his lap. "No," he said quietly. The expression on his face was so vulnerable, as open and exposed as a trusting child, I froze, unable to move. A stone-cold killer, a creature who had been intentionally conceived to be faster and stronger than any human being, Halton would obediently walk back and place his neck meekly on his creators' chopping block.

He'd been right, there would never be a fabricant rebellion. His makers had ensured themselves against that, and Halton knew it very well.

I burst into tears, unable to stop myself.

Instantly, he had his arms around me, holding me tightly. "I'm sorry, I'm sorry," he kept repeating in a small, frightened voice. I hugged him, trying to squeeze the trembling out.

"Shut up, Halton," I whispered. He did. "You didn't do anything wrong. I should be saying I'm sorry, except it's not my fault, either. Damned creeps should fry in hell."

We held on to each other, drowning souls clutching at straws to keep our heads above the sewage.

"This sucks, Halton," I said finally, my face against his chest. "I may be old and slow, but I'm not some stooge CDI can jerk around. I don't like being used, and I don't like using other people." I sighed. "Too bad we can't just pack it in and run off to someplace like the Moon, be pioneers in the asteroid mines or something."

He stiffened. I looked up inquiringly. His face had gotten that impassive dead look again. "If you want," he said simply. "However, I believe if the motive is to find a secure refuge away from CDI, off-Earth would not be a viable choice." He was reciting with about as much animation as a textbook. "CDI exerts far more control over off-Earth Stations and lunar colonies than on the planet itself. I would suggest searching for a sanctuary on Earth first."

"I wasn't being serious, Halton," I said. I pulled away from him, shivering in the sudden chill, and started dressing. "Even if I were, you couldn't go with me anyway. You're still a CDI fabricant, your first allegiance is to the Hill, hardwired in, right?"

"Not exactly." He started dressing as well. "I'd be useless as His Excellency's bodyguard if my commitment to him could not be guaranteed, but intelligence implies a certain amount of autonomy of thought, what you could call 'free will.' Without it, fabricants would have no more flexibility than AI machines." He buttoned his shirt, watching his hands. "What *is* hardwired in me is a strong *need* to belong to someone or something. I'm absolutely loyal to whatever or whomever I recognize as being my legal owner."

Finished with his shirt, he looked up at me. That strange, cold look flickered in the back of his eyes. Totally inhuman. "At the moment," he said calmly, "you are still the legal owner of record."

The implications began sinking in. I suddenly felt sick. "If I say 'Go,' you'd go, just because I wanted it, is that right?"

"Yes."

Bile stung the back of my throat, turning the inside of my mouth sour. "So, all this"—I waved a hand at the tarp on the sand-covered *madja'* floor, two indentations still marking the depressions our bodies had made—"*this* was just because CDI programmed you with some weird sense of loyalty?" I could feel the outrage churning up into fury. "You wanted to fuck me only because I wanted it, and whatever *I* want, like a good little dog, you've got to give it to me? My obedient slave, is that it?" I was crying now in anger. "*Is that all it was, you bastard?*"

He looked startled at the idea, and hesitated, deliberately analyzing the idea. "I don't know," he said finally, his voice low, troubled. "I don't know." He couldn't even lie, the son of a bitch. Not even that.

It was worse than all the perverts and the drunks who had used me as an easy lay, then tossed me aside. At least then I'd had no illusions about the desperate humiliation I'd allowed myself to wallow in time after time. The pride I'd had to swallow so many times along with bitter semen was nothing compared to the betrayal I felt now. It was worse than rejection.

I'd let my guard down, *again*, and once again it was being rubbed in my face that it simply wasn't possible for a man to feel for me anything like I felt for him. Even a goddamned *fabricant* could only get it up for me if something else were in control, some other need, some other degenerate perversion calling the shots.

I was crying, hurt and furious, years of alienation turning me into a pillar of salt tears. I walked out into the violet gloom of desert twilight and lit a cigarette, drawing the smoke in to try and sear the pain out of my chest. All it did was ache.

Halton came out, folded the tarp and placed it in the back of the sandjeep behind me. I didn't turn around. I heard the sandjeep's tires creak as he leaned against it, waiting silently. Stars were beginning to pop across the cobalt-dark sky. I lit another cigarette with the butt of the last and sent the stub arcing out with a flick of my fingers, red ashes glowing like a miniature missile. It splattered a tiny fire when it hit in the darkness, and faded away.

Sand crunched under Halton's feet as he finally walked up behind me. "Kay Bee . . ." he started.

"Hey." I turned and cut him off. I had my shoulders back and chin up, tears dried and a sneer plastered firmly on my face. "Let's just forget about it, okay?" The tough little street kid was back. "I don't need to hear it."

"I'd like you to listen to what I have to say." He sounded angry.

That surprised me. It got my attention, anyway. I looked at him narrowly, his face hidden in shadows. As I drew in another lungful of smoke, the red glow briefly illuminated the hard line of his jaw. "Okay," I said, spiteful. "You have a captive audience."

"You said you kept forgetting I'm not real. That's not true." The meek, obedient Halton had vanished. This Halton was mad as hell. "What you keep forgetting is that I'm a fabricant. It's no sin, and it's no crime. I'm not ashamed of what I am. I have no more desire to be human than an elephant wants to be a hedge-hog. I'm not a little wooden Pinocchio hoping my good fairy will turn me into a real human boy if I keep my heart pure and do kind deeds."

*Ouch.* He was getting good with the sarcasm.

"I don't have human rights, because I'm not *human.* I never will be."

"You're as smart as a human, probably smarter."

"So are some species of whales. No one is sentenced to life in prison for killing one."

"That's a bunch of bullshit sophistry, Halton." I laughed, harsh and humorless. "Boy, when the CDI ran your brain through the rinse cycle, they fucked your head up *real* good."

"That's right," he said. The chill was back in his voice. "I love the CDI. They created me. They raised me and trained me and gave me a purpose for existing. They are my mother and my father and my family. And I'm fully aware that I have no choice in how I feel about this. I've been designed and conditioned to feel this way; even the thought of doubting the CDI physically hurts me."

I took another long drag on the cigarette, lighting up Halton's face, the stark shadows making him appear haunted and callous. "So if you won't resist them, and you love them so much, just what the fuck do you expect out of me? Why are you getting me involved in all this crap? All I was supposed to do is escort you to Khuruchabja and deliver you to Sheikh Larry. *That's all.* What the hell am *I* supposed to do about it?"

I was pissed off all over again. "But you've been drawing me deeper into the shit, baiting me with Government secrets, telling me your life story, even seducing me, you son of a bitch. Certainly it's not because of my lovable and charming personality, so just tell me, why *me*?"

"Because my family, who has given me life and everything I hold dear, is planning to destroy me," he said bitterly. "Because I want to live. Because I'm alone, and there is no one else I can turn to for help."

I didn't say anything for a moment, taking a last puff on the cigarette before I set that one arcing away, another little missile flung into the night. The anger had been punched clear out of me. "You don't know for sure." His silence told me he did. "But why?"

"I don't know why," he said quietly. His own anger seemed

to be spent as well. "But I do know CDI doesn't send out fabricants on first assignments without a trainer, or at least another CDI operative. They don't send them into high-risk countries without extensive prior experience."

The wind was coming up, moonlight cast through the rising dust in the distance looking like ephemeral genies let out of their bottles to play.

"My specialty is languages, Kay Bee," Halton said. "I was designed primarily for learning a great many languages quickly and accurately. But I'm only a linguist. All these other abilities I have that you seem to think extraordinary are standard for every fabricant made." I shivered in the sudden cold, the heat sucked away into the vacuum of night. "I'm not Super Spy, I was never intended to be. My sub-sector is part of CDI's exclusive quota; I'm not even supposed to be lent outside my own department, never mind given to foreign governments or civilians. I had expected to spend my life in Langley, sitting with a jack in my ear translating covert conversations. That's all I ever wanted to do. There are other fabricants specifically designed for active espionage. But that's not me. I shouldn't be here."

I shuddered, just imagining what *they* must be like.

"Two previous John Haltons were terminated," he said, his anger lost, "because somewhere their training failed, they deviated too far outside the acceptable parameters. I think the series is still good enough to be salvageable, but used simply as one-shot weapons. Then they're discarded. Thrown away . . ." He faltered. "Killed," he finished softly, trying the word out gingerly.

I lit another cigarette, then clamped my arms around my chest to hold in my shaking. My teeth started chattering. Halton walked to the sandjeep and came back to hand me my jacket.

"It doesn't make sense," I protested, and gratefully shrugged into the padded jacket. "A fabricant must cost *millions* of dollars. Even if you were going to be used only once, it's just not worth blowing that much money over this little piss-ant country."

"You were here during the last war, Kay Bee," Halton said. "How much money was expended in high-tech weapons used against the secondhand planes and missiles the Behjars put together from reject parts bought in India?"

"That was different. The Behjars had infrafusion bombs, thanks in no small part to your bosses. They certainly didn't get those by building them out of do-it-yourself mail-order kits." My long dormant journalist brain cells were starting to nag at me. "The Behjars had to be stopped or they'd have wiped out far more people than who did get killed. Diplomacy wasn't getting anywhere. You can't reason with madmen. They didn't leave us with any other choice."

What the hell was really going on in Khuruchabja that the CDI would waste a fabricant over? And why had a microflake which cost even more than a fabricant been risked by being so precariously smuggled in? And by whom? We were caught in a crossfire we couldn't even see. Was Sheikh Larry's ludicrous dream of an Islamic *wirtshaftswünder,* or CDI attempts to frustrate it, really worth throwing away this much money?

True, this wasn't the billions of dollars spent on eradicating a small group of deadly fanatics, but nobody squanders that much money without a damn good reason. Not even the U.S. Government.

And why was *I* here? Never mind what Somerton had said, they didn't really need me at all to plant Halton inside Khuruchabja. They could have parachuted him somewhere over the desert, had him walk in disguised as just another nomad shepherd, and no one would have known the difference. But Somerton was right, somehow, that I was a part of the setup working for the benefit of CDI, and I wasn't even getting the company dental plan out of it.

Halton could hear the rusty wheels squeaking in my head, letting me think. "But why me?" I mused. "Why would they team you with me?" I said, slowly, balancing puzzle pieces in my head. There were too many missing elements to make the picture clear. Halton was quiet. "They want a thick-headed, burned-out journalist here for more than just making a simple delivery. I'm being used, too." I glanced at him suspiciously. "You knew that, didn't you?"

He took a breath before answering. "Except for the details, I had that part figured out fairly quickly, yes."

I snorted, looking away back at The Mothers, demurely shrouded in the evening darkness.

"And of all the things you did tell me, that wasn't one of them." I wasn't angry, honest. My cigarette had burned down far enough so that my fingers could feel the heat. I flicked yet another tiny rocket off into the night air. It hit the ground, rolling embers before it vanished in the dark. I hadn't chain-smoked like this in ten years, and the nicotine rush was making me feel slightly vertiginous.

"I was afraid to," Halton said, his voice low. I turned to face him. He wouldn't meet my eyes. "If I'd told you I was part of a plot CDI was setting you up for, would you have been willing to try to help me then? Would you have even believed me?"

"Probably. Possibly. Shit, Halton, I don't know." I sighed, and then shook another cigarette out of the package. Four left, I was getting low. The lighter cast a wavering yellow glow over his troubled features. I inhaled deeply, feeling about twenty more cilia curl up and die in my lungs. The smoke looked like pale silk billowing on a slight breeze. "Tell me something. Whose idea was it to seduce me, yours or theirs?"

"Mine. I think."

I chortled, painfully. "You don't even know that?"

"I can't tell you the exact reason, Kay Bee. Maybe it's true, I wanted to have sex with you only because I'm preconditioned that way. Or maybe I deliberately wanted to create a psychological bond between us, calculated to make you more attached to me, to manipulate you. Maybe that's part of my programming, too." He looked at me, his eyes glittering in the dim light. "Maybe I just wanted to fuck, and it's no more complicated than that."

That stung. "Jeez, thanks, Halton," I sneered. "All those possibilities make me feel *so* much better."

He suddenly reached out and grabbed me by the arms, jerking me around to face him. My cigarette spun out of my hand, unnoticed. His fingers were tight, but not painful, just hard enough to let me know I wasn't going anywhere.

"I wasn't trying to make you feel better, Kay Bee. I was trying to be honest with you."

"That's what friends are for, right?" I said cuttingly.

He held me trapped in his grip for a long moment, seemingly frozen into place. That weird look had come back into his eyes, not seeing me, an ominous *emptiness*, frighteningly alien. "Friends?" he repeated, as if the concept was completely foreign to him. "I have no friends. Friends are people who trust each other." I could feel a sudden tremor in his hands. "Do you trust me, Kay Bee?" he whispered. "*Are* we friends?"

It was part defiant challenge, part a desperate plea. And part something I couldn't decipher.

I believed he wasn't lying about wanting my help, not playing a role in some complicated CDI plot. But he was still a CDI spook fabricant. Despite all the secrets he'd told me, I still knew nothing about how his head was really wired. How could I believe this wasn't just part of some devious manipulation outside his control? How could I be sure he wasn't acting exactly the way CDI had intended him to, whether he knew it or not? If he'd deviated this far from "acceptable parameters," bucked his programming this far to resist his makers, how could *I* be sure all his mental equipment was in working order?

How could I *trust* Halton?

I had a sudden intuitive flash: If I said no, I'd condemn him to death. He'd simply give up and walk in front of a firing squad without a fight. If I said yes, I'd end up taking on the entire CDI with a stolen biomachine already proven to be lethally dangerous, possibly even renegade, having to rely on its uncertain guarantee not to kill me or get me killed.

I gave the only answer I could.

Putting my hands around his waist, I drew him gently to me in a calming embrace. My head tucked under his chin, he held me tightly against his chest.

"Looks like it's just you and me against the world, kid."

# SIXTEEN

"Rule Number One of staying alive is C.Y.A., Halton," I said. "It means 'Cover your ass.' Self-preservation." I jabbed him in the chest with two fingers. "Get some. I have too much, you have none at all. Understand?"

"I think so," he said earnestly.

"Hmph." I'd been racking my brain for the better part of a day to come up with ideas for a way out of this mess with both our skins intact, and so far hadn't done much more than bluster. We had less than four more days to think of something before I had to turn Halton over to Sheikh Larry. But what actual constructive action I was going to be able to take, I hadn't a goddamned clue.

I'd wanted to confer with Arlando, hoping to set up some preventative maintenance on his end, but Halton had emphatically nixed that idea. He had no idea what hold CDI had on my boss, but he knew enough about the internal workings of his own organization that any discussion of our problem with Arlando would only tip them early that something wasn't kosher.

He made it clear that as soon as CDI suspected their fabricant of making any attempt to defect, they would waste no time in wasting him. Not that there were many places to defect to. While there had still been a Vice-President's Council on Competitiveness to pressure for relaxing of Federal regulation of biotechnical products, the CDI had been busily buying up patents on human DNA through the back door, ignoring the loud screams of various Greens and the EPA. The industry's safety regulations were too burdensome to business, came the official statement from the conservative White House. The free market economy was too eager to grab their lion's share of the world's multibillion-dollar biotech boom to bother worrying about a bunch of leftist pinko crackpot environmentalists.

But Clinton had abolished the Council, global warming steamed up, a forty-mile-long ice cube dropped off the Antarctic shelf, and by the turn of the century, environmental protection had become as sacred an American icon as Mickey Mouse and Michael Jordan. Once the Ripe Tomato Gene disaster of '02 had devastated half of the entire Midwest's farm crop with an accidental mutation, the pendulum completed its panic swing totally in the other direction. The Environmental Protection Agency had had no trouble pushing their Public Health and Safety Act through Congress. Biotechnological regulations now included instant seizure and destruction of any genetically engineered products even slightly suspected of being defective, whether they were proven to be or not. If it turned out they *weren't*, well, better safe than sorry, right? Everybody could sue each other for damages later.

It was meant for medical gene-splicing and viral pesticides, but it covered *any* defective artificial biological product. Halton was an artificial biological product. He was also quite defective.

That didn't leave us a whole lotta options.

What kind of "trust" did Halton believe we had? On the one hand, while his entire life had been rigidly controlled by humans and he obeyed their orders without question, he was neither stupid nor naive enough to believe we were smarter than he was, or infallible. It wasn't so much that he had confidence I could somehow get him out of a lousy situation as it was he was trusting me to *try*. If I failed, it would be circumstances, not betrayal. He would be satisfied with that, even as it killed him.

It didn't make *me* feel any better.

We apparently had alarmed the watchdogs by slipping our leashes, and were being much more closely followed since we got back from our little field trip in the desert. We had led them around for an hour after we left the hotel without shaking them. But we weren't trying that hard, really. At the moment, we sat on the long shelf bench ringing the Nok Kuzlat War Heroes Memorial Square in the Old City, talking while we watched our keepers pretend to read newspapers.

"You told me fabricants have a certain amount of free will, right? So exercise it. Get creative. Think about ways to protect yourself, not just whoever you're assigned to. You're no good to anyone if you're dead. Then find ways to make yourself indispensable to the right people, making getting rid of you a losing proposition."

He thought about that for a moment. "Like blackmail?"

Yup, he was learning. But I wasn't really being too creative about thinking up exact details on operating instructions. I didn't know much about the nuts and bolts of extortion, not being a blackmailer either by nature or profession. Halton probably knew it, but he sat, listening solemnly and nodding in the right places.

Pigeons pecked at scattered crumbs, their heads bobbing as they strutted jerkily across the square like wind-up toys. Well-dressed children with healthy round cheeks squealed and chased the birds as their parents strolled across the wide, ornately paved square. Men in expensive business suits or impeccable qaftans walked together, some chatting as their hands gestured with energetic animation, while others played with strings of amber prayer beads, Arab hands always busy, even if not actually doing anything. An occasional rich man's wife, enveloped in lightweight silk robes, her face hidden behind an embroidered yashmak and h'jab, followed at a discreet distance behind her husband. Probably the highlight of her week.

The square's main feature was an immense scrubbed metal sculpture at its center, an avant-garde artist's interpretation of the folds of a tent blown by a violent wind. Water jetted from nozzles placed along the pleated edges, spraying rainbows in the air before drizzling into the huge basin below.

Kids wearing miniature versions of their father's three-piece business suits played with motorized boats in the water. A tiny girl, dressed in a dozen layers of crinoline petticoats under a pastel-pink dress, baby hair drawn up into two pink-ribboned ponytails, tottered along the plaza, tended by an anxious-looking Filipino woman wearing the mandatory black aba'ayah that Khuruchabjan Islamic law required all foreign women to wear. Red was reserved for native citizens. The nanny's bad Markundi was muffled by the cloth around her head clenched tightly between her teeth. Only the top of her face was visible, pretty Oriental eyes tired and nervous. The child giggled, lurching away on chubby legs to escape her restraint.

*Enjoy it while it lasts, kid,* I thought sourly.

At each end of the square a pair of Khuruchabjan army soldiers in fancy dress uniforms stood at the ready, jaunty red berets at an angle, uniforms crisply creased, burnished machine guns cradled in their arms. They looked like statues themselves, pointedly ignored by the people in the square. But no one doubted that under the mirror-shades their dark, sullen eyes constantly scanned the crowd.

I scanned the crowd as well, keeping tabs on our shadows, and it was with mixed feelings I spotted Thomas Andrew Hollingston Clermont, Esq., strolling across the wide, paved park in deep conversation with two Arab men in white and gold robes. I grimaced and shifted in my seat, ducking my head in the hope he would overlook us, but his eyes widened and he smiled, changing direction.

"How very pleasant to run into you again, Mr. Halton, Mr. Sulaiman . . . Kay Bee," he said in his exquisite accent. He then switched to Markundi, managing to sound equally posh as he introduced us to his companions, high-ranking men who worked in Larry's government and liaisoned with the British Consulate.

Which meant, of course, they were in reality a couple of Larry's snottier relatives skimming a healthy percentage of baksheesh off the Brits in exchange for awarding outrageously priced bids on Khuruchabjan construction projects to favored companies. The real work would be done by poorly paid non-blueblooded Khuruchabjans supplying any physical labor necessary, and other maltreated foreign "guest" administration workers needed for the skills the Khuruchabjans were sadly lacking in.

So it has always been. *Yah zhsa'ara.*

We smiled and shook their hands, murmuring the correct social phrases, returning polite salaams. Clermont exchanged a few more pleasantries with the two Arabs before they sauntered off in search of other kickbacks.

Clermont took out a silk handkerchief from his pocket and dusted off a spot on our stone ledge before sitting down. He turned his face up to allow the sunlight to fall full glare upon his skin. Blinking against the harsh light like a cat stretching itself, he said, "So different from London. I adore the sun."

He had the tan to prove it, too.

"I've always tried to avoid it, myself," I said, wrinkling my nose. "Ozone depletion, skin cancer, all that."

He smirked, turning to look at me with a depreciating gleam in his eye. "So, what brings you two to the Heroes Square?"

It was his tone. Very casual. Too casual. Did he think we were meeting someone?

"Just out stretching our legs. Do some site-scouting, soak up a little of the local color, you know, the usual touristy bullshit," I said offhandedly.

Clermont went back to absorbing ultraviolet rays on his face. "I *had* expected you to give us a ring. We could have helped you to make arrangements for any site locations you might need for filming. You've disappointed me."

You probably are not the only one, luv, I thought. "Sorry about that, Tommy," I said lazily. "I'm just one of those stubborn cusses who likes to do things on my own, get the real flavor of a place rather than the sanitized official tour. Know what I mean?"

When he looked back again, the sun had done nothing to warm up his eyes. "I'm terribly sorry if I left you with that impression, Kay Bee," he said, his voice not matching the look. "I thought I'd shown you an indication of my sincerity, giving you the tip on His Excellency's wife's unfortunate demise." He waited.

If he was attempting to make me feel obligated, or guilty, it didn't work. He raised an eyebrow, then shrugged.

"I'm sure we could have provided something more out of the ordinary for you. Perhaps meet anyone you liked, film anything at all in Nok Kuzlat. For instance, you might be surprised to know His Excellency has detained without trial a few of his political opponents right here in the capital. A judicious word and goodwill gesture in the right places, you could have done an interview with some of Khuruchabja's more interesting dissidents from deep inside the Islamic gulag, so to speak. Definitely off-limits to the usual Western reporter. You still have time. Perhaps I might still be of some assistance after all . . . ?"

He was playing dirty. I'd have given my eyeteeth to get something in a slipclip with more substance than Sheikh Larry's perspective on tiddlywinks. He also knew it wasn't too likely I'd be visiting the neighborhood again any time soon, so didn't need to struggle with the dilemma of most journalists, the endless balancing act between the craving that politicians and despots have for favorable public exposure and the risks taken by members of the press—their careers, visas, confidential sources, and even on occasion, their lives—for the facts. I was about to jump on the offer before it scuttled away, when I noticed Tommy looking at Halton with more than casual interest.

"And when His Excellency discovered I was taking a little meeting with his enemies in jail on your say-so, they could go ahead and make up another cell for the three of us, Tommy."

"Nonsense." Clermont dismissed the notion. "His Excellency might be inconvenienced, but he could cope with any minor external embarrassment as long as internal politics remain stable."

I snorted. "Which means there isn't really anyone who could cause him much embarrassment, is there?"

*Embarrassment* . . . Something in the word tickled a brain cell awake. "You must have some unusual authority to be able to get Western reporters into political prisons, Tommy."

"A better word would be 'influence.'"

"Mmm. Say there was someone of interest I could interview, just what would you expect in return if you did us this favor and used your 'influence' to pull the right strings?"

He eyed me for several quiet moments, then looked up serenely at Halton. "Perhaps if you . . . knew anything that might be of some mutual interest . . . discovered some useful information we could both benefit from . . . ?" he suggested coyly.

"I can't imagine what that would be, old son."

His gaze slid back to me. "Oh, just anything. A stray microflake, for example."

I hadn't exactly been prepared for that. Not with the funny looks he'd been giving Halton. I thought he wanted to know about CDI's planting an unorthodox agent in Khuruchabja. The skin along the back of my neck stood up, a chill like ice. Clermont smiled his direct-hit smile, amused and dry.

"Microflakes are such a growing fad these days, aren't they?" I said. "Seems like everybody on the block wants one to keep up with the Joneses. Personally, I think they're overrated."

He didn't seem pleased with my answer. "Some are more valuable than others. One in particular has already cost me a dear friend." He looked at Halton again, and for a moment his face was naked, his hostility bare. A few pieces of the puzzle clicked into place, which made me none too comfortable.

Khatijah had been his lover.

Somehow, she had known about the flake, but not about Halton.

Clermont hadn't known about either one. Now he knew about both.

Halton had killed her and her friends, but the only one who knew that had been Elias Somerton. The *second* Elias Somerton.

Clermont knew Halton was a fabricant, but he didn't know I'd already given the flake to Somerton. He thought we still had it, and was bartering for it.

Desperately.

None of this fit together in any kind of pattern. The situation still looked totally enigmatic. Every time I turned around, the puzzle just seemed to grow larger and larger. For all my wisecracks and the dislike I felt toward Clermont, I suddenly worried I'd given away the flake too soon. Maybe even to the wrong person.

"You didn't just run into us by accident, Clermont. How did you know we were at the Square?" I demanded abruptly. I was through playing verbal games. I nodded at the men across the Square, still busy studying the sports pages. "They yours?"

Clermont glanced at them. "No." He nodded to another set of men in business suits strolling and chatting by the fountain. "They are. Or rather they work for the Consulate. The Square is close by, they let me know you were in convenient range. I went for a walk." He didn't seem embarrassed.

Why should he have been? He had his own team of babysitters traipsing after him, their own set of newspapers tucked under the bulging armpits. No foreign official could so much as jog down to the corner for a bottle of milk without an uninvited entourage sniffing at his heels. It was a traditional way of life for any foreign government staff here.

Half the crowd in the Square must have been assorted snoops all bumping into one another. A scrawny kid in a cutoff qabah and Levi's hawked the same newspapers that the shadows seemed to patronize heavily, the Square being a sure place for brisk business that day, I'm sure. Who knew, maybe the baby in crinoline was actually a spy on someone else's payroll. Too bad for the newsboy that she was too young to read.

"We must stop meeting like this, Tommy," I said. "People might start talking."

"I know you consider me a prize asshole, Mr. Sulaiman," Clermont said abruptly. I looked back at him, startled. The muscles in his face were hard, grim. "I'll be frank with you. I'm not overly fond of myself at the moment, either. Self-loathing is always an occupational hazard for diplomats dealing with the Middle East."

At that moment, I almost liked him. An alarming thought.

"I need that microflake. I could put pressure on you through official channels, but I'd like to think my honor is still sufficiently intact that I needn't stoop to that. I find it distasteful enough being reduced to dealing baksheesh like some common *tah'jeer* peddling scraps in the suuqs," he said, spitting out the word as if it left a bad taste in his silver-spooned mouth. Actually, I suspected, he had never entertained the slightest notion of leaning on me; the less people who knew anything the better.

"I'll promise to do whatever is necessary to get you interviews with whomever you like in Nok Kuzlat," he said, "whenever and wherever you choose. That much is indeed within my power. I'd like to point out that I and my government will suffer certain consequences for it with the Khuruchabjans, but we can sustain the damage."

Sun-bronzed skin or not, Thomas Andrew Hollingston Clermont was still a card-carrying member of the pasty-faced twit club. I didn't like him, he didn't like me. His disgust with being forced to bargain with me was only surpassed by his haughty contempt for this backwater country he obviously found far beneath his due.

"In return, I'm only asking that you consider what I need. That's all, nothing else. Only *consider* it."

What a gent. Problem was, I didn't have the flake anymore.

I stood up, stretching my back in the sunshine. Clermont was looking at me with his resentment and hope thinly veiled by his arrogant upper-class polish.

"Sure, Tommy. I'll think it over." I said. I jerked a thumb at all the watchdogs scattered about the Square reading papers. "If I find interesting knickknacks lying around, I'll place an ad in the classifieds so you'll be the first to get the news."

I grinned cheerfully at his disappointment, disguising the leaden feeling in my stomach, and walked away. Halton said nothing, as usual. We passed the young boy peddling his Arabic-language newspapers.

"Buy a newspaper," the kid said.

"Thank you, no . . ." I tried to brush him off, but he danced in front of me and thumped the paper against my chest with a firm slap.

"Buy a newspaper, get the TV guide free," he said insistently, his aggressiveness a bit too urgent. Wasn't there anybody here who was what they were supposed to be? I fished the coins out of my pocket and bought the grimy rolled-up newspaper, barely four pages of it. The kid tucked in a TV guide three weeks out of date.

Oh-kay.

The kid then turned away to try and sell his papers to the tag-team shadows following us. I made it a point to stop and wait for them, tapping my foot with feigned impatience and grinning as they scowled.

Close to the Square was a Salon du Thé, which was about as Parisian as the tiny Muslim saint's tomb next to it. Halton and I took a table outside and sipped mint spiced tea from gold-scrolled tea glasses as old women wrapped in red aba'ayahs prayed and gossiped by the small dome over the shrine's square base. A couple of our snooper troopers took a table at the far corner, conversing quietly while pretending we didn't know who they were.

I handed the paper to Halton, and leafed casually through the TV guide. Someone had marked various random words in both Arabic and the comically translated English. This obviously wouldn't be from Hamid; not only was it not his style, what with our chaperons, if Hamid were around, he wouldn't come within a hundred yards of us.

I smiled as I started working my way through the secret message, amused by the Captain Clandestine comic-book safeguards, knowing this had to be the work of Ibrahim's little computer club. Halton folded the paper over to read the middle section, scanning the small Arabic script casually. I stopped smiling when I had enough words in a row. Halton glanced up at me from over his newspaper. "Anything interesting?"

I wasn't taking the chance our shadows didn't have spikemikes. "Not much. Missed a good show last night. Our feathered friend has flown south for the winter," I said nonchalantly. "After having contracted a slight fever."

Halton understood my cryptic remark, although I hadn't been strictly correct. Gabriel didn't *have* a virus. Gabriel *was* the virus.

The AI program had been ARC'ed onto the flake, and when it rewrote its own programming, it had unraveled like a spring, copying itself from the flake straight out onto the kids' electronic bulletin network.

Had it been only the small infrastructure of friends and their antique computers, there wouldn't have been data storage connected by modems big enough to hold Gabriel. But the network was also hooked into the government's computer library system, courtesy of the cousins working as data entry clerks. They had been busily probing files and stealing software off the government's computer network for years, and now Gabriel had escaped to infect the bits and bytes of Nok Kuzlat's entire computer communications systems.

So far, the message read, Gabriel hadn't done anything. It sped through the electronic chains like a ghost, popping up here and there to open and close various files and programs harmlessly and unchanged, undetected by the government.

So far.

Abdullah had managed to engage it in a conversation, of sorts, and had asked it what it was doing.

The answer made me shiver.

The Archangel Gabriel was looking for the Mahdi.

# SEVENTEEN

We were ready for our appointment with the Boy King, HoloPak and PortaNet at our feet while we sat eating leftovers from the room service breakfast and discussing our alternatives. The Raid box blinked like a Christmas tree ornament on the trolley. Now that "they" knew I had it, there was no sense in putting up with eavesdropping vermin infesting the flower arrangements.

I could feel some kind of nasty surprise CDI had just for us lurking in the background, but I still hadn't come up with a plan. Telling CDI and the Sheikh to piss off, and running away together like Huck Finn and Jim down the Mississippi River on a raft was not a viable option. But there didn't seem to be much of anything else, either.

"We're just going to have to go through the motions and try dealing with it as it comes, Halton. I don't know what else to do," I admitted finally. "Looks like you've backed the wrong horse." I looked over at him, realizing by his detached expression that he didn't understand. "I don't know how useful I'm going to be at helping you. I'm not sure how useful I am even to myself."

I was in a shitty mood, feeling sick with self-disgust, not even a flippant joke ready to lighten my mood.

Halton studied me with calm eyes, finally getting the

idiom. "I'm backing the only horse there is, Kay Bee," he said. "We still have a week left."

Then it was showtime.

Halton and I arrived fifteen minutes before the appointment. Americans are notoriously on time, and get peeved when others don't run by the same internal clock. For some reason, the palace military guards took their sweet time searching our equipment and ordering us to walk through the sensor repeatedly. They did a thorough pat-down, making me sweat. I passed inspection, and when they were finally satisfied with both of us, we followed a pair of machine-gun-armed guards as they swaggered down the long hallway.

Then we cooled our heels for the better part of two hours after our scheduled appointment in one of the endless number of brocade-curtained *ma'gâlees*, this particular tiny reception room done up as a miniature replica of the Sistine Chapel, complete with Jehovah jump-starting Adam with His mighty finger. It was a curious room to find inside the palace of a Muslim monarch, but Larry wasn't your run-of-the-mill Muslim monarch, either.

When one of the ancient attendants to His Excellency finally showed up, we were escorted to yet another small room, this one almost plain by comparison. Sheikh Larry lolled on a small love seat under a stained-glass window opening out onto a small, quite lovely garden. He was dressed casually, his jeans in slightly better condition than the previous pair, and a T-shirt with a newer icon of the flame-haired lead singer of Brain Damage, which seemed to be his favorite rock group. Our elderly escort hobbled to stand at one side, his twin on the other. A high, round table in the center of the room was covered with assorted documents.

"You brought the papers?" His Excellency said unceremoniously by way of greeting.

I drew a complete blank, taken entirely off-guard. "What papers?" Then, of course, I understood. "Oh. Yes, I have them. They're in my Net." I patted the PortaNet hanging from my shoulder.

"Okay. Let's do it." He rose from the sofa and stood on the opposite side of the table.

"What . . . ?" I stammered. "Wait a minute. I thought we had until the end of the week . . ." I glanced at Halton. He looked alarmed. "I *need* an optics man, your Excellency. . . ."

Larry frowned, annoyed. "Look, just hire another photographer; there're always a bunch hanging around. You can keep him until you've finished the interview this afternoon, but I'd like to get the formalities over with now, privately." He grinned. "Sorry to break up a great team, but I get what I want, when I want it. I'm the friggin' king, you got it, Sulaiman? So don't go giving me a hard time. *Capish?*"

This was not the spoiled rich brat boorishly shoving his daddy's money around in Beverly Hills. An insolent little Beverly Hills cretin I could have decked. Sheikh Larry was still the head of state of a country not generally known for its mercy or benevolence toward infidels and other lesser beings.

"Got it," I said sourly.

Halton was standing as rigid as oak as I dug the Transfer of Title papers out of the PortaNet's side pocket. One of the twins filled in the Arabic half of the contract, while the other dotted the *i*'s and crossed the *t*'s on the English half.

The Boy King read it, smiled, and slid the papers toward me, a 24-karat gold pen resting on top. I picked up the pen with numb fingers, and pretended to read the words on the contract I couldn't even focus on.

I had the pen poised over the dotted line when Halton said softly, "Kay Bee . . ."

Looking up, I met his wide eyes. He was staring at me in distress, frightened, a silent plea for help. I felt like a complete shit.

There was nothing I could do; Halton knew it. The wall slid back into place, his frantic appeal replaced by cool indifference.

I signed the goddamned papers and sold Halton's soul to another devil.

If Sheikh Larry noticed any of this, he was too wrapped up with the excitement of his new plaything to pay it any mind. One of the two elderly advisors gathered up the papers and discreetly retired from the room. The other stepped back, hands behind his robe at dignified attention. We stood around that small table staring at each other wordlessly until Larry suddenly flicked several bright somethings into the air with a magician's sleight of hand.

Without moving from his place, Halton grabbed them all in a neat sweep. He then held them out toward the king, and I saw they were five silver dinar coins. I saw the advisor's eyes bulge in surprise. The Boy King laughed with delight.

"Now bend one," the Sheikh commanded.

Halton held one up with thumb and two fingers, bending the thick coin into a perfect right angle. After handing that one to the king, he bent another, then straightened it back into shape. Not even a stress line showed where the coin had been crimped.

"Man, this is rilly great!" Larry said elatedly. Halton looked at him, silently impassive. I closed my eyes.

Next thing you know, the kid would be ordering him to sit up, roll over, fetch. *Play dead.* I was trembling.

Sheikh Larry was speaking to me. I opened my eyes, willing myself to remain calm. "Your Excellency?"

"I said Mustafa will take you back to the waiting room. Both of you. I'll be holding court in an hour, which you will film." He wasn't asking. "So be ready."

Mustafa bowed to the little bastard, and we trotted out behind the old man back to the same *ma'gâlees* we'd already spent hours admiring.

Halton sat inanimate, carved from marble. I felt miserable. "I'm sorry, Halton. Jesus, I'm so sorry."

His head turned slowly, as if someone had forgotten to oil it recently. The dead expression was back in his eyes. "What for?"

"For signing the goddamned papers. For not telling His Excellency to go screw himself." I felt my short nails digging into the palms of my hands, they were clenched so tightly. "For letting you down, Halton," I finished softly.

"It was not unexpected, Kay Bee. I realize nothing else could have been done," he said without energy. "You didn't let me down."

"Now what are we going to do?" I hated the forlorn sound in my voice.

"We?" That made me glance hard at him. "There is no 'we,' Kay Bee. You've signed over the title. I belong to His Excellency now." His tone was completely devoid of any human emotion. "I assume you will continue your work as a journalist, and I will become His Excellency's bodyguard. I'm no longer your concern."

It was as if he'd dumped a tub of cold water over my head. I stared at him, realizing that strange plastic look was back. His eyes were bland, vacuous, and his mouth had frozen back into that goddamned bogus half-smile.

"No longer my concern . . ." I repeated thickly. Anger

seeped up through the ice. "That's it? After all the shit you've put me through, asking me to help you, I sign a lousy piece of paper and you're no longer my concern?"

He regarded me silently. "Yes," he said finally.

"It was all for nothing. All of it, even at the *madja'*?" I hissed between clenched teeth. "This is your idea of friendship?"

For a moment, I thought I saw a crack in the shell, a hint of strain in his eyes. Then it was gone.

"I sincerely hope it was not for nothing," he said firmly. "Please believe me, I'm very grateful you were my friend."

*Were*.

I sat back slowly, refusing to look at him. I listened to the sound of blood pumping in my ears, counting heartbeats.

*Past tense*.

"Okay, fine, if that's the way you want it," I said slowly. "Fuck you very much, Halton."

He didn't react, and we sat without speaking until Mustafa returned for us. Halton adjusted the HoloPak, ready to shoot, and I had the PortaNet ready.

We were escorted to one of the biggest rooms I've ever seen. A gold domed ceiling towered overhead; a double row of slender columns kept the roof up. Cathedral-huge and octagonal, it was bisected by a long carpet in a native Oriental design that ran the length of the hall, terminating at one end with a raised dais.

At the top, the Magnificent Servant of Allah, the Beloved and Glorious Leader, Monarch and Commander-in-Chief of all Khuruchabja, His Exalted Excellency Sheikh Larry sat with his forearms positioned on a large gilt-and-green velvet chair like a teenaged pharaoh carved in ice, his face arrogantly impassive, frozen in a regal scowl. His hair had been slicked back neatly, and he had changed from his T-shirt and jeans back into another of his wedding-cake military uniforms, this one generously festooned with ribbons, medals, various baubles, bangles, bright shiny beads, the works. I half-expected the Mormon Tabernacle Choir to start singing hosannas from Dolby speakers.

On the three lower levels from the throne, various robed men sat on cushions, as orderly as if they'd been placed in position by a choreographer. At ground level, a crowd of more than a thousand men filled the hall on either side of the wide carpet, with enough room left over for twice as many more. Some wore immaculate qaftans and richly embroidered qabahs, with gold-thread *burda-ts* covering their shoulders. Others were seated cross-legged in Western business suits and ties under their kaffiyehs. Behind, with increasing degrees of shabbiness, hundreds more filled the hall, until those pressed at the very back of the hall, next to the huge entrance, were dusty *al-wabahr* straight off the desert, the musty smell of old sweat and sheep dung still permeating their robes.

I had the PortaNet hooked into a standby relay channeled through a multilink satellite to some bored feed-in editor monitoring a dozen other such dull transmissions all at the same time. If Larry had some exciting surprise proclamation up his sleeve, at least we'd have it live.

Halton had the HoloPak up and running as we marched across a marble inlaid floor. As we approached the royal personage, he smiled disdainfully, a practiced pose, his shoulders wedged firmly back, head held high so as to look down his thin, curved nose at the flyeyes poking from either side around the top of Halton's head. We were seated about halfway down the dais, to one side. At a distance of ten feet we were out of the way but still positioned at a satisfactory angle to film. Larry's good side, I noticed.

We proceeded to film about three hours of Larry holding court, Arab-style, listening quietly to complaints, nodding and frowning thoughtfully, then dispensing justice however he saw fit. One by one, or in groups of three or whole clusters, men stood, walked to the foot of the dais and began arguing heatedly among themselves until Larry had had enough, judgment was made and written down in a ludicrous big vellum book, and the plaintiffs retreated with varying degrees of smugness or dissatisfaction on their faces.

As much as I disliked the kid, I had to admit he was a decent administrator. Hot disputes over government regulations between opulently robed civil service officials devolved to arguments over banking laws and company contracts by men in business suits and kaffiyehs. Merchants disputing delivery and inventory rivalries were eventually supplanted by villagers quarreling over goats and camels, all sides claiming various degrees of kinship with the Boy King and his corresponding obligation to decide in their favor. How he could keep the boredom off his face was beyond me. But the spoiled brat had vanished, replaced by the haughty young ruler expertly balancing the demands of justice with the need for expedience. Impressive, but dull. Not a prime-time grabber.

I had to suppress a yawn, standing to one side next to Halton, the PortaNet humming to itself. My mind was elsewhere, thinking of where I could make a private call to Arlando, changing my flight schedule to get out of Khuruchabja. I'd done my bit. To hell with the rest of this cloak and danger bullshit. To hell with Sheikh Larry and CDI's backstage manipulations. To hell with the microflake and Somerton and Clermont.

To hell with Halton.

So I wasn't paying attention when a particularly raggedy-looking *fhalell'h* walked up the aisle on trembling legs to stand before his regal lord and master. Having spent the past hour listening to other peasants just like him bicker vociferously over fences and water rights and which son got what number of lambs and whose family hadn't paid what dowry price, I didn't imagine this grubby little man had anything of overwhelming importance to petition.

He seemed terrified, eyes rolling whitely in a deeply tanned face, drooping mustache on a quivering lip. For the first time, Larry smiled—a warm, open expression—as if to calm the man's fears and encourage him to speak his mind. The peasant abruptly fell to his knees, forehead pressed to the step, babbling nonsense. One of the ministers started to stand, ready to remove the hysterical man, but Larry waved him back with a peremptory flick of his hand. The minister sat back, annoyed, as the peasant scuttled on hands and knees closer to the king. Larry leaned forward, as if to better hear the terrified man's gibbering.

"*Allah ahk'bahr!*" the man suddenly screeched, straightening up with a half-meter-long pigsticker clenched in his fist. He lunged toward the Boy King barely a foot away.

And was brought up short by Halton's hand clamped around his wrist. From a good four meters away, Halton had ripped off his HoloPak and sprung across the distance to block the man's attack, the tip of the blade stopping short a fraction of an inch from Sheikh Larry's throat. He twisted the assailant's wrist sharply, the knife clattered to the floor, and the man ended up on his back with Halton's knee planted firmly on his chest.

After a second of stunned silence, the hall erupted in pandemonium, the would-be assassin screaming incomprehensibly over the din of panicked noise. Adrenaline was pumping through me as I had the PortaNet blipping directly into GBN's news-feed, my journalist's instincts taking over before my brain could figure out what was going on.

"An assassination attempt in Nok Kuzlat has just been thwarted," I said into the relay, yelling to be heard over the chaos, scrambling with the other hand at the fallen HoloPak transmitting only stampeding feet. "In a dramatic—" Suddenly I stopped.

Ministers on either side had tripped over themselves falling backwards, as if they'd been blown over by the breath of a cyclone. Larry was pressed back into his ornate chair, eyes wide and astonished, but, I noticed, not frightened. Halton was staring up at the kid, poker-faced, the assailant still writhing in his grip and howling. And I saw, unheard over the cacophony, Larry laughing heartily.

*So be ready.*

It had been a setup.

I cut the transmission without another word. I could almost hear GBN's feed-in editor cursing me from half a world away. I took two steps toward Halton, when a couple of olive-green military guards emerged from the mayhem to form a protective shield around him and the king, blocking my view.

Driven along with the crowd, I was being forced back by the guards shoving people with the side of their machine guns. The shrieking "assailant" was dragged away, and the king had vanished. I fought to swim upstream of the crowd being hustled out the doors, but ended up with the rest, outside the locked palace gates.

On the street, the crowd grew thicker, gossipers anxious for the news from eyewitnesses eager to embellish, at the top of their lungs, their assorted tales of near-assassination and a miraculous rescuer. I pushed my way back toward the armed guards stationed on the other side of the iron gate.

"Kay Bee Sulaiman!" I was shouting over the noise, waving my press credentials at one of them. "GBN News! I had an appointment with His Excellency . . . !"

The guard grinned nastily. "Go away," he ordered.

"My optics man is still in there!" I was pointing toward the palace, my voice hoarse from shouting.

The guard pulled back the bolt on his machine gun meaningfully, an ominous solid thunk. "You go away now. *J'ahkzhil!*"

he shouted back, still grinning. The barrel of the gun was pointed at me.

Right. Hey, no problem.

I went.

# EIGHTEEN

I spent the rest of the week in the hotel. Alone. His Excellency's palace didn't return my calls. The kid had what he wanted, I could go whistle Dixie. I didn't even have an optics guy anymore, and Halton still had the HoloPak.

I called Arlando on a secured line to bitch and moan, which made me feel like shit and didn't achieve much, either. What could I tell him, anyway? I'd done my job, delivered Halton, even had an exclusive, such as it was, on the so-called assassination attempt.

I was stuck here, he spelled out in words of one syllable. That was that. For crying out loud, Kay Bee, you're supposed to be a *journalist*, so make the best of a bad situation. Be a pro.

At least he had the grace not to tell me to stay out of trouble.

There were any number of other reporters and optics men staying in the Grand Imperial, so I puttered around buying drinks, such as *they* were, and putting out a couple feelers for a freelancer. Then I sat in my room waiting by the phone. To pass the time, I downloaded some files out of Cairo Relay's archives onto the PortaNet, studying the possibilities of who I could hit Clermont up to interview.

The hotel's TV system was an old-fashioned internal cable, with very new jammers filtering out all but the most tightly beamed satellite feed. Not even one of Carl's toys could get any of the Western news channels through the hotel's jammers with any degree of clarity. I had to settle for the meager Nok Kuzlat local news on a bad Chinese holoset set at low volume, at uneven intervals between the interminable prayers and two-year-old soccer matches.

The Boy King's sensational survival made the top of the hour, the anchorman gushing with equally effuse praise for Allah, His Excellency and Halton, who had been honored by being immediately offered the job of His Excellency's personal bodyguard, for which he was so obviously qualified. There wasn't even a good holoshot of the rescue, just the endlessly recycled GBN picture of the kneeling assassin seconds before he jumped the king, then a reeling blur of noise and sound as the HoloPak hit the ground when Halton jumped.

The assailant had been promptly tried and publicly executed. They did have wonderful footage of that. Good lighting. Nice sound.

I got a nibble from a freelance holo-optics buddy of Carl's who was also staying at the hotel, and made arrangements on the phone with him while finishing up the tenth archive clip from Cairo to make my choice of political prisoners I might finagle an interview with.

There weren't many who were suitable for the kind of piece I had in mind; most of them were the usual out-of-favor hydrophobic clerics advocating terrorism as the only legitimate catalyst for change, in whom the vast majority of GBN's viewing public had little interest or sympathy for. The rest were routine smugglers, murderers and thieves, run-of-the-mill common criminals, with only the barest veneer of political oppression about them, waiting years for Warhol's fifteen minutes of fame, fleeting and fatal as it was. The Boy King didn't keep that many troublesome political prisoners romantically languishing in his dreary dungeons. He seemed to prefer having those few liberal dissidents, doctors, college professors and, yes, journalists who annoyed him, promptly shot instead. Keeps the public entertained while cutting down on the overhead.

I'd settled on an elderly ulema who had been in jail for more than five years for certain unkosher religious views, a bit too popular and frail to have executed without a PR scandal, when the latest Khuruchabjan news flash playing in the background caught my eye. The anchorman was replaced by a superb holoshot taken by one of Nok Kuzlat's very own.

Nathan R. Mitchell, a dastardly British national working for an unscrupulous Canadian export company in Nok Kuzlat, had been arrested for attempting to bribe a number of our virtuous, upstanding Khuruchabjan officials over a contract grant. The cheerful voice-over described the degenerate Brit's heinous crimes as military officers hustled the suspect down the office building steps, hands cuffed behind him.

The lens zoomed up for an excellent shot on his pale and drawn face, hollow eyes staring back at the camera in disbelief. Then he was shoved roughly into an official car, cameras, PortaNet microphones and HoloPaks waving around the car as boxes of "evidence" followed the culprit into the back seat.

It was Elias Somerton. The second.

I had to root through the junk accumulated in the hotel room to find the card Clermont had pressed into my hand.

The British Consulate's line was busy, and I kept the phone on constant redial until I got through.

"I'd like to speak to Mr. Thomas Andrew Hollingston Clermont, please."

"May I ask who's speaking?" The phlegmatic young man at the other end could have been interchangeable with any number of other lowly government receptionists in embassies around the world.

"Kay Bee Sulaiman." I didn't bother with the "GBN News."

"One moment, please . . ." He put me on hold while the screen showed a panorama of green English hillside, bursting with flowers and lush trees, a river trickling merrily in the dappled sunlight. Haydn's "Water Music" played in the background.

The glum receptionist returned. "So sorry, Mr. Clermont is in conference and cahn't be disturbed. Would you care to leave your number, sir?"

I did. His meeting must have lasted all day, since by the time I called for the third time, he'd gone home, and the embassy receptionist was *veddy* apologetic—he couldn't possibly release Mr. Clermont's confidential home number, please ring back in the morning.

The next morning, I didn't bother making the call, knowing full well Clermont was going to be in conference regardless of what time I called. Leaving the PortaNet in the hotel room, I carried another of Carl's little devices, a miniaturized recorder, the mike pickup disguised as a button on my shirt, the chip disk hidden in my belt buckle. The chip itself, he'd assured me, was protected against crippling devices like the Raid box.

Downstairs, I had the desk call a taxi, eyeing one of the watchdogs reading a newspaper in the lobby as I waited. Finally, I walked to where he was seated and stood directly over him. He looked up in ill-concealed uneasiness.

"Where's your partner?" I asked.

"I beg your pardon, sir?"

The taxi pulled up, and the imitation Mameluke doorman opened the lobby doors and looked at me expectantly. I looked around the lobby with exaggerated care.

"Still in the can, is he? Well, look, if we get separated," I said helpfully, "I'm just popping over to the British Consulate for an hour or so, so he doesn't need to hurry and risk catching his dong in his fly, okay?"

The watchdog glared at me with sheer hatred in his eyes. Sure enough, his cohort shuffled hastily out of the men's room, jiggling the zipper on his pants.

I knew it wasn't smart to hassle these guys too badly, and to be honest, my heart wasn't much into it. It was more for form's sake, to cover up my own nervousness.

The security screen at the British Consulate didn't pick up the micro-recorder, but they confiscated my Swiss Army knife and a ballpoint pen in my shirt pocket before a British military officer escorted me to the main desk.

"Kay Bee Sulaiman," I said to another of the stoic carbon-copy receptionists. "I'm here to see Mr. Thomas Clermont, please."

The receptionist picked up the phone, speaking briefly to someone on the screen I couldn't see before he hung up and laced his fingers together primly. "I'm sorry, Mr. Sulaiman, it appears you haven't an appointment. If you'd care to make one, I'm sure . . ."

I was getting pissed off. "Call him back and tell him I'm a close personal friend of Elias Somerton. I really think Mr. Clermont would like to see me."

"Sir, really now. I . . ."

"Just do it."

The receptionist regarded me with disdainful eyes for a long, hostile moment. When he set the phone down the second time, he said icily, "Mr. Clermont's offices are on the third floor, to your left. The sergeant will escort you."

Clermont didn't keep me waiting in his outer office, not even long enough to make a point. When he opened the door to the waiting room, he looked haggard.

"Sulaiman," he said shortly. I stood up.

"Hullo, Tommy—"

He cut me off. "We can talk in my office," he said, turning on his heel and walking off.

I followed him down a corridor, offices on either side with no names on the door. The hallway terminated at a medium-sized office, its door likewise blank. Inside, the room was strangely barren of any personal items. He closed the door carefully behind us. The desk was uncluttered, no photos of family, no personal mementos or paintings on the wall. A room to meet people from the outside, sterile and safe. Clermont sat down behind the desk, and I sat in one of a pair of chairs so unused, the new smell had yet to wear off the fabric.

"I came to take you up on your offer, Clermont."

"What offer would that be?" His eyes were spiritless. No doubt the room was thoroughly bugged.

"I want to interview one of Nok Kuzlat's prisoners. The Brit who was arrested yesterday, Nathan Mitchell."

He didn't react. "I'm sorry, that's not possible."

My eyes narrowed. "I thought you said you could arrange it so I could see anyone I wanted being held by the Khuruchabjan authorities."

He stared at me, his face devoid of expression. "You misunderstood me, Mr. Sulaiman. In any case, the welfare of British nationals is the concern of the British government, not GBN News, nor yours. I'm sorry, it is simply impossible for you to see Mr. Mitchell at this time."

His voice was completely neutral, the practiced tone of a diplomat. It didn't match the hollowness in his eyes. The same kind of troubled look Mitchell had worn on camera the night before.

There was something missing here. "Is it you won't, or you can't?" I insisted. "You *know* I know who he is. What the hell's going on, Clermont?"

The arrogant, disdainful man I'd talked to in Heroes Square was gone. He looked tired and shaken. He sighed, his eyes drifting around the barren room to avoid looking at me.

"Unfortunately, Mr. Mitchell suffered a heart attack shortly after his arrest," Clermont said in a dull voice. "He died early this morning. His Majesty's government is making arrangements with the Khuruchabjans for the return of the body to England."

My skin chilled. "And I'll just bet the coroner's report is going to say any unusual marks on the corpse were from some overly enthusiastic first aid, right?"

Clermont's eyes bored into me. "Mr. Sulaiman, I really have no idea what you're implying."

"That a fact. And you don't know anything about a microflake, either?" I put as much scorn and skepticism into my words as I dared.

He stood up. Strangely, he was not angry. "Mr. Sulaiman, I don't think we really have anything further to discuss."

I stayed seated. "You know I don't have it. You know who had it last. And you know why Mitchell was killed, if that's even his real name." He walked toward the door, as I added quickly, "Talk to me, Clermont, maybe we can help each other. I don't want to have to keep nosing around until someone tells me something."

He stopped with his hand on the doorknob, his eyes averted. "I would strongly advise you to desist from this line of questioning."

"Or what? I'll end up having a heart attack, too? Or maybe a fatal 'car accident' like Khatijah? Who killed Mitchell?"

He didn't open the door, turning to face me. He wasn't angry.

He was scared.

"Listen to me, Sulaiman," he said in a near whisper. "You're in over your head, you haven't any idea what you're involved with. As a representative of His Majesty's government, I feel obliged to give you some advice. You're a reporter, that's fine. Report whatever news you want. But you're not a police detective. So keep your mouth shut and your eyes open, that's all. *Don't get involved.*"

He was sweating, his eyes darting around the room again, clearly wary of saying too much, or too little. "Too many things are going wrong, and people are starting to be hurt. I don't know where you get the idea that journalists are immune to bullets, but if you keep shoving your way around, you're going to find out very quickly you can be hurt, too."

"Is that a threat?" I said quietly.

He stared at me. "No. It's a friendly warning. Sticking your nose where it doesn't belong is going to get it cut off, and other people killed, good people." He sounded desperate. "People I'm responsible for. People I care about."

I stared back at him. "I got dragged into this mess against my will, but I'm not going to be scared off now. Talk to me, Clermont," I pressed.

For a moment I thought he might. He hesitated, shaking, his face bloodless under his tan, turning it an odd shade of gray.

"My sources are kept strictly confidential, Clermont. I swear you can trust me. Journalists are capable of keeping secrets, too, you know; probably even better than you can."

He laughed, a harsh bark that sounded like a groan.

*"Talk to me . . ."*

He shook himself, as if struggling to wake up from a bad dream. "Go home, Sulaiman," he said in a low voice. "Get on the next plane out and go home."

"No."

"Then you're a fool."

He opened the door, and I followed him as he walked stiffly down the short corridor.

"Clermont . . ."

He opened the outer door, and spoke to the uniformed British officer. "Please be so kind as to escort Mr. Sulaiman out of the Consulate," he said before turning around to walk away without looking at me, his spine tense.

I was very cordially and graciously tossed out of the building, left fuming with impotence at the polite, iron refusal to allow me back in to speak to Clermont's superior.

When I got back to the hotel a flock of intrepid tourists bused in on an obscure tour group were blocking the doorway with the usual glut of baggage, all quarreling at top volume with the harried desk clerk in a tongue I'd have guessed was either Punjabi or Urdu. No doubt Halton would have known which, I thought sourly.

The two shadows I'd needled had been replaced with a new pair of shadows infesting the lobby, tucked behind their newspapers. The freelancer friend of Carl's was also waiting nervously in the lobby for me, standing up like a jack-in-the-box when I stomped in.

"Sulaiman? GBN News?" he asked with a jittery smile.

I stuck my hand out automatically to shake his. "You the

new optics guy?" I had to raise my voice to be heard over the noise.

"Yeah," he said, hesitated, then added, "I mean, actually, no."

"Come again?"

"I'm sorry, I got a conflict. I can't cover for you. I'm really sorry . . ."

"This is kind of short notice, kid," I said, not pleased. "Think you can recommend somebody else?"

He grimaced, uncomfortable. "Ummm, well . . . not really."

Then I understood. I wasn't going to find *any* optics man in Nok Kuzlat. In a business where people only survive by taking care of each other, this was most unusual. A few seconds later, I discovered that the optics kid hadn't been frightened off by threats. He simply knew I wasn't going to be around long enough for him to work for and if *he* wanted to keep on working in Khuruchabja himself, he wouldn't try, either.

"Mr. Sulaiman." The Khuruchabjan in the colonel's uniform shouldered his way through the gaggle of angry tourists and strolled over to hand me a large, single-paged document. I was being pinged: PNG, persona non grata. "Your visa into Khuruchabja has been revoked. You are expected to leave this country no later than tomorrow morning or you will be arrested as an illegal foreigner suspected of espionage."

I scanned the paper quickly. In both Arabic and English, it spelled out clearly, "Yankee Go Home." When I looked up, the optics kid had faded away. A few of the tourists were staring curiously.

"This is ridiculous. Why?" I demanded. "For what reason?"

The colonel smiled humorlessly. "None. We don't need one, Mr. Sulaiman. We simply don't want you here anymore."

"Clermont's behind this, isn't he?" I cursed.

The colonel looked offended. "The Khuruchabjan government does not need approval or permission from the British to expel any undesirables from our own country," he said indignantly.

Maybe not. The order sure got here goddamned fast if Clermont was behind it.

"I'm going to file a formal protest with my government and with my news bureau," I warned him, frustration making it hard to speak.

He shrugged. "As you like," he said, unconcerned. "Just be

on that plane tomorrow morning." He didn't bother to add the *or else* as he took a step back, saluted me sardonically, and left.

The two watchdogs smirked at me over the top of their papers as I headed for the elevator. Once in the room, I did a quick extermination sweep with the Raid, pried the recording chip out of my belt with a fingernail and wired it into the PortaNet.

At least I could replay the conversation with Clermont, listen to the words again for anything hidden in them, maybe run it through a voice-stress analyzer, *anything* . . .

Except there was nothing on it but static.

I stared at the Net uncomprehendingly, then checked the chip again with a growing sense of dread, just to make sure I hadn't screwed up, but the Net was working okay.

There was nothing wrong with either my PortaNet or the chip. It had recorded all right, but there was nothing on it except a steady hiss of white noise.

I vibrated with sudden anger. The rage I'd been keeping in check for so long took over, a mindless white haze of fury, and I found myself standing breathless and exhausted half an hour later. The hotel room was completely trashed. Feathers drifted from torn pillows, the curtains hung in shreds. I was drenched in sweat and panting, grinning like a maniac but with no trace of good humor left to account for it.

Let CDI pay for the damage, screw them. I shook the broken glass off the bedspread and began calmly packing my bags in the middle of the wreckage.

# NINETEEN

I had a peaceful dinner at the hotel restaurant overlooking the beautiful rooftops of Nok Kuzlat. After I'd finished, I took the PortaNet out under the bright stars to sip strong coffee and make a private call to Arlando, top scramble.

I had expected him to show more enthusiasm after I'd poured everything out I could about the faked attempted assassination and Halton's "heroic" rescue, the strange circumstances surrounding Somerton-Mitchell's death, Clermont possibly being behind getting my visa pulled.

Most of the conversation was in the cryptic tongue used between journalists. Even so, for some reason I held back on spilling my guts about actually *cracking* the microflake at Ibrahim al-Ruwala's little computer-hacker club, or the circumstances surrounding the untimely death of the Sheikh's wife. I also didn't bother going into much detail about Halton's suspicions over his employer's intentions for him.

Arlando sat unresponsive until I was finished.

"You got anything on clip, Kay Bee?"

"Like what?"

"Like the so-called assassination attempt? Any way to prove it wasn't just what it seemed? Can you trace who the poor schmuck was they set up? Interviews with witnesses? Hard documentation of *any* kind on this Mitchell guy? Who he really was or who he was working for? Or Clermont? *Anything?*"

"No." I was reluctant to say it.

"Then you've got nothing. Allegations and hearsay are not a news story. You know better than that."

"Come *on*, you know something fishy's going on. This place is like a firecracker with the fuse going. I can *feel* it!" I couldn't believe it. "You're not going to even try to follow up on this, Arlando?"

He frowned and shook his head. "Not without something a lot harder. *Responsible* journalism, Munadi. We don't do yellow sensationalism, okay? So you got your visa revoked, big deal. It's an occupational hazard, happens all the time. You've done what you were supposed to do. Now get on the plane and come home."

I stared at him with my jaw hanging open, speechless. "You haven't just been blackmailed, Arlando," I finally blurted out. "You're *collaborating* with those bastards. I can't believe it! Who's side are you on, anyway?"

His stony expression didn't waver. "Your side, whatever you believe right now. Listen to me. You're tired and upset. You're not thinking straight and you're losing your objectivity. You're no good there, so get on the plane tomorrow and come home."

"But . . ."

"Get the hell out of there, Kay Bee." He didn't raise his voice. It was much scarier that way. Suddenly, I *was* scared. "Just get on the goddamned plane and get your ass out of there, you got that?"

"Got it."

"Good."

I didn't sleep well that night.

The puddle-jumper going out of Nok Kuzlat to Cairo only stopped once a day, scheduled tomorrow for ten-thirty in the morning. If I missed it, I'd have to wait until the next day, which meant arguing with the authorities about my visa from inside a jail cell. I decided to leave for the airport six hours early, entirely too familiar with small Middle-Eastern carriers' idiosyncrasies, and nervous about a screwup. I'd rather be half a day early than a single minute too late.

The front desk rang the room to say they had my ticket at the desk and a taxi waiting as I snapped the last latch on my PortaNet. I grabbed my suitcase on the way out the door. Even while I was being ignominiously kicked out of the country against my will, I was still very glad to be going home.

I signed the bill without bothering to check over the extensive itemization, adding that there might be additional charges after the maid went up. The dark-eyed night clerk frowned; not even the two 500-Khuru rial notes I laid on the counter alleviated his apprehension. He rang for the bellhop before scurrying off to investigate the damage for himself. No doubt it would be added retroactively to the bill, along with a few more inflated items in reprisal, but that was just fine with me; CDI was paying for it, anyway.

I glanced around the lobby for the pair of shadows, but they were nowhere to be seen. Except for the sleepy-eyed bellhop, the lobby was deserted. That didn't necessarily mean anything.

At four-thirty, the air was cool, a pearly-gray sheen in the early morning sky. The traffic was light, lethargic pedestrians on the streets returning from predawn mosque. An old man leading two tasseled and heavily burdened camels weaved his way around cars parked with scattered disorder against the curb, on the sidewalks, sprawled half in the street wherever their drivers had abandoned them for the night. Leaving early would avoid the rush-hour destruction-derby.

The taxi driver had already transferred his spare tire into the front passenger seat. His taxi doubled as a rolling 7-Eleven, and the open trunk was near-full with various crates of illicit merchandise he sold on the side to supplement his taxi earnings. He was having trouble rearranging the goods to make room for both me and my luggage. The bellhop had taken my single small suitcase three yards and set it down on the sidewalk, waiting pointedly for a tip before shambling back into the hotel.

I had the PortaNet strapped to my shoulder, drumming my fingers against its case impatiently as the driver explained apologetically, shifting this box of powdered orange drink, that carton of AA batteries, when Halton materialized from the shadows of the hotel's shrubbery. I didn't see him until he touched me on the arm, scaring the bejesus out of me. I muffled a shriek as I recognized him.

"Well, hello, John," I said, pouring as much contempt into my voice as I could. "Come to see me off? How thoughtful of . . ."

"I think I'm in trouble, Kay Bee," he said quietly.

The taxi driver finally slammed the trunk of his taxi shut, and looked at us expectantly.

"Ain't that too bad," I sneered, hating myself for it. "You're no longer my concern, isn't that what you said?"

He stood with his back to the driver, his eyes obscure in the early morning light leeching everything of color. "I can follow the taxi," he said, as if he hadn't heard me. "Have the driver stop anywhere, before you get out of the city limits, but tell him to go on to the airport."

"Forget it, Halton. My visa's been yanked. If I miss this plane," I said heatedly, "I'll be thrown—" The words died as he pulled open his jacket.

Somebody had shot him. Blood covered the front of his shirt in a dark shiny stain.

"Please," he said, closed the jacket and vanished.

I got into the taxi and started for the airport.

He was not my lover, I reminded myself. I didn't have any obligation to him. He was not my friend, either. He wasn't even a human being, for shit's sake. It's just a biomachine, an artificial fabricant spy, I didn't have to involve myself in this crap anymore, I'd done dood my duty, I didn't have to risk getting tossed in prison or even worse, I was *outa* here. The Old City wall loomed ahead in the fragile morning mist.

"Stop here," I said impulsively and leaned over the front seat, peeling off rial notes without bothering to count them. "I want you to go on to the airport and put my luggage on the plane to Cairo for me. If anyone stops you, you tell them I left on a bus headed for the American military post at Sa'deqi, okay? You didn't see anyone else, and you don't know anything else. You understand?"

The driver was staring at me, eyes pale in the rearview mirror, nodding quickly. I shoved the thick bundle of notes in his hand.

"Come back to the hotel tomorrow. If you've done what I've said and kept your mouth shut, there'll be four times this for you there." That would give me twenty-four hours. I hoped. I grabbed my PortaNet, glancing through the back window as I cracked open the door. "*Rah*," I said—"Go"—and was out and crouching in the shadows as the taxi took off.

I cursed under my breath, hugging the walls as I trotted hurriedly down the alleyways, turning at random. I hadn't the foggiest notion of where I was, and if Halton didn't show up, I was going to have a hell of a time getting out of here. Turning a corner, I spotted a tiny coffee bar, elderly men just from mosque slouched at the tables outside, down hunting jackets over their qaftans against the morning chill. They blinked rheumy eyes at me as I slid into the smoky interior.

I walked to the far end of the counter, where I could watch the door. Before I'd gotten halfway through ordering a coffee, Halton came in. "Let's go," he said, grabbing my arm and hustling me out the back way. We jogged through more mazelike alleys. It seemed just as aimless as my route had been, but I knew Halton couldn't be lost.

The alley terminated in a small square bustling with men setting up their fruit and vegetable stalls under a ramshackle covered bazaar in preparation for the day's open market. With Halton's hand still tightly clamped around my forearm, we walked quickly to a garage at the other end. Inside, two young men dressed in blue coveralls and black grease glanced up from the open engine of an ancient Yugo three-seater. I recognized one of Ibrahim's numerous cousins. Wordlessly, he nodded, jerking his head toward a key hanging from a hook over the tool counter.

Halton snatched the key and we left. A few blocks later, he pushed open the door of a nondescript apartment house set in a complex of project-like apartment houses, all grim, barren and reeking of poverty. A single flyspecked light bulb hung in the entrance hall, doing little to brighten the rickety stairway leading up into the gloom.

For someone who'd just been shot, Halton looked pallid, but not out of breath. I was the one winded by the time we reached the garret floor. Halton slid the key into the lock, and we walked into the tiny room.

A narrow bed had been shoved against one wall, unmade and obviously well slept in. A Pakistani calendar three years out of date hung on the wall, adorned with the holoprint of a kohl-eyed movie starlet barely covering her modesty with misty-focus veils. A gravity-fed sink dripped in the corner, staining the chipped porcelain with rust from the converted gasoline-can water tank bolted to the wall over it. Clothes were piled in a heap in one corner. Dozens of books in Arabic, a few in French and English, lay scattered about, and a desk made from bricks and scrap-board supported one of the most ancient personal computers I'd ever seen outside a museum. A modem had been rigged to it, the wire running out the single window, where it had been spliced into a phone line. A few pieces of clothing fluttered from the wire to disguise it, unconvincingly, as a laundry line.

Halton stood immobile, listening. I could feel him trembling through the hand still clasping my arm. He looked suddenly exhausted, and released me to sink heavily down on the narrow bed. Moving slowly, he unzipped his jacket, peeling it gingerly off his shoulders.

The whole front of his shirt was soaked with blood, still damp. He hadn't been shot that long ago. Three small rips in the shirt showed where the bullets had gone in, a direct hit to the chest. He should have been dead. Blood smeared his shaking fingers as he tried unbuttoning his shirt.

I shook myself, and squatted down to help him. "Jesus Christ, Halton, we gotta get you to a doctor . . ." I said, my own fingers fumbling from the oozing slickness. The fabric clung to his skin as I peeled it gently away from the wound.

"Not necessary," Halton said thickly. "He missed the heart."

I used the shirt to wipe away the clotting blood, then stared, astonished. It looked like he'd been shot with an Eclipse, all right, the shells' backlash gouging babyfist-sized holes out the front of his chest. But the bullet wounds had already begun puckering over, inflamed pink skin sealing the punctures shut. The scar tissue over the wounds writhed like maggots burrowing underneath.

I felt like I'd just stuck my hands into a nest of cockroaches, and shuddered away from him. My skin crawled, twitching in witless revulsion. I found myself pressed back against the primitive desk, gulping air through a constricted throat. I threw the shirt away from me and wiped my stained hands together in reflexive horror.

Halton reacted as if I'd slapped him. "It's only nanos, Kay Bee," he pleaded. "That's all, just the nanos . . ."

We stared at each other while I shuddered, then pulled myself back under control. It was just so unnatural, perverse. "Jeesuz," I spat out. "Takes a lickin' and keeps on tickin'." Not my best, but it was the only way I could deal with it. My media-art education was wasted on him anyway; he didn't have a clue what the hell I was talking about. "Who shot you, Halton?"

He shook his head. "I don't know." He grimaced with pain

as he reached into the pocket of his discarded jacket, and held up a single slipclip. "I hoped you'd help me to find out."

I sat down in the room's single chair, pushing the small computer to one side to open out the PortaNet. Halton watched from behind me as I slid the slipclip into the playback flat screen.

Halton hadn't wasted *his* education, however. He'd stripped the HoloPak down to essentials, redesigning and rewiring his assortment of flyeyes into hidey-holes and corners of Larry's private rooms, triggered into individual feeder Paks by motion sensors. If he couldn't be there personally, his own private security system could. I wondered if this had been for Larry's benefit, or some newly developed sense of self-preservation.

This Pak had been covering the hallway leading out from Larry's playroom, filming from a strange angle, a fly on the wall. For most of the clip, we were entertained by the lopsided figures of military messengers stomping self-importantly along the corridor, servants dusting furniture, a flock of berobed elderly men walking slowly, heads down and muttering to each other as they came and went, a shot of Larry skate-boarding along the long hallway. Then the clip cut from a security guard in uniform schmoozing one of the veiled cleaning women busy ignoring him while vacuuming along the walls, to Halton walking in front of three other men. The light had shifted, and the tiny digital numerals in the lower corner indicated the time had changed from late afternoon to well after midnight.

Larry came out of the games room, shut the door and turned. He was dressed in his usual casual clothes, and didn't look as if he'd been to bed. He seemed mildly surprised to see the other men with Halton, but not afraid.

"Damn," one of the men said quietly in English. The flyeye recorded it, but His Excellency didn't seem to have heard.

"What's up, John?" he said, the flyeye picking up the sound perfectly. "I thought you—"

Halton withdrew an Eclipse from under his jacket and shot Larry point-blank in the chest. The Boy King's arms and legs jerked out from under him, his expression dumbfounded, and he crumpled to the floor.

I looked up from the playback, gaping at Halton. His face was ashen. "That's not me, Kay Bee," he said, shaken.

The Halton on the screen bent over Larry's body, stripping

the clothes from it quickly and efficiently while one of the men behind him withdrew a bundle of army uniforms from under his robes. "Hallway's as good as inside, I guess. Hurry up," he said in a clear American accent. The voice seemed familiar. "C'mon, c'mon . . ." Halton stripped off his jacket, and pulled the uniform on quickly. He took the second uniform and began dressing the corpse.

An alarm went off, shrilling in the background. "Right on time," one of them said, glanced at his watch, then turned to look behind him. The flyeye picked up his face clearly.

It was Cullen Laidcliff.

Halton had finished dressing the dead king in the second army uniform, picked up the Eclipse from the floor and stood up, facing the three other men calmly, the gun in his hand hanging limply by his side.

"Ready?" Laidcliff said to the one on his left.

"Yeah," the man said, and reached over the body to take the Eclipse away from Halton. The fabricant looked at the weapon indifferently, making no move to protect himself as the man shot him.

In the chest. Three times.

"It wasn't me, that *can't* be me . . ." the Halton behind me murmured. His knuckles had gone white clenching the back of the chair. I thought any moment he'd crush the cheap aluminum tubing.

A second later, one of the three had discarded his robes, and I got my second shock. It was His Excellency, Lawrence Abdul bin Hassan al Samir al Rashid. He was gazing down unemotionally at the two fallen bodies as the man with the Eclipse twisted the barrel, then stepped across the body to fire a wide-angle blast into the dead Larry's face, ripping it to mangled, unrecognizable shreds. He turned, and the flyeye recorded the second man's almost delicate features clearly, green eyes, sandy hair.

"We can't have two," he said, and shot another wide-angled discharge into Halton's face, nearly tearing the head off the body. Halton's legs jerked; then he lay still, the obliterated face oozing dark blood and brain matter. Now there were only two anonymous dead army soldiers lying on the hallway floor.

The muffled sound of shouts, someone pounding outside an unseen door, could be heard over the still-blaring alarm. The sandy-haired man slapped the Eclipse into the living Larry's hand, and grinned. "That's it, you're on, boy," Laidcliff said sardonically. "Make it look good."

His Excellency slowly twisted his head, looking straight into the flyeye. An impassive cold drifted through the inhuman eyes, a glacial look I knew so well sending shivers through me. I rubbed the hairs standing up on my arms.

"We are being recorded," the replacement Larry said, his voice colorless.

The two other men twisted around, staring up at where the fabricant was gazing, their faces crystal-clear on the clip. "Son of a *bitch*," the sandy-haired man cursed. He snatched back the Eclipse, raised it and shot out the flyeye, the tape going dead.

"I didn't kill him, it wasn't *me*," Halton was still whispering to himself. He looked as if he were in shock, pale and stupefied.

"Not unless you've got nanos that can scoop brains back into your skull, Halton," I snapped at him. "Calm down, get a grip on yourself." He blinked rapidly, focusing slowly on my face. "Well, this is another fine mess you've gotten me into," I said, and rubbed my eyes with the palms of my hands.

"Kay Bee . . . ?"

"Just tell me what happened, everything you remember," I prompted him.

"A little before one A.M., His Excellency sent me to wake al-Hasmani, the Minister of the Interior." Halton took a deep, shuddering breath, visibly settling down. "The old man he plays . . . played hologames with. Al-Hasmani has his apartments connected with the palace, off the main building, so that he can be summoned whenever His Excellency was in the mood for a game. It's in a secured area, only family members or trusted ministers. No one could have gotten in or out of the palace at that time of night without either my approval, or by direct order of His Excellency."

Halton sat back on the bed, his panic quelled. He distractedly picked through the pile of clothing on the floor and selected a shirt from it, shaking the wrinkles out to examine its size.

"I arrived at the Minister's offices and woke his secretary. He said the Minister was in the lavatory, he'd be back soon, that I should wait. I sat down to read a magazine. The Minister is an old man, he sometimes needs a few minutes. The secretary got a phone call, spoke in Markundi. He left immediately afterwards on an errand, said he'd return in a moment. I looked up when the door opened a few minutes later. The man in the clip—not Mr. Laidcliff, the other one, I don't know who he is—shot me. Twice."

Halton's forehead creased with concentration, his hand flitting to his chest, where three inflamed punctures in his skin continued their bizarre wriggling. "I stood up, and fell facedown on the floor. The man pushed me onto my back with his foot, stood over me and shot me a third time. My nanosystem took over, and he must have thought I was dead."

Halton glanced at me, troubled, apologetic. "He had the Eclipse set for narrow fire, or I would be dead. He missed the aortic arch by millimeters, nicked the pericardium. The sternum gladiolis deflected most of one shot, but the other two ruptured the left anterior segmental bronchus and part of the left upper lobe of the lung. The nanosystem is triggered by acute trauma, drops me into a catatonic state, no heartbeat, no breathing, temperature drops, barely any brain activity, while it—"

"Don't bother me with the technical details, Halton," I interrupted. "Just get on with it."

He nodded. "I don't know how long I was unconscious. When I woke, I could hear the alarm going off in His Excellency's palace. I still had severe damage, but by then I was able to walk. The Minister's secretary was standing in the doorway; al-Hasmani was behind him. They both started screaming when I stood up. I pushed them out of the way, and ran back toward the main hall, where I had left His Excellency. I heard Mr. Laidcliff coming with another man. They were talking about the timetable being screwed up now, about the other fabricant, and Larry's body and mine, about finding out fast where the damned flyeye led to."

Halton hesitated, swallowed. "That's when I knew His Excellency was dead," he said quietly. The thought seemed to cause him some pain. I waited for him to go on.

"I'd set up the flyeye for the main hall, to transmit short pulse to a feeder Pak in one of the anterooms off the corridor. I headed directly for the Pak, got the clip out of it just as they traced it." He had calmed and pulled the rumpled shirt on. It was slightly too small; his fingers bumbled with preoccupation in buttoning it.

"I had the clip in my hand when I turned; there was Mr. Laidcliff and the other man." His eyes were remote, remembering precisely each detail recorded in his eidetic memory.

"They seemed surprised to see me still alive. They didn't say anything. The other man started to bring the gun up. I picked up a chair, threw it through the window and jumped out. There was a tiled roof two stories below. I landed on it, ran as far as I could, jumped the space across to the roof of the next building. It was dark, the spotlights were turned on, someone began shooting. The perimeter stone wall has electrified razor-wire. I had to climb over it to jump onto another roof . . ." He focused back to me in the present. "I ran," he finished simply.

"Straight to me."

"Yes."

"The first place they'd probably expect you to go."

He looked stricken. "What else could I do, Kay Bee?"

I didn't have to answer that. The next second, he was off the bed, pushing me behind him. Footsteps pounded up the stairs, and a voice yelled out in Markundi, fists banging on the door.

"Sirs! Sirs! You've got to get out of here, *j'ahkzhil* . . . !"

Halton jerked open the door, and a barefoot teenaged boy in a T-shirt hastily thrown on over torn jeans appeared, out of breath from his flight up the stairs. "Yousef's been arrested," he babbled. "Mahmud telephoned they came to the garage and took Yousef Mahmud got away but they've gone to Yousef's mother's house she's sure to tell the police about Yousef's room we're all in a lot of trouble if you don't leave. *Hurry—*"

The boy had pushed into the room, hysterically jerking the modem wire from the window and gathering up the antique computer equipment. He stopped, his arms full, as Halton said quietly, "It's too late. They're already here."

Many running feet were thumping up the steps, and the shouts of men echoed in the street below. "Oh, Allah, what am I gonna do . . ." the kid wailed, and ran out the door. I heard a clatter as he jerked open another door, and flung the equipment in, my last sight of him a pair of frightened eyes before the hall toilet door slammed and the bolt slid into place.

Halton shoved the door to the garret room shut, dragged the bed in front of it, then toppled the brick-and-board desk over that. I had popped the clip out of the playback reader, stuffed it into my pocket and started breaking down the PortaNet.

Halton had the window open. "Leave it," he said, looking down.

"You've got to be joking," I said unbelievingly. "*You* may be able to stop speeding bullets and leap tall buildings in a single bound, but not *me*." Someone began yelling, pounding on the door.

Halton grabbed me tightly by the waist, yanking me to him and said, "Hang on," and out we went.

"Hang on" was right. Seven stories up. I had my legs wrapped around his middle, my arms squeezing so hard around his neck I thought I'd strangle him. He carried me piggyback, his hands and feet scrabbling frantically for purchase as he descended the outside of the building.

Above us, the door was kicked in. I heard angry shouts and the sound of wood shattering and broken glass. Now Halton was panting. I could feel his sweat against my cheek. A gun cracked below us. The bullet smacked into the wall by my face, powdered brick splintering.

I saw what he was planning a split-second before he did it, just enough time to scream "NO!" and squeeze my eyes shut. He turned like a spider monkey in the jungle, pushing off from the wall as he leaped across a four-meter-wide chasm to the next building. He hit the opposite wall with a pained grunt, his hands grabbing onto a window frame. I almost lost my grip around his neck as we jerked to a stop, hanging five stories above an alley by one hand.

"Oh God oh God oh God," I was gibbering. Halton had one arm around his back, keeping me from falling as I tightened my grasp on his neck, the other hand clawed over the lip of the window. We dangled there for a moment before his legs skittered up, dragging the rest of his body along with mine in through the window.

Falling onto the floor, we rolled to our feet as a woman shrieked. We ducked as she threw a pot at us. I caught a glimpse of open-mouthed children as the pot splattered dark gooey stew against the wall. Then we were out of the apartment, sprinting down another stairwell, out into a garbage-strewn back alleyway. Halton boosted me by the ass over the fence, and we clambered down the other side, landing in muddy goat-urine puddles.

"*Yah!* There they are, get them! *J'ahkzhil!*" somebody shouted, and we were off and running again. Halton knew his way through the twisting suuqs and alleyways probably better than the Khuruchabjans chasing us. I just trusted him to get us the hell out of there.

I ran until my lungs were seared to ash, ran until my ears burned, then stumbled along blindly. I ran until I staggered and fell, unable to take another step. I smoked two packs a day, I'm overweight and over forty—what the hell did I expect? My heart pounded in my ears, and I felt so sick I didn't care any longer if they shot me or not.

A second later, I was curled up with Halton's arms around me, my back against his injured chest, his knees crushed against either side of mine. The smell of musty wool was the only sensation my brain was registering other than sheer agony.

I heard men shouting, and Halton turned my face away, pressing my cheek into his sweat-dampened shirt, his hand covering my face. My hands gripped his arms locked around me, my nails digging into his flesh. I took huge gulps of air, whimpering, my eyes squeezed shut, tears leaking past the lashes. I heard his heart thumping wildly, his quick breathing in my ear as his head bent over mine.

"Shh," he said. "Shh." He sounded like an anxious father hushing a newborn infant crying in his arms.

A machine gun sputtered nearby, making me jump. Halton clamped his arms tighter around me. I was sobbing, more from pain than terror, into his chest, sweat running in hot rivulets down my heaving sides. Three cars roared by, men shouting in anger and others in alarm. Another burst of gunfire echoed, but now in the distance.

Then it got so quiet, I could hear a bird trilling.

"Praise be to Allah, Lord of the Worlds . . ." I heard a quavering voice say.

Opening my eyes, I found myself staring at a pair of dusty ankles, callused feet shod in leather strip sandals.

"The Beneficent, the Merciful, Owner of the Day of Judgment . . ."

Folded piles of woven rugs were stacked to either side of where we crouched, hiding beneath a market stall. An old man stood trembling in front of us, the veins of his exposed calves under the hem of his qaftan standing out in knobby relief. I was recovering my breath, although I shivered uncontrollably, exhausted.

"Thee alone we worship, and Thee alone we ask for help. Show us the straight path . . ."

I continued looking up, meeting the eyes of a frightened

rug seller, eyes wide over his gray beard. My mouth began to move as I stared at him.

"The path of those whom Thou hast favored . . ."

"Not the path of those who earn Thine anger . . ." I heard myself saying it with him, words my mother had repeated every day of her life. I prayed with the old man, my heart never more into it as it was at this moment. "Nor of those who go astray."

The old man stared for a moment at us, then smiled, broken teeth stained black with tobacco.

I thought he was beautiful.

# TWENTY

Halton had taken us the long way back to the same market square only a few blocks from the run-down apartment projects. We had been lucky in all the confusion that the instinctive reaction of the frightened vendors when confronted with military police was to instantly lie, point and babble and send them careening down the wrong streets and away from the open market. After their fear had subsided, curiosity and excitement bubbled to the surface. The old rug dealer held an energetic conference with the other merchants, his social importance suddenly elevated by our choosing his particular stall to duck under, and therefore his responsibility as well. After some rapid debate, we were hustled off to find Mahmud, the friend of Ibrahim's arrested cousin, hiding in his sister-in-law's house off the market square.

He was still dressed in his grease-monkey coveralls, oil stains on his knees and elbows matching the ingrained grease in the lines of his hands. His older brother, Majid, went through the motions of the coffee service, his eyes a little glazed. My hands shook so badly as I took the little cup from him, I nearly spilled it. I sipped methodically, then passed it on.

"They came to the garage with a holophoto of Mr. Halton," Mahmud said, his voice low. "Then they arrested Yousef, said he had conspired with Mr. Halton. They said that Mr. Halton was a traitor and an American spy who murdered two of the palace's Personal Guards and tried to assassinate our Sheikh." Mahmud looked up at Halton, eyes troubled, silently asking him to deny it.

"I'm not a traitor," Halton assured him. "I didn't kill anyone." I noticed he left out the part about being a spy, but Mahmud visibly relaxed, satisfied.

"How did they know to come to the garage?" the older brother asked, aggrieved. So, it was *his* garage. It was still a good question.

Mahmud looked at Halton thoughtfully. "It had to be King Kong," he said finally. "That's how you knew, too, wasn't it?"

Halton nodded.

"Who?" I asked.

Mahmud grinned, less shaken now. "There's a lot of people on-line who aren't part of the Young Islamics," he said. "Not the core, anyway. Ibrahim had the computer network set up so that if one database terminal was found and confiscated, the others couldn't be traced. All the modems were connected by low-pulse codes, not really using enough energy to alert anyone looking for them. But if one was broken into, the rest would automatically self-destruct all the links. That protected our equipment."

I passed him the tiny cup of coffee; he sipped and passed it to his brother before going on. "Abdullah wrote a dormant virus into all the programs sent over our lines. If the connection is broken, after the computer network goes back on-line recognition codes have to be entered before trying to communicate again. If they aren't, the virus goes active and immediately destroys all the files in that database. That was to protect our information. That way, no one could steal our files."

An elaborate, but probably necessary precaution.

"Each of us only knew of the others through telecode names, even family members. That was to protect *us*. No one knew where the other databases were located. Even Ibrahim doesn't know where they all are. Except everybody knew about King Kong."

"And King Kong was . . . ?" I had already guessed.

"His Excellency, Sheikh Lawrence Abdul al Rashid." The royal computer hacker, who else?

"King Kong only knew one of us by our real names. Yousef. Ibrahim was very angry when he found out; he threatened to expel Yousef from the group. But about the only thing King Kong was ever interested in was hologame programs—I don't even think he knew much about any of the political communications. That's probably the only reason Ibrahim let Yousef stay."

"But it still left a weak link in the chain."

Mahmud nodded glumly. "Yeah."

And dollars to donuts, his good buddy and playing partner, al-Hasmani, had been monitoring King Kong's on-line conversation for some time. No one else would have had either the access or the expertise to know what Larry was doing.

Except Halton.

I thought about telling Mahmud about Larry's death, then decided that might be a bit touchy. "Mahmud, I'd be very careful about communicating with 'King Kong.' "

He snorted wryly. "Tell me about it!"

"What I mean is, if King Kong comes back on-line, I would have serious doubts it's really His Excellency." That's about as close as I could come to the truth. Mahmud looked surprised, then chagrined as if he should have thought of that himself.

A woman appeared in the doorway, Mahmud's sister-in-law, I would have guessed. Her eyes over the yashmak were frightened. Her husband didn't admonish her for breaking into a meeting of men, but stood looking at her.

"Ibrahim's been arrested," she said, almost whispering.

"*Yah sa'laam, khalah damm'aq,*" Majid breathed. Loosely translated it meant "We're knee-deep in shit now."

"The computer network?" I asked Mahmud sharply.

He shook his head. "No way. Khalid got Yousef's computer out before the police got to the room," Mahmud said firmly. "When he broke the modem connection before entering the code, it's a signal. Everybody else's disconnects. They won't be able to trace anyone through our network." He looked glum. "Ibrahim is Yousef's cousin. They're probably just arresting all of Yousef's relatives—that's what they usually do."

Majid turned to us grimly. "But too many people know about the garage. It's only a matter of time before they come back." He left unspoken what I already knew. If the military police found us here, they would throw his entire family in prison, tear down his garage, destroy his house and, if he was lucky, summarily execute him. We had to leave.

Majid looked at his wife, and she nodded wordlessly. "My wife will take our children and go where it is safe. I must stay.

Everything must seem normal. If I leave also, when they return they will know something is wrong."

"They'll have the airports covered by now," Halton said to me.

"Maybe a public bus, or a train, if we disguised ourselves . . ." I was thinking as quickly as I could.

"I have another car," Majid said reluctantly. "Not a great car, but it runs. I bought it from my uncle in Shardamuzh. You can go there; he will know this car. It's near the border; you could leave it at his house. He'll take you to where you can walk across." He smiled, his first smile that evening, and a bleak one at that. "At least I may be able to save my uncle's car."

He left to get the key, speaking rapidly to his wife as she followed him.

"I'm sorry, Mahmud," I said to the boy. "I've put you and your family at risk with my problems."

He shrugged, false bravado barely covering his worry. "This is Nok Kuzlat," he said. "You learn how to live dangerously, or you don't live. We're strong. We'll be all right."

I inhaled, gauging my next words.

"Mahmud," I said, "I have to ask you to do something else, something which is very important and also very dangerous." Cautiously, he glanced up at me. He had no reason to do me any further favors, but after a moment he nodded sharply.

"I left my PortaNet at Yousef's place when the police came."

"They've probably taken it, then," Mahmud said.

"Check. If they haven't, take it to Ahmat; he knows how to run it. If they have, find a TVN reporter called Jefferson Carleby." I took out the call card from my wallet and fished the slip-clip out of my pocket, knowing I was trusting him with my only hope for protection. "Tell him to blip this to the GBN Cairo Relay station, and tell the man on the other end, 'Sailor's in trouble, make a multiple SDB.' You got that?"

"GBN Cairo Relay, Sailor is in trouble, multiple SDB." Mahmud's English would do. He was nodding earnestly.

"It's important, Mahmud, not just for us, but for you and your country. But if you don't get this blipped to Cairo, Halton and I will die, and so will anyone who's caught with it." Mahmud's eyes looked as if they'd fall out. "We'll make a run for the border. You've *got* to get this sent to Cairo, Mahmud. Then destroy it."

"*Wijh-hya'at abuuya*," Mahmud said. On my father's life. He stared down at the slipclip in his hand as if he were holding a scorpion with a hangover.

Hopefully, my smartass American friend would be working the Cairo station, and would know to relay the clip into several of GBN's "safety deposit boxes" scattered around the world, each spinning off another copy of itself before it moved on, growing fractally at random. It was the only hope I had of taking out any sort of life insurance for Halton and myself.

"We'll owe you a big one, Mahmud," I promised him.

He pushed the clip into his pocket and nailed me with a hard look. "Damn straight," he said. Nothing for nothing, not here.

Majid returned with a couple of striped qabah and two frayed kaffiyehs over one arm. He handed me a key with a paper tag tied to it with a twist of wire as Halton pulled on a qabah, then adjusted one of the kaffiyehs around his head.

"It's a Volvo, behind the garage," Majid said. "My uncle's name and address is on the vehicle registration in the glove box."

Mahmud had the curtain over the little window lifted by a finger, glancing down into the road. "*Fi'ih râagihl bzkarrah*," he whispered. I skittered over to the side of the window, looking out sideways. He was right, there was a man outside. He stood in front of the house, looking at a sheet of paper in his hand, then up at the house. He disappeared from our view as he walked up the stairway and knocked on the front door.

Mahmud and Majid exchanged looks, then woodenly, Majid left the room. We crowded near the doorway, barely breathing, straining to hear the low voices. For a second, I had the bizarre image of ourselves as we might have been, in a different time, different place . . . a different people. Jews trembling behind a door, yellow stars sewn on their clothes, as the Gestapo officer interrogated the landlord.

Majid returned with a relieved smile. "It's the father of the Toyota Tri-star coupe with the bad differential," he said to Mahmud. "His son asked him to pick it up for him today." He turned to Halton and me. "My wife will show you out the back way. Be gentle with the transmission, I didn't have time to repair it." He hesitated, then said, "*Mazha-sala'ama.*" Good luck.

That we were putting him and his family in extreme danger

wasn't mentioned. It was the will of Allah and a matter of honor now, our fate bound with theirs.

*Please, God,* I prayed. *Whichever God You are.*

The change of clothes was a poor disguise, but we wrapped our faces with the kaffiyehs, and walked calmly to the garage. I wished desperately I could have been born about two inches taller. I felt like Mutt and Jeff next to Halton, and conspicuous as hell. Around the back, we found the ancient little Volvo, its gray hulk dented and rusted. The doors squealed as we got in, and had to be slammed hard to catch. The floor was littered with trash, empty fast-food wrappers, a child's comb with most of the teeth missing, empty Coke bottles and bits of anonymous things that didn't bear close inspection all soaking in a greasy puddle of black motor oil.

A large square of sun-faded green-and-gold plastic had been glued over the dash and decorated with plastic flowers. Someone's souvenir from hadj, a quote of Qur'anic scripture. "A Pilgrimage to the House of Mecca is a duty unto Allah for mankind, for him who can find a way thither," it read. "Whence soever thou comest forth, turn thy face toward the Holy Place of Worship, and where soever ye may be, turn your faces toward it. Fear not but Me, and so that I may complete My Grace upon you and ye may be guided."

I giggled, more from nerves than humor. "I don' care if the hot winds blowerin', s'long's I got mah plastic Qur'an sittin' on the dashboard of mah carrrr . . ." I sang off-key. Halton looked at me quizzically as he jiggled the key into the ignition. Before his time, I guessed.

Majid was not fastidious, but his skill as a mechanic was evident as the engine started up with only the slightest of grumbles. An ancient CD disc whined to life in the car's music deck, a woman's ululating voice quavering its way through the halftones of an Arabic love song. I winced and turned it off as Halton slipped the old car into gear and eased it out onto the alley behind the garage.

Halton drove, since his ability to navigate through Nok Kuzlat was superior to mine. It was slow maneuvering down the narrow back streets, through the maze, out on the ring peripheral road leading north out onto the long stretch of brown highway.

"Oh, shit," I said. We had stopped at the tail end of a roadblock, uniformed soldiers with machine guns wandering up the long column, bending over to peer into cars and interrogate the drivers. We couldn't turn around without calling attention to ourselves. Stupid, stupid, stupid, I cursed myself silently. Of course they'd have cut off the roads. I unwrapped the kaffiyeh from around my head, knowing it wasn't going to work.

"They're going to have holophotos of us, Halton," I said, glum.

Halton leaned down and rubbed the palm of one hand in the pool of filthy oil while adjusting the rearview mirror with the other. Quickly, he dabbed the blackened grease onto his face.

"What the hell are you doing?"

"Utilizing available resources in the attempt to improvise a credible disguise," he said, then ran his oil-stained hand through his hair, using the remaining teeth on the child's comb to slick it down on his scalp. He hesitated for a moment, considering, then wiped his hands artistically on the qabah.

He turned to look at me, smiling grimly. The grease had filled in crevices in his skin, accentuated the stubble on his face. He sucked in his cheeks so that his features were sunken, the bones of his jaw in sharp relief. I gasped as he bugged his eyes out, one of them slowly twisting away.

"Jesus Christ, Halton. More of your goddamned nanos?"

"No," he said. "Just good muscle control. What do you think?"

You ever see that 1931 classic black-and-white where Dr. Jekyll starts grimacing and turns into Mr. Hyde right before your very eyes without the aid of high-tech FX? What Fredric March did for Hyde, Halton was doing for Marty Feldman in *Young Frankenstein*. Halton's own mother wouldn't have recognized him, even if he'd had one.

I glanced at the soldier casually sauntering up to the window of the car three ahead of us. We didn't have a lot of time.

"Lovely." I shuddered. I wasn't going to be able to do likewise; my membership at the local health club didn't include facial aerobics. "You got a fake mustache in your pocket for me?"

"Get in the back seat."

I crawled over the back, and crouched down. There was no blanket or tarp, nothing to hide under. "Great idea," I said. "*Now* what?"

"Lift up on the seat. It comes up."

I did, and was surprised to find he was right. "How'd you know that? Never mind . . ." *Get it out of books.*

The space underneath was for storing tools and oil cans, a

round indentation showing where the spare tire took up the back end of the little trunk behind me. I rifled quickly through the assorted junk, but there still was nothing I could use to hide under. I risked looking over the front seat toward the soldier strolling up to the car in front of us, before dubiously eyeing the filthy small space.

"Damn, damn, damn!" I started tossing everything out of the storage space onto the floorboards of the back seat, and tried crawling in. It was not made to accommodate human bodies, and I was no contortionist anyway. There was no way I could shut the seat completely over me, no matter which way I scrunched.

Halton had turned the music back on and was already rolling the window down on the car. "What is happening?" he demanded in loud Markundi over the wailing song, his peasant's accent the right mix of respect and aggravation. "Why have you stopped everyone?"

I couldn't see more than a thin line of light through the crack between the storage space and the seat. I held my breath, not trusting myself to make a sound. Which was just as well, since the exhaust fumes seemed to collect in the small nook and I was in imminent threat of asphyxiation.

"We're looking for a dangerous criminal," I heard the soldier saying. "An American spy who tried to assassinate His Excellency."

"Allah preserve him!" Halton breathed fervently.

"Turn that crap down," the soldier demanded with the contemptuous tone of a superior to an inferior, "and let me see your license."

*Oh, shit.* I heard Halton scrabbling around in the glove box, and the rustle of papers.

"This is only the registration," the soldier said.

"But this is me. Look here, here is my name, Salim Fareed—it says so right there." Halton was jabbing at the paper. *Thwack, thwack.* "See here?" *Thwack.*

"You need a license," the soldier insisted.

"A license, a registration, they are the same, only pieces of paper. Why do you need my license when you can see with your own eyes this is my registration?"

"Show me your identification," the soldier persisted, his tone growing angry.

"All right, here. Does this not also say I am Salim Fareed?" There was more rustling of paper, a long silence.

"Where are you going?" the soldier sounded less antagonistic.

"To my sister's house in Zaqihab," Halton answered promptly, his voice quavering slightly with anxiety tinged with injured pride. "It is not far. I did not think I'd need papers just to go so little distance to see my sister." Halton sounded like a querulous, stubborn peasant whose honor had been wounded. No doubt the exact impression he was trying to give the soldier. "I don't know anything about American spies. I am an honest man. You can search my car, then, for your American spy, if you must . . ."

*Christ, Halton, don't overdo it!*

"Look there, you can see I am a respectable mechanic. Look at my tools. I must take all my tools and extra oil to help my nephew rebuild an engine. Look here, see—look at these cans of oil." The springs in the front seat were squeaking as Halton turned toward the back where I was hiding. No doubt he was waving a hand toward the jumble of cans I'd tossed out onto the floorboards. I willed myself to shrink, regretting my earlier wish to be taller, as Halton babbled on. "He says it is a cracked block, I know about cracked blocks on engines because I am a good mechanic, that is a very difficult job, a cracked block . . ." He was starting to sound slightly hysterical.

"Okay, okay," the soldier snapped, bored and irritated. He had no interest in the fine points of engine repair. "Go on through."

The car rumbled around me, and we lurched away. I held my breath as long as possible, until little black spots whirred around the edges of my sight. Taking a deep breath, I started coughing immediately, doing my best to stifle the sound.

"Stay down," I heard Halton say, and choked quietly to myself. The bumps in the road translated to bumps on my head and hips and shoulders and knees and elbows, as the loose seat rattled and banged.

A few miles later, he gave the all-clear, and I hauled myself painfully over the front seat, sliding down to cough.

"Next time, I drive, *you* hide in the back seat," I wheezed out.

"I wouldn't fit," Halton said solemnly, keeping his eyes,

both of them now, looking straight ahead on the road in front of him. His face had relaxed back into his normal features.

"Jeez, Halton." I let it go. "What the hell did you give him for identification, anyway?"

"A hundred-rial note."

I laughed.

Halton didn't. "It won't keep him long," he warned.

"You think he believed you?"

He shrugged.

I rubbed my aches and stayed quiet as we drove across the desert. The cars thinned out after the roadblock. Shardamuzh was two hours from Nok Kuzlat, a few miles from the border with the only one of its neighboring countries semi-friendly to Americans. Mile after mile, we squinted through the harsh sunlight and tails of dust kicked up by the vehicles occasionally passing on either side of the two-lane road.

Desperadoes on the run, I thought. I yawned, the heat making me drowsy against my will. If this were a movie, I let my thoughts wander sleepily, this part would definitely end up on the cutting room floor. I had to fight to keep my eyes open.

Then suddenly, an ancient rusting pickup with a kneeling camel tied to the bed of the truck drew up alongside the Volvo, the driver risking life and limb to overtake us as a large tractor-trailer coming in the opposite direction honked in protest. My hands clawed into the dashboard, and I caught a glimpse of the wild-eyed kamikaze trying to pass us. If Halton had been a true, self-respecting Khuruchabjan, he would have sped up, refusing to give an inch of road, and forced the pickup to either fall back behind us or get creamed by the semi. But Halton was a civilized driver, tapping his brakes to make room for the careening pickup wobbling beside us to cut in front.

The pickup lurched over ahead of us at the last moment, its bumper inches away from ours. The semi's horn blared indignantly as it passed, huge wheels churning up sand from the shoulder of the road. The pickup driver waved a defiant fist out the window, middle finger extended in the universal gesture at the semi, at us, at the world in general—who knows? Sand and pebbles pinged off our dust-coated windshield. The adrenaline had snapped me completely out of my heat lethargy.

I stared at the camel in the pickup now in front of us as it chewed methodically, small brown eyes glaring down the sides of its bulbous nose thrust in the air. Somehow, it reminded me of the late king. I started to giggle.

"What?" Halton looked over at me curiously.

"I can't believe we got away with it," I said lamely, not able to explain my sudden impulse to laugh.

"We haven't yet," Halton said. Ever the killjoy.

We passed several routes leading away from the main road, before finally taking one that looked about the same as the others. The green and white road signs were half-obliterated by blowing sand and rusting bullet holes made by passing shepherds for target practice. I had to trust Halton's sense of direction. We drove over the rise of a small hill to find Shardamuzh in the distance, a squat, mud-brick town.

As we got closer, I could see where old bomb damage had taken its toll on the village: bricks piled haphazardly at the foot of crumbling walls, empty windows and doorways. The modern bridge which once spanned the river had never been repaired after being hit by a bomb; by the extent of the damage, I'd guess a French-made Feu-du-Dieu spearhead missile. Instead, a rope suspension bridge not made for motorized vehicles hung between the pilings, being traversed by cars anyway.

"Nice," I said, watching the bridge sag dangerously under the weight of an ancient two-door Skoda being pushed across by several men. "Good thing we stop here."

Halton asked directions to Majid's uncle's house, and we were directed toward the edge of town, down a dirt road, past what looked like an automobile graveyard, to a small house. Several cars in the three-sided garage were on blocks, chickens clucking and scraping the sandy oil-stained ground around the hulks. Except for the chickens, the place seemed deserted. We parked the Volvo, and Halton turned off the engine. My ears buzzed in the sudden quiet.

A fairly new sandjeep was parked in the back, and a dark, mustachioed man leaned against it, smoking a cigarette. He looked up indifferently as we came toward him.

"We're looking for Salim Fareed," Halton asked.

The man nodded his head at the house, wordlessly.

We thanked him and walked toward the house. It was very small, no more than a couple of rooms, and I knocked on the wooden door.

"Come on in!" I heard someone call out cheerfully in Markundi.

Halton stopped short as I pushed open the door.

My eyes adjusted to the dim light to make out Cullen Laid-cliff sitting in a chair at the far end of the room, grinning over the barrel of a very nasty-looking Eclipse special.

"Don't," I heard someone say softly behind me, and knew that someone was holding what was probably the Eclipse's mate to Halton's head.

"Hello, honey," Laidcliff said, voice oily. "I hope you've been faithful . . ."

# TWENTY-ONE

**W**e'd done this routine before, in Nok Kuzlat, where Sheikh Larry's wife wound up sprawled on a derelict cafe floor lit up like the lead dancer in *Swan Lake*. The question asked was pretty much the same as well, only this time, Laidcliff had plenty of time.

The green-eyed, sandy-haired man held his Eclipse pressed firmly against Halton's temple. He leaned in to breathe into the fabricant's ear, "Next time I *can't* miss, asshole," and chuckled as if he'd said something funny. Halton didn't react, his eyes on me.

"How'd you find us?" I demanded, trying to keep the fear out of my voice as Laidcliff tied my hands behind my back. "How could you possibly get here ahead of us?"

"It wasn't hard," Laidcliff said patiently. "You just can't trust these sand-niggers to get anything done right, too busy raking off bribes and buggering each other. So we set up scanners to automatically trace every license plate going out of Nok Kuzlat. Ran 'em through the police computer until something popped up as a little too coincidental." He jerked the last knot painfully tight. "Besides, a hundred rials just doesn't go as far as it used to."

He was grinning as he turned me around and pushed me down into a chair. "We paid a little visit to your friend Majid, asked him a couple of questions. With a little chemical persuasion, he was more than happy to tell us anything we needed to know."

My stomach sank. "Is he dead?" I had to keep my voice low to stop it from quavering.

"Not when we left," Laidcliff said from behind me, sliding my arms down around the back of the chair and anchoring my wrists to the seat. I was staring at Halton standing motionless, the sandy-haired man keeping his grip tight, the muzzle of the gun pressed hard against the side of Halton's head forcing it slightly to one side. "But I can't vouch for what the Khuruchabjans will do with him." He didn't much care, either.

"Once we knew where you both were headed"—he came around to kneel down to tie one of my ankles to the leg of the chair—"we just hopped on a helicopter to the Qurzon airbase, picked up a sandjeep and got here, oh, about an hour before you." He grinned up at me. "You missed lunch."

"Where's Salim Fareed?" I didn't want any more people hurt, helpless to stop it.

"Taking a nap." Laidcliff nodded toward a closed door. He patted me gently on the cheek. "Don't worry about him, sweetie. When he wakes up, he's going to have the honor of claiming he killed two American spies. A hero of his country." The last pat ended up a hard slap. I yelped more from surprise than pain.

Halton didn't blink.

If we had been in a *civilized* country, Laidcliff explained, he wouldn't have had to waste all his best pharmaceuticals on a bunch of camel jockeys. He could have made it painless and easy for me, a few questions asked under the correct dosage of gentle chemical persuasion, followed by a quick lethal shot in the arm to go flying out on. But they were all used up, all except the lethal stuff, and there wasn't a corner Thrifty to trot down to and pick up some extra truth serum. In primitive conditions, one just has to improvise, doesn't one? He chortled happily, enjoying himself as he tied my other ankle to the chair.

"That's all you really needed me for, wasn't it, Laidcliff?" I said while he tightened the ropes. "Bring in one Halton Larry would trust so another could assassinate him, right?"

Laidcliff laughed, jerking the ropes painfully taut.

"Wrong, sugar," he said, and stood up. "The original plan was exactly how we laid it out. Larry needed a watchdog, and we had a custom-made puppy wrapped up just for him. We wanted somebody stupid to bring him in. You were our man, so to speak. The only reason we needed you was to give Halton a good excuse to get close enough to the Sheikh when the time came to 'rescue' him.

"If you'd just stuck to the rules, nobody would have gotten hurt. But then Halton started acting wonky, and you brought down some extra illicit baggage and were nosing around where you didn't belong. You were so sure there was some sort of conspiracy going on, you helped stir one up on your very own. Too many things were going wrong, and that changed the whole game plan."

"I don't have the microflake anymore," I said. Not that that was going to stop him from beating the slipclip out of me.

"That's okay." He grinned, and pulled the flake out of his pocket to brandish it. "I do."

Now I knew who had killed Somerton.

"See, by the time old al-Hasmani gave us a call, gibbering about weird microflakes and flying tomatoes and computerized spirit messages taking over their data networks, we'd already decided we ought to get our butts over here and do something to straighten this mess out. Larry was getting a bit too uppity anyway. He somehow got himself convinced he was some kind of holy messiah about to stomp the shit out of us, so we just went to Plan B."

Laidcliff leaned forward, speaking in a conspiratorial stage whisper. "But you want to know something really funny? The flake's worthless. We didn't have to cancel the kid's ticket after all."

I must have looked very bewildered and idiotic with my mouth hanging open, and Laidcliff's delighted laughter confused me more.

"You want to know what's on this thing, honey?" He held it under my nose. "Garbage. The kikes sold the ragheads a bunch of phony AI plans for infrafusion bombs that won't work. The kid had *nothing*! The rest of the flake is just empty space."

He thought this was outrageously funny.

Laidcliff didn't know we'd already cracked the flake.

*Gabriel hadn't liked the accommodations . . .*

It hadn't just rewritten its own programming, it had abandoned the flake altogether. That's why Halton couldn't coax it back out again; it simply wasn't there anymore. It had dumped itself wholesale into Ibrahim's computer-bulletin network system, escaping into the electronic ethersphere to search for its Chosen One. Gabriel had almost found him, too, but Laidcliff had just assassinated the object of the AI's fondest dreams. Gabriel was still out there, futilely looking for the Mahdi.

And it had been the Israelis who had created Gabriel.

*Shalom, Gabriel.*

I thought that was rather humorous myself. I laughed.

Laidcliff didn't enjoy sharing the joke. He backhanded me. Then he got down to the rough stuff.

"Where's the slipclip?" Laidcliff said for the third time. I was crying. I have a tendency to do that when someone beats the shit out of me, but I don't confuse pain with stupidity. Or bravery. I knew as well as he did that if I told him, he'd kill me, then Halton. Then anyone else he could make me name. The idea, see, was that eventually he could convince me dying would be a pleasant reward for talking. I wasn't so sure he couldn't, either.

Halton hadn't moved when Laidcliff started in. The sandy-haired man held him in a firm throat-lock, the Eclipse never moving a fraction of an inch away from Halton's head.

But someone else had made the mistake of thinking he could hold him like that. Maybe the man's arm got tired. Maybe his attention wandered, distracted by the entertainment. Once, only once, as I sagged against the ropes and wept, I saw Halton go very still, radiating an aura of serene tranquillity. The next time I screamed, I heard a muffled crack, and a hiss of breath being sucked in for a curse.

Laidcliff spun around, and said, "Johnny, stop . . ." in a strange, friendly voice. Halton froze into complete catatonia. Laidcliff's muscle-boy was holding his wrist, and had to extract himself very carefully from Halton's rigid grip.

"Jesus, fuckin' son of a *bitch!*" the man swore loudly, grasping his injured hand and dancing around the room—"I think he *broke* it"—before he remembered a minor detail. He stopped, and gently pulled his Eclipse out of Halton's paralyzed other hand. Then he glared at Laidcliff resentfully. It was the second time the fabricant had gotten the better of him, and he didn't like it.

"I told you fabricants were fast, Ed," Laidcliff said scoldingly. "You let your guard down. You're damned lucky you're not dead."

"Shee-it," the man sneered, but eyed Halton suspiciously anyway as he slipped the Eclipse back into his armpit holster with his good hand.

"Now, get away from him," Laidcliff said. Ed was holding his injured wrist against his chest gingerly. "Go get that wrapped—find a split or something—there's a first-aid box in the jeep. I'll call you if I need you." He sounded disgusted.

"Mr. Laidcliff . . ." Ed said dubiously.

"Don't worry about it. He *can't* hurt me." Laidcliff showed teeth in a vicious smile. "The sound of his master's voice."

Unconvinced, Ed left. Alive.

Well, hell. That trick wasn't going to work twice. Halton stood immobile, muscles quivering. A line of sweat trickled down from his forehead, dripped from his nose.

"What have you done to him?" I said, lisping wetly through swollen split lips.

Laidcliff sniggered. "Nothing. Nothing at all. Nothing he wasn't designed to do in the first place." He walked over to Halton, put a hand on the fabricant's shoulder and said sweetly, "*John*neeeey."

Halton straightened up slowly, and looked at Laidcliff, terror in his eyes. Laidcliff *tskked* and shook his head ruefully. "What's the matter with you, boy? You've been behaving very strangely. Young Lawrence of Arabia is dead, right?"

"Yes," Halton croaked. "He's dead."

"So his contract is null and void, terminated, isn't it?" Laidcliff's voice was smooth, obscenely soothing. Halton heard *terminated* and visibly trembled. He didn't answer, and Laidcliff went on. "And what happens if the subject a fabricant has been allocated to becomes deceased? . . . Johnny?"

"The legal ownership of the fabricant reverts automatically to the manufacturers," Halton said, reciting brokenly. He was staring at me, horrified.

"Who is . . . ?" Laidcliff patiently prompted him.

"CDI."

"And I am . . . ?"

"My CDI trainer," Halton said, swallowing and turning his eyes slowly to look at Laidcliff. "Sir." It hurt him to say it.

"That's right, very good." Laidcliff smirked. "So now why don't you be a good boy and tell me where the slipclip is, Johnny."

Halton stared at him, unblinking. "I don't know, sir," he said thickly.

Laidcliff's eyes narrowed. "Where's the clip, John?" he said, the smirk and his arrogant condescension vanished.

"I don't know, sir," Halton repeated.

"Johnny. Don't lie to me," Laidcliff said in that same tone that had first paralyzed Halton. "Where is the slipclip?"

"I don't know, sir," Halton repeated again. There was a faint edge of panic in his voice, which I'm not sure Laidcliff heard.

Laidcliff simply stood in front of the fabricant for a long moment, studying him. I was sweating in terror, sure Halton would crack in a second. I forced a contemptuous laugh.

"You asshole, Laidcliff," I jeered, forcing his attention back to me. "Are you really so stupid you think I'd trust my one and only safety net to a goddamned spook fabricant, especially one you were so inept in planting, it was *obvious* you'd set me up?"

Oh, that got his attention back, all right. And Halton stood there watching helplessly as Laidcliff decided I should repent my words a little. It was primitive, but it was effective.

He didn't rape me, nothing so simple as pushing a protruding part of his body into a concave part of mine. But he didn't need to. He wasn't planning on keeping me around afterwards, so he didn't have much concern about permanent damage. He was careful not to create an injury I could actually die from. Not then. Not at first. He systematically broke several of my fingers, pausing between screams, then expertly squashed my nose into pulp.

He'd just gotten started. He took his time, carefully, methodically, and crushed in one side of my face, knocking a couple of back molars loose. I blacked out when he smashed my cheekbone. He took a break, waiting for me to wake up. When the pain pushed me unwillingly back to consciousness after a few moments, he had stepped back, panting slightly after his exertion. I wept and drooled blood.

He cupped his hand under my chin, forcing my face up to look at him. "I won't ask you what you've done with it, sugar," he said to me. "That was just to remind you where you stand. Now, we'll get serious." He smiled and wiped a tear away from my one good eye with a gentle finger. The other eye had already been buried under swollen flesh. I couldn't help whimpering.

"I didn't blind you," he said, "because I want you to watch something . . . just watch, and think about it."

He walked around Halton like a dog sniffing a strange object. Stopping behind him, he pondered for a moment, then kicked the back of Halton's knees so that the fabricant dropped to the floor.

"Hands on your head, Johnny," he said mildly.

Halton complied wordlessly.

Laidcliff sat down in the chair, one ankle propped on his knee, and fished a knife from his pocket. Ten inches long, black-and-chrome, unadorned and functional, he flicked the switchblade out, then eased the blade back in with his thumb, then—*click*—out, slide it back in—*click*—out, over and over. A schoolboy bully's toy. Halton just watched, kneeling on the floor, his hands laced behind his head like a POW.

"You damned fabricants," Laidcliff sneered finally. "You all think you're so fucking great, don't you?"

Halton had to clear his throat before he answered. "No, sir."

"Don't get cute, Johnny."

"I'm not, sir."

"You think you're so superior to us poor humans with your fancy designer genes." Laidcliff grinned, amused by his own pun. "Anything the best of us can do, we've just wired into you—add water, shake and presto, instant Superman." He tapped the blade of the knife under Halton's chin, just grazing his neck. "You're not all that extraordinary, Halton. You're not jack shit. You know that, *boy*?"

"Yes, sir," Halton whispered.

Laidcliff was jealous of fabricants. I know I'm stating the obvious, but I had some time to sit there and watch, part of my brain wondering how someone like Laidcliff could be so goddamn *mean*.

I had considered Laidcliff as just some CDI lackey, which was true. He had risen as far up the ladder as he was competent to go, but not near far enough to satisfy his ambitions. Laidcliff was the kind of man who carries around an inferiority complex his whole life, hiding it behind a façade of bravado. He remained obsequious to his superiors while hating them, and took out his frustrations as much as he could get away with on those further down the chain. It was bad enough when it was just other people like himself, then along came the fabricants. I mean *I* was envious of fabricants—who wouldn't be? But it seemed to have sent Laidcliff over the edge.

He had been nasty the brief time we'd met, but not necessarily sadistic. I had written him off as unimportant, and forgotten about him. He obviously had not forgotten my little jest at the Orbital airport.

Normal legal constraints, like going to prison for the rest of your life for murdering someone, are usually enough to keep the minor Laidcliffs of this world at least socially tolerable. His anger and inadequacies had just been exacerbated by fabricants; they were better at doing the job *he* had wanted to do. He was being supplanted. I could understand that fear. Then I'd added insult to injury.

Now the restraints were off: Laidcliff was allowed to do whatever he wanted, and in his furious resentment there were no holds barred.

"I can't believe you actually fucked this ugly bitch," he said, and turned his head to grin at me. And laughed at my astonishment. "You did, didn't you?" He *was* guessing after all.

"Yes, sir."

Laidcliff *tsk-tskked*. "And I'll bet you just gave it away for free, too, didn't you? After all the really nice girls I set you up with, you learned nothing." Halton flinched. Laidcliff pimping for his fabricant hadn't been one of the secrets of his love life that Halton had revealed to me. "You at least have a good time, Johnny? Was it good for you?"

Halton was shivering uncontrollably. "Yes, sir."

"Monotonous, isn't it?" Laidcliff suddenly said to me, and mimicked in a high voice, " 'Yes sir, no sir, anything you say, sir.' Got about as much imagination as roadkill." He turned back toward Halton. "Johnny . . ." It was that tone.

Halton's face was bloodless. "Yes, sir?"

"You have become psychologically contaminated."

"No, sir . . ."

"John Halton. Indigo. Faubourg. Salicylic. Pentacle. Go."

At first, nothing happened, then Halton's eyes rolled up in his head, spine arching as he fell backwards, twitching violently.

"What are you doing to him!" I screamed, appalled.

"*I'm* not doing anything to him." Laidcliff laughed. "He's doing it to himself." Halton was drooling, hands clenching and unclenching in uncoordinated rhythms, muscles spasming. "Every fabricant has built-in fail-safes. The nanos. Fabricants have them from before they're even born. It's so closely fitted to their fancy tailored genetics, they can't tell the nanos apart from their biological bodies. They don't even know how many different designs they've got floating around inside them."

He jerked a thumb at the convulsing fabricant. "That's a little army of nanos marching around inside his Grade-A Prime brain, been sitting there waiting to be called into combat all this time, and he never knew it," Laidcliff said conversationally as Halton's feet drummed the floor. "They're triggered by the specific sound of my voice repeating a preset sequence of words." He grinned, holding up two fingers like a pair of scissors. "Snip. Snip. That's the sound of thousands of little nanos cutting neuron connections. Snip—whoops, there goes another one. Snip . . . Like Alzheimer's in fast motion. Snip . . ."

"Stop it, stop it!" I was screaming. "*Stop it!*"

"Hey, no problem. That's easy." He turned, and said in the same tone, "John Halton. Stop."

Halton shuddered violently, then lay still, staring at the ceiling, his chest barely moving, struggling for breath as if he'd forgotten how his lungs worked. I was sobbing, hysterical, while Laidcliff idly played with his switchblade and enjoyed the show.

"C'mon, Johnny," he said finally, nudging the fabricant with his boot. "Get up off your backside."

Clumsily, Halton managed to roll himself upright, sat on the floor, feet tucked under him, and slowly locked his fingers behind his neck. He swayed, slightly unstable, his head bowed, his face glazed in a stunned expression.

"So, sweetheart," Laidcliff said softly to me. "Honeybun, sugarlips, you ready to tell me what you did with the slipclip, or would you rather watch me slowly turn your toyboy into a vegetable?"

"You bastard." I knew he'd gotten to me, knew it was hopeless. Fucket. There wasn't going to be a miracle, no cavalry riding over the hill to save us at the last minute. It was pointless and stupid to keep on resisting when we were just going to die anyway. Maybe by now it'd be too late. I could hope. For a moment, I gave up, trying to figure out how to make a deal, trade the slipclip for quick, painless deaths for us both.

Laidcliff was watching me, gloating over what he saw in my face. He didn't see Halton raise his head. He didn't see the single tear run down the fabricant's cheek, or see his mouth move, a silent desperate *No*.

Jeez, the amount of trouble and abuse people will tolerate for someone else that they wouldn't put up with for two seconds for themselves. "Go fuck yourself," I said weakly. I wasn't up to being creative at that moment. Laidcliff was, however. He ripped my shirt open, buttons pinging on the floor.

There was a point when he'd backed off to admire his work, knife clenched in one bloody fist, where I thought *nothing* could be worth this. Blood was pooling between my legs from the decorative calligraphy he carved on my breasts and stomach. I had to fight to keep thinking this horror would have to be over sooner or later. If I could hold on, I could go knowing I'd screwed over Laidcliff and the CDI on my way out.

Laidcliff took a breather, sitting back to smoke a cigarette while I hung tied in the chair and bled, crying quietly to myself. The acrid smell of bad Turkish tobacco hit my shattered nose with almost as much pain as the torture. I hadn't had a smoke for hours. I wanted one, even in the condition I was in.

*Goddamn it*, I thought, disgusted with myself. *I really gotta give it up* . . . and almost laughed.

Halton stayed kneeling on the floor, stonelike. Laidcliff decided it was the fabricant's turn again. "Even if I didn't need you at the moment for leverage, Johnny, we'd have to terminate you, anyway—you understand that, don't you?"

Halton slowly looked away from me to stare at Laidcliff.

"Fact is, you've brought this all on yourself. It's your own fault. You fucked up, boy. The minute you started giving away company secrets to little Miss Perilous Pauline here during that really classy dinner up on the Station, you dug your own grave."

He leaned over to wipe the blood off his switchblade onto Halton's shirt. The fabricant didn't flinch.

"That's right, we heard you. You don't have little nanocameras in your eyes"—he turned momentarily to look at me—"although I like that idea. We'll have to think about that one"—then back to Halton. "We've got a complete range of other ways to keep tabs on our little boys and girls. You broke the rules, Johnny. Your whole design went under review, and you know what? Your entire series had to be yanked. You were all flawed and unreliable. Contaminated. Defective. Malfunctioning. You understand, don't you?"

"Yes, sir," Halton said. He didn't bother to hide the despair in his voice.

*Don't believe him, John. Don't believe him* . . .

But of course, he had to. He was designed to.

Laidcliff was a puppeteer, too. Halton was his own personal

bubblehead. Hey, Lew, you think *you're* audio-sensitive, watch this!

Laidcliff wasn't paying attention to me; he was busy having fun jerking Halton's strings. I felt something cold move inside me, my muscles going numb, a powdery-weird sensation. Something deadly glacial, something like what I imagined a fabricant might feel, slid along my nerves, quiet and subtle. I was watching the pulse in the curve of Laidcliff's neck, feeling my legs turning to numb posts. I pressed my feet solidly on the floor, an icy, metallic snake coiling around my spine. I had no thoughts, no plan in my head. Time seemed to slow. I felt utterly calm. Peaceful.

"Johnny," Laidcliff said, caressing the word.

"Yes, sir . . . ?" Halton whispered, terrified and helpless.

"John Halton. Indigo. Faubourg. Sali . . ."

I pushed off the floor, chair and all, like I was jumping out the door of a parachute plane. I could distantly feel my muscles ripping from the strain. My mouth open as far as possible, I screamed as I catapulted into Laidcliff. I caught a quick glimpse of his startled eyes as he turned toward me before I clamped my teeth down on his throat.

I hit him hard enough to ram him off his chair. We tumbled to the floor. The chair I was tied to broke, and I wriggled frantically to stay on top of him. I felt his skin give, my teeth driving through, the bulge of his windpipe under my tongue. Distantly, I could feel my broken cheekbone rasping as the muscles of my jaws ratcheted down. The tang of warm blood bubbled into my mouth, which for once wasn't mine. My nostrils filled with it, and I couldn't breathe, drowning in the taste of his blood.

I didn't care. Laidcliff was struggling, trying to both stab me and wrestle me off him at the same time. His collapsing windpipe vibrated under my mouth as he tried to shout, only a muffled hiss by my ear. Sharp pain sliced in deep underneath my arm, and I grunted, clamped down harder. I felt cartilage cracking under my jaws. Laidcliff's legs kicked out under me once, twice, and went limp. I had my teeth buried as far as they could go into his flesh, biting harder, unable to breath, not about to let go.

I couldn't believe he was dead, I couldn't have killed him that fast, the son-of-a-bitch had to be faking . . .

"Kay Bee . . ." Halton said softly, tugging at me.

Amazed, I relaxed, letting Halton drag me off Laidcliff's

body. I retched, vomiting up blood, the pain from my broken cheek kicking back in with a dizzy vengeance. But my mind seemed unusually clear.

It was astonishing how easy it was to kill him I didn't think someone could die that quick from being throttled maybe I'd hit an artery or something . . .

But when Halton pulled me away from Laidcliff's body, I noticed there was something seriously wrong with the dead man's face. Halton had jammed both his forefingers straight down into Laidcliff's eyes, smashing through the thin orbital bones beneath them, burying his stiffened fingers deep into Laidcliff's brain. One eye had burst, like a deflated water balloon; the other dangled by the optic thread out of its broken socket as if trying to look over the dead man's shoulder.

Halton's hands holding my shoulders were sticky. Pieces of grayish brain matter mixed with his own bright red blood where the sharp edges of shattered bones had gouged the fabricant's fingers.

*If you cut me, do I not bleed . . . ?*

Halton got the switchblade and was behind me, sawing through the ropes tying me to the broken chair. My hands came free as I heard footsteps. Without thinking, I reached over Laidcliff's corpse with both broken hands to slip the Eclipse out of his armpit holster.

Ed opened the door and took in the scene in a single glance. He was smart enough not to reach for his own gun. There wasn't a chance he could get it out before I could shoot him.

"Shut the door, Ed," I said, kneeling next to Laidcliff, my crippled hands holding the Eclipse out unsteadily. I was trembling violently, the hysterical strength quickly evaporating. I could barely grasp the gun, my fingers not working properly. I had my middle finger, one of the few Laidcliff hadn't snapped, on the trigger. In a few moments, I knew I would drop it. He did, too.

He stepped inside and shut the door very carefully behind him, flicking his gaze toward Halton, then stared at me, eyes narrow, thinking. I could see the wheels turning, how to get the gun away, who to take down first, analyze the situation, take advantage of any weakness. He looked more mechanical than any fabricant.

I shot him.

That wasn't why. I shot him because I was tired and hurting, and because I knew it was likely that if I did the humane thing and attempted to take him with us as a prisoner, he would find a way to kill us. I shot him because he was inconvenient.

The Eclipse quietly made a neat, round implosion crater in Ed's chest as he thudded back against the door, amazed.

"Oh, hell," he mumbled, and died on his way sliding down to sit on the floor. The Eclipse sagged from my fingers.

I made myself watch as Halton went out and shot the unarmed native man leaning against the sandjeep, waiting patiently for the two *Americhurja* to finish torturing the enemy infidels. Through the open door, I could see the driver's face, his mouth an astonished O, before he seemed to leap backwards like a gymnast over the hood of the jeep. His legs quivered slightly and then he rolled slowly off onto the sand.

It wasn't a casual thing. Nor was it strictly killing in self-defense. We deliberately murdered them both. I knew I'd have my share of nightmares and the shakes later on. At that moment, the physical pain simply overwhelmed any emotional considerations.

Halton and I didn't spend much time in idle conversation. He checked the two other rooms, and found Salim Fareed snoring away peacefully on a tiny bed. The old man would be all right, but he was going to have a hell of a headache and a bloody mess to explain away later.

Halton also found Laidcliff's little medical kit. The son of a bitch had lied; there were plenty of chemicals left. He'd just wanted to get his jollies torturing us before he had to resort to more civilized means. Halton injected me with a small amount of painkiller, the worst of the pain dulling almost instantly.

There was little useful in the jeep's first-aid kit, bug-bite cream and Band-Aids in with a few rolls of crepewrap, one of which had already been used on Ed's broken wrist. Halton unwound it from the dead man, and splinted my shattered hands before he rolled the unconscious old man aside to strip the bed. He ripped the threadbare cloth into bandages to stanch most of my wounds, covering it with Laidcliff's shirt until we could get something better. Except for the one gaping stab under my arm where Laidcliff had cut deep between the shoulder blade and ribs as we struggled, the incisions were all superficial. I'd need stitches, but he had been careful not to cut into any vital body cavities.

With my chest and stomach wrapped tightly, Halton helped me struggle out of my ripped and bloody pants and into a pair of Salim Fareed's too-long pants and an oversized qaftan. Blood was already leaking through the bandages, but the dead men had soiled their clothes. I preferred blood to shit. Still, it was going to be interesting trying to think up explanations.

"Where now?" Halton asked as he gently assisted me into the passenger seat of the sandjeep. I was feeling a bit fuzzy from the drugs, as if the pain were being held three inches all around from my body, but my mind seemed almost abnormally lucid.

"Back to Nok Kuzlat," I said.

Halton looked surprised.

"Any country friendly to Americans is going to be friendly with CDI," I explained. "We try to cross the border here, we'll either be arrested or shot. I'm sure of it."

"You need medical help," Halton insisted. "Soon."

I could feel warm blood spreading out on my back, leaking out of the stab wound. "I know. I won't get it here. They won't be expecting us to go back to Nok Kuzlat." The words were slurred, my face oddly numbed. I could feel the break in my cheekbone grinding against the effort to speak. "Hamid's," I said simply.

Halton nodded.

We drove away from Shardamuzh, heading back toward the slums of Nok Kuzlat. I dozed off, waking when the narcotic began wearing off, a throbbing pain in my side. The clearheadedness had gone, my face one solid misery. I had Halton stop for a moment, and help me light one of the cigarettes I'd taken from Laidcliff. He had to hold the cigarette to my mouth, my splinted fingers too swollen and blue to handle a thing. I sucked the harsh smoke into my lungs gratefully. It was the first rush of pleasure I'd had all day, easing the fogginess in my head a little.

Halton was staring at me, a strange, lost look in his eyes.

"What is it? What's the matter?" I said sharply.

"Who do I belong to now?" he asked, forlorn.

# TWENTY-TWO

Halton pulled the sandjeep off the road miles outside of Nok Kuzlat, homing in on the city with his own internal sense of direction. The sky had darkened to deep cobalt, the first stars popping out. It was a bumpy, agonizing ride, but we managed to bypass the roadblock, and got to within a few streets of Hamid's.

My head pounded, the pain worse than any hangover I'd ever self-inflicted. I'd lost enough blood now that I was shivering, my skin cold and clammy. My ears burned, but I was aware enough to recognize the signs of shock. We ditched the sandjeep in a squalid area of Nok Kuzlat's districts where I knew it would be stripped anonymously bare within minutes. Then we walked to the little store.

Or actually, Halton walked and I hung on to him for dear life. Somewhere, I was conscious enough to be aware of noise in the distance, the streets in the Nok Kuzlat slums strangely dark and empty. Curtains twitched while impassive eyes followed us behind carved screens and bleak windows. They would see nothing.

Hamid took one look at me, and rushed me through the back rooms, up the narrow stairs into the family's apartment. Three other men, teenagers actually, stood up as Halton half-carried me into the family's *ma'gâlees*, and pushed me gently down on the living room sofa.

"Did Ahmat send it?" I asked.

"Hush," Hamid said, his eyes aghast as he opened Laidcliff's shirt and found the strips of cloth completely soaked in blood.

I fought to sit up, ignoring the stabbing pain in my arm. *"Did he send it?"*

"Yes, yes, all has been done as you instructed. It is sent," Hamid said impatiently. "Now lie back, my friend." He started calling Allah's name and Jamilah's with equal fervor. "Get my wife," he ordered one of the young men. The boy darted from the room immediately. The other two hovered over Hamid's shoulders, looking down at me.

"We can't stay, Hamid," I insisted. "We just need to make a phone call. We'll be gone before the military police find us." I had some half-baked plans to call GBN for help. "I can't put you in any more danger, *please* . . ."

"You are not leaving, not like this," Hamid said firmly, again pushing me back onto the sofa. He started working the blood-soaked shirt off my back. "You'll be as safe here as anywhere, God willing."

"We should call a doctor, at least," Halton suggested.

"You can't call anyone," one of the boys said. "The phones are dead."

"Dead?"

"Forget about doctors," Hamid snapped. "All the telephone lines in Nok Kuzlat have been cut, the electricity, too." Then I noticed the light came from kerosene lanterns which every house in the slums kept on hand for the frequent power outages. "The streets are not safe. The city is in chaos. I wouldn't worry about the police; they have other things to occupy their attention at the moment."

I was trying to work that one out, when his wife appeared in the doorway, flanked by wide-eyed children.

She spotted Halton and drew up her yashmak over her mouth reflexively before she realized who he was, then stared at me while holding it in place with one hand. Her eyes widened as she finally recognized me, and dropped the embroidered cloth. "Merciful Allah," she breathed.

"I'll say the prayers, woman. I need some clean cloth, a needle and thread. Hurry up!" Jamilah turned and fled, small children hugging the door frame excitedly. They hadn't seen this much activity since the Khuruchabjan civil war, which some of them were too young to remember. "You two, get Fuad and go," Hamid said abruptly to the boys. "Be careful and get back quickly."

They nodded and left as Hamid started peeling away the bloody bandages on my chest. Uh-oh. Halton read my thoughts. "I'll do that," he said. "Could you please bring some warm water?"

"Of course, yes," Hamid said, and quickly left the room, batting at the children clustered around the door as if brushing away a flock of pigeons. He bellowed for Jamilah, what the hell was keeping that lazy woman, you kids get out of the way, miserable good-for-nothing wretches . . .

Jamilah brought an armful of clean linen, probably their own towels and bed sheets, and laid them on the table next to the door. She kept her horrified eyes averted and tried to pry some of the more inquisitive kids away from the door. Hamid bustled back with a large saucepan of warm water, tugging it away as Jamilah dutifully attempted to take it from him.

"Leave me be, woman. Go and get more, make yourself useful," Hamid scowled at her, but his sharp eyes had seen how shaken she was. She glanced at him thankfully before she hurried off.

Once she had left, he began sponging the worst of the blood from my skin. "She is a good wife," he said under his breath to me, "but she is not used to this." He looked at me. "City women," he explained. "They are too delicate." For a fleeting moment, I saw the Hamid I used to know. Then he was yelling at you goddamned kids get the hell away from the door right this minute.

It was strange to see my friend so deep in his role as Old Hamid the Grocer. What had happened to Hamid the Assassin, dour and silently grim? Or maybe that had always been the invented role, and this compassionate family man had been the real Hamid all along.

But if he kept peeling bandages away, he'd shortly discover I had a secret identity of my own I'd just as soon keep. I did some fast talking, something about Halton being a medic in the Marines— Could we have some privacy? I didn't want to shame myself in front of my good friend by weeping like a child as I got stitched up. Halton was already drawing up another syringe of painkiller from Laidcliff's kit, handling the medical equipment like a pro. Hamid, being Hamid, retreated and closed the door without protest. I could hear him stamping around in the hallway issuing curt orders to hide his anxiety.

Laidcliff had done some ornate work, and it took some time for Halton to sew me up. The injection took the edge off, but he had no local anesthetic. It hurt like hell. I'm not a tough TV cowboy type, biting the bullet bravely in dignified silence. Besides which, I couldn't bite down on anything too hard, since Laidcliff had ensured I was going to make my future dentist a very rich man. All I could do was lie there, sniveling and whining as Halton got to work. I did try to hold it in as best I could after I happened to look at his stoic face, tears running down to drip off his chin as he stitched methodically.

I tried to think of other things. "You lied, John," I wheezed out. He was concentrating on his needlework. "You told Laidcliff you didn't know where the slipclip was."

"I didn't know," he said. He didn't elaborate.

"Yes, you did. You knew I gave it to Mahmud."

"He asked me if I knew where it was, not if I knew who had it." He pushed the needle through a flap of skin, trying to line it up with the other side as it oozed fresh blood. I held the fingertips of one bandaged hand against his arm, stopping him. He looked at me questioningly.

"You're so fucking literal-minded," I said. He stared at me soberly. "Thank God." I couldn't very well kiss him just at that moment, so I fumbled, my hands wrapped the size of baseball gloves, to place his chemical-sensored palm down against an uninjured area of my body. I don't know if there is such a thing as gratefulness pheromones, but he understood anyway.

The obscene graffiti Laidcliff had slashed on my chest and stomach stopped oozing blood fairly quickly after Halton had sewn the wounds shut, and all but one of my fingers were simple breaks. My face and the big stab wound under my shoulder blade were going to need some real medical attention soon, however. There wasn't much Halton could do for my face, but he packed a bed sheet against the stab wound, tying it as tightly as he could without actually breaking my ribs. Then he tied a double sling, cradling my broken hands against my chest like a pharaoh's mummy to immobilize them. That would keep for a few hours. I hoped. It would also help to camouflage my tiny, hairless boobs.

Hamid returned with two of the young men, and Ahmat. The boy's dark eyes burned with anger as he stared at me, jaw clenched.

"We did as you asked, Kay Bee," he said, voice thick. "Mahmud found the PortaNet. They had thrown it down the stairs when they found it was empty and left it, but we got it to work again. Your friend in Cairo has relayed the clip. He says it is in several places, and it will be safe. He says he understands."

"And the slipclip?"

"We burned it." He pulled out the melted casing of the thin slipclip from his pocket, the one that caused me so much trouble. He placed it carefully on the small table.

"Majid is dead," he said simply to Hamid. I closed my eyes, squeezing out the light. "He was drugged, too slow when they got the prison open. The guards shot him."

Hamid merely nodded.

"It's my fault," I said softly, staring at the charred remains of the slipclip. "He died for that."

"I know," Hamid said. He was neither going to blame me nor absolve me; it was never that simple.

A small boy, a half-naked dirty urchin much like any of anonymous thousands swarming through the back alleys of Nok Kuzlat, pushed his way through the crowd and peered in the open doorway. Hamid immediately rose, pulled the child to one side and questioned him in a low voice. The child nodded quickly, and vanished.

"The palace was taken fifteen minutes ago," Hamid said quietly. "The Sheikh cannot be found." He glanced meaningfully at one of the teenagers. The boy nodded, and slipped quietly away.

Hamid looked at me and smiled gently, the corners of his mouth tugged up under his graying mustache in a cynical lopsided grin. "The government has cut the power and the telephones," he said, "thinking that is enough to paralyze the city.

They are all like my son, forgetting the old ways." Ahmat didn't seem chagrined. He had aged since the day I'd met him, the adolescent resentment lost from his brooding eyes. "What do old men know of computers and electronics? That is for young men. The old men have other ways to communicate which have no need of electricity or telephones. But together . . ." He put his arm around Ahmat and smiled proudly at his son, leaving the statement unfinished. I could suddenly see how much the sullen boy resembled the Hamid I'd once known.

"Where's my PortaNet?" I asked Ahmat.

"Downstairs. It is safe."

I smiled, something I hadn't done for a while. It hurt. "How'd you like to keep it, Ahmat? You and your friends. How'd you like to be the first bureau chief of GBN in Nok Kuzlat?" The boy blinked; his dark eyes widened, instantly seeing the possibilities. "You film and blip your own stories, cover the news here in Khuruchabja. However you want."

"Yes!" he said fervently. "We could show the world the truth, *yah, in'shallah*; we will fight back against those who would keep us enslaved with their foul lies and tyranny . . ." I recognized the rhetoric from all Ibrahim's propaganda posters. His eyes smoldered with a proselytizing fire. I'd seen that look far too many times in the past.

I shook my head, stopping the tumble of words. "Just a few words of advice, my friend. Be cautious. Be fair." *Be objective*, I heard Arlando in the back of my head. "There is no sense in all you young martyrs being willing to die for the cause if in the end the cause has no one left to live for it. And be careful you do not become one of your own enemies in your zeal to rid the world of evil and injustice."

"I understand," he said quickly. No, he didn't; he just said the words to reassure me.

But his father did. Hamid nodded slowly, his hand firmly on Ahmat's shoulder. "We understand, Kay Bee." Ahmat wouldn't like it, not at first. But if he was lucky, he'd grow up and learn. Maybe he'd even turn out to be a good journalist.

Jamilah had returned with clean clothes, a Khuru-styled qabah tunic and Western men's pants. I shook my head. "The equipment is not strictly a gift, Hamid," I said. "In return, I need a woman's dress."

Hamid was startled, doubtful. "You wish to disguise yourself as a *woman*?"

"It has been done before by better men than me, Hamid," I reminded him. "What better way to conceal myself? They will be looking for two men, one with injuries like mine." I pointed with one finger poking out from its sling to my bruised and bloody face. "But who will see them if they are hidden behind an aba'ayah and yashmak? And if I've got two black eyes, well, that's a wife's private affair with her husband, *w'alah*, isn't it?"

Hamid looked uncertainly at Halton, who smiled tightly, and began speaking in Markundi, his accent one of the mountain dialects to the south. "I would ask for a simple man's dress as well, my friend," he said. "Something that the army guards along the border will not think unusual. Perhaps also some small packs with goods to carry, papers to show them."

Hamid was surprised, and impressed. He nodded. Yes, he was thinking, I was small and dark. A woman would not speak; my atrocious accent could be kept quiet. His lips quirked up, the audacity of the scheme amusing him. It was possible I could pretend to be a woman. It *might* work . . .

Jamilah fetched one of her older dresses, winter-wool voluminous and heavy. Hamid wouldn't allow her to touch me, however, and the two men tried to drape the henna-dyed garment around my body, fumbling around my splinted arms to get it adjusted, while Jamilah hovered by nervously. I yelped in pain when Hamid inadvertently touched my broken cheek attempting to adjust the yashmak around my ears.

"My husband, please," Jamilah said finally, in frustration. "It is not quite right. These are women's things. May I be allowed . . ."

He waved a hand impatiently, and she stepped up close to me to arrange the h'jab head scarf and thick embroidered veil across my face. Her fingers brushed my skin, and for a moment, we locked eyes. *She knew*—in that moment, she knew. Her eyes widened slightly. She nodded almost imperceptibly with the tiniest hint of a smile. I wondered if she would tell Hamid later.

I stayed in the house until after dark, sipping tea and resting until I could manage. Bulletins continued to arrive at Hamid's via his network of young men and ragged street urchins. The palace was occupied, but under siege from the army, bloody fighting in the main streets. How much Hamid had to do with coordinating the running battle, I didn't know and didn't ask.

I didn't want to be involved anymore.

I had dozed, only the injections pushing the pain far enough away for me to have slept fitfully. A little before sunrise one of the younger men drove us into the mountains in the south within walking distance of the border.

The roads around the capital had filled with people escaping the worst of the fighting, but had thinned out to makeshift camps parked along the highway shoulders. People sat in their cars listening to their radios, smoking and gossiping, mothers rocking children by camp stoves, all waiting to see if it would be necessary to flee the fighting in Nok Kuzlat any further. But as yet it was too early for refugees to begin pouring across the borders. The fighting had not reached the rural provinces, no one sure yet how far any civil war would spread. Villages stirred to life sleepily as we passed, a few lights in the windows, unconcerned.

Two miles from the border, the young man put us aboard a small bus already filled with migrant workers on their way to a day job in a neighboring country where money was more plentiful. The rickety bus bumped its way down the dirt road, stopping at the border.

The Khuruchabjan side of the checkpoint was empty, the army having abandoned its posts. Its neighbor, however, had doubled their guards, and I could see heavy armored vehicles in the early morning haze being brought up to line the narrow mountain pass. We were all brusquely ordered off the bus at machine-gun point, and Halton and I limped in line behind the migrant workers. I stayed the respectful distance behind Halton, my head down, extra clothes tied into padding around my middle to make it look as if I were pregnant.

The guard glanced at my bruised eyes, and laughed at Halton's carefully feigned surliness. He took the papers out of Halton's grimy black-nailed hand and examined our day visas, worn documents with holoflats of our faces pasted on the back. The photos were nearly obscured after they'd been carefully tarnished with grease; they could have been anyone's picture. He squinted at us, not as if he suspected the papers of being forged, but to see if we were worth the bother of hassling. My heart beat rapidly as he searched Halton's small pack, confiscating the few coins he found there. Then he waved us through to reboard the bus.

I entered Khuruchabja as a woman disguised as a man. I left it as a woman disguised as a man disguised as a woman. . . .

How's that for schizophrenia?

# TWENTY-THREE

We took the bus to the end of the line, getting off with the rest of the unwashed day workers heading toward the agricultural fields. They went in one direction, we headed in the other, and slowly walked the long miles to a relatively civilized town.

There was no American embassy in which to seek sanctuary, even if I could have trusted it, diplomatic relations having been broken yet again in the past several years. However, the UN ran a small clinic on the outskirts: twenty or so army cots crowded in a one-room hut, every one of them occupied, some with more than one patient. Halton managed to get me to it before I passed out.

The lone doctor, a young overworked Indian, clucked his tongue disapprovingly and glared at Halton in silent accusation. But he asked no questions while he splinted the fingers of both hands in a rudimentary plaster cast and sewed up my stab wound, while I hid the others with a pretense of modesty. To him, I was just another hapless peasant woman caught in a violent culture.

He probed my broken cheekbone cautiously, muttering in frustrated Hindi to himself. I knew I needed some delicate surgery which he hadn't the equipment for. He gave me an address for a charity surgical hospital run by Médecines sans Frontières in Tanrasda, four hundred miles away. Other than that, all he could do was tape up my face as best he could and give me painkillers.

After putting in a plastic drain tube to draw off any infection, he rebandaged the stab wound and gave me a bottle of antibiotics, instructing me on how to take them in a tone one would use with a particularly stupid child.

"You must come back in four days to have the drain removed. Do you understand?" he said in his exasperated singsong voice. "I give you more pills to make you feel better if you come back . . ."

Yes, yes, we assured him, and he sighed, knowing full well we would not return. Then we got the hell out.

We found a cheap hotel, the kind of run-down place catering to indigent pilgrims slowly wending their way on hadj to Mecca. I had hidden the handful of Khuru rials as well as a limited amount of *écus* we had left in the clothes tied around my waist. Here, all we could use the rials for was toilet paper. Halton got me into the single, narrow bed and left to exchange half the *écus* at an extortionary rate. He also took the red Khuruchabjan wool robe with its beautiful embroidered yashmak and traded it in the street for a few coins and an ordinary black cotton aba'ayah, worn and plain. Anonymous.

Although we needed to save as much of the local cash as we had left, we paid extra for the luxury of having a private room. Minimal at best, it was still the only room with an antique coin-operated handheld telephone bolted to the wall. With the last of my strength, I made a series of phone calls. I didn't phone my "safety deposit box" contact in GBN (don't ask me, I'm not going to tell you), since they'd get the message on what to do next from oblique sources. I didn't doubt that CDI would have everybody under surveillance by this time.

Then I allowed Halton to take care of me. Even while I lay in the lumpy, lice-infested bed, sweating and feverish, I knew something unusual was happening. The only ones who had known about the slipclip had been Laidcliff and his sidekick. But as soon as the clip had been deposited, a copy had automatically been sent directly to CDI, addressed politely to "Chief Asshole in Charge." It certainly got someone's attention, judging by all the commotion still going on in Nok Kuzlat.

I was in no condition to go anywhere. While I slept, loaded to the gills with painkillers, Halton wandered the streets, listen-

ing to the excited rumors. The stories were garbled and contradictory, but it was clear all hell was breaking loose in Khuruchabja.

By the third day, my fever broke, and I knew I was going to
live, because in spite of the pain I was hungry. The hotel had a
small kitchen on the ground floor, a sort of communal dining
room, front desk and lobby. The food was atrociously bad and
outrageously priced. An occasional chicken wandered in, clucking and pecking at the fallen crumbs of its erstwhile coop mates.

The diners packed the room, but spent most of their time
staring at a single flat-screen television, wired into one corner,
so as to ignore the rancid taste of the heavily spiced food they
were shoveling into their mouths.

The hotel pirated channels wherever they could, and the
Khuruchabjan news service came in coherently, if not clearly.
Mixed with partial broadcasts stolen from CNN and GBN, reports were sketchy. Between the eager rush of words, I pieced
together what was happening.

The Archangel Gabriel had found its Mahdi.

The AI had been lurking quietly in the data systems, until
Yousef's disconnect signal alerted it. Then it had gone into over-
drive, stirring up an electronic whirlwind in search of the Chosen One while all the turmoil and confusion boiled out onto the
streets of Nok Kuzlat. The phony Sheikh Larry hastily disappeared within hours after the copy of the slipclip got to CDI.
The army had tried to stage a coup d'etat. Someone had shut
down telephones and electricity, not to stifle communication between rebel factions, but in an attempt to kill the troublemaking
AI invading the government's data system.

It hadn't worked. Once Gabriel had escaped, putting the
cork back in the bottle wasn't going to stop the genie. I guessed
it was most likely Abdullah who cracked its recognition code.
During the height of the revolt, Gabriel had appeared in all its
glory at a mosque, and someone had stepped forward, speaking
the correct passwords. Gabriel acknowledged him before the astonished eyes of the faithful as the legitimate heir to Sheikh
Larry and the Royal Presidential Throne of all Khuruchabja,
true descendant of the Prophet Muhammad, champion of social
justice to the world, midwife of an Islam rebirth, the once and
future Mahdi.

Guess who? Ibrahim al-Ruwala.

Someone had gotten a shot of this on an amateur handheld

video camera, and even the few wobbly, out-of-focus moments taken through the doorway over hundreds of bobbing heads still managed to capture some of the impressiveness I knew the AI could inspire. After this miraculous appearance, Gabriel vanished in a flash of dazzling heavenly light, disappearing forever. The AI programming self-destructed, leaving no incriminating evidence behind that this had been anything less, or anything more, than a genuine miracle.

The country exploded in a frenzy. The uproar expanded like ripples outward, pilgrims on their way to Mecca suddenly deciding to make a slight detour to the mosque in Nok Kuzlat to see where the phenomenon had occurred. There they could argue the merits of whether this had really been a miracle or a fraud, and in either case what did it mean? One of the things it meant, I knew, was that CDI was going to have a bitch of a time keeping the lid on. And, hopefully, they'd be a little too preoccupied to spend much energy tracking down Halton and me.

On the fourth day, Halton snipped the stitches and pulled the drain from the puckering wound under my shoulder blade and replaced the bandage. The break in my cheekbone had started knitting together, leaving my face oddly flattened and making my eye water constantly. I still hurt like hell, but I was healing rapidly enough. We weren't ready to move on, though, until CDI knew whose balls I held in my broken little fist.

Halton had to dial while I held the phone awkwardly in my bandaged left hand, fistfuls of coins dinging merrily. After long arguments and explanations to various international phone operators in assorted degrees of English, I got through to CDI through a GBN secure line. The line hissed static as I waited for the call to go through. Halton sat on the edge of the rickety bed, the little baggage we had by the door ready to go as soon as I hung up. A woman answered the call, a receptionist's cool voice.

"Yes, good afternoon," I said in my best professional voice to the woman at the other end. "Would you please connect me with the Chief Asshole in Charge?"

She didn't even stop to gasp. "One moment, please."

They had been expecting my call. "Kay Bee Sulaiman?" a deep, masculine voice said. Such a lovely voice, exuding warm confidence.

"You got it on the first guess," I said. "You *must* be the Chief Asshole."

"Ms. Sulaiman," the sympathetic voice said smoothly, "I think there has been a grave misunderstanding . . ."

"Aww, jeez," I said, disappointed. "You must have gone to the same college I did. James Cagney, Media Art History 201, right?"

There was a baffled pause.

"Maybe it was James Coburn. I can never remember."

"Ms. Sulaiman, I'm very relieved you called. I think it's of utmost importance we talk this over . . ."

I knew they would want to keep me talking as long as possible to try to break through the GBN shield and trace the line. Not that it made that much difference; I knew I was safer from the CDI while staying in a hostile country than I was in the good ol' U.S. of A. "Then talk fast, because as soon as I hang up, we're gone. The only question is, which direction we go next."

"All right," the voice said. "We're both reasonable people. I'm willing to negotiate. Surely we can come to some mutually acceptable arrangement—"

I cut him off. "You've obviously seen the same stupid spy holos I have. There's only one deal: You leave us alone, I leave you alone. Take it or leave it."

"By 'us,' I assume you mean the fabricant."

Even with a single line handphone, Halton had good ears. He reacted visibly, shuddering. I muffled the phone against my chest and said quickly, "Get out of range of his voice. *Now.*" As he stood up and went to the farthest end of the room, I said into the phone, "Yes, I mean John Halton. He's mine. I'm claiming him. Finders keepers, losers weepers. You got a problem with that?"

"None at all," Mr. Smoothie said. "If you'll allow me to speak with him, I can assure him that it's all in order, he should consider you the legal registered owner . . ."

I laughed, sharp and unamused. "Laidcliff is dead. But he played some interesting tricks before he went. You can send the paperwork in the mail, if you like. That should be adequate."

There was another pause, this one longer. "Ms. Sulaiman, I think you should know Cullen Laidcliff was a rogue agent. He was not under any official orders, and operating entirely outside our authority, I assure you." It might even have been the truth, but it would be typical CDI routine to disavow all knowledge of Laidcliff's activities once the agent had thoughtlessly deceased on them. I wondered which part of the schism Mr. Slick was on, then decided it didn't make a hell of a lot of difference to me or to Halton.

"Laidcliff was out of control," the CDI man went on. "He abused his authority and was using his fabricants illegally for his own reasons. By the time we were alerted, you had unfortunately already been caught in the middle. I wish I could express how truly sorry we are for that."

Sure. Don't confuse incompetence with conspiracy. "Even if that's true, not a goddamned one of you has given me any reason to trust you . . . except John," I said coldly.

"I understand your misgivings, but I can't warn you strongly enough, Ms. Sulaiman," he pressed. "You don't know anything about fabricants. Your life is very much in jeopardy. Laidcliff sabotaged their training; their conditioning is impaired. Halton is dangerously defective." He sounded *so* concerned with my welfare. "It's not simply a matter of stolen Government property, which in itself, I'm sure you realize, is a felony offense . . ."

I snorted.

"You don't seem to understand the grave danger you're in. The entire John Halton series has malfunctioned, lethally. He is *not* a human being, you cannot trust him. The fabricant could turn on you at any time without warning—"

He was starting to sound shrill.

I cut him off. "I'll take my chances."

Long pause. "All right." The man's voice had cooled discernibly. "Suit yourself. It's your neck. As to the film, it's no longer as much of a problem to us as you seem to think it is."

"Then you won't mind if we air it on prime time news, will you?"

Mr. Suave seemed to take an awfully long time thinking it over. Another dramatic pause. "Really, Ms. Sulaiman, I believe you're making more out of this than is really . . ."

"Look, infeedel," I said, putting on my hokeyest TV Arab villain accent, "I get very good pictures of imperialist *Americhurja* do very bad things. See all you faces very clear. I show this to great American peoples, they rise up and strike you like scorpions in the desert, infeedel traitor—you blood run like rivers in the sand, maybe you have beeg troubles with Congressional funding next year . . ."

There was another long pause. Finally he said, "Perhaps it would be better if we agreed that this slight embarrassment could be kept quiet for the time being."

"Perhaps it would. Perhaps you should think about cleaning up the mess you've made. Perhaps I can come home and you guys don't bother me no more, huh?" There was another of his theatrical delays. "Hello, hello? Maybe I'm not talking to the right guy. You seem to be having to wait for permission or something . . ."

Mr. Slick finally got a bit irritated. "We'll eventually find all the copies, Sulaiman," he snapped, his nice polite company voice gone. "Even if we don't, we'll soon have this whole affair neatened up. In a few months, a year at most, that clip will be worthless. The world isn't going to care what happened in some backwater country. It's already yesterday's news."

"I'll worry about tomorrow, tomorrow. Meantime, it's just like the script, you got the idea? Anything happens to me or my friend, we're all going to be real famous two hours later."

"I got the idea," he said sourly, and slammed the phone down.

"Oooo!" I said, jerking the phone away from my ear. "What a rude man. He didn't even say goodbye."

John was having trouble again understanding my sense of humor.

# TWENTY-FOUR

**W**e headed out with a band of pilgrims on hadj, seeking safety and anonymity in numbers, then took a sharp right turn and aimed for Turkey. The UN soldiers at the border examined our American passports with skepticism, eyeing a short, badly beaten up woman in a black aba'ayah and a peasant man in dirty, baggy pants and an embroidered qabah tunic. By now, Halton had grown a thick, Arab-style mustache which didn't match his passport photo. They made us wait at the police station until someone from the nearest GBN bureau could come out from Urfa and vouch for us. By the time they got us to the airport at Ankara, I was in really lousy shape.

As soon as we hit American soil, GBN speedily packed me off to a private medical clinic in New Mexico while our lawyers fended off warrants to take me into Federal custody for questioning—sort of a New Mexican stand-off. I filed my report on the last moments of the ex-Sheikh, handing it to Arlando from my hospital bed just before they wheeled me into surgery.

He didn't argue with me about the editorial content, either. He knew all the rest of the details I hadn't been able to tell him from Khuruchabja. But we didn't discuss the reasons he'd sent me out in the first place, and I didn't give him any lengthy explanations of why I was careful to edit out John Halton and the

CDI agents' activities, as well as downplaying certain other parties' particular roles. Co-opted, or wiser, I'm not sure which.

Nonetheless, swathed in bandages, my bruised face and ruined hands gave the extra added touch of pathos, the Dedication of the Press to Truth and the Public's Right to Vicarious Thrills that can masturbate the ratings into new highs. The Feds and their subpoenas discreetly vanished and I got a brief, revived burst of celebrity with the renewed world attention on poor little Khuruchabja.

After I'd filmed my last slipclip as Kay Bee Sulaiman, I went under the knife. Kay Bee Sulaiman was excised and they stitched Kay Munadi back together again. Except for Arlando and my very own GBN security team, my only nonmedical company during the two months I stayed in the clinic was John. I would rouse briefly from the sedatives my bloodstream seemed to be saturated with most of the time, my bandaged hand in his, my first sight always his relieved, anxious face.

There was nobody John could have seen for a medical check-up, however, although we both knew he had been damaged. The first time it happened, I had been half-dozing from a shot of painkiller while watching the endlessly recycled newsholos. John had been standing by the bulletproofed window, gazing fixedly off at the mountains in the distance. I yawned, and flicked off the tube with the remote.

"John . . ."

He didn't react. My heart kicked in to attention, and I called his name softly a few more times before he finally responded. He turned slowly from the window to look at me, as if he were swimming in molasses. His body moved mechanically. His eyes were lifeless, that strange, barren expression I'd seen so often before drifting steadily through them. Pure ice. Deadly. *Inhuman.*

"John?" This time I whispered his name stone-cold terrified. My hands were still helplessly encased in steel and plastine. I couldn't have defended myself had I tried. For a fleeting moment I thought of screaming for the guards outside the hospital door. The image of them bursting in and shooting him down stopped me. "Halton . . . ?"

He blinked, as if awakening from a dream. "Yes?"

"Are you all right?"

He looked at me, puzzled. "Yes, of course."

"Where were you just now?"

He started, suddenly realizing he'd come out of his trance. "Inside myself," he said, frightened. He wasn't able to explain it any better than that.

Physically, the doctors have given him a clean bill of health. Even the three bullet scars have vanished. But once in a while he slips away, like a fabricant's version of epilepsy, unable to control it, lost inside his mind, unaware until after it passes. Sometimes he thinks it's beneficial, a flash of insight, a new neural pathway discovered. That's his theory, anyway. Sometimes he just comes out of it trembling and scared. The only people who might know what's wrong or how to repair the damage that Laidcliff's booby-trapped nanos have done are CDI.

In a bizarre way, Laidcliff did *me* a favor. My face was so ruined, they had to rebreak the bones and start over. I needed some heavy-duty plastic surgery just to rebuild the architecture. I'd always dreaded surgeons and dentists, doing my very best to avoid both. Now that I had no choice, I thought, What the hell, while they're at it . . . So I had them install those really high, model-type cheekbones and the classically straight thin nose my mother always wanted me to have. I'm still making regular donations to my dentist's Swiss bank account, but the replacement clones he implanted are far, far better than the original set.

I've got a killer smile.

They also did some nips and tucks when they removed the worst of the scar tissue graffiti on my front, and I had them rearrange and transplant some fatty tissue, flattening my tummy while enlarging my breasts. No amount of plastic surgery is ever going to make me into a raving beauty, understand—that much is still within the realm of fantasy. I'm still homely, to put it kindly, but now if I tried dressing up as a man, I'd look like a woman dressed up as a man. And I'm beginning to like what I see in the mirror.

The funny thing was, it didn't make one goddamned bit of difference to John. I felt somewhat insulted by his lack of appreciation when I'd gone through so much pain and trouble to look nice for him, but he really didn't see any difference. When John says it's my mind that drives him wild, he honestly means it.

The news and public interest in Khuruchabja died down as CDI scrambled to sweep as much of their dirt under the Persian rug as they could after deep-sixing their pseudo-sheikh. The local clergy once again had trouble digging up a suitable nominee to counter Ibrahim's claim, various contenders busily killing off their rivals. Ibrahim's future on the Presidential throne was shaky at best, and the Israelis were being very quiet. It looked disappointingly like it was going to be just the same old same old after all.

*Yesterday's news.*

After I was discharged from the hospital, GBN moved us into a smallish house inside a high-security complex on the outskirts of Washington, near Mount Vernon. It's similar to the kind of safe-zones the Government usually reserves for union Mafioso informants, exiled foreign dissidents, and paranoid politicians having scandalous affairs with holo stars whom they'd prefer keeping out of the limelight.

GBN's private complex protected mostly ex-Government sources who had been burned and a few foreign political refugees not in favor with our Government, who were in the process of writing their exposés.

And us. Halton and I tried to adjust to life in the security complex, as much as two people who expected to be murdered at any moment could adjust. The house itself is nice enough, despite a security-screened gate around it. With enough acreage to buffer one property from the next, infrared cameras in the trees and motion sensors in the flower beds, it's the kind of miniature prison-palace I might have daydreamed about when I had the freedom of not being able to afford it.

We have twenty-four-hour personal bodyguards with bio-tailored guard dogs, repellent electronic fences, top-of-the-line scan cameras, filtered phone lines, ultrasound motion detectors, bomb sniffers, fortified walls on the houses—you name it, we had the works.

I didn't feel safer in the least. John holed up like a clam, afraid to go into the city, afraid to open the door or answer the phone or read the mail, cloistered away in the house reading trashy novels all day like some depressed hausfrau.

Despite the fact I'd fucked up royally in Khuruchabja, GBN does take care of its own. But protecting us was more than simply fraternal altruism or forgiveness on their part. They had a special investment in safeguarding us. No other journalist in the world had her very own fabricant, and, so far as I know, there's only ever been one CDI fabricant defector.

GBN sold my beloved city apartment for me, and had my things moved to our new house. The house is comfortable as well as secure, but it lacks the charm and individuality of my funky two-bedroom apartment with its peeling wallpaper, squeaking floorboards, leaky faucets, and windows that needed propping open with spare books on a hot summer day. I even miss the neighbor's bad-tempered cat who liked to crap in my flower boxes.

My possessions seem somehow out of place here—temporary, vaguely alien. Like me. Like both of us.

Of course, CDI knows exactly where we are. If they really wanted to make an all-out effort, all that the security toys would do is slow them down and possibly embarrass them. GBN made no effort to hide us, only defend us, while continuing to make the benefits of killing me or Halton of limited return. Living on the run sounds romantic, but in real life it's a heavy strain on the nervous system. The best we could do was to cover our tender asses, and let GBN watch *them* watching us.

We knew CDI was—is still—watching us. Watching John. Maybe they really are concerned that he was damaged and might suddenly mutate into a berserk ax murderer. More likely, they don't relish the idea of all that secret shit John's carrying around inside his body outside their iron-fisted control.

But they actually did send the goddamned Transfer of Title listing me as John's legal owner. I couldn't believe it. I couldn't have cared less about that; I was furious they'd sent it openly to the correct address—just another little aggravating form of intimidation, telling us they knew exactly where we lived.

I also remembered the bit Laidcliff had mentioned about possession of fabricants reverting to the manufacturer on the death of the registered owner, and had GBN's legal department revise it. The way the title is set up now, GBN as a corporate entity has a lien against John, with me being listed as having the controlling interest. If I should end up untimely demised, GBN retains its rights to John with my controlling interest divvied up equally among two dozen or so individual GBN employees as shareholders. Any nefarious plan CDI might have had to get John back by killing me, our legal beagles assured me they've scotched it. Not unless CDI is willing to murder dozens of high-profile people just to get their fabricant back, the lawyers snickered. I didn't laugh; I wouldn't put it past them.

The documents did seem to make John feel better, though. there are some things hard-wired into him he'll never escape. I gave him my copy of the title, and he put it away carefully with the rest of the papers he's collected: his phony passport, his GBN employment contract, a special social security number, his brand-new union card—the kind of paperwork people accrete their whole lives and never notice until they need it. Sometimes he sits and goes through the papers as if they were old love letters, trying to get a sense of the person he's supposed to be.

After sitting around convalescing for a couple of months, I decided to quit smoking. I drove us both crazy going cold turkey, then moped around the house because there wasn't anything else to do. Jeez, Kay Bee, go outside and play . . .

Finally, I went back to my old job as an anonymous Broadcast Editor on a feed-in desk, only on a part-time basis, however, since I was still in physical therapy. When Laidcliff had broken my fingers, he'd damaged the ulnar nerves in my left wrist, making me clumsy. He'd also managed to nick part of the trigeminal nerve in my cheekbone, numbing half my face. Ironically, part of my physical therapy included a set of biomedical nanos injected along the damaged nerves. My fingers still hurt on cold nights and sometimes I have trouble holding a pencil, but at least I've gotten the feeling back in my face, and my hands do what I tell them to.

But I *had* to go back to work. I'd become obsessed with keeping my name far enough up in the public consciousness to make killing me an ill-advised proposal. I mean, who's gonna murder St. Cronkite or a latter-day Peter Arnett with impunity? But I was certainly no bubblehead and I was in no shape to go back into the field again, not immediately, if ever. I, of all people, am fully aware of just how short the viewing audience's attention span is. I sat behind a feed-in Net, worrying and being paranoid, before Arlando cordially pointed out that I couldn't watch a Netline while simultaneously looking over my shoulder.

We were miserable.

Then Arlando suggested something I should have thought of. *I* was no bubblehead, but why not Halton? He was certainly the right physical type and he could anchor in any language we needed. No one had to know he was a fabricant, and the higher visibility would give us both some measure of protection. I explained about John's occasional problem, and Arlando brushed it aside.

"We deal with crazier problems than that every day, and make it all look seamless. If he fritzes out on the air, we'll work around it. Don't worry."

I said I'd see what he thought about it, although we both knew John would do whatever I told him to. Arlando wouldn't push me, and I refused to push John.

I outlined the plan to John, staying carefully neutral, and let him wallow through the stress of making up his own mind. He'd have to get used to it sooner or later. The next day, we took our security-driven car into GBN together.

He picked up the necessary anchoring skills with as much ease as he'd learned holo optics, and two weeks later I stood up in the engineering gallery behind Penley, chewing my now-manicured Chrysanthemum Amethyst–polished nails to the quick. Penley jacked into his Netline and ran a few checks, doing his best to ignore me hovering over him. I could see Arlando in the visitors' observatory, hands deep in his pockets. More than the necessary number of my co-workers seemed to be attending this particular debut, and I wondered how many knew what Halton was.

On the broadcast monitor, Clark Fitch in Rio was mouthing silent words earnestly; off-air monitors flickered in the semi-darkness of the studio. Below us, in a brightly lit circle, Halton was being seated, his equipment adjusted, next to a moderately disgruntled Tricia Kwong. She had been mollified with the assurance that Halton was only there to learn the ropes from one of the best.

Clark's face was replaced by quick real-time footage of rebels in South America, as John and Tricia were cued. Tricia pasted on her professional smile, and John seemed utterly at ease, looking steadily at the camera.

Penley looked up at my red-tinted reflection in the booth's glass. "If you don't stop biting your nails," Penley said quietly, "I'm gonna throw your butt outa here, Munadi. You're making *me* nervous."

GBN's self-promotion theme music played tinnily through the monitor, the engineer pointed a finger at the couple impaled in the bright light, and the red ON THE AIR light flashed.

"I'm Tricia Kwong in Washington," Tricia said, and turned her head to smile at John.

"And I'm John Halton," John said, his voice professionally polished. His face held exactly the right mix of personal warmth and authority. It sent a wave of delightful shivers up the back of my neck. "Welcome to our viewers around the world to the Friday morning English edition of GBN Global News Report."

God, he was *smooth*! "Medical scientists at Johns Hopkins announced today a major breakthrough in their research into DVS Syndrome which has cost the lives of so many innocent children." John looked and sounded like he'd been doing this job for years. I noticed Penley whispering names, but John was reading straight off the text display, taking in whole lines without even a twitch of an eyelid to give him away. "We now go live to our correspondent in Maryland, Will McDawney, who is with Dr. Victoria Czaktiz. Will?"

John's face on the broadcast monitor was replaced with Will's own blond cherub features. "Thanks, John," he said, and turned to the woman in a lab coat smiling fixedly into the camera, the whites of her eyes visible around her irises. "Dr. Czakitz"—Will pried her gently out of her rigid stage fright—"you've headed the DVS research team at Johns Hopkins for the past two years, right?"

"Yes," the doctor agreed, and took a quick inhale. "We've been working on detecting the gene sequence of various DVS retroviruses which we've isolated in the laboratory in order to tailor an inhibitor to nullify the effect, and eventually a splicing agent to remove the virus from the cells of affected patients."

"One to stop the disease and another to cure it, yes?" Will said, putting her words into a more easily digestible sound bite.

"That's right. But what we discovered is, an active DVS viral infection has more than one specific gene sequence causing the disease, and we were surprised to find that not all of them are generated by the same factors present for puberty to occur, which was what we had originally hypothesized. Some children can be infected with part of the viral code, and never get the disease. It's the combination of DVS viral infections triggered by hormonal activity in pubescence which activates the disease. While we have yet to discover the method of transmission, we have definitely isolated those particular DVS genes working in synchronicity with others which produce the deadly effects. . . ." Once jolted into the story, Dr. Czakitz relaxed on familiar grounds.

On the off-camera monitor, Tricia Kwong shuffled the paper files set in front of her, looking uneasy behind her plastic smile. Her puppeteer sat three Nets down, whispering soothingly into her ear mike. John simply waited, following the text display and watching the tiny broadcast screens on the panel below camera level while waiting for his cue. Penley sat quietly, then glanced once at me and shrugged. Halton didn't need any handling. I had a sudden rush of sympathy for Tricia.

Fabricants could do a lot of things better than us.

Over the next three hours, I stood alternately clenching my hands and wiping my palms on my skirt, itching to push Penley out of the chair and take over, although there wasn't much to do other than edit the Net through onto the text display, and give Halton the correct pronunciation of unfamiliar names. It was a slack morning, few real-time blips breaking into recorded stories. Tricia finally warmed up, she and John handling the live cut-ins as if they'd been working together ever since Zworykin had been in short pants.

Then it was over, the eleven to three crew already in place. The floor crew unplugged the two anchors from their mock-up desk, and I watched Tricia stand stiffly for a moment before jutting out one formal hand toward John. I couldn't hear her from the booth, but I watched her speak, saw John smile, nod, shake her hand and say something polite in return. Tricia looked relieved.

Penley unjacked from the Net. "Your boy's okay, Munadi," he said laconically. "Bet he gets a thousand mash notes from the blue-rinse brigade by the end of the week."

He got more than that. Before the perfume-drenched love letters from geriatric widows swamped Halton's in-box, Arlando got an indignant call from CDI about the illegal use of classified material, dire threats and stern warnings. Arlando told them to go fuck themselves. Within a month, John Halton's ratings were high enough, I started to feel more optimistic than I had in a long time.

I got a call myself not long after Halton's debut. One of the sound techs called down to the editing booth where I was struggling to make my fingers finish working the board before the extra-strength aspirin etched an ulcer in my stomach.

"Hey, Munadi," he said. "Somebody on line four asking for Kay Bee Sulaiman. You wanna take it?"

My first reaction was to have all the blood in my face drop to my feet. The second was to get mad as hell. Goddamned CDI sure had a lot of chutzpah. I grabbed the handheld and punched the picture, although I kept my holoscreen off. "Who the hell is this?" I barked into the phone.

The man on the other end was a deeply tanned Arab,

brown eyes widening in surprise before he squinted dubiously at the blank screen on his end. "Ah . . . Kay Bee Sulaiman . . . ?"

"Who wants to know?"

Then he grinned, white teeth under a dark mustache. "GBN Cairo Relay. Maybe I shoulda asked for Sailor . . ." His English was more than perfect, it was natural, with just the slightest spice of an accent. "Just thought I'd do a follow-up, make sure your deposit went through okay."

I'd never seen him before, nor spoken directly on the Por-taNet's handheld. I had just assumed he was an American expa-triate; Arabs simply couldn't be capable of speaking English that fluently, certainly not well enough to crack jokes.

Well, hush mah mouth, Kay Bee. You're a *racist*.

After a moment, I opened my screen. His grin widened as he saw me. "I'm sorry," I apologized. "Yes, it arrived just fine. Thanks, really, thanks a lot." Then I blurted out, "I thought you were an *American*."

He laughed. "Hey, I'll take that as a compliment. Sorry to disappoint you, but I'm Egyptian. Lots of Egyptians work in Cairo these days." He eyed me for a moment before adding, "I'll plead guilty, too. I thought *you* were a man."

I was. But how was I going to explain that one? "Anyway," I said quickly, "you really saved my life." An expression, for once, meant literally.

"No problem," he said. "Just glad to know everything's co-pacetic."

We'd already broken the connection before I remembered where I last heard that.

*We repay our debts . . .*

It gave me chills that lasted for weeks. When I tried to con-tact him again, he had vanished without a trace. Nobody knew who he was or where he went.

I never even caught his name.

# TWENTY-FIVE

John settled comfortably into his job, and we were slowly relaxing, once in a while even venturing outside of our boring old pseudo-suburbia (with our bodyguards, of course). We started pretending maybe we might have a chance at a normal life, a future with real freedom, when we were reminded that CDI was still out there—they hadn't forgotten us and didn't want us to forget *them*.

John and I were out shopping downtown for who remembers what now, standing in the middle of Isako's Department Store, everything for the contemporary American home.

I turned around to John and said, "Hey, whaddya think of this one?" and looked up.

Except it wasn't John.

It was John-sized and John-shaped, exactly—even a strong facial resemblance, but it wasn't John. He looked down at me, arctic wastelands drifting endlessly through cold blue eyes. The thing *radiated* inhuman power—oily, smooth, deadly. He had the same plastic smile I knew so well.

I stood there immobilized, clutching some gadget absolutely essential for the modern kitchen. A warm hand took me by the arm and John, my John, was standing next to me, silently regarding the other fabricant. I was shaking like a leaf, but the two of them just stared at each other, a pair of stone idols claiming the same god. The sudden rustle of bodies materializing around us indicated that our bodyguards had belatedly realized something was amiss, and there were a lot of hands being tucked into jacket armpits. A few fellow shoppers glanced at us with wary curiosity before moving discreetly out of harm's way.

"Joseph?" A refined gentleman with a rich man's cultivated voice materialized behind him. I barely saw him. Some high-level Government functionary, no doubt. He was with the fabricant, not the other way around. His face was puzzled, worried. "Is there a problem?"

"No, sir," Joseph said, his eyes steadily locked with Halton's. "No problem, Mr. Oberly."

The fabricant ignored the tense group of bodyguards surrounding us, while the Government pen-pusher tugged anxiously at his sleeve. CDI had gone far beyond the obsolete Halton series, and they wanted us to know it, to rub our noses in it. This *thing* could have leisurely killed every armed guard we had, barehanded, before it got around to pulling the wings off John and me. It was a soulless killing machine; we were nothing in its path.

Then the fabricant, the Joseph fabricant, smiled tightly and inclined his head just a fraction. An acknowledgment? A challenge? A warning?

Or maybe it was the look that Cro-Magnon man gave the last Neanderthal. *There's a new sheriff in town, boy. The last dinosaur leaves at noon. Be on it.*

The Joseph fabricant glanced over at me, turned away and left. We haven't seen him, or any other fabricant, since.

I thought I was the one with the shit scared out of me, John had been so cool and calm. But that night I rolled over and woke up. The bed was shaking. John was sitting up trembling violently.

"John . . . ?"

He turned to me, face pale in the darkened room.

"Maybe it's true, maybe the nanos have destroyed something, cut something in my brain, and that's why I could kill Laidcliff, and maybe I could kill you and not be able to stop myself. . . ."

I sat up and tried to hold him. "Oh, John. C'mon, it's okay, calm down. . . ." It was like trying to hold on to a greased rock underwater.

"They can do anything, Kay Bee, *anything*. And I can't stop them. What if there are other people who can trigger the nanos? What if there are other nanos inside me, something worse? What if they've got his voice on digitape, and the phone rings sometime, and I pick it up . . ."

I held him tightly, pulling his head down to my softly augmented chest, stroking his hair like a child, which in many ways he still was.

"What if a safe falls on your head tomorrow?" I said, my cheek against his hair. "What if I get run over by a truck? What if a bolt of lightning comes through the window right this minute and crisps us both to french fries? John, if it's gonna happen, it's gonna happen. There's not a whole hell of a lot more we can do than what we have."

"I could hurt you," he whispered hoarsely. "You can't ever trust me." His tears wet my arm, and my throat suddenly ached.

I kissed the top of his head gently. "I've never trusted anyone in my whole life," I said. "So why should I start now?" His hand curled around my forearm, gripping so hard I knew I'd have bruises the next morning, but I winced and rocked him back and forth, murmuring, and let him cry.

Maybe he's right, maybe someday the upstairs wiring will completely short out, and he'll turn into a drooling maniacal killer. Or maybe it was just like Mr. Slick said: What happened way back when in Khuruchabja, that's yesterday's news, who cares anymore? Maybe someday John's ratings would drop, and we'd end up as a convenient auto accident on the obituary page. A lot of blue-rinse ladies would weep copious tears, but people die every day from unfortunate accidents. Maybe they'd just jerk off on watching us worry ourselves to death.

John finally went to sleep, still holding on to me like a life preserver, while I spent the night spinning my own "maybe's" in my head. There really *wasn't* much else we could do.

I continued working three hours a day as John's English feed-in puppeteer, which was about all the strain my damaged hands, nanos or no, could handle on the Net. John worked full time doing voice-overs and occasionally anchoring the Arabic, Japanese, Chinese, Spanish, Finnish, Swedish, Dutch, French, Italian, German, Lithuanian and Russian-language broadcasts, which gained him even more celebrity, including a two-page article in the *TV Holo Guide*. The Wonder Kid from Nowhere, the Mystery Man with the Golden Tongue.

When the news broke on Khuruchabja, I wish I could say

that it had been Halton who'd been on the air. But that sort of ironic serendipity only happens in cheap fantasy novels and holoshows. We were sitting at home with our feet up on the coffee table watching the tube while choking down another of my gourmet Suzy Homemaker failures.

The breaking story wasn't even on GBN. We watched the excited face of Jefferson Carleby covering the hottest news flash, reporting live! From Nok Kuzlat, Khuruchabja! For TVN Cable News! I always hate to see a rival reporter get the jump on GBN, but I had to admit I was glad for Carl. I saw myself as I could have been, probably should have been, too many years ago. I wished him well.

Just when things looked like they'd fallen apart, Ibrahim al-Ruwala had thrown a new monkey wrench into the works. The man who would be Royal President had diverted attention from the squabbling, outraged clerics (who had been baffling the hell out of most Khuruchabjans anyway, with their contradictory decrees and condemnations) by adamantly refusing to ascend the Imperial Throne—which he had only the most precarious claim on anyway—unless he was first legitimately elected by the entire population.

To prove the sincerity of his intentions, he proclaimed magnanimously that these elections were to be overseen by an international watchdog group to ensure their absolute fairness. Khuruchabjans would decide for themselves, in their first guaranteed democratic election, who they wanted to lead them to a glorious new future. Men *and* women.

Supplanted by the novelty, the controversy over the Archangel Gabriel's reality was conveniently forgotten, and skirmishes erupted over which country's observers should get the job, whether or not the women's vote was in violation of Islamic shar'ia law, and who, if anyone, should run against the leading candidate. But the issue of Ibrahim's legitimacy was neatly buried, and Ibrahim became a hometown hero for a slim majority of the voting public, the women's vote rounding out the lead. A few weeks later, he was inaugurated as Khuruchabja's very first lawfully elected Royal President.

He immediately took another abrupt left turn, throwing more of the unwary off the wagon by abolishing the Royal part of the Presidency, then undercut any potential rivals by slicing up his own power base and sharing it out. Inviting the Americans to send ambassadors was more to prevent the CDI from assassinating him than it was to renew diplomatic relations. With the American public busily applauding, he sent the rest of the West into waves of ecstasy manifesting itself in promises of billions of dollars- and *écus*-worth of nonmilitary foreign aid.

Shortly after this latest update, Arlando called Halton and me into his office. He didn't seem happy.

"President Ibrahim al-Ruwala has indicated he'd be willing to give an exclusive interview to GBN," he announced.

"That's great!" I was all for it. The more attention on Khuruchabja, the better.

Arlando wasn't as thrilled. "He's asked to be interviewed by GBN's one and only Kay Bee Sulaiman."

*Uh-oh.* I wasn't as thrilled, either. "Then we got a problem." I had permanently retired my Kay Bee Sulaiman persona, and was plain old Kay Munadi again. Just another anonymous Broadcast Editor.

Arlando gauged Halton. "What about you, John? You want to tackle interviewing the President of Khuruchabja?"

John glanced at me. "I'm not sure that would be a good idea, sir," he said quietly. "If CDI felt I was in a position to compromise them, it's possible they might decide it worth the risk to divulge what I am and my connection to them in order to undermine the new government of Khuruchabja. And GBN." No one would believe the fabricant wasn't still a tool working for the CDI; John's credibility with the public would be instantly flushed down the tubes.

Arlando was nodding. "So let's beat 'em to the punch," he said calmly.

"Say what?" I didn't like this.

Arlando's smile was ironic. "We tell the exclusive inside story of daring Secret Agent John Halton and GBN's very own Kay Bee Sulaiman, intrepid reporter, going boldly in disguise where no woman has gone before, thrown together by fate and patriotism, heroically risking their lives in order to bring out the truth from the very capital of Khuruchabja."

"This isn't funny, Arlando. I ever go back, they'll *kill* me."

"What, you had plans to buy a vacation home there, Munadi?"

"No . . ."

"Then so what?"

"So I've met Ibrahim al-Ruwala. And so has John. He believes I'm a man, and he's not going to appreciate having been made a fool of," I said hotly.

"He's not going to do a goddamned thing. He's got his own little secrets he'd like kept off the record. Think about it, Kay. You really believe he's willing to publicly admit it was his group that cracked Israel's Gabriel microflake? Tinkered with it in order to hoodwink his constituency and steal the Presidency?"

No, I guessed he wasn't. The silence grew a little strained.

"What about John?" I asked finally. "You reveal John's 'secret agent' identity, that would certainly rocket GBN straight to the top. Then what? CDI comes out and exposes him as an extremely dangerous malfunctioning biomachine? John could kiss more than his job goodbye, Arlando." I glanced at John, his face as unreadable as ever. "How long do you think it would take the EPA to confiscate him under the Public Welfare act? Maybe pull his plug for good? I don't really think *we're* ready to take that kind of risk. We just can't afford to tell the whole story."

Arlando shook his head. "Nobody even knows what the whole story *is*, Munadi. Do you?" He looked at John. "Do you, Halton?"

"No, sir."

Arlando leaned back in his chair, leather creaking. He turned to gaze out the transparent walls of his office. Monitors and computer screens flickered, people walked by as if unaware there was anyone in Arlando's glass cubicle. Selective blindness.

"Kay, you've been in this business long enough to know the real news is not always what gets on the air."

Truth is just as vulnerable to market forces as any other product. Viewer appetites and short attention spans, commercial economic needs, the lack of time boiling stories down to only bare essential facts, the caprice of popular fashion, are far more powerful editors of news than simple political pressure or corruption.

"There's a whole hell of a lot we're never going to know," Arlando continued. "And for the same reason other pieces are going to drop through the cracks, to protect the innocent and a lot of not-so-innocent people from getting themselves unnecessarily killed . . . like you and John, just for example." I winced.

His voice softened slightly. "No one has to know he's a fabricant, Kay." He looked at Halton as he spoke. "At least not yet. Maybe not ever. CDI *could* cause us a lot of trouble and inconvenience, but there's nothing illegal they could pin on us, John, and they know it. I seriously doubt they really want to kick up a fuss now."

John nodded. I wasn't sure if he was agreeing or consenting.

"At the moment, we have the upper hand. All we have to reveal is that John was actually a CDI secret agent, now honorably 'retired' and hired by GBN, and who was instrumental in bringing about the current political changes going on in Khuruchabja. Change that is very popular right now. Give CDI the opportunity to take a few bows for themselves, a little noble credit for some of it. Whether they deserve it or not. They've already been pushed into cleaning house. The President is still furious with their screwup in Khuruchabja, Congress is furious at the White House for trying to sneak covert actions by them yet again. CDI'll have to be submitting their fiscal budget proposals to Congress soon and it would be good PR, which they need at the moment. It just might help to reduce some of the friction between you two and the CDI."

"They'll never go for that . . ."

"They already have," Arlando cut me off coldly.

John had taken my hand, his fingers tight and chill, but his face impassive. I stared at Arlando, speechless.

"Jesus," I finally squeaked out. "Who's idea was this?"

"Mine. They owe me," Arlando said quietly. "Listen to me, Kay. *Everyone* has dirty linen they'd rather not see aired on the evening news; politicians having affairs, movie stars with drinking problems, Supreme Court Justices who like to dress up in lace garters and handcuffs. But if no laws are being broken, if it doesn't involve the public welfare, then it's not *news*. There's a line between informing the public and invasion of privacy."

What's your secret, Arlando? I wanted to ask. I didn't because I didn't want to know the answer.

Arlando stared back at me, eyes hard, gauging. "A large part of news is also timing, Kay and you should be enough of a journalist to know that. Thousands dying of famine in Africa doesn't have the same punch during a hard domestic economic recession as a story about a dozen Americans losing their jobs because some billionaire Wall Street trader has junk-bonded a small company into oblivion. You don't get ratings with bad timing.

"At some point, it's possible we may want to go ahead and reveal John's 'secret identity.'" He smiled thinly. "It would indeed boost our ratings, timed right. It would also take away one more threat CDI has hanging over our heads. But not now. Not all of it at once."

" 'The truth is not there to be seized in one piece at a time,' " John recited softly. " 'The truth emerges, and that is how it is supposed to be in a democracy.' "

Arlando looked surprised. "Walter Lippmann," I said, attributing the quote.

"So you *can* read instead of just watching old movies," Arlando said to me and smiled at John. "Nice to see you're having a good influence on her."

John returned his smile. *"Today and Tomorrow, The Life of a Newsman,* a made-for-TV miniseries, Gene Hackman, Sophie Hargood. French American co-production, shot in Canada," he said. He glanced at me, almost apologetic. "Won an Emmy for Best Set Design," he added.

Arlando laughed. I didn't, but a lot of tension crackling in the air had dissipated. John's fingers squeezed mine gently.

"Goddamn it, Arlando. I hate this, I really do." I tried to keep the whine down to a minimum. "In my heart of hearts, I've always believed my job was to tell the truth, expose other people's nasty secrets. Not cover our own asses with lies of our own."

He smiled wryly. "Your *job,* Kay Bee, is to report as much of the news as you can, in a responsible and professional manner. The public's right to know does not extend to the point where people get needlessly hurt. That's what *responsible* journalism means."

"And who makes those decisions, Arlando?" I asked. "Who takes responsibility for what goes public and what doesn't?"

He shrugged. "Better you and me than the Government. If someone else can do a better job, they're welcome to it." He leaned back in his chair, hands laced together across his stomach, fingertips rubbing his knuckles. "This is the way it's going to happen, Munadi. You've just been promoted. Congratulations, you're now GBN's Chief Middle Eastern Analyst and Commentator. We do a splash feature on you and John a few days before you interview al-Ruwala. That'll kick the ratings up high enough we should have the biggest market share for the interview, and believe me, it'll be worth it."

"I don't even have a choice?" I said in a low, aggrieved voice.

"None at all."

For some reason, John smiled. I didn't ask.

They did the story. It hit the air right after the latest news flash from Khuruchabja, an endless roller coaster on the holo-tube that no one dared to look away from for a minute. Arlando even used the goddamned clip I'd deposited as our insurance, voices and faces obscured with digitalized scrambled pixels. And what a spin he put on it! CDI came out looking like *they* personally had thwarted an attempted coup, patriotic heroes one and all.

Events happened fast after that, so quickly and flawlessly, it had to have been prearranged. When our special aired on American prime time, it was the wee hours of the morning in Khuruchabja. Within an hour, Ibrahim had used the disclosure to arrest the top brass who had helped him into power, most of them treacherous and corrupt schemers themselves, tossing them into jail still dressed in their pajamas. His own loyal guard handcuffed the army, stripping it of its major weapons. Rather than throw a hundred thousand soldiers into prison, most of whom had been in popular support for him during his rise, he promoted everyone a rank, passed out new uniforms and pop-gun pistols and turned them all into traffic cops.

By morning, the few dozen political prisoners were instantly released and granted amnesty to great fanfare, even those rabid anti-government clerics still calling for al-Ruwala's head on a plate. It was a cynically calculated move aimed at increasing Ibrahim's popularity, and it worked. The more resistant *mutawin* and remaining army officers with a fondness for coups would later find themselves either quietly exiled or six feet under, but the rank and file, tired of the pointless violence, were more than happy to go home to the wives and kiddies and sing Ibrahim's praises from the safety of their front porches.

Of course, this also meant he was vulnerable to attack from any belligerent neighbor with a grudge. One or two rattled their sabers just to gauge the American reaction. The United States immediately made it clear they would not feel the slightest obligation to be sucked into any war on Khuruchabjan soil; this was not their affair, they'd had enough in the past. The jackals grinned.

It looked suicidal.

But Ibrahim was kind enough to save his coup-de-grâce for me and GBN. There was no way on earth I was going to fly to Khuruchabja for the interview, so it was done with a satellite up-link. My hair had now grown out long enough to style, the sweat on my face was covered with heavy camera makeup, and I sat in a skirt and silk jacket in the studio as the techs wired me thoroughly into place. When the holo of Ibrahim al-Ruwala solidified in the chair beside me, his electronic eyes widened slightly, amused but not surprised. Somewhere in Khuruchabja, my own hologram sat nervously facing the real Ibrahim.

He had changed as well. The quick, street-smart man in worn jeans had been replaced by a well-groomed, composed dignitary in an expensive Western suit. He nodded graciously.

"Good evening, Mr. President," I said nervously, finding it hard to get the words to come out smoothly. "Thank you for joining us. 'Ana 'asz'heed geeddan, it's a great pleasure for us and our viewing public in countries around the globe."

"'Ana 'asz'had," Ibrahim replied. "Not at all. The pleasure's mine."

"Mr. President—" I jumped in by reading the first question off the monitor. "You've stunned the entire world by abolishing the Khuruchabjan monarchy and establishing a Parliament to be democratically elected with real legislative powers to balance your own Presidency. Just in the past few days, you've made radical changes in your country's military command, in effect demilitarizing your armed forces with a civilian controlled authority. How do you explain this sudden modernization you've undertaken for your country?"

"There are many 'modern' countries which are not 'democratic,' " Ibrahim's hologram said. "Democracy is not the only form of modernization." He smiled self-confidently. "But as Churchill pointed out long ago, democracy is the worst possible system of government . . . except for all the others."

"You see yourself as an Islamic Winston Churchill?" That wasn't on the script. My ear mike whispered warnings.

"More as an Arab Charles de Gaulle. As you well know, it takes far more than free elections to make a true democracy. My goals for my country and my private aspirations are happily quite compatible. My ambition is to create a government to suit my own personal tastes and preferences," he said honestly, "which will then work without me for the benefit of my people when I decide to retire."

I blinked at that. He grinned.

Then he dropped the bomb.

"Could you explain the reasons behind your rather drastic military disarmament, Mr. President?" Like a good little bubblehead, I had gone back to following the list of questions flickering on an isolated prompter off-camera. "It appears you have left yourself vulnerable to attack by any hostile factions."

"There is no longer any need for Khuruchabja to maintain such an extensive offensive military force as we have in the past, which has drained our economy and only encouraged animosity from our friends. We will certainly maintain a limited civilian defense reserve sufficient to repel any unlikely invasion of our sovereignty, which I intend to model on the Swiss example. Slightly improved, of course. We have taken these steps to prove our willingness in declaring a national policy on Islamic nonviolence, a willingness I trust my brother Muslims will respect. There is simply no reason for Muslims to fight each other."

I looked at him skeptically.

He smiled, and steepled his fingers. A thin blue transmission line glitched briefly through his figure, the only flaw in the illusion that he was not right there in the studio with me. "As far as our enemies are concerned, internal or external, Khuruchabja will be the first to recognize what should have been obvious all along. For too long we have tried to divide the secular from the religious in our countries, each half vying to vanquish the other. It is like the right half of the body trying to defeat the left, futile and foolish. It is not possible or even desirable to separate the secular and the religious from a modern Muslim government. Those who have tried have blinded and crippled themselves."

This was some speech, and I let him talk for himself, ignoring the irritated prompting in my ear to cut it up into sound bites.

"The independent and sovereign nation-states of the Middle East are a day-to-day reality, what in certain Muslim tenets could be called the *zâhir*. But Islam also teaches us to see the greater reality, the divine *bâtin*, the truth underlying what we see only with our eyes, not with our hearts. The Europeans understand this with their Common Market, the United States has its own Unified American Trade Alliance with Canada, Mexico, Central and South America. Even the former Soviet Union and its mutinous republics finally understood the wisdom in the American phrase 'United we stand, divided we fall.' It is time for us Muslims and for the world to recognize that each of our individual nations is, and has always been, and will always be, part of the unified whole, a Common Middle East. Each nation is itself only a separate *millet* within the Greater Islamic Empire."

*Huh?*

"Including Israel," Ibrahim added, and sat back to smile like the Cheshire cat while I stared at him speechless for a moment.

"Does this mean your government is officially recognizing the current borders of Israel as it stands as an independent, sovereign nation?" I asked slowly, not following the frantic prompter blinking wildly. I winced, the mike in my ear suddenly too loud.

Ibrahim waved the question away with a grimace. "Borders and nationalism are a Western concept imposed on us by colonialism, which has never been wholly accepted in the Arab world. We are traditionally a society of peoples, united by faith and by blood. Borders are illusions, certainly not worth dying over. Khuruchabja recognizes the current borders of Israel as being representative of a historical *millet* of the traditional Islamic Empire, a sort of 'Jewish quarter,' if you like. A fairly *big* Jewish quarter, but it is an autonomous region within the Greater Islamic Empire just the same. As is Khuruchabja.

"We have already taken official steps in negotiations with the state of Israel to sign a formal treaty to this effect, guaranteeing the people of Israel their historical place within a unified Middle East, with all the privileges and obligations Jews have always had the right to expect under such a unified Islamic whole. The government of Khuruchabja not only is prepared to recognize the right of the Jews to their separate *millet*, but we are prepared to defend it against all aggressors, with every means at our disposal, as we would for any nation who joins with us in this Islamic unification."

My jaw dropped at this one, and simply hung there.

"Of course, as non-Muslims, the Israelis would be expected to pay a religious tax to Khuruchabja, as well as to any other Muslim nation within the Greater Islamic Empire who perceives the truth of the situation . . . in the form of military protection."

Ibrahim's eyebrows rose fractionally, as if defying me to ridicule this preposterous "truce" with Israel. Except we'd both seen Gabriel. And I knew who had made it. Maybe he did, too.

I don't remember much more of the interview, except that someone was screaming in my mike until I had to dig it out of my ear, and I found myself shaking my head at the smiling hologram as it winked out of existence.

I was still trailing wires when I stumbled out of the brightly lit holo booth. My eyes unadjusted, I was blinded as I stepped past the sound panels into a clamor of people arguing intensely. Then John's arms were around me, hugging me gently while plucking hook-ups off with a now-practiced hand. I was only too glad to let him.

". . . Are you *kidding!*" a voice said sharply next to me. In the semidarkness, I recognized him, more by sound than sight, as one of the techs. "The Israelis are never gonna go for that bullshit Muslim mumbo-jumbo. The guy's a lunatic . . .!"

"Well, maybe he *is* crazy, but crazy like a fox. He's got something up his sleeve, that sort always . . ."

"This is just some kind of scam to pull the rest of the Gulf states back into a war, gang up against Israel, trick 'em into thinking this time you really are gonna bring an olive branch, then *wham* . . ."

"Try that, America would vaporize that little podunk country in two seconds flat . . ."

"Not if it means the entire region is joining forces. We aren't gonna fight the whole goddamned Middle East . . . !"

"Come off it, these guys have never been able to get it together long enough to decide how to split a lunch tab . . ."

"Gotta be the CDI behind this—this guy's just a puppet—they gotta be the ones pulling his strings . . ."

"Hey, Munadi! You're the Chief Middle Eastern analyst now." The group had spotted me. My eyes had adjusted, their faces reflecting red and green highlights from the monitors. "Give us your expert opinion."

I wasn't sure if they were making fun of me or not. "I think you might be overlooking one other possibility," I said quietly.

"Yeah? What?"

"It could be he really *is* the Mahdi."

I kept an absolutely serious, straight face. It wasn't hard. Their eyes bulged in incredulity as they stared wordlessly at me for a long moment. Then I let them off the hook and grinned.

*Still* . . .

# TWENTY-SIX

During the following days, John had the pleasure of reporting the Israelis' response in the United Nations. Far from laughing their asses off at this absurdity and telling the Khuruchabjani government to stick it where the sun don't shine, much to the world's surprise, Israel promptly praised the move. They announced they were extending blanket military protection to the recognized (and disarmed) tiny Republic of Khuruchabja, vowing to repel aggressive action taken by *any* nation against the newly formed democracy. *Including the Americans*, was the unspoken threat. And they had the nukes to back it up.

GBN beat out all rivals over the next few weeks, for the very first time climbing to the top of the news heap as we all competed to keep up with the coverage. Ahmat al-Hamid began filing reports from Nok Kuzlat, eagerly polling the man in the street. Appalled at first, then grudgingly accepting, the average Khuruchabjan didn't *really* mind. Just so long as those despised Zionist dogs stayed at their end of the desert where they belonged and minded their own goddamned business, which Israel was more than happy to do.

Cautious negotiation, both public and covert, opened up between Israel and her more powerful and alarmed neighbors, however. The advantages in a unified Middle East had always been secretly acknowledged by all parties concerned; the "solutions" forced on the Middle East from the outside had never worked.

Israel had good reason to want a real truce in the Middle East. The perpetual hostility was beneficial only to Western countries with their military bases on foreign soil in order to keep their thumbs firmly inserted into the oil pie. Decades of fighting Hamas and Hezbollah and Behjars all by themselves had left the Israelis with a permanent case of national paranoia. Israel wanted good relations with their traditional ally, the United States, but for their own security they *needed* the cooperation of the Islamic countries bordering them on every side. The issue of Jerusalem and the occupied territories had always been a sore point, but with the formation of a Common Middle Eastern Parliament similar to the Europeans', the issues could be wrangled over endlessly without anyone required to don black or white hats.

Israel, with its massive military technology and infrafusion nuclear capability, was the only country with any chance of standing up to pressure from the Americans, and they didn't appear to be interfering in Khuruchabja's internal politics. A pax with the little Zionist Satan was at least better than the big American one, which had been Israel's intent all along.

Hesitantly, grudgingly, the Gulf states were forming a true Middle Eastern Common Market. There was now even some open talk about closing American and British airbases in the Gulf, much to those governments' consternation. Ibrahim's peaceful economic jihad was slowly becoming a strange reality.

Given breathing room, the new Republic of Khuruchabja had a good start. With the extension of automatic and full Khuruchabjani citizenship to any Arab Muslim who previously had no nation of his own, the trickle of skeptical homeless from a variety of countries turned into a small but steady stream of immigrants. Only some of them were educated or skilled, but all were eager to trade the violence and poverty of refugee camps and city slums for a fresh start. Those who were not doctors and nurses, engineers, college professors, writers, artists, were given community service jobs and community housing while they built roads, badly needed housing, and sanitation faculties—the infrastructure of a modern life. To keep prejudice and fear at a minimum, native Khuruchabjans profited almost immediately from the benefits of an enlarged labor force, artfully tided over by grants from certain advocates from the West.

Those who arrived trying to hide behind covered faces, importing the bigotry and hatred with which they had terrorized their own people, found themselves not tolerated by either their compatriots or their new countrymen. Even the threat of a drain on slave-wage labor in various rich countries dependent on their "foreign residents," many of whom had been born there, alarmed several governments enough to add a few civil and legal rights along with economic incentives to keep their lower-class workers happy.

Other than extending special visa privileges to Khuruchab-jani pilgrims visiting the great mosques in Holy Jerusalem, Israel stayed scrupulously out of Khuruchabja's Islamic internal affairs, and made sure everyone else did so as well. If the fledgling nation was to succeed, it would have to do it by itself. Or not at all.

The nuts and bolts would take longer and be less exciting, but interest in Khuruchabja persisted; the country never returned to its original obscurity. There would always be fanatics, Jewish or Muslim, resisting anything that looked even slightly like capitulation. The kind of "The only good fill-in-the-blank is a dead fill-in-the-blank" extremist. Centuries of mindless prejudice and hatred will not be washed away overnight.

Khuruchabja still has a long, long way to go, the usual nepotism and business by baksheesh too ingrained to disappear instantly. The career of Islamic leaders has never been an enviable one; the balancing act between religion and secularism exhausting and often unrewarding. Those few who manage it without resorting to despotism and bloodshed are admirable and underrated heroes.

Of course, Ibrahim's rivals still have an unfortunate tendency to mysteriously disappear when they get too pesky; what was left of Larry's family prudently decided to retire along with their Swiss bank accounts to the ski slopes of Europe; and ulemas of every sect, understandably, were incensed at this perversion of Islam with its corresponding usurpation of their political dominance.

Ahmat continued filing reports for GBN, slowly toning down the wild rhetoric as his English improved and he grew more sophisticated. GBN added decoders for several Arabic dialects to their list of choices as homemade satellite dishes began popping up like mushrooms all over the tiny desert country. Hamid's network kept CDI and any vestiges of disgruntled out-of-power factions from killing the kid, or oppressing his news-hungry neighbors, until his television-fused tribe had grown so large, former enemies did the age-old, two-step shuffle and joined the side that was winning.

Little Khuruchabja began experiencing its first economic growth in centuries. It was hard to argue with the flourishing middle class as Khuruchabja's burgeoning electronics industry brought a burst of economic spring to the parched desert. But in the face of this growing prosperity, the ulemas seemed some-what surprised at the open reception the New Age Islam received. Ibrahim had meant what he'd said, no matter how cynically he felt about it privately. One by one, the clerics gradually gave up their futile struggle to turn back the clock and started looking for ways to fit that old-time religion into the new succession. Those who continued to preach violence and murder in the name of Allah found themselves cut off from support, in more ways than one, while those who preached the tenets of Islam based on a love of God were heavily endorsed by Ibrahim's government, both politically and financially. Islam Studies Institutions rapidly expanded throughout the country. The government constantly emphasized that Islam had tradi-tionally integrated politics and religion, this was an *Islamic* flow-ering, an *Islamic* revival, that Ibrahim had declared his country was on a peaceful *Islamic* economic jihad.

It was ambitious as hell, and there are still a discouraging number of problems, but Khuruchabja is just beginning to slowly pull out of the medieval tarpit they'd been sunk in for centuries and come into their own blossoming Twenty-first–century Islamic renaissance. By all accounts, Ibrahim's new gov-ernment seems to have gotten off to a vocal, heated start, squalling as lustily as any healthy newborn baby. With luck, it'll survive.

And so, it seems, will we.

After the feature and the GBN interview with Ibrahim, I had a sudden rush of fame which made me feel both relieved and massively uncomfortable. CDI got a badly needed shot of public goodwill, which helped tremendously when budget time came around. The Director in Chief of CDI sent me a strange, reserved note of congratulations, meticulously avoiding all men-tion of John. A shaky truce, but a truce nonetheless.

Arlando threw a celebratory party for Halton and me (and all our little bodyguards) at the security complex. I'd had enough of the contrived best wishes and congratulations in about ten minutes flat, and spent the rest of the evening OD'ing on vacuous conversation and egotism.

I stood grinning frozenly, empty champagne glass clenched in one hand, while listening to some exiled South American generalissimo do "My secret's better than yours but I'm not telling you without a really good book contract" with some Mafioso informant under wraps until he's called to testify flanked by his lawyer and his investigative reporter. When I couldn't stand it anymore, I wandered around to find John.

John had become rather popular with the ladies at GBN Center when he'd started working as a new anchorman. His instant celebrity and glamour as an ex–CDI spy had just upped his desirability factor by ten. I found myself having to fight not to get ridiculously insecure and jealous whenever some buxomy blond brain-dead bimbo made a serious play for him. I didn't always succeed, and that, combined with my smart-assed mouth and hot temper, made any real friendships problematical. John always managed to turn them down gently. He gets along with just about anyone; they all think he's so mellow, so sweet and wonderful.

Couldn't hurt a fly.

I spotted him trapped in the corner going through some intense socialization ritual, trying to puzzle out all the sexual innuendoes and invitations from the bored wives of absent, shady millionaires off finking on their even wealthier and shadier bosses. Not all of his most ardent admirers were female, I noticed, which amused me.

By the time I'd wormed my way through the crowd of too many sweaty bodies pressed together to rescue him, he'd vanished. Oh, well. I turned, and glanced out the French doors into the garden, where several guests had fled in search of some fresher air.

One of the guests Arlando had invited to the party, a little man with strange skin that looked as if he had had the wrinkles surgically stretched out of it one too many times, was working his way toward me, thin lips stretched in a predatory smile. He had been badgering me all night for the film rights to produce some kind of fictionalized TV holo series based on our exciting True Life Adventures in Khuruchabja. Lotsa money, he'd wheezed furtively while surreptitiously squeezing various unerogenous parts of my body. *Lotsa* money.

Suddenly the garden seemed like a good idea to me, too.

I discovered John standing by himself at one end of the garden, staring unblinkingly at a stack of trussed up rosebushes left by a gardener to be planted the next day. He'd fallen into one of his trances. I stood a few yards away and watched.

Although the attacks had gotten less frequent, he could be triggered into a dream state by just about anything, a spot on the wall, a button on his shirt, a bundle of rosebushes stacked against a fence. Maybe the stress of the party had provoked it, I don't know. I'd learned to simply leave him alone when his mind checked out for lunch. He stared with absolute concentration at rosebushes in bondage while people strolled by, laughter and the heavy smell of lilac lingering on the night air.

He'd also caught the rapacious eye of one of the better-known holo stars who frequently visits her political friends here when she's not out decorating films and overdosing on fame. I intercepted her before she reached him.

"Hi," I said cheerfully, blocking the path between her and John with a big, friendly smile and my short little body. "Wow, it sure is hot in there, isn't it?"

"God, is it ever," she said with forced courtesy, resentful I'd prevented her from seizing a few private moments with John.

"Yeah. Really hot," I agreed vacuously.

I could feel her eyeing me, wondering what a young, good-looking hunk like John could possibly see in an old bow-wow like me. She had about four extra inches on me, all of it leg, and ten less pounds nicely distributed on the rest of her body. She had on a rather skimpy dress to show off her perfect curves, the kind of slinky outfit I'd love to be able to wear but would look ludicrous in if I tried.

She smiled her dazzling white, perfect teeth at me, but kept batting her eyelashes seductively in John's direction. How disappointed she looked, I was pleased to note. Her sly, and not too subtle attempts at catching John's attention right under my nose sent my blood temperature higher, but John remained catatonic. Not even the lure of her tanned, smooth thighs rubbing together suggestively could break that spell.

"Is he like part Indian or something?" she said, admiring him over my shoulder, stuck with trying to be nice to the ugly little wifey. She had some chutzpah, no doubt about it. "I mean from India, not American Indian, y'know, into Buddhism and meditation and that kinda thing?"

"You could say that," I agreed. You could say anything you wanted. John continued gazing at the rosebushes, locked into his private reverie.

"I knew it. He's like, y'know, so in tune with nature and all."

I smiled politely and didn't bother to enlighten her. John doesn't actually *see* much nature. He wants to understand it, he wants to understand everything, but "in tune" with nature, he's not. He's got a hard enough time trying to get in tune with himself. Maybe he was looking for his own Mahdi in the nano-torn recesses of his mind.

She finally gave up, giving me a withering look that made her appraisal of me infinitely clear before wriggling back to a more appreciative audience. When John blinked his way back to the real world, scared and silent, we ditched the party and went home.

That was a few years ago, and up until the other day he hadn't had another of his attacks.

I wear a ring on my left hand, and endorse my paycheck these days "Kay Munadi Halton," as in "Mrs." We're not married, not legally, since John isn't legally a person. It doesn't matter.

We got our bank checks in the mail with both our "married" names emblazoned on the top. John sat down and held the checks in his lap, staring unblinkingly at them for over an hour. I made myself a cup of coffee and leaned against the doorjamb, waiting patiently for him to come out of it.

My coffee dregs had gone cold, and I'd just about decided to give up, when he looked at me, his eyes as round as a child's.

"What is it?"

"There's only one," he said, wonder in his voice.

"Only one what?"

"Only one John Halton."

That's right. They'd killed all the others; he was the only one left in the whole world.

"I'm unique," he said, awed.

I sat down next to him and took his hand. "You always were."

FIC
WOO          WOOD
Looking for the Mahdi.

| | | DATE DUE | |
|---|---|---|---|
| | | | |
| | | | |
| | | | |
| | | | |
| | | | |
| | | | |
| | | | |
| | | | |
| | | | |
| | | | |
| | | | |
| | | | |
| | | | |